Ho

Adam Baron █████████████████████████ and
comedian. As ████████████████████████ron
Brothers, he █████████████████████████ *now*
and *The Lenny* ████ ████████

His first novel, *Shut Eye*, was published in 1999 and is
also available in Pan Books.

Praise for Adam Baron and Shut Eye

'Classy and able debut thriller, with crunchy London
backgrounds ... An agile, ingenious plot ... Decent,
vulnerable hero, credibly in love with fiancée of crippled
brother. Forecast for series is excellent.' *Literary Review*

'Urban Noir has arrived in London, and Adam Baron is
one of its finest proponents.' *Independent*

'It is Rucker's disillusioned monologue that makes [*Shut
Eye*] stand out among the myriad of formulaic thrillers,
and adds up to an accomplished first novel.' *The Times*

'A treat.' *Evening Standard*

'Rucker is an intelligent, reflective hero, a man well
worth keeping an eye on.'
Donna Leon, *Sunday Times*

'This thriller stays in the mind even when you're not
reading it.' *Front Magazine*

'Good, gritty stuff.' *Crime Time*

'Great atmosphere ... a surefire hit.' *Aberdeen Evening
Express*

By the same author

Shut Eye

Adam Baron

Hold Back
the Night

For Steph!?

all my

love

PAN BOOKS

First published 2000 by Pan Books
an imprint of Macmillan Publishers Ltd
25 Eccleston Place, London SW1W 9NF
Basingstoke and Oxford
Associated companies throughout the world
www.macmillan.co.uk

ISBN 0 330 39117 8

1 3 5 7 9 8 6 4 2

A CIP catalogue record for this book is available from
the British Library.

Typeset by SetSystems Ltd, Saffron Walden, Essex
Printed and bound in Great Britain by
Mackays of Chatham plc, Chatham, Kent

For Naomi, with love, thanks and diamonds

*'Good things mostly leave no trace,
but something always comes of evil.'*

Knut Hamsun, *Growth of the Soil*

Part One

Part One

Chapter One

It was the hottest summer since 1976. London seemed to groan at the weight of itself, like a woman pregnant with triplets. The tube was packed and bad-tempered and a strike by council workers had left the streets draped in the smell of fermenting bin bags, which lay piled outside houses and shops, spilling onto the street, pulled open by kids or dogs or the homeless or the rats that us Londoners are never, apparently, further than ten feet away from. There was dog shit everywhere and our hard-working water suppliers had imposed a hose-pipe ban. The newsreaders spoke of standpipes, and every other ad on TV seemed to show a pretty girl running out of the sea with a can of overpriced glucose in her hand.

Those who could afford to fled at the weekends. The rest seemed to crowd outside the pubs like buffalo at the watering hole. A lot of people griped about the heat just as much as they had griped about the lack of it the year before, scowling at anyone who came too near to them, clutching onto their space as though the people surrounding them were a different, alien species.

But apart from the insomnia, and the traffic, which made driving more like sitting in a peat oven, and the fumes, which made cycling just plain toxic, I didn't actually mind it. I wasn't working that hard and my occupation means I get to spend a lot of time outside anyway. It also meant that the people I was looking for would be right there, outside, in front of my face, not huddled round gas fires in dingy squats or skulking around in video arcades. The summer was easily the best time for them, made better, the better the weather stayed. Pollution and stink were nothing to them compared to bone-numbing days outside the tube stations and long nights in freezing doorways. The heat drew them out and made my job easier. All I had to do was walk around in the sunshine, in the places they were likely to be, until I found them.

Except there was one girl the sunshine wouldn't show me, no matter how hard I looked. Not, at least, when I was searching for her. The night wouldn't give her up, the night that called to her and surrounded her and penetrated her completely. That led her by the hand through foul pastures and laid her down to lie where the sun could not reach her. Where the rats were closer than ten feet and bolder. Far bolder. Drawn by the stink of a part of her that was slowly rotting, because it had died within her a long, long time ago, and was just waiting for the rest of her to catch up.

I found her though. I found her twice.

Chapter Two

If I'd had to guess the age of the man sitting across the small, round, French-style bar-table I would have had to think about it. At first I would have put him near sixty, but that would have been too high. His collar-length hair was the patchy white/grey of a young seagull but the forehead it fell over was smoother than I would have expected, leading me to think that the greying was a genetic thing. He also looked weary; his milky blue eyes were rimmed with red and they both sat on what looked like two thumb-smears of soft charcoal placed just above his cheekbones. Even though I'd never seen him before I could tell that he looked drawn, his features given sudden and stark prominence by a lack of sleep and sustenance. His face looked made-up, badly made-up to look old.

I didn't have to guess the man's age, however, because I already knew it, exactly, to the day. I also knew why he had asked to meet me, what he wanted me to do for him, and beyond that I knew that I would agree to do it and then shake his hand. Still, I heard the man out, nodding now and then, writing the odd thing down. When he'd finished he sank back into his chrome chair, and though he wasn't a heavy man, so much weight settled back with him that I couldn't imagine how he would ever lift himself out of it. I took the cheque he offered me and then left him there, staring through the smeared windows at all the cars and the buildings and the people walking past, possibly wondering how it all kept going; why the people hadn't all stopped dead, why the buildings hadn't just collapsed in broken heaps all around them. Why this had only happened inside of him.

As a small gesture, one that I knew would not mean anything to the man, I paid the bill at the till on the way out. It was only a few cups of coffee. Call it a birthday present. Then I walked out into the world that was still standing and thought about the morning, nearly two weeks before, when I had sat in another café in a different part of London, and how with strange fluidity the commonplace events of that morning had led me there.

I had got up quite early on a Thursday and left my flat in Clerkenwell before eight. I'd bought a paper, got in the car, which started, and then gone to sit in a greasy spoon on Camden High Street. I had a bacon sandwich and a cup of tea, and I was keeping a loose eye on the pavement opposite for a young girl called Donna Appleby, when something down a side alley caught my eye. It was a door, thrown open, and a body rushing out of it. A boy, a skinny white boy with a floppy bowl haircut, tripped on a couple of old boxes and went sprawling. He was followed out by a big fat, white guy, in his mid-fifties, unshaven, dressed in those huge jeans and a yellow, short-sleeved shirt straining over a taut belly. He landed the boy a toe in the ribs as he went to get up. The boy scrambled up against the right-hand alley wall as the fat guy stood facing him, blocking his escape onto the High Street.

My tea rested in mid-air as the fat guy tried to get hold of the boy. But the boy was good, he ducked and bobbed. I tried to make out if I'd seen him down at Sal's gym, where I train sometimes, but I didn't recognize him. I pulled my camera out of my holdall and took a few shots, not really knowing why. This had nothing to do with what I was there for. Then the big guy managed to land a big right on the side of the boy's head and it looked like it was over. The boy went down hard and he didn't move. Fat guy landed more size tens on the boy's side and head, and I swore to myself, about to go over there, when suddenly the boy sprang up. He was past the fat guy in a second and even though Fat tried for ten yards or so, there was no way he was ever going to catch him. The boy legged it off up the High Street, stepping off the pavement into the road, spots of blood trailing back over his shoulder from his mouth and landing on the tarmac behind him. The fat guy stood watching him for a second before walking back up the alley, breathing hard, swearing to himself. He stepped back in the door he had thrown the boy out of and it shut hard behind him.

People walked past the top of the alley engrossed in their own thoughts. I sighed with relief and put my mug down. Strange what you see when you're looking for something else.

I was about to order some more tea when, as they say, bingo. Four hundred pounds came and sat down on the other side of the road.

I took about ten snaps of Donna, eight more than I

needed, getting close in with the zoom of my brand new second-hand Leica. Then I just focused, and looked at her through the camera lens. She was pretty, with clear skin, and bright green eyes. Pulling back I could see that she was about sixteen, but that she could easily have got a child travel-card without much fuss. She was petite, fairly well dressed in jeans, trainers, scruffy tee shirt and former-Ginger Spice hair tied in the rat braids they do up by the Lock. She looked just like any teenager waiting outside the M&S, for her mother maybe, except I could see that below the frayed cuffs of her jeans her ankles were dirty, even though she was wearing a garish pink polish on her toes. She also had a small cardboard carton in front of her that had a quantity of coins in it.

I put the camera down on the table next to the brown sauce bottle and reached into my bag for the photo I had of her, which her mother had sent me. Just to make sure. Then I looked through the lens again and yes, this was the same girl. Miss Donna Appleby of Keswick in Cumbria. I watched as a youngish blond man, walking out of the store with a carton of fresh juice in his hand, stopped to give her some money. The guy walked off, running a hand back through his hair, perhaps thinking to himself what a benevolent, in-tune kind of person he was. If that is what he was thinking I would have agreed with him. I kept the camera steady on the girl, her face blinking in and out of the picture as the hurried queue of people being sucked towards the tube like so much dust into a Dyson moved past her.

In the photograph Donna's hair was longer, and it wasn't a fake caramel but a pleasant, natural brown that people who have hair that colour call mousy. She was standing with her back to a field. In the field were two ponies and behind the field was a big, ivy-covered Georgian house with a large, new-looking conservatory holding on to the right-hand side. It had eight long, airy windows. Donna was looking straight down the barrel and her face was fixed in a laugh, making her look carefree and happy. Her mother had told me that the photo was only six months old, however, so she can't have been that happy. A month or so later she had disappeared from the home in the picture and her whereabouts had been a mystery to her family, to the police, and to the large firm of investigators her father had hired immediately to find her.

But then, as I like to say, along came me.

I held the Leica steady again and studied her. I felt the slight, erotic tinge of guilt you get when looking at someone, particularly their face, when they don't know you're doing it. The face was remarkably clear, without even a single freckle that I could see, which is a shame because I like freckles. But I liked Donna's face. I liked her. She had an open, sunny expression. She grinned at people if they gave her money. I liked her especially though for the fact that she was exactly where I had been told she would be, at almost exactly the right time. My kind of girl. I paid the woman for my tea and sandwich, asked her to mind my bag for a second, and walked outside.

It was only nine fifteen, but on the street it was already starting to get hot. I waited for a couple of cars to pass and then I crossed over the road, kicking aside a Coke can and stepping over a tyre-flattened smear of recycled Pal. I walked past Donna, casually.

'Can you spare any change please, sir?'

I stopped, turning round to notice her. I looked down into her eyes and then dug my hand in my pocket. I pulled out a pound coin, but as I reached down to hand it to her I pretended to hesitate. I think I did a good job. My brother used to be an actor and I like to think I collected a little dissimulation DNA myself. The girl's face changed. She looked a little worried, like I had decided not to give her the money. But not surprised. I stared down at her for a moment before letting out a breath.

'Listen,' I said, 'what's your name?'

Very slightly, her jaw hardened.

'Natalie,' she answered, after a second, looking at me like 'What the fuck do you want?'.

'Natalie,' I said, trying to sound concerned, 'my name's William. Bill. Billy. I was just sitting over there having breakfast when I saw you sitting here.'

I hesitated again, and laughed self-consciously.

'Listen,' I went on, 'I don't like giving money to people. You understand? But would you like me to buy you some breakfast? No strings, of course. I just felt guilty eating my bacon and eggs.'

I laughed again, a little embarrassed. I ran a hand through my hair like the blond guy had done, but met a little less resistance than him due to yesterday's two, one. I smiled down at the girl and stood with my hands on my hips. She looked unsure for a second, but I imagine she thought there wasn't much anybody could do to her in a café. So she stood up, gathered her things, and followed me across the road towards the greasy spoon.

I bought Donna, or Natalie as she had become, a

vegetarian special: toast and coffee. I had another tea. I told her I was glad she'd come over with me. I told her she could order what she liked. I didn't tell her that I was a private investigator who specialized in locating stray teenagers and that her parents had hired me to find her. I told her that she looked pretty young to be out on the streets, although that was a lie, and I asked her if she had run away from home. Being a stranger she found it easy to tell me about herself, where she was from, even why she had run away. She told me what sometimes happened behind the airy windows of the house she'd been standing outside, in the picture that was in my bag only two feet away from her. She didn't tell me where she was staying now though, which might have been useful at a later date. I made the observation that while I understood, and I sympathized with her deeply, I thought she should phone her family and tell them she was fine.

'Your mother at least,' I said.

Donna looked down at her plate. The past seemed to arrive on her clear, soap ad face for a second, like a grey cloud, closing it in. But she blew it off. The sun came through. She said she would think about it. She finished eating, and asked me if she could have a can of Lilt to take with her. We talked, and then we went outside.

I said goodbye to Donna-Natalie and told her to be careful. She said she would be, and thanks, and then she crossed back over the High Street to her pitch. I watched as she sat down and set her stall out again.

I felt a pang of regret as I hitched my bag over my shoulder and walked the short distance to my car. I don't know if the regret was because I had deceived the girl, or because of what she had told me, or simply because I had enjoyed chatting to her and felt bad about leaving her where she was. Whatever. I blew it off. I got to my old Mazda, opened up and stepped in. I wound the windows down. I turned round in the side street I was parked in and pulled out onto the High Street. I saw the big man drive by in an old silver Jag, trailing a hand down the side of the door, a cigar burning furiously. I drove up towards where Natalie was sitting.

As I got level the lights turned red, and while I was stopped I watched as another girl walked up to Natalie and started speaking to her. The girl looked about sixteen too, she had a denim mini on that stuck out at the sides, a vest top, and one of those tiny rucksacks made out of silver vinyl that girls used to wear in clubs, and probably still do in smaller towns. She was tall, with long lean legs, no bra, and a firm, tan stomach. As she'd walked up to Donna I saw that she had a big mouth, teeth. Teeth. Her hair was a shortish bleached blonde, clamped to her head in the kind of tight bunches I always think look like electrodes, but which did in fact suit her strong features. As she bent over to give Donna something I got the briefest glimpse from behind of a triangle of clean, bright white cotton knickers.

Summer. Jesus. Lock me up and throw away the key.

A horn behind me sounded. There was a space in front of my car. Donna looked up and I waved at her through the window. She waved back. The other girl straightened up and looked at me. Then I put my foot on the pedal, turned the wheel away from the hot, angry bee box that was now Camden Town, and drove home.

Chapter Three

Home is on a side street behind Exmouth Market in now very fashionable Clerkenwell. It's a former photographic studio that I acquired about six years ago. When I got back from Camden I parked my car and left the morning's film with my friend Carl at the repro shop I use. I strolled back up to the market and bought a carton of milk and then asked some workmen what the shop they were refitting was going to be. Some kind of interior design place, mate, I got with a shrug to go along with it. Just what we need round here, I told them, before going upstairs to my flat.

Once inside, I switched the kettle on and sat at my desk, listening to a piece about child labour in Bangladesh on *Woman's Hour*, which was followed by one on how to make your own marmalade. What I didn't do was get on the phone to Mrs Appleby and tell her that I had located her daughter Donna in Camden Town, outside Marks and Spencer, or that she was now called Natalie, had dyed her hair, and made up at least a portion of her income begging for change. I could have, but I didn't, which wasn't unusual behaviour on my part because I never tell my clients where their children are. I used to, when I first started. But often a kid has run away from home because a father, or an uncle maybe, has been cruel. Or violent. Or raping the shit out of them. Male and female. If they are under sixteen I sometimes tell the police where they are. If they're in trouble. If they are over sixteen I don't tell anybody. I just find them, photograph them, and, if they will speak to me, tell them to think of their mothers and phone home. Then I send the photograph I have taken to my client and I give them an honest description of how their kid is.

For this service I charge a flat rate of four hundred pounds, inclusive of update reports if I happen to run into their kid again, in the near to nearish future. I suppose I lose a lot of work this way, not telling where I have located my quarry, but I'm not sending some fucked around teenager back to a vicious weekend alcoholic who likes to act tough when his team loses at home, or an uncle with a very shaky hold on the concepts of age difference and family ties. I made this decision after I had found a thirteen-year-old girl living in a squat in Streatham and I'd taken her father down there. Now, the life the kid had been leading in Streatham was probably not exactly pleasant, but there was still a mixture of resignation and terror in the girl's eyes when she saw her father. All the guy said was 'Outside. Get in the car,' in a voice that told me the kid would have been a lot better staying where she was. The kid did go with her father but I could tell that having had the courage to leave once, she would be on the road again pretty soon. Or at least I would if I'd have been her. Once, if you like, I was her, and when I'd finally had enough, nothing could have got me to go back.

My reasoning is that kids run away for a reason, but this causes a lot of pain, and not normally to that reason but to someone else. Usually, but not always, to a mother. I try to help without hurting the kid, and in the meantime make a living. It isn't ideal, not for the kid, or the parents, or even for me. It's not what I dreamed of doing, although I do have reasons, reasons for being on my own, for only doing it the way I want to do it. Most of it is bound up with why I left the police force, and a man who had done something wrong but didn't have to pay for it. And my brother. I don't think I'll do it for ever but right now it seems to suit me as much as anything else I can think of doing. Actually, to tell you the truth, at the moment there isn't anything else I can think of doing.

Instead, I called my friend Nicky, who had left me a message on my home machine. I could hear the sound of chairs being taken off tables, and the rush of a dishwasher; he was just opening his bar. Nicky wanted to know if I was around that night but as I was meeting Sharon I had to decline. I sat looking out of my window as we chatted for a while, at the rooftops and the office buildings going all the way down to St Paul's. Looking out of the window made me think of Donna-Natalie, and the photo of her home. I was glad I'd found her, but I was also glad that she didn't have to live in that house any more. I hoped that one day she would have the courage to go back there though, and deal with the reason she'd left. I saw her face for a second, changing so quickly and so completely the way it had, like one of those old-fashioned weather houses. I marvelled at how anyone could ever look so cheerful, even for a second, when they were holding inside of them the knowledge that Natalie-Donna was. It depressed me that someone so young had had to take something like that into herself and just accept it as one of the shit things in life, like rain on your birthday or flu.

I said goodbye to Nicky, telling him that I'd stop by over the weekend.

'Don't bring that girl Sharon with you though,' Nicky said. For a second I thought he was serious.

'Why the hell—?'

'Because it disgusts me to think that anyone so beautiful and intelligent should bother hanging around with someone like you.'

'I'll convey your concern,' I said. 'Anyway, are you still seeing that lap dancer?'

'Fuck you,' was the last thing I heard my friend say. I put the phone down.

After which I had my shower, letting a tired stream of lukewarm water run all over me. For some reason I picked up a bottle of shampoo that Sharon had left round here, and I used that instead of my shower gel. I don't know why. The smell of it made me think of her.

When I was all dry I dressed again and walked back to my car. I parked in the forecourt outside the building I rent my office in, locked the Mazda, and walked up the two flights. My office is opposite the tennis courts up by Highbury Fields in a 1920s clothing factory that looks like an ocean liner and has been broken up into business units, which are mostly occupied by dance companies and small design studios. I keep it because I pay no rent on my flat and can afford a small space to do business from, and because it's good to have a place to go, on the few occasions when returning home is not advisable. It also gives me a reason to get out of bed in the morning, all of my non-personal mail being sent there. I rent a small, light, bare space with a desk, and a phone, a couple of chairs as well as a sofa bed. There are also two filing cabinets, full of people. Mostly young people. Young people I have looked for and found, or else looked for and missed. Young people who have either grown older than they appear there, and changed a lot, or who have stayed the same age as the photos there show them to be. Who will always be that age.

I followed my footsteps down the empty corridor and then dug in my pocket for my keys. I shut the door behind me and let down the straw blind against the glare coming in from the window. It was still only elevenish, and having already done something that day made me feel hard working and energized. I picked up the mail from the cold wood floor and sat down at the desk to read it. One of the cheques and a rates bill that would not quite get covered by it. There was also a request from a woman to find the son I had found a couple of years ago, and send another picture. I remembered the son; a married man of forty with two young children. I wondered if he was still living in the comfortable semi in Greenwich where I'd seen him before, washing his car on a Sunday with his young daughter to help him. I took out his file and had a quick look at the pictures I'd got.

I made a couple of notes to myself and leant over my desk to the answerphone. As my finger hit 'Play', however, I caught sight of the face of my brother Luke, staring straight at me from the newly framed photo that for the last two weeks had been sitting on my desk. Luke's face stopped me for a second, until the voice on the machine interrupted my thoughts.

The voice was a very plummy voice, and it belonged to a Mrs Bradley. She didn't give a first name. Mrs

ADAM BARON

Bradley said she was waiting in the café for me, and could I join her there as soon as I got in? She sounded worried. Or, rather, late for something. I had no idea who Mrs Bradley was, but seeing as the café is only four doors along from my office I decided that yes, I could definitely meet her. After Mrs Bradley there was a message from Andy Gold at the Station and then one that surprised me, even though I had actually been expecting one like it for a week or so now. It was from a woman called Lisa March at the *Daily Express*. Lisa said she would be very pleased if I would call her on a number I didn't bother writing down.

I played the messages over, wrote more notes to myself, and walked out into the grey tiled hallway. I smiled at one of the girls who had recently taken the studio next to mine, heading towards it with a can of lemonade in her hand. Then I stopped outside the café.

The café exists to serve the business units. It's small and cheerful with more potted palms than the place really has room for, and is a great help to me. It means that people like Mrs Bradley have a place to wait if I am out or late, and it also means that I manage to maintain a balanced and nutritious diet, largely consisting of coffee and Italian cakes. I looked round the doorway of the café, and then stood leaning against the frame. The breakfast rush was over and the lunch rush was an hour away so Ally and Mike, who run the place, only had one customer. I used my incisive powers of deduction to come to the conclusion that this was Mrs Bradley. I watched her for a second, conscious of the fact that, as yet, I knew her but she didn't know me. It was a little like looking through a camera at someone. When she turned to look at me I walked towards her.

'Mrs Bradley?' I asked, proffering my hand. 'William Rucker. Would you like to come into my office?'

Mrs Bradley stood up and shook my hand but didn't say anything. I stepped back and held the door for her. Mike, who was cutting sandwiches, gave me an eyebrow as we walked past him.

Once inside my office I pulled out a chair for Mrs Bradley, walked round the desk, and sat down myself. Mrs Bradley was a well-dressed woman of about forty-two/three, her still dark, shiny hair tied back severely and a handbag over her shoulder even though she was sitting down. She wore a black, fitted skirt suit over an electric-blue silk blouse, and a thin gold necklace round her firm, though slender neck. She had quite a long face, with a good-sized mole an inch below the right corner of her mouth, which some women would have had removed. She was still attractive or, to someone who has a penchant for more mature women, she was now as attractive as she had ever been or was going to be. She sat there with a quiet, detached, slightly furious expression and her back was straight as a nun's. She didn't look the sort who would just stop by on the off chance and I wondered why she hadn't phoned me first to set up an appointment.

'Now then, Mrs Bradley,' I said, charmingly I felt. 'What can I do for you?'

'You can find my daughter,' she replied. 'My daughter Lucy. She's run away from home.'

Mrs Bradley sounded impatient and rather grudging, as though she hated asking people for things she couldn't do herself. She had a hard, deep voice, a touch too loud for my small room. She reached into her bag for a cigarette, which she lit, before adding to the tiny fan of wrinkles heading from her top lip to the bottom of her nose by pulling on it.

I leant back and opened the window behind me.

'Lucy has always been a difficult child. She hates the countryside and ever since I can remember she's talked about being where it's "at". But then, when she failed her A levels—'

'Please,' I interrupted, holding up my hands. 'Just a second.'

I wanted to tell Mrs Bradley how I worked. She sat quietly while I explained to her that I charged per case, not by the hour, and that no matter what, I would never tell her where her daughter Lucy was. She listened carefully to everything I said and she didn't seem surprised. She looked at me all the time with hard, grey eyes, the eyes of a successful politician. Or a boxer. Her eyes left me only once and very briefly, to take a look round my office. There wasn't much to detain them and I don't think their owner was hugely impressed by what they showed her.

Without making any comment on what I'd said, Mrs Bradley explained again that Lucy, who was seventeen, had disappeared from the Bradleys' home in Sussex just over two months ago. She hadn't been seen since. As she spoke to me, Mrs Bradley seemed curiously removed from what she was saying. She wasn't the bundle of terror and self-flagellation I was used to calming down over the phone or sitting across from me. She was angry and impatient rather than worried and distraught. She also had very full, and still firm breasts, breasts a little too noticeable to be absolutely proper for a woman of her age and obvious social standing. It was a body slightly too young for its face. I noticed this, you understand, because it is my profession to notice such things. A conscientious investigator has to notice everything.

I asked Mrs Bradley why she thought her daughter had come to London and she told me she'd found a bus timetable in Lucy's bedroom. For some reason she pulled it out of her handbag and showed it to me. I looked at it politely, nodded sagely, and then asked her if she was happy with the way I worked, and therefore wanted to employ me.

Mrs Bradley waited a second, studying me with her lips pursed, like an art critic looking at a bad forgery.

'You're very young,' she said finally. 'You don't look like a private investigator, or whatever it is that you call yourself.'

I smiled.

'How would you know, Mrs Bradley?'

'I went to Sirius first,' she stated. 'They're all fifty-five, with beer bellies and cheap suits, or shirts with sweat down the sides. You look about thirty, at most, and you don't look like you own a suit.'

She stared at me. No longer thirty, quite. I was wearing a white tee shirt with a rip in the front, cut-offs and trainers.

'It's part of the uniform,' I told her. 'When you're looking for young people it doesn't pay to look ex-police, even if that's what you are. In fact you've caught me on a good day, I shaved last night.'

I smiled again. I believe I have a disarming and relaxing smile. Mrs Bradley sat there, looking just as armed as she was before.

'You say you don't charge until you send the picture?'

'No, but I make you sign a contract saying that you will pay me when I do. It's binding.'

'I see,' she said. 'And you don't concentrate on one case at a time, you look for all the people you take on at once?'

'I go to the places where they are going to be. I can get into them and not look out of place. I don't care too much about background, or what sort of girl she is, although that can often help. I just know where to look, and I keep looking. There are places in London that young people are drawn to, and I know what they are. Sooner or later I usually run into them or I get a tip-off as to where a particular one might be. That's if they are there to be found,' I added. 'I do OK, I think.'

I sat back in my chair, trying to look nonchalant, trying not to think of the bank statement I had read that morning. Trying not to think that it might be a lot of fun looking for a seventeen-year-old version of the haughty, attractive woman sitting in front of me.

'Well,' Mrs Bradley said, reluctantly I thought, 'I suppose I have nothing to lose. The police said you were the one, when I asked. Your name was volunteered. Off the record, as the man put it. But tell me this. How much would it cost to hire you exclusively?'

Mrs Bradley looked straight at me. This woman must be into politics at some level: she was treating a very emotional matter as if it were simply a business deal, and she had just ignored everything I had been saying to her. I told her again how I worked, but this time added that that was the only way I worked. I told her she could hire someone else if she wanted, that I had more than enough to do at present. Just as I finished speaking, however, she reached into her bag

22

and took out a cheque book. She opened it and started scribbling.

'All right,' she said, 'but I will pay you in advance, and when you find her there will be a bonus. That might make you look harder.' She scribbled some more and then snapped off the cheque like a gamekeeper putting a rabbit out of its misery.

Mrs Bradley seemed to have finalized the arrangement. I didn't argue with her, although I did have the strange and sudden urge to tell this hard, determined lady to fuck right off out of it. Instead I opened up a notebook and wrote Lucy's name at the head of a new page. As I did so I saw Mrs Bradley glance at the cigarette she had hardly touched, the ash piled improbably high like a chimney just before the charge blows. She looked round my desk, presumably for an ashtray, but she was never going to find one. I left her to her discomfort for a second or two and then I leant forward. Very gently I reached out my hand and took the cigarette from her, carefully. I leant backwards towards the window and knocked the ash out of it. Then, just as gently, I placed the cigarette back in her hand, our fingers brushing slightly as the pressure on it was exchanged from me to her. Mrs Bradley held it for a second and then turned away.

She rummaged in her bag with her free hand, and then handed me a photograph. I was expecting another picture of a posh-looking girl at a party, or outside a nice house in the country, but that is not exactly what I got. The picture was of a girl straddling a stationary motorbike, in a ripped denim jacket and wearing bright red lipstick, sticking the finger up to whoever took the photo. It seemed a strange picture for the austere Mrs

Bradley to be handing me. I looked at it, hard, and then I got Mrs Bradley to sign her contract, and write down a few details about her daughter Lucy, her height, what kind of music she liked. I did this as quickly as I could. I had intended to ask her some standard questions about herself and her family, whether Lucy had any friends in London, stuff like that. But I didn't. I told Mrs Bradley I would call her and that I would be happy to meet her again very soon but that I had an urgent meeting to attend and couldn't talk to her now. When she'd given me her card and told me when to call, I almost lifted her out of her seat and threw her out of the door. It took some courage, believe me. I pointed her towards the lift. Then, without bothering to lock the office behind me, I took the back stairs six at a time and jumped into the Mazda.

It started.

The traffic was a nightmare, especially on the Holloway Road, and I wished I'd had another bike at the office as well as the one I keep at home. My new tee shirt stuck to the back of the seat and rather than a breeze, all that came through the open window was the dirty heat generated from all the other vehicles. When I finally got back to Camden High Street the doorway outside Marks was occupied by a frail old woman trying to play a penny whistle.

Donna-Natalie was gone.

I wasn't surprised really. She'd looked to be making quite a lot of money before and who wants to sit in the baking hot sun all day? But it was a shame. She may have known where the other girl I had seen her talking to hung out.

The other girl's name was Lucy. Lucy Bradley.

I turned the car round. If only I'd had the good sense to snap Lucy, as well as the Early Morning Fight Special, I could have earned her mother's little bonus without leaving the office. Shame. How bizarre, to have seen her like that. As I looked through the rolled down side window at the old woman making thin music from her pile of stained blankets and ragged clothes, I had a sudden image.

A flash of bright white knickers.

It's funny what you see when you're looking for something else.

Chapter Four

I pulled the car into a bus lane and sat for a minute thinking what I should do with myself. It was still only twelve-thirty but it seemed like I'd already had a long day. I wanted another shower; my tee shirt had become a permanent part of my body, and my hands felt slimy on the wheel. But I couldn't go back home *again*. I had things to do, I was a detective for God's sake. I thought about going down to Greenwich but there wouldn't be any point, not in working hours. I thought about strolling around Camden, seeing if I couldn't spot Miss Bradley anywhere. Good plan. I parked the car where I'd parked it earlier, slung my bag over my shoulder, and walked up towards the Lock.

I wandered around the Lock, up and down the High Street a few times, and I looked in some of the shops that seemed to be selling the type of clothing Lucy nearly wore. She wasn't around, or if she was I didn't see her. I also kept an eye out for Olly, Camden's finest *Big Issue* salesman, and the purveyor of sometimes useful information, but he was nowhere either. I tried to decide whether Donna-Natalie knew the girl I was now looking for. I couldn't really tell, but when Lucy had given her what I took to be money, she had handed it to her rather than tossed it into her box. I hadn't seen what it was but I had seen Donna-Natalie's hand reach up for it. Did that mean anything? Probably not. I hoped it did though; Donna-Natalie had been easy to find and if she knew Lucy then she wouldn't be too hard to track down either.

I bought an old copy of the *Tao Te Ching*, a book I have been meaning to read for as long as I can remember, and then ignored a cup of black 'coffee' in the greasy spoon I had been in before, hoping that Lucy would walk by on her way back from wherever she had been going to when I saw her before. No joy. I did see a lot of other teenagers, some of whom looked to be living rough, and I'm sure there were people out there who would have wanted news of them. But nobody was paying me to find them. I paid for the coffee and walked out into the heat again.

I hung around for a while, taking in the lazy, nonchalant tawdriness of Camden Town. The heat seemed like a giant insect, slowly sucking on my resolve to do anything useful. I found myself standing outside the café/bar on Delancey Street where my brother Luke worked for a while, about six years ago, before the accident that left him in what the doctors call a persistent vegetative state. A state he has never escaped from. I stood in the doorway, peering in through the smoke, confronted by a hubbub that sounded like a BBC sound tape backed by the spoilt whine of an espresso machine. I didn't go in. It was here that Luke had first met his one true love, the girl he went out with for two years, whom he eventually got engaged to but never got a chance to marry. The young, earnest lawyer, whom Luke loved to wind up, because she would always take things seriously. The

27

girl with the deep blonde hair, who sent Luke's heart spinning, but gave his life a grounding, who encouraged him to apply himself more, to get what he wanted. The girl who turned him from the meandering, noncommittal path he'd been ambling along, whom he credited for all of his eventual acting success and for getting his poems in the magazines. The girl whose eyes, he said, were fresh and green like river moss in the sun. I tried to decide which table she'd been sitting at when Luke had walked over to take her order, and, as he told me later that same day, he just fell in love with her there and then. The table he had then proceeded to spill cappuccino all over because he was so nervous. I couldn't decide, but I didn't have to think about it too hard, because if I cared enough about it I could ask her. I was seeing her later.

Thoughts of Sharon spread a sense of calm through me, which seemed to turn the volume down on the traffic, and dampen the noise crashing out of the rattling bar. Sharon's eyes really were like that, something that astonished me when I first saw them, which still does, now that they look at me far more often than they look at Luke. I thought about the first time that I ever woke up and found them open to me. Sometimes, when I think of Luke, trying to imagine the dark and lonely place he must inhabit inside his head, I wonder if he remembers them. I wonder if he sees them, like Catseyes on a road. I hope he does. I couldn't ever imagine not seeing them.

A waiter serving one of the outside tables asked me if he could get me anything, but I said no. I looked at my watch; it was after three. I walked back to my car. I stopped outside the M&S again but now even the old woman had gone. All that was left in the doorway was a couple of orange flyers for a night at York's, a big warehouse-type club venue in that no man's land between Camden and King's Cross. Reasoning that they wouldn't have belonged to the old woman, I picked one up and stuffed it in my pocket. By now it was at least eighty degrees, or whatever it is in Celsius, which I'll never get used to, and when I climbed into the car again my thighs got third-degree burns from the plastic seat cover. Once again I cursed the state of my company vehicle, an old, shit-coloured Mazda that had belonged to my mother. Oh for air conditioning, a sunroof, an engine that didn't make it seem like you were playing the Lottery every time you tried the ignition. This time I was a winner. A sign at the end of the street claimed that I could not turn right but it was wrong because I did turn right and then I was at the lights again.

Back at my office I pulled on yet another fresh tee shirt before getting down to my typing. I walked down the hall for a cup of tea but the door was shut. I was about to push it open but I could hear the sound of Ally's high-pitched Italian voice battering itself against Mike's slightly rounded London vowels. I'd heard this yesterday too; the heat I suppose. Working together every day in such a cramped environment must get really tough, I thought, especially seeing as Mike and Ally also share a none too spacious one-bed apartment. I thought they would rather have the privacy than the trade so I went without my tea and sat down again. At about four, the phone rang. Acting on one of those bizarre telepathic telephone instincts that sometimes inexplicably tell you the identity of the person calling you, I let the machine get it.

'Mr Rucker, this is Lisa again, at the Express. *I'll be in the office till about six if you could call me, or else I'll try you again tomorrow. Thanks a lot. My number is 020 7811 4325.'*

Luke smiled at me from the centre of the frame. I ignored the number and erased the message.

* * *

There's something friendly about the night-time in summer, something completely opposite to the long, miserable nights in winter. The buildings and the people seem to relax from the heat of the day. When I came out of the gym that night the air felt good, even though the gym is only a step away from King's Cross Station. I felt good too, having put in a full workout, and then managed not to get my teeth knocked out by a guy called Des Formay. Des had once actually tried to make boxing his career, and even if it hadn't taken too long before he was made to realize that he'd never be anything more than a very good amateur, I was pleased to be able to live with him for a few rounds, even if I knew he was getting the best of it. It felt good that Sal, who owns the gym, had been there to see it. Afterwards she unlaced my gloves and massaged my fingers for me.

'What did I tell you? You're better than you think you are, Mr Rucker.'

'Thanks, Sal. You don't have Don King's home number, do you?'

'Ah, you may jest. But who knows what could happen if you just put some work into it?'

Work? I was down there three nights a week at the moment, and if it wasn't work I was doing on the bag, the rope, the mill and the machines, I'd like to know what the hell it was. I thanked Sal for her encouragement and went to shower. On my way out I went to find Des to thank him too, but as he was having a medicine ball dropped repeatedly on his stomach I didn't bother interrupting him.

Back in my flat I dressed quickly with the TV on, listening to a smoky-voiced actor give the impression that he was ten feet away from the polar bears someone else was filming. I sat for a while, mesmerized by the fluffy, dapper-looking creatures. I watched a polar bear pounce on a baby seal and then begin to pick at it, the seal's flippers flapping uselessly. I watched a mother, buried under the snow, suckling something white and helpless, small as an albino chihuahua. Apparently, the mother had given birth to another cub too, but made the decision to let it die. I watched the same mother six months later, teaching her cub how to go for the seals. The mother brought another baby seal back for the cub and let the kid get on with it.

When the programme was over I flipped through my new copy of the *Tao Te Ching*. *'He who knows how to live can walk abroad without fear of the rhinoceros or the tiger.'*

Not much use, I thought, to a baby seal.

Before leaving I called the number that Mrs Bradley had given me. It was a London number, and I wondered whether she was borrowing a friend's flat or the family

31

kept a place in town. Mrs Bradley was out, so I left a message for her to call me tomorrow.

I met Sharon in the little French place opposite Sainsbury's at the Angel, a place you go to for the cramped, left bank atmosphere as much as for the food. I walked up there with a spring in my step, thinking that it had been a week and a half at least since I'd actually seen Sharon. It hadn't seemed that long because we'd spoken on the phone, but now, walking to meet her, it did. I realized that I was almost bounding along, and the feelings I was having embarrassed me slightly, making me feel no more than about fourteen years old. I slowed down. As I crossed over to the restaurant a young lad asked me if I wanted a copy of the *Big Issue*. I already had the one he was selling but I dug out some change for him anyway.

Sharon had been in court today and she still had on her simple black fitted suit with trousers, which she hopes makes her look neutral before the members of our largely sexist and patronizing legal profession. I didn't tell her, but I don't think Sharon could look neutral in a mail sack, which probably makes me as bad as they are. Sharon had given me a fleeting smile when I'd entered, and touched my cheek with hers.

'It's great to see you,' I said, as we sat down.

'You too,' she said. 'Are you hungry? I'm starving.'

We were at a small, dark table in the back. Sharon had her mud-blonde hair raked back severely and she wore no make-up. I reached forward and brushed the tiny, dark mole that sat just above her left eyebrow, which she hated and which drove me wild. She studied the menu, biting her top lip. Rather than look at my menu I watched her. It had been a long time since my eyes were able to do this, and the effect she had on me was to scour my head clean of anything except what I was seeing. All I could think of was how simply and completely beautiful she was. Her face stopped me, like an early Giacometti drawing you just can't walk past, and for a second I couldn't get beyond it. I was brought back to the present by a waiter taking our drinks order.

The way Sharon looks is something that used to unnerve me when we were 'just friends', both trying to get over what had happened to my brother. I used to register it, but not let it in. Now it still unnerves me, but not in the same way. The beauty of Sharon's face, the simple way it is laid out, scares me, because though I know it is irrelevant, a genetic accident, I can't help but feel that, somehow, it *means* something. Sometimes, I even wish that Sharon wasn't quite so startling to look at, and not because of insecurity or jealousy or what I see in the faces of other men. It may sound bizarre to say it, but once I got to know Sharon, I began to feel that it didn't quite suit her, this beauty that rested on her features unbidden, which seemed to come from another place. I think she even feels this herself, though she would never actually admit that she was beautiful. I think she finds it irritating, an irrelevance, because it's something she doesn't give a shit about in anyone else. I think she hates the way it makes people instantly define her, and the way it makes some people behave when they meet her. Men and women. She is the only woman I have ever met whom I am careful never to compliment on the way she looks, except to say that I like a particular thing she may be wearing. Whenever I have, unable to contain what I feel, a look of impatience shadows her face and I lose her.

Sharon's mother once told me that one afternoon Sharon disappeared from school. She was ten years old. A search eventually found her in the tool shed. She was with the old man who used to tend the gardens. Nothing had happened to her, Sharon swore to that. The old man had just asked her to stand there, in front of him. Apparently, when the teachers found them, he was sat on a stool, three feet away from her, his head in his hands, crying. The governors were apparently very worried, not having a reason to sack him, but it didn't matter. He walked out of the shed and never came back.

Apart from looking sensational tonight, Sharon looked stressed. The candlelight deepened the already strong hollows her green eyes sat in, and showed me the tiny channels curving down from the centre of her eyes towards her cheekbones. Sharon looked serious, as though the menu were a ten-page legal document. I leant forward and took her hand.

'I'm so glad you could make it,' I said, smiling. 'God, it seems like ages since we've spent any time together.'

'I know but I've been busy, Billy, I really have. What with this course I'm doing and the summer's a bugger anyway . . .'

'Hey,' I said, 'I know, I know. I wasn't blaming you, I understand.' I smiled again. 'Someone has to stand up for truth and justice in this wicked world.'

'Don't take the piss, Billy.'

'I'm not, God. I'm sorry. All I meant was it's good to see you. I'm happy to see you.'

Sharon took a breath, closed her eyes briefly and nodded. Her lips were pursed as she said, 'And you. I'm sorry. It is, it's really good to see you too, Billy.'

She did her best to brighten and to smile at me, her mouth closed, before looking down at the menu again when I tried to catch her eye.

I don't remember what we ate. I probably had the *gazpacho* because of the heat, and Sharon is a fan of shellfish so it's quite likely that she had the clams. The starters came and went and were followed by the main courses as starters usually are. Sharon, in contrast to her stated hunger, picked at her food like a rich woman at a jumble sale, and her lack of appetite soon infected me. It was pretty obvious that there was something wrong. We sat in silence for a while, with a brittle awkwardness at the centre of it that I hadn't felt with her for a long time. It was made worse by the image that sat alongside it, a warm, expectant, intimate evening with the girl I was in love with. I couldn't think of a natural way to break the silence, and I left it to Sharon to do so. Finally, she asked me what I was working on at the moment.

I told Sharon about my week and my day, how I had seen Lucy Bradley that morning and then gone back to find her. I returned the question and Sharon said oh, just dull stuff, but then expanded when I told her that I never found her work stories boring. Sharon works as a lawyer for the Refugee Legal Centre, defending asylum seekers from deportation orders, trying to get them resident status on the grounds of political, racial, or religious persecution in their own country. She told me the story of a woman who had somehow escaped from China to avoid being sterilized for giving birth to twin girls.

'The problem is that the Chinese deny that sterilization is a government policy, it's all done on a local level.'

'Right,' I said. 'But you might be able to help her?'

'How do I know?'

'Well, from past cases, I don't know . . .'

'Listen, it's all really complicated, Billy.'

'Right, right,' I said again.

Sharon wasn't really there. She was just going through the motions. There had been times in the past when I had listened to her for hours as she told me of the difficulties of getting help for genuine refugees, but tonight it could have been the football results she was telling me. I decided that she must just have had enough of legal stuff. I realized that I'd made a mistake asking her about work, but then I made a bigger one. I tried to lift the evening, to bring it round to something that meant a lot to us, which was something we had both planned, both made happen. I asked her if she was ready for the 15th.

Sharon stopped. It was like an arrow that went straight to the centre of her thoughts, the ones she was keeping to herself. I was reminded of times on the Force when I'd done the same thing to a suspect, suddenly coming out with the right question, sometimes by accident, after going round the houses for an hour. I wasn't interviewing Sharon though, and the comparison made me feel shitty.

Sharon put her fork down and looked straight at me for the first time that evening. Her eyes flickered like she'd seen a ghost, and her teeth caught hold of her lip again. Everything inside her seemed to settle on this question I had asked her. She looked at her wine glass, resting her hand on the stem. Her expression shocked me, for a second I thought she was going to break down. And then, somehow, the look on her face prepared me for what she had to say, even though a second before it would have been the last thing in the world I would have guessed she'd come out with.

'I don't think I'm going to come, Billy,' she said, in as firm a voice as she could manage.

I left a second. The waiter came over and cleared away our plates.

'What?'

Sharon fought against a tremor in her jaw. 'I've thought about it some more. I just—'

'But we've already discussed this, Sharon. I thought we'd agreed that though it'll be hard, we're going to be there. I thought—'

'I know, Billy, I know. But things have . . .' She took a breath. 'I've changed my mind, I don't think I'll be able to deal with it.'

'And you think I will?' I wanted to try and understand, not shout at her. I tried to make my voice sound reasonable. But I couldn't. 'I thought we'd both decided to say fuck it! We're not doing anything wrong, we're not ashamed, and no matter what anyone says we're not going to get into any of that Oprah Winfrey bullshit. So it's OK if we go.'

'I know but—'

'It was you who decided. You said to hell with them.'

'Yes—'

'And it was you who wanted to get them published in the first place, when you knew I was against it. And

37

now you're saying that I have to go to the frigging launch on my own. That I have to deal with all the bullshit myself.'

'You don't have to go either.'

'What? But I want to go, because in spite of what I used to think, you persuaded me to be proud of Luke, proud of his work, and so to hell with the rest of them. I'm not missing the launch of my brother's book and I can't believe you want to miss it either.'

'Well, I'm sorry, Billy, I just don't think . . .' She took another breath. I could feel my face set tight against her. I was wound up now, wound up tight, and I could feel myself ready to pounce on the next thing Sharon said, whatever it was. She must have felt it too. She sat back.

'Listen, Billy, I'm sorry. I'm probably just being stupid. I'll think about it. I will. I shouldn't have said anything. I'll probably want to go when it comes to the day. I just . . . I'm sorry, Billy, I'm probably just being stupid.'

'Sharon—'

'Please, Billy, don't. Just let me think about it some more, OK?'

'OK, but—'

'Billy!'

I shrugged my shoulders and drained my wine glass.

Sharon didn't want dessert, or coffee. I ordered an espresso, but just so that we didn't leave the place feeling the way we were feeling. I didn't really want it. I took my time sipping it, trying to ignore Sharon's occasional glances at her wristwatch. She obviously wanted to leave but I wanted to talk, about Luke, and the launch of the volume of poems that Sharon and I had collected together from the ones he had already published in magazines, and others she had found in his notebooks. This had to be the reason she was behaving like she was. I thought I'd better wait until we were back in my flat though, where Sharon didn't have to worry about making a scene, or letting go of the clenched knot of doubts I could see inside her. I wanted her to tell me the reason why she didn't want to go. Then I could argue it with her, we could scream at each other and then she could tell me what the real reason was, the reason she probably didn't even know herself yet. Then we could talk about that and there wouldn't be this sheet of ice between us any more.

Once outside, however, Sharon told me that she wanted to go home.

'Billy, I'm just so tired.'

'OK,' I said, not that it was. 'OK.'

'And I'm sorry about before.' Her eyes tried to find mine but I pretended not to notice.

'It's all right. I know it must be hard for you. It was just a surprise, that's all.'

Sharon took my hand and squeezed it. We stood for a second. I felt very defensive towards her but told myself I was being stupid. I met her eyes and then went to kiss her, but she turned her head towards a cab coming along the Liverpool Road. She put her free arm up and it slowed. The cab stopped beside us and Sharon climbed in the back.

Sharon gave me that closed mouth smile again as the cab moved off.

I stood outside the restaurant for a while, gazing blankly at the shapes inside the all-night supermarket opposite. Just as I had done any number of times since

I'd first heard from Sharon that Luke's book of poems was going to be published by Faber, I pictured myself standing at a party, cheap Chardonnay in hand, without him. Only the week before the publicist had called to tell me when the event would be.

Luke had never really spoken to me about his writing, he'd never told me that it was his burning ambition to get his work published. I'd always just assumed it was his acting that meant the most to him. But when I read the proofs of the book Faber had produced, I knew how proud Luke would have been to stand in front of a display of the finished work, as its author. That Luke could not come and do that simple thing was something that I had to live with. I'd be damned if I wasn't going to stand there in place of him. That much I owed him at the very least. I didn't care about all the shit I might get. I knew what questions I'd be asked and I knew what the answers I'd give would be.

'And, Mr Rucker, can you tell me again the circumstances of your brother's accident?'

'I was a member of the Metropolitan Police. I was on a case when, through various circumstances, my life was in danger. My brother found this out and he tried to warn me. He borrowed my car and drove across London, but he was followed by some of the people I was investigating.'

'Who were these people, Mr Rucker?'

'They were never caught by the police. Anyway, they must have thought that my brother was me, and the car was rammed from the side, sending it over a flyover. Luke sustained the injuries that have left him in a persistent vegetative state. A coma, if you like.'

'And where is your brother being cared for now?'

'I can't really see any need to tell you that.'

'Finally, Mr Rucker, can I ask you about Luke's fiancée?'

'His former fiancée.'

'Yes. Sharon Dean. You and she have remained friends since the accident, haven't you?'

'Yes. Yes, we have remained friends.'

And if I thought the questions would end there I was kidding myself. If they didn't I would answer them truthfully and without any apologies or embarrassment, because to deny something I wasn't ashamed of would have been wrong. Not to answer would have been to tell them what they were hoping for anyway. That some years after Luke's accident the friendship that had helped both Sharon and myself get through what had happened had changed into something else, and even though we both tried, neither Sharon nor myself could do anything to prevent that change. Or stop ourselves being glad about it. I knew that the questions would come, perhaps veiled in concerned-sounding crap about the closeness that helped sustain us, or perhaps not. Whatever, I was ready for them, and the self-satisfied newspaper articles that could very well follow. No newspaper article could do anything to hurt my brother, and if what they said was the truth then how could they hurt me either? The sanctimonious glee might be hard to stomach but I knew I'd get over it.

One thing I hadn't anticipated, however, was that I would have to go and answer these questions on my own; that Sharon wouldn't be there to answer them with me. I didn't think this was like her, she was not the sort of person to run away from things. In all the images I had of the event, Sharon had always been there, standing beside me, or giving me a look from across the room. But now it looked like she wouldn't be. I didn't think it was fair, either, that she'd run off back to West London rather than talk about it.

I didn't really want to go home yet. I'd had the image of a different ending to this evening in mind and I wasn't ready to go and deal with the less than appealing alternative just at the moment. I thought about a drink down at the Old Ludensian, but Nicky would only ask where Sharon was. Instead, I decided to go back to Camden, to hang around the Lock or outside a pub until it shut, and then sit in a late café or stand outside a hotdog stand. I crossed the road and walked down St John Street before turning right into Chadwell Street, towards Middleton Square.

The night was quiet and I could hear the muted sound of my Salomons on the pavement as I strolled along, as well as a sharper sound behind me, given a slight resonance by the neat brickwork of the imposing flats and houses of the square. I stopped opposite the big, sombre box of the church, to tie my shoelace, and the steps behind me came to a halt. This surprised me; I hadn't stopped on purpose. I didn't think too much of it, but when I moved off again the steps started up again, not getting any nearer to me, even though I wasn't walking very fast. Then, when I sped up a bit, this time definitely on purpose, they didn't get any further away.

Now, I was thinking much of it. I went the wrong way round the square before turning back on myself a little and crossing over Amwell Street. The footsteps stayed directly behind me. I tried to snatch a look over my shoulder, but I couldn't get round far enough. If they got any closer to me then I'd definitely turn round. I took a left out of Lloyd Baker Square down a cut-through passage towards Margery Street, and walked through Wilmington Square.

My car was parked outside my flat. I rolled the window down, started it and waited. After a second or two I heard another engine come to life, back up on Exmouth Market. I pulled the Mazda up towards Rosebery Avenue and then out towards the lights. I could have made the lights but I didn't want to. I waited while they went through red again, as an electric-blue Peugeot 205 pulled up behind me. Then, when the light turned green I turned right onto the last stretch of the Farringdon Road and then made sure I arrived at the next set of lights just as they turned red too. I stopped. I checked my wing mirror. I waited.

And then I backed my car up fast so that it was right up to the grille of the blue 205 behind me and I got out quickly. I managed to reach the other side of the car before the person in it could either back up or lock the passenger side door. I pulled the door open fast, got in and looked to my right. It was an impulsive thing to do and I really don't know what I expected to happen after I'd done it, but there was one thing I certainly wasn't prepared for.

Lucy Bradley was sitting behind the steering wheel.

Chapter Five

My hand was on the gear stick, keeping the car in neutral, and I was about to reach over and take the keys out when I stopped. I stared at Lucy Bradley. My mouth opened stupidly and my mind did several of the gear changes I was preventing the car from doing. A horn behind me sounded and I looked up to see that the lights had turned to green.

'Put your hazards on,' I said.

The girl beside me reached forward and touched a button. More gear changes. The cars behind began to make a detour round us. I looked at the girl's face again.

'Jesus Christ,' was the best I could come out with.

It really was incredible. If her hair had been shorter than her sister's and not longer, I wouldn't have even begun to doubt that she had had it cut that day, and re-dyed black from its glam blonde. But as you can't make your hair three inches longer in the space of a few hours, the only conclusion I could come to was that the girl I was suddenly sitting next to wasn't Lucy Bradley at all but someone else, and the only person she could possibly have been was her sister. Maybe, if I'd seen her after speaking to her mother properly, then I would have been prepared. I would still hardly have believed it though. Identical doesn't seem anywhere near strong enough.

I sat with my hand on the gear stick of the 205 staring at the girl. The girl herself didn't look too frightened but she did look caught out, like a sixth-former found smoking dope by the deputy head. I wasn't about to tell her off though. I was still stunned by her physical resemblance to her sister, even though I'd only seen the girl once in the flesh, and once in a photograph. I finally did get it together to reach over and take the keys out of the ignition, though I didn't really think it was necessary.

The girl who wasn't Lucy relaxed a little when she realized that I wasn't going to give her a lot of shit for following me. She reacted to my astonishment with a weary, though understanding smile.

'Don't worry,' she said, slight sarcasm trying to cover up her nerves. 'Everyone's like that. At least to begin with. Then they're just confused. After that they can tell us apart but its only because of what we wear, and the kind of things we like doing.'

'And your hair,' I said.

'And our hair.' She pushed a wedge of it behind her left ear, releasing a pocket of fresh, Body Shop perfume. Her hair was a deep, lustrous black, softer than her mother's but without so much of a shine. She smiled nervously, not a big smile but still showing me columns of straight, firm teeth. 'Although I don't know what Lucy's done to hers recently. It could be anything, knowing her.'

I didn't tell her that I knew exactly how her sister was wearing her hair these days.

'There's also the fact that your sister probably

doesn't go around following people to restaurants and out again, halfway round Islington and then along the Farringdon Road.'

'No,' the girl said. 'There's that too, I suppose.'

Her name was Emma. I told her to take a right and then park the 205 at the bottom of Lloyd Baker Street. We then walked back to my car and I drove up to my flat again. My space was gone, but there's a delivery bay nearby that's safe overnight so I left the car there. We walked back down Exmouth Market towards Fred's, a café at the Farringdon end of the street that's open late from Thursday through the weekend. As we walked in the door I nodded hi to Alberto, who was leaning against the bar as usual, and he waved and walked over. He looked at Lucy's sister.

'Hello again,' he said, surprised.

Emma looked embarrassed.

'I was in here earlier,' she said to me. 'You get a good view of the top of the street you live on.'

'Some more coffee?' Alberto asked her.

We took a table by the window and Alberto sauntered off to forget about our drinks for a while. I eventually drank the top third of a glass of syrupy Belgian beer while Emma sipped nervously at a Coke. As we spoke I tried to dredge up the image of Lucy from the morning, but I couldn't get any further than the face in front of me. Emma had a long, geometrical jawline. Her nose was impressive with a slight ridge that made her eyes seem set back a little too far. Her eyes were two dark almonds that I could tell were stinging her. Unlike her mother, Emma's face was younger than her body which, though it was perfectly well advanced, she still carried like a teenage girl, covering her breasts with her arms, relaxing her posture into a hunch that belied her height. From the brief glimpse that I'd had of her sister I had the impression that while they were physically interchangeable, she'd had an older, more confident bearing.

Emma played nervously with her straw.

'I'm sorry I followed you, Mr Rucker.'

'Billy.'

'I'm really sorry I followed you, Billy.'

'That's all right. There's only one thing worse than being tailed.'

'What? What's that?'

'Not being tailed. Oscar Wilde.'

Emma smiled and I was glad. I was actually annoyed at her for trying to follow me, but the nerves she had shown at being discovered by me, and the fear that I'd be angry about it, had slowly begun to wear off to reveal a far deeper concern beneath it. I could guess what it was.

'How did you know where I live?' I asked.

'I looked you up in—'

'I'm not in the phone book. Listen, I don't give a fuck, OK? You followed me and I caught you, end of story.'

'All right,' Emma said. 'I'm sorry. But I don't want you to think that my mother had anything to do with this.'

'I see. I think I see.' I went through it quickly. 'You were waiting outside my office?'

'Yes.'

'And you followed me back from there to my flat. I have to say you did a much better job that time.'

'There was loads of traffic. I thought I'd lost you a few times.'

'And then you waited here, watching my street, and then tailed after me on foot up to the Angel.'

'Yes. Yes, I did. I was really worried. I thought you'd be bound to look round.'

'I had other things on my mind.' I sat back in my chair and took a sip of beer. 'You mentioned your mother.'

'She doesn't know,' Emma insisted. 'I didn't tell her. I just knew when she was meeting you. She didn't know I was going to follow you. It was my idea that she employ you. Mine and my dad's.'

'But not your mother's?'

'No. The policeman told Mum that you wouldn't tell us where Lucy was. Mum couldn't see the point of that. Dad could, he just wanted news of her, any news.'

'And you?'

'I thought that if Mum employed you, then maybe I could follow you and if you did find Lucy, well then I could wait till you left and then talk to her. I could maybe persuade her to come home. I really want to talk to her.'

A swell rose up in Emma very suddenly, like a wave of nausea, which she just got under control.

'You must want to very badly.'

'I do. I do.'

'Apart from obviously wanting to see her, is there any particular . . .?'

'I made my sister run away,' Emma said, before the next wave crashed through and out of her, and over the table all around us.

Emma leant over forwards with her head in her hands, pressing her elbows into her ribs. Her dark straight hair hung forwards on both sides like two meat cleavers and began to sway gently. Emma had large, strong hands, and when she didn't stop crying I reached forward and gently prized one away from her, holding it on the table top, squeezing it tight. At that moment Alberto walked past and was about to come over to chat when he noticed what I was doing. He saw that Emma was in tears and he stopped, giving me a shocked half comic grimace as he walked through into the kitchen.

Emma held on to my hand, crying like a very young child, and then, when she had calmed down, she took hers back self-consciously. She used it to dust away some tears from her eyelashes, which didn't smear because, contrary to appearances, they were not made up. She straightened her back, set her jaw against a few dying tremors, and breathed in deeply through a nose that I'd noticed was red even before this bout of tears. Her hair was bothering her and she pushed it off her face again.

'Bloody stuff.'

I stayed still for as long as it took her to focus on me.

'Tell me all about it,' I said.

Emma and I sat in Fred's for an hour while she told me why she thought she was responsible for her sister's sudden disappearance. I sat listening, nodding my head now and then and thinking how ready the human mind is sometimes to heap guilt upon itself. Guilt that hangs in the air because no one else seems to be claiming it.

'Lucy messed up her exams,' Emma said, as if that was the explanation for everything. 'Then she just disappeared, about two months ago. We weren't too worried for a day or two because she often stays out, never telling anyone where she is. After a while Mum phoned a couple of old boyfriends, the few she knew the names of. They hadn't seen her, so she phoned the police.'

'And then a big detective agency.'

'She told you?'

'She did. But she didn't tell me she was still employing them, which I imagine she is.'

Emma looked uncomfortable. I didn't want her breaking her mother's confidence so I didn't push it. It was annoying though, knowing I might get my toes trodden on by the big boys.

I tried to send my mind back fourteen years.

'I didn't think the A-level results were out yet. I mean, how did Lucy know she hadn't done well? I mean definitely?'

'She didn't write anything,' Emma said, after a second or two. 'She just sat there looking at the papers. Apparently she didn't even write her name at the top. She didn't even show up for the last one.'

I nodded again. 'How did you know? About her not writing anything? Did she tell you?'

'I . . .' Emma hesitated. 'I was in the same hall. At least for History and English. I wasn't sitting next to her but my friend Clare was both times, and she told me. I . . .'

The swell rose up again but this time Emma contained it, quickly getting hold of herself. She blinked strongly, forcing air into her lungs. There was a definite look of steel in her face and I saw a resemblance to her mother that I hadn't noticed up till then. She also had that preoccupied look that told of thoughts way off to the side, intruding on the centre. She held them back.

'I think I made her run away,' Emma said, her voice strong and even.

I shook my head. 'How, Emma? Did you have a fight?'

She nodded. 'At home. We were always having fights, at least we used to. Now we just don't talk much at all. But we had a fight and after Lucy said something nasty about me I just yelled back that at least I'd finished my A levels.'

'And that made her leave home? I don't think—'

'Mum heard. She came and asked me what I meant and I told her. I told her what Clare said, about leaving the papers blank. I knew I shouldn't have told her but I wanted to. I really wanted to hurt Lucy, and it was the only way I could think of. Lucy's normally so . . . so untouchable. And Mum went mad, she went really mad. Lucy ran out of the house and she never came back.'

I looked at Emma and shook my head again and smiled. I remembered how important we think we are when we're young, how we think we're the cause of everything.

'You weren't to blame,' I said. 'And you know it really. No one runs away for this long after one argument. What would have happened when the results came out, your mother would have found out then, wouldn't she?'

'I suppose,' Emma said.

'These things build up, they don't just happen. But I can understand why you want to find Lucy.' I felt like telling her that I'd seen her sister, that she was all right. I was about to when Emma cut me off.

'I'm glad you stopped me following you though,' she said, thinking about it. 'I am. I'd have probably messed it up with Lucy if I'd spoken to her. Actually, no probably about it.'

Fred's was getting busier now, as the pubs were shut. The noise level had increased and the manager had turned up the sound system to counter it. Just then, two men asked if they could share our table. We moved up for them. When we settled down again Emma was smiling at me.

'I'm glad I saw you as well as Mum,' she said.

My faced must have registered something.

'How was it with her?'

'Scary,' I admitted.

'She's OK though,' Emma said, quickly.

'I'm sure.'

'It's just that she never shows her feelings to people. She's odd that way.'

'It's OK,' I said. 'I could tell that underneath she really does care about Lucy.' Could I tell that?

'She runs her own company, you know, a software firm. She's always doing things, making things happen, telling people what to do, where to go. I'm glad I saw you as well. I want to show you how upset we are. I want to ask you to really try to find Lucy. Not tell you the way Mum probably did.'

Emma's focus shifted again.

'And if you do find her, will you tell her something, just from me? Will you tell her that I'm sorry?'

'We've already established that it wasn't your fault.'

'I know, but not for that. I don't know.' Emma looked me hard in the face. 'I want you to tell her that I'm sorry for who I am.'

'I'm not sure—'

'There are photographs of us at home,' she explained. 'When we were little. Together. In some of them, no one, not even Lucy or I, can tell who is who. I can't tell you how weird that is. At junior school we used to have to wear name tags. Lucy, of course, made fake ones with my name on to get me into trouble. But even though we looked the same, I always knew we were different, really different. We used to fight like hell, all the time. Lucy was so high-spirited, always getting told off. I was quieter, I worked hard at school and got better grades than she did. She used to say that it was all crap, that all they were teaching us was how to think like them, and seeing as they were a bunch of flabby failures what was the point? I remember her making that very point when we were fourteen. To the geography teacher.' Emma smiled. 'She hated the fact that anyone should have control over her.

'Outside school, if we were out anywhere, Lucy always took charge. She knew what to say to people. She was so confident it was amazing. And then, when it came to boys . . .'

Emma laughed to herself at some memory. And then another one came like a wave crashing into it and she laughed even more.

'She was outrageous. Mum was always catching her. She slept with the art teacher, though Mum never found out about that. She used to sneak out of the flat we've got in London and I'd hear her come in again at three in the morning. Once I was at home on my own, on a Sunday afternoon, and when I went into my bedroom there was this naked man on my bed. Lucy had given him a key and told him that my bedroom was hers. He

ADAM BARON

didn't know about me and her being twins and he just wouldn't believe I wasn't Lucy. He grabbed me, and started trying to kiss me. I screamed like anything and eventually phoned the police and he ran down the drive trying to put his trousers on.'

I let Emma finish her story and then stop laughing. I didn't think it especially funny. It could have had a different ending.

'I was the classic quiet one, you see. And I always got As in everything. And everyone always used to tell her to be more like me.'

'I see.'

'And that used to really bug me. Can you imagine, in class, or at parents' evening or bringing our reports home together, can you imagine how it made me feel? And I was just as jealous of her! I even tried a bit of rebellion of my own but it just didn't feel like me. I didn't like smoking and I don't like clubs much. Dope didn't do anything for me and I'm too scared to try anything else. I was always a haircut behind, too. I guess I'm just the square one.'

'Me too then,' I said, 'at least these days.'

Emma smiled. Then she looked serious again. She rested her hands on the table.

'I want you to tell Lucy that I'm sorry I was always there for people to point out how useless they thought she was.'

'OK,' I said, 'I'll tell her if I can.'

'And tell her too that I don't think she's useless. And I never, ever thought she was.'

The two guys sharing our table had a friend who'd dragged a stool over and pretty soon it was their table not ours. I didn't mind; there wasn't really anything else Emma had to say to me, although she did go on telling me about various scrapes her sister had got herself into. Eventually I excused myself and went to find Alberto to get the bill, but Emma followed and insisted on paying it. I couldn't dissuade her, and it felt odd to be bought a drink by a seventeen-year-old girl, especially as Emma did it somewhat awkwardly. I stood next to her as she searched in her purse for enough pound coins.

Alberto looked at me strangely the whole time. I could tell he was trying to add up everything he'd seen that day in relation to the young girl and me. And Sharon, I suppose. He's an Italian, so I didn't have much doubt as to what his conclusion would be. He tried to catch my eye as I followed Emma to the door but I ignored him, and didn't look back as I shut the door behind me.

Outside it was warm and the sky was unusually clear for London. Orion stood up in front of us, tall and naked. Apart from him, there weren't many people about. I walked Emma back down to her car, and we chatted away, and as we did so I got a feeling that I get only very rarely. It was a feeling of animosity towards the person I was looking for. I saw her again, Lucy, walking down the street looking sassy and cool, a summer chick. And here was her sister, wrung tight with guilt just because she was a pleasant girl people got on with, and she got good grades at school. I was sure that if I ever met Lucy she would give me ample reasons for her behaviour but at that moment I didn't know them. I was just trailing in her wake amongst the debris.

Emma thanked me for listening to her. She said that

talking about Lucy had really helped. I said anytime, if she was in London. She said she would be, until Lucy turned up. I gave her directions back to Chalk Farm and then watched her drive away up Lloyd Baker Street.

At home I took off my shoes and sat for a while. I left the lights off and just sat in the dark staring at the ceiling. I did my best not to think about anything. One thing in particular. I sat there for an hour or two, maybe more, letting the small sounds of my flat, and the muffled sounds of London run through my head. I flicked a lamp on and tried reading the *Tao Te Ching*, but nothing in it grabbed me. Eventually I got up and went to bed. And then I couldn't help it any longer; my thoughts went back to the restaurant, and to Sharon, that smile she'd given me as the taxi drove away. A quiet, dark lake sat heavy inside me so that I didn't sleep for a long time.

Chapter Six

I got up the next morning quite late, at tennish, and after making a couple of calls I wandered down the empty market to the Sand Bar for my breakfast. The refuse strike had spread from Camden to Islington over the last few days, and already the bags were beginning to pile up. They looked like blackheads, bursting up through the paving slabs. It was a relief to get inside the Sand Bar, where the cement floor seems to keep the place cool. It was also a relief to find it quiet, which it generally is at that time of day. I sat on a bench to the left side of the plain white room with a coffee and some raisin bread, reading the paper for a while but not really engaging with it. I was thinking about Sharon. I'd thought we'd finally managed to sort out everything concerning Luke and her, and me. I couldn't help wondering what these new doubts she had were about. She'd been so defensive. Being with her last night had been like cruising on an open sea and hitting a rock I had no idea was there.

There was nothing I could do about it though, at least not for the moment, so I turned my thoughts to Emma Bradley instead. I was glad I'd spoken to her. Having done so gave me a clearer picture of her sister. She was a party girl, someone likely to be where she thought it was at. A provincial girl only in the city for a couple of months, but who would try to get into the swing of things as quick as possible, maybe through a boyfriend. She'd certainly looked confident enough of her surroundings, strolling along Camden High Street, and the fact that she hadn't had any stuff with her meant that she must have had somewhere to stay.

But like Emma I was also glad to have spoken to her because it made the whole thing more human. Sometimes, when I'm busy, my job can seem very functional, like tagging birds. Just find them, snap them, send the picture. But I only had one other case on at the moment, which was probably going to be pretty simple, and it gave me an added spur to meet the twin sister of the girl I was looking for. I no longer felt any animosity towards her, and it felt odd that I had, having only ever got one fleeting glimpse of her. Who knows what she was thinking? It all seemed like a whole series of crossed wires to me, and it would make me feel good to pass on her sister's message to her.

I picked up the pictures of Donna-Natalie from Carl and drove up through Islington towards Highbury Fields. The Earl of Warwick, which had closed a month ago, had reincarnated itself in the form of yet another of those tacky 'Irish' theme pubs. Christ. Upper Street was no longer a street but a theme park, with all the standard, patented generic leisure experiences where once there were places to go and have a drink, or something to eat. Were people really that easy to satisfy? Were they really so lonely, so scared of the city that everything had to be immediately recognizable? Or was it just the simple disease of the age? Pure, unadulterated laziness.

I drove past O'Neills, and All Bar One, and the Pitcher and Piano, the Something and Firkin, the Slug and Lettuce, the Dôme, Café Rouge, Nachos, Pizza Hut, and all three branches of Oddbins that the street supports. What these places all used to be before being bought out and gutted I didn't know. If once I did know, now I've forgotten. What would be the point of remembering?

Once in my office I drank half a litre of mineral water and took four deep breaths. Then I dialled the number Emma's mother had given me the day before, and also left on my machine that morning. I was confronted once again with the arresting tones of Mrs Bradley.

'Ah, Mr Rucker. Any progress on Lucy?'

Mrs Bradley's voice still sounded too big for my office. I didn't like the way it seemed to get right at me, put me on my back foot.

'Maybe,' I admitted. 'It's going to take a bit longer than a day though.'

'As long as you're doing everything you can.'

'You can count on it, Mrs Bradley. Now, I need to know if this is a permanent number that I can reach you on.'

'For the time being. Either myself or my husband will be here or else there will be an answering machine I can access.'

'I see. I take it that you own the flat then.'

'We do, but I don't see—'

'So Lucy will have been there before with you?'

'Many times.'

'Right. Where is your flat?'

'Oh, it's in Chalk Farm. Near Primrose Hill.'

59

'And did Lucy ever stay there alone at all?'

'No, never. We only ever came to London as a family. Or else I came alone on business.'

'Your husband?'

'Never. He works from home. In Sussex. But I can't—'

'I see. So, when you came to London, were there any areas that Lucy seemed particularly keen on?'

There was silence for a second. I liked the sound of it.

'Well, I don't know, I mean, we just used to go to museums and to restaurants. I used to take the girls shopping. I may not have told you that I have another daughter, Emma.'

'Right,' I said. 'So nowhere Lucy took a particular shine to?'

'Not that I can think of,' Mrs Bradley said.

'Or any shops she was particularly keen to visit?'

Another silence.

'Camden,' Mrs Bradley said finally. 'Lucy went to Camden once with James. No, a couple of times. My husband. While I was at a meeting. It was a terrible mistake, especially the second time. She talked him into buying her some truly horrible clothes.'

'I see,' I said.

Camden.

I allowed myself a smile.

I didn't think that Lucy was going to be too hard to find. Neither did I have a lot more to ask my employer because Emma had told me what kind of girl Lucy was last night. Mrs Bradley didn't seem to know that Emma had recently failed her entrance test for MI5 and I couldn't see the point of mentioning it. I didn't think

Mrs Bradley would be angry with her daughter for following me, but she probably would have been for not telling her. And more so for getting caught. After asking her what bank her daughter used, and the name of her branch, I told Mrs Bradley that I would get in touch when I had any more to tell her.

It was almost midday. Andy Gold had told me earlier that he'd be by before then so I figured he wasn't coming. It wasn't as if it was urgent, at least not for me. I wandered down the corridor for a quick coffee and was surprised to see him in the café, leaning up against the counter with a mug of tea in his hand. He was talking to Ally. Ally was laughing, quite obviously insincerely, at something he'd said, her arms folded, her mouth open a little to reveal teeth that all pointed inward ever so slightly. My little shark, as Mike called her, when he wanted to annoy. She turned, relieved, and smiled her perfect smile when she saw me walk in.

Andy put his half-empty mug down.

'Billy,' he said. 'So you are in.'

'Coffee, Billy?'

'Thanks, Ally.'

Ally reached behind her for my special mug, the one with Kojak on the side, which she and Mike had brought me back from New York, and given me for my birthday. It is a good, big mug, thick enough to keep the coffee warm. What's more, Kojak's lollipop changes colour when you pour the coffee in.

Ally's long slim hand reached towards me with the cup and then went to put a tick in her tally book. It then pushed a coil of curly black hair behind a pale, delicate ear, revealing a small gold, tear-shaped earring. Andy stood beside me. He followed me across the small room, and when I held the door for him, he turned back and winked at her.

'Who loves ya, baby?' he said.

Ally's professional smile again, wearing thinner. I lifted my eyes towards her before following Andy out into the hall.

The sun had eased round to batter the other side of the building, so I pulled my blind up. I pushed the window open further. I sat down, and as Andy sipped his tea I reached into the bottom drawer of my desk and slipped out a fifty-pound note from beneath a copy of *Hunger*, which Luke had once given me. I left it on the corner of my desk while Andy inspected his finger-nails, and went out to use the toilet. When I came back it was gone.

'Pretty, isn't she?'

Andy was holding a photo of Lucy Bradley. My copy was still in my bag so it must have been one her mother gave to the police. It was the same shot.

'I'm not sure pretty's the word,' I said.

'No. Not pretty. Pretty stunning. A tough life is it, Billy, trawling the streets for this kind of thing?'

I shrugged.

'I tell you what though, mate, I wouldn't mind a finder's fee paid in *that*, I can tell you. Wonder what I'd get for fifty quid though?'

Andy sat back in his chair and scraped his finger-nails back through his coal-black hair, with its natural Brylcreem effect. I took the chance to look my former colleague over. Andy didn't look good, although whether this was the heat, his health, or just the day he was having I couldn't tell. Andy is one of those people whose appearance can vary dramatically, even on one given day. Working, he always looks like he either just got out of bed, ready dressed, or else had been up all night pulling information out of hapless minor crims in the sort of soul-shivering interview rooms I was all too familiar with. From both sides of the desk. Right now he was wearing a cheap suit, a grubby white button-down and a tie he could have recently taken back from the kittens he had given it to play with some weeks ago. He looked just like a copper and he even smelled like one too. I was getting coffee, smoke, sweat and Dettol. His eyes were tired, and his flat, Mediterranean complexion looked dirty and yellowish. He was putting on weight, and as usual he seemed to be between razors. All in all, Andy was a walking advertisement for a life outside the police force. I knew, however, that if I met him in the pub later, after a shave and brush up, he could well have lost five years and be smelling as sweet as a widow's handbag.

'You'll call me if you see her?' I asked him.

'If I do,' he said. 'But I certainly won't be looking for her. She's over sixteen, got nothing to do with us. She could be getting banged up the arse by the Archbishop of Canterbury five times a day and we wouldn't be interested.'

He put the picture down on the desk.

'A point I'm sure you made to her mother.'

Andy smiled. 'Not *quite* in those terms. We explained our legal problem, but said we'd keep an eye out for her. Let her know if she's OK, if we happen to run into her.'

'The chances of that being?'

63.

'None. Unless she happens to do something we would be interested in, in which case she is legally entitled to request us not to contact her family.'

'So it's all down to me then?'

'It is. Thanks to our nanny state legal system you can go and find people and tell whoever you like about it. But not us. We've got more rules to go by.'

That was true. It was why I left. Because I had something to do, something a policeman should have been able to do, but which he couldn't. Something I had to do as a representative of myself, and no one else.

'I remember,' I said.

'Really? I don't remember you remembering.'

'Sorry?'

'That there were any rules,' he said.

Andy Gold glanced to his left, at the photo frame on my desk, angled just far enough towards him that he could make out a face. He looked surprised.

'Bit odd isn't it, Billy? Keeping a picture of yourself on your desk? Shouldn't it be one of that lawyer bird you're shtupping?'

I looked from the picture to Andy.

'It's Luke,' I said.

'Oh.' Andy raised his eyebrows. He reached over and picked the photo up, holding it on the desk in front of him. He bit his lip.

'I don't remember you looking this alike,' he said.

'Some people said we were similar. Others not.'

'Not that I knew him, of course. I only met him once or twice.' Andy suddenly looked confused. I couldn't tell if it was real confused or not. I guessed not.

'Wasn't . . .? Hmm.' He stared hard at the picture. 'I seem to remember that it was your brother who was with that girl, not you. I thought she was his girlfriend, not yours. I must have got it wrong.'

'No,' I said, evenly. 'That's right. She was with Luke. They were engaged.'

'Right,' Andy said. 'Right.' He put the picture back where it was. 'They were engaged. And she's with you now?'

'Yes,' I said, 'she is.'

I sat back in my chair and looked at Andy in a frank, come-on-then-ask-me kind of way. After a second his eyes turned away from me and he put his hands on the sides of his seat.

'Well,' he said, 'I'd better get back on the job. Can't sit around shooting the breeze with my old mates all day. Thanks for the tea though. I got that Italian piece to put it on your slate. Didn't have any change.'

He stood up.

'Don't mention it.'

'And thanks for the other—'

'Or that,' I said. I looked at him. 'You don't have to come all the way over here, you know. I'm happy to meet you. Wherever.'

'Billy!' Andy said, holding his hands up. 'You don't think I come and visit you just to pick up the occasional minor gratuity, do you? Really! What a cynical man you are, Mr Rucker.'

Andy picked up his mug.

'Better take this back,' he said. 'Wouldn't want young Alessandra to think I'd forgotten about her. I bet she's stood there right now, longing for my return.'

'Undoubtedly.'

'Yes, undoubtedly.' He looked thoughtful. 'By the way. Have you got to her yet?'

Andy walked out into the hall.

As his footsteps trailed away I stood up and pushed the door shut. Then I sat down and rummaged through my filing cabinet for a hard-backed A4 envelope. I didn't exactly relish Andy's little visits, and would have felt much more comfortable meeting him in a pub somewhere, but it wasn't difficult to see why Andy came over to my office. I had recently been implicated in a very nasty case involving, among others, rent boys, airline pilots and MPs. There was no way I was guilty of anything, a fact that Andy's boss had finally had to admit, but even so some very dodgy things had occurred around me. To Ken Clay, Chief Inspector of Islington Police, this made me suspect, something that I had actually been to him ever since I had left his tutelage some years ago.

'I can smell stuff on you,' he'd once said to me, through a cloud of cigar smoke and Aramis.

And so Andy came over to see me, because he had enough faith in his own powers of detection to believe that he would somehow be able to tell if I knew something that I wasn't sharing with the appointed forces of right and just order. I felt it was a shame. I could never admit to having actually liked the man 100 per cent, but when we were working together we had got on pretty well. Friends even. As time went by, however, a professional gap had grown between us. Whereas Andy used to do me favours, which I would compensate him for out of my own sense of obligation, now it was just minor business to him and, more importantly, a good way of keeping tabs on me.

I found an envelope and addressed it to Mrs Juliet Appleby of Pennerton House, Pennerton, Keswick, Cumbria. Then I slid open the envelope that Carl had given me that morning. I pulled out all the copies, and looked at them, sliding the top set off and setting the duplicates aside. Taking one set, I used a ruler and a scalpel to crop any that gave away anything about the picture's location. I discarded two that showed some give-away green store-fronting, and I removed from another an old lady who was carrying a bag with the Marks and Spencer name and logo on it. I also cut away the back of a goods van that had a Camden number on the side. I was left with four pictures of Mrs Appleby's daughter Donna, now known as Natalie, sitting in the doorway of an anonymous shop, in a pair of jeans and a tee shirt. Two of the shots were full body, and the other two were close-ups of the girl's face. A very pretty face, undoubtedly, in spite of a rather cheap hair dye and the regrettable absence of even one freckle.

I placed the glossies on top of the addressed envelope, and then took out some headed notepaper from my desk. I took a pen and wrote a description of Donna, as I had seen her. I said that she looked well, appeared cheerful, and that she seemed to be eating. She didn't look noticeably thinner in my photos than she had in the one her mother had sent me. I said that I had spoken to her and had tried to get her to re-establish contact with her family. Finally, I said that, as the pictures showed, I had found her begging for change, but that I felt she was doing OK, and that while Mrs

Appleby was right to be worried about her daughter, a life on the street was not necessarily as bad as she might think, especially if it was only for a while, and the weather was fine.

I did not tell Mrs Appleby that Donna was now calling herself Natalie. Nor did I say that she had told me the reason for her sudden departure from Pennerton House. Mrs Appleby almost certainly didn't need to be told what that was.

I signed the letter, folded it, then slid it into the envelope on top of the photographs. I stamped it and left it on the front of my desk for posting. Then I picked up the remaining pictures, intending to file them, and it was only as I did so, noticing their comparative weight, that I remembered the other shots I'd taken. Of the kid in the alley. I'd forgotten to tell him not to bother, so Carl had made duplicates of these as well. I took them from the bottom of the pile and spread them out on the table, for no other reason than I was curious. They meant nothing to me, except for the fact that when a fifty-year-old man beats the hell out of a kid in his teens, something has to be awry. If I were Ken Clay I would have said that I could smell something. It was the sort of smell that even an ex-policeman finds difficult to ignore.

I had shots of the kid on the floor, and two of the kid successfully dodging a couple of hay-makers, one with a duck and the other with a nice pivot backwards from the waist. I also had a clear shot of the man, standing at the mouth of the alley after the kid had legged it. He was standing with his hands on his hips and a look of pure disgust on his face. I suddenly wondered something that hadn't occurred to me at the time: was he the boy's father? He could have been. Was he mad at the boy for something; for smoking, or talking back, or coming in late? Was that his idea of administering a reprimand to his teenage son?

I didn't know. At the time I hadn't stopped to think what was going on. My sympathies were all with the kid; he was the one getting the kicking. But I'd only been in at the denouement, I hadn't seen the whole play. I looked into the man's face. Was his disgust at letting the kid escape, or for what the kid had done, or even directed at himself, for the violence he had used? I didn't know. Maybe he'd caught him trying to rip off a car, or shooting up, or skipping school again. Maybe he'd had too much, nothing else had worked. Maybe he'd just cracked, after years of trying to deal with the boy more reasonably.

Or maybe he was just a vicious bastard, whether he was related to the boy or not.

It was a habit of mine to draw things out, to let my mind run down avenues of its own invention starting from an incident, or a picture. I did it with the kids I came across, those I held in my viewfinder for a second and then let go again. What did they do when I'd turned away from them? I tried to trace them out, the friends they had, the things that were precious to them. I watched them sitting in doorways and wondered what they thought of the people who gave them money, and of those who didn't. Or not to sit in doorways but to stand in them, and then to give head in the back of BMW estate cars littered with picnic rugs and plastic footballs, beneath the gaze of stuffed Garfield toys sticking to the windows. And the men who drove these cars home, a half hour late, what did they think, sitting in front of *EastEnders*, saying yes, love, no, love, have you done your homework yet?, a gin and tonic hissing on a coaster, waiting for the ping of the microwave?

I gathered up the pictures and put them back in the envelope Carl had given me. I didn't know where to file them so I put them in with Donna Appleby. Then I walked out into the hall and locked up my office behind me. I had begun to think about Lucy Bradley, and the kind of life she might have been living over the last two months. But I didn't want to imagine it, to make it up in my head. I wanted to find it out.

Chapter Seven

I walked round Camden again and still didn't get anywhere. It was busier, and even hotter than the day
before, but still not that crowded. I did run into Olly
though, who was selling the *Big Issue* outside the tube
station. I gave him the twenty I owed him for Donna,
and then showed him the picture of the girl on the
motorcycle; the lipstick, the hand held low, the finger.
Olly had hardly glanced at it when he started to laugh.
He even laughed with a Manc accent.

'You're asking if I've seen her? This bird?'

I nodded. Olly twisted a thin finger round the
long, wispy goatee that made him look as though
someone had recently conjured him up out of a tree.
The effect was intensified by his eyes, which are the
brightest, most disconcerting blue I have ever seen.
You got the impression that if you were to look away
from Olly, even for just a second, when you turned
back he might be gone, having simply vanished into
the air.

'Yeah, I've seen her.'

'When?' I said.

''Bout five minutes ago as a matter of fact.'

'What?' I said. 'Where!?' I looked round quickly.
'Here?'

'No,' Olly said, holding up his armful of magazines. 'Here.'

He handed me a copy and I opened it.

'Towards the end,' he said, enjoying my disappointment. 'Before the classifieds.'

I flipped to the end and saw what Olly meant. There were three photographs on the 'Missing' page, and Lucy's was one of them. Her sarcastic grin greeted me alongside the face of a worried-looking middle-aged woman, and the broad smile of a young pale-skinned black boy, probably not yet in his teens. The editor had cropped the photo, however, so that only Lucy's face was included, not her expressive left hand. It wasn't only me who censored his pictures, it seemed.

'That'll be a pound please, sir,' Olly said.

I looked at him.

'It's not like W.H. Smith,' he said. 'You can't browse through the material and then decide you don't want it.'

'No,' I said, 'of course not.' I dug him out a coin. 'But, Olly, if you do see her . . .?'

'I will immediately call the Missing Persons Helpline, as instructed there.'

'You do that, Olly, by all means, and see what they give you for it.'

'No, you're all right as it goes. I'll give you a bell.'

'Thanks.'

He looked down at the magazine I was still holding.

'I'd never call that lot,' he said, with unexpected venom.

'Oh. Why not?'

'You,' he said. 'You don't snitch on them, do you?'

'No.'

'You don't tell them where they are.' He took the

72

magazine out of my hand. 'You know what,' he said, 'every time this comes out I look at this page and I'm bloody terrified, and d'you know why? It's because I'd fucking hate to see my picture there. My own face. Knowing people might see me and call that number. I wouldn't go out for a week.'

We were interrupted by a girl who wanted to buy a copy. Olly handed me back mine and gave one to the girl, with a smile. When she was gone he said, 'They're bringing out a special "Missing" Issue soon, full of people. I don't agree with it. I was an abused child. I haven't seen my parents for six years and I never want to see them. Not fucking ever. It's not for us,' he said, 'that number. It's for the bastards who fucked us up, and what I say is, let 'em suffer. Let 'em suffer not knowing. That's what I think. Because it's like, what are they going to say to me? "I'm sorry, darling. Won't you come home?" I don't think so.'

Olly shook his head and looked to the side, suddenly embarrassed. I thanked him for his time and took another walk up to the Lock.

Before leaving Camden I found a phone box, which was down a side street and therefore relatively quiet. I didn't want to use my office phone. I asked directory enquiries for the number of Lloyd's Bank, in Arundel, Sussex. I wrote the number down and then dialled it. I asked to be put through to accounts.

'Hello, Jane Hart speaking.'

'Good afternoon, Miss Hart,' I said. 'My name's Inspector Clay, of the Met's missing persons unit, and I was wondering if you can help me.'

'I'll do what I can.' Jane's voice was clear, and hopeful.

'You might want to write down my warrant number,' I said. 'It's WXC358769.'

'Right.'

'Now then. I'm trying to trace a young girl called Lucy Bradley, who has an account at your branch.'

'Yes,' Jane said, uncertainly, 'I understand. Yes.'

'She has been missing for a while now, and I want to try and get a hold on her recent movements. I was wondering if you could tell me if there have been any cashpoint withdrawals from her account, and if so, their location.'

There was a pause.

'Miss Hart?'

'Sorry, Inspector. It's just that these requests are supposed to be put in writing.'

'Yes,' I agreed, 'they are usually, yes. But the delay caused often means the information we receive is useless. I think we're close to tracing Miss Bradley, but these young people move around a lot, do you see?'

'Yes, yes I do.'

'So you see my problem. And I can assure you that we have the full co-operation of her mother and father, and indeed that of her sister Emma, who is very keen that we find Lucy.'

Another pause.

'Yes, Inspector. Yes. I know the family. It's a small town.'

I was hoping this would be the case.

'So you will perhaps be able to appreciate what the Bradleys are going through right now.'

'Yes, yes I can. But—'

'You can contact the family by all means. I'll hold. I have a number for them.'

She thought about it. Then: 'Well, no, I can't do that. But if you wait a moment. I can't really see the harm.'

'Thank you very much,' I said.

In a lowered voice, Jane told me that Lucy had made three withdrawals from her account, in the last week, all from the same machine, and all of the maximum amount her account would allow; one hundred pounds on each occasion. Her account was now in the red, and drawing very close to its overdraft limit.

'I see,' I said. 'I'll suggest that Mrs Bradley supplies more funds to the account, but also lowers the weekly limit on it. Thanks very much for your help.'

'You're welcome,' Jane said. 'And, Inspector, I hope you find Lucy. She's a very nice girl.'

'We'll do what we can, Miss Hart.'

I left the phone box and within five minutes I was standing outside the branch of Lloyd's Bank which Lucy had drawn all her money out of. The last withdrawal had been yesterday, at ten minutes to midnight. The bank was on the High Street, at the junction, almost exactly where I would have been standing if I hadn't had to abandon the idea of coming to Camden because Lucy's sister Emma was following me. It was the second time I had come close to her, the second time I'd missed.

I took my wallet out of my pocket. While I was there I used the machine myself. I had no idea that two days later the real Ken Clay, warrant number WXC358769, would be getting in touch with my branch in order to find out just exactly where I'd been that day.

* * *

Sharon was at her parents' for the weekend so I spent the evening sitting on a stool in the Old Ludensian, which is a bar and a restaurant at the bottom of St John Street, close to Smithfield. My friend Nicky owns the bar, but I'd probably go there if he didn't, even though it is a little too close to the City for my liking. The food's good, and the place manages to have a modern feel to it in spite of the absence of the usual chrome chairs and cement walls. It was another busy night in there, and I knew a few faces to say hello to.

I sat at the bar, ate a bowl of pasta and chatted intermittently with Carla, one of the waitresses, with whom I once had a brief thing, but with whom I have now reverted to minor scale flirting. I didn't stay late, only about ten minutes after Nicky was collected by a very elegant black woman who was about three inches taller than him. We said we'd see each other properly soon. I chatted away to a few of the other regulars but I wasn't really in the mood. I couldn't help wishing Sharon was there with me. It was still only about tennish when I walked outside to my car.

I drove up St John Street, but I didn't turn down Rosebery Avenue towards my flat. Instead I went down to King's Cross, getting through the lights quite quickly, and then heading up towards Euston, where I took a left towards the Victorian training hospital that is attached to UCL. I showed my pass to the security guard, and steered the Mazda into the staff car park, stopping just outside the entrance I wanted. I left the car there and walked into the shadowy doorway of the blackened, red-brick annex, where I was waved into the building by an old man who had seen me several times before.

My brother Luke is normally housed in a quiet, leafy hospital about twenty miles north of the M25. For the last three months, however, he has been living here, at the training hospital, and will be staying for another three. The hospital asked my permission to have Luke there for training purposes, and so that they could perform some tests and a couple of simple, non-invasive experimental procedures on him. It didn't take me long to agree. While I was sad that the nurses treating him would be different, and I valued their contribution highly, it would mean that I could visit him more often. When the hospital said that I could basically come and go whenever I pleased, I told them to go ahead and move him.

I didn't stay long with Luke. I sat on a chair by his bed in the quiet ward and held onto his hand for a while, slowly stretching his fingers and wrists out of the pronounced contraction that was now their natural state. The ward he was in was much sparser than his usual home, with much more of a clinical feel. I was glad it was only temporary. I chatted away and of course he made no response of any kind. I told him about the invitation I had received. I told him I was going to go and take all the praise for him. I didn't tell him about the argument Sharon and I had had. Instead, for some reason, I found myself telling him about the documentary I had seen, about polar bears on the TV. The big furry mama and her little rat, both buried beneath the snow, totally cut off from the world and totally caught up in each other until the snow began to melt. I told him how the mother taught the young cub how to rip baby seals to bits, and how cute the furry little thing looked when it did so.

Pretty soon I ran out of things to say. I kissed Luke's cold grey forehead and left him there in the flat dull night-lighting of the still ward. The old man didn't even look up from his paperback as I walked out.

At nine thirty next morning, Donna-Natalie Appleby was sitting exactly where she had been before, outside the Marks and Spencer on Camden High Street. This time I didn't approach her though, and I even sat in a different café so that she wouldn't see me if she stopped by for a cup of tea. I chose a classier affair a few doors down that I figured was out of her range.

At about eleven Donna stood up and gathered her things together. She scooped up the pile of change she had been given and dropped the cardboard cartoon onto a pile of refuse that was now twenty feet long and three bags high. The bags were beginning to merge into one another. I'd heard on the news that morning that the government was considering getting the army in, or else using young unemployed people on back-to-work schemes to clear it up. One thing they were apparently not considering was releasing more funds to the council to give the bin men a pay rise.

As it was a Saturday the tide had changed in Camden. Instead of sick-looking people moving in a straight line towards the tube, the pavements were awash with aimless souls spilling into the road, hardly caring about the crush of cars trying to move through Camden up to Hampstead and Belsize Park. I walked out onto the street, the crowds and the traffic stabbing my ears with their noise. I followed Natalie at a distance, stopping when she stopped, keeping about twenty feet, and a hundred people, behind her. There was no way she was going to see me, and even if she did, she wouldn't have been able to tell I was following her. There were too many people. I'd just say hi, and smile; another Camden resident strolling around the market.

I was keeping an eye on Donna in the hope that she was a friend of Lucy's. I *had* seen them together. If she was I might see her, if not, well, I would have been looking round Camden anyway. I followed her past more trash mounds, up to the Lock, where she bought some freshly squeezed orange juice from a stall, and then a foil tray of what looked like noodles from another. Every ten paces brought a different smell: Thai spice, sweat, frying onions, pizza, leather, petrol, smoke, incense, rubbish, perfume. I squeezed myself past Germans and Italians and French people and Scandinavians and ultra hip Japanese and Gap-clad Americans, tuning in and out of accents and languages like a Belgian radio ham. I couldn't decide whether Camden Lock on a Saturday, with its clothes stalls and new age stands, its food stalls, junk stalls, art deco shops and Goth palaces, its general buzz, was a pretty cool place or actually hell on earth. I told myself it was cool, even though I couldn't remember the last time I'd actually been there by choice. It was without doubt tatty and claustrophobic, but it was the kind of place I would have visited if I was in a foreign city. I could see people all around me appreciating it for its peculiar brand of Englishness, one that I definitely preferred to most of the other kinds.

Donna had doubled back on herself, and then stopped on the bridge to chat with a girl doing hair braids, probably the girl who did the ones she wore herself. I took the chance to get my own carton of juice, and I stood at the far end of the bridge sipping it. When Donna moved off I followed her and watched as she absent-mindedly reached out for a flier someone was passing out. I couldn't see the someone, only a hand. I saw Donna smile, fold the flier and stick it in the back pocket of her jeans as she was about to move off. She stopped though, when the hand reached out and held on to her arm. Donna stood and chatted for a while. Then she did leave, walking with a little more purpose than her previous ambling, probably going back to her pitch.

I followed Donna but when I got level with the hand I had seen passing her the orange flier I stopped. I forgot all about her.

The hand reached out to me.

'What's this then?' I asked.

'York's,' the boy said. 'Tonight. Only a tenner with this.'

He lifted the flier up towards me. I didn't take it yet.

'Who's playing?'

'It says on there, mate. Pete Tong. Christian Vogel. Boy George.'

'What about you, do you play?'

'No mate.' He shook the flier at me.

'Just work there?'

'Sort of. Do you want one of these?'

'Thanks,' I said. 'Only a tenner you say?'

'Yeah, with that.'

'I suppose you get in free. That why you do the fliering?'

'Yeah, we don't have to pay. Here you are, love.'

He pushed his arm past me, towards a girl who ignored him. He forgot about her instantly and pushed the flier on someone else. He avoided looking at me as he slid another from the pile in his left hand, and held it out to the side of me. I could tell that I was annoying the boy, standing close and right in front of him, but I wasn't ready to leave just yet. I studied his face as his eyes darted out and round me. He didn't have as many marks as I'd have thought he would. Just a plum for a left eye and a badly swollen lower lip. I also thought I saw a shadow on the side of his face, just beneath a flop of greasy hair.

'You get many girls at this place then?' I said, making him catch my eye. He stopped what he was doing and looked at me, sizing me up. A knowing smile split his broken lips.

'Yes, mate, I get plenty of girls at this place.'

'I might see you there then,' I said.

'It's a big place.'

'Pretty easy to score down there, is it? Or should I sort myself out first do you reckon?'

'Don't ask me, mate, never touch the stuff.'

'Of course not,' I said.

Then I finished my juice and dropped my carton in the road. All the bins had been full days ago. I put the flier in my bag.

I walked all round Camden but didn't find Lucy. Donna was at her pitch again. I sat in another café, opposite the bridge, and stayed there until about seven. I had a sandwich and a couple of coffees and the waitress didn't bother me. I thought that Lucy might come by, possibly to relieve the boy. The flier he'd given me was the same as I'd found in the doorway of

81

the M&S, after I'd seen Lucy there with Donna. Fliering for clubs seemed like the sort of thing Lucy would have got into. It would be a lot easier to get her picture taken here, rather than trying to find her in the dark amongst a crowd of sweaty teenagers. But she didn't appear. When the boy left I paid my bill and went to find my bike. I wheeled it up to the tube, intending to speak to Olly again.

But where Olly had been standing there stood a lean, athletic-looking girl, with a worried expression. She was leaning back against the tiled wall, impatiently squeezing her hands together, looking round in all directions. For a second I was annoyed; had she followed me *again*? But no, not on my bike. It was her mother. Yesterday I'd made her mother think that Lucy might be in Camden and she'd mentioned it to Emma, who had come to look. I didn't blame her, it's what I would have done myself.

I nearly stopped to speak to Emma but I thought better of it. Instead, I rode past, but once I was out of sight I stopped at the nearest phone box and called Mrs Bradley. I left a message to the effect that her daughter Emma was outside Camden tube station looking for her sister, and that perhaps Mrs Bradley might want to drive past there by accident and maybe notice her. It wasn't the kind of thing that I usually did, and Olly would no doubt have disapproved, but Emma hadn't run away, she hadn't actively made the decision to leave her family. She was just a rather naïve and worried young girl willing to believe anything. There are people who can smell vulnerability from a hundred yards, even somewhere as commonplace and busy as Camden High Street on a sunny Saturday evening.

Emma might have been planning to stand out there all night for all I knew. She stood out like a lily in a cesspool.

I got back on my bike. I pushed my way into the traffic and weaved up through the lights. Donna-Natalie was grinning up at shoppers and passers-by. A hot filthy breeze ran through my tee shirt as I cycled home.

Chapter Eight

I was feeling annoyed as I struggled with my bike through the street door to my flat, frustrated and annoyed at not finding Lucy. I didn't know why. I often went months before spotting someone I was after. I suppose it was because I'd been close, even seen her, and had then missed her by chance, and would now have to stay up all night. I also felt the urgency of her family, and there was one other reason. I'd been paid in advance, something I never feel comfortable with. I don't like feeling obligated to people, and I wanted to discharge my obligation as soon as possible. I don't like people who say things like 'as long as you're doing everything you can'. I wasn't doing everything I could. I could have skipped meals and got up at six a.m., I could have posted pictures of Lucy all over London. No one ever does everything they can.

I'd left before the mail arrived that morning, and there was one letter addressed to me sitting in the box on the floor of the small hallway. I spent a second or two pointlessly wondering what it was, and then I took it upstairs, opened it, and pulled out a largish, well-printed invitation card.

Dear Mr Rucker,
You are invited by
Faber and Faber
to attend the launch of our Poet's 2000 series
at 7 p.m. on 15 September 1999 at
The Century, 32 Lisle St NW6
The new young poets in the series are:
James Walsh, John Harding, Jennifer Sales,
Monica Hartson, William Bowen, Annette Charles,
Jeff Jones and Luke Rucker
Yours sincerely
Josephine Smilie, Editorial Director, Poetry.
RSVP

At the bottom of the card were eight small photographs, one of which was the shot of Luke, sitting on an upturned boat, which was also in a frame on my desk. The launch was Faber's new concept; to sell poetry like art, grouping together a bunch of young writers in a form of private view. All of the poets looked suitably attractive, or at the least fashionably pierced and menacing. Sharon had been told that this was a very important part of the publishing process these days, and had been asked for the best photograph of Luke that she possessed.

I took the card and left it by the phone. Then I dialled Sharon's number.

'Hello.'

'Oh,' I said, surprised. 'Sharon. I didn't think you'd be home.'

'Then why did you phone?' Her laugh was the 'I don't understand' kind.

'I . . . was just going to leave you a message. I thought you were going to Hampshire.'

'I came back,' she said, 'I've got a ton of work.'

'Oh, right.' I said. 'How are your folks?'

'Fine,' she said. 'They're fine.'

'How's Mick's canoe coming on?'

'What?'

'The canoe he's building? In the garage?'

'Oh, God, I don't know, I didn't ask. Well?'

'Well what?'

She laughed again. 'What message were you going to leave, Billy?'

'Oh.'

I looked at the card by the side of the phone.

'Nothing much, just welcome back, how about dinner tomorrow night?'

'Well, I'll see if I'm finished. I should be. Thanks. I'll call you tomorrow.'

'OK,' I said, 'but not too early.'

'Oh,' Sharon said, 'so Nicky's taking you out to one of his glamorous dens of iniquity tonight, is he?'

'I wish,' I said.

I made another call, and then got my things together. I spent a couple of hours in the gym, ducking the howitzer shells my friend Mountain Pete was trying to land on my head, peppering him with mortar shots in his ribs. I spent an hour on various of the machines, and pretended not to notice when Sal disappeared into her office with a couple of serious-looking types in soft leather jackets, who left quickly and anonymously ten minutes later, without taking any sort of interest in the hustle and bustle of the gym. I didn't think they were there to sign up, although both of them could have done with losing a few pounds. What they were there for was anyone's guess; anyone's guess, that is, but mine. Sal's business interests extend a lot further than the gym she runs, but my interest in her extends just as far as the bag and the ropes and not one inch further. The fact that she is widely thought to have carried on her husband's business, shortly after his death four years ago, has nothing whatsoever to do with me.

I took a long shower and then drove back up to the Falcon on the Farringdon Road, just by the *Guardian* building. The workout had helped dissipate some of the shapeless frustration I'd been feeling, but because I couldn't actually pin that frustration down to anything, it started to come back to me. The place was rammed, and the guy to my left kept blowing smoke in my face because his girlfriend had complained about him blowing it at her. I would have turned my back on him completely if it weren't for the guy on my right, who couldn't quite decide which of his two topics of conversation was the more enthralling, his new Suzuki Renegade, or the landmine he'd nearly trodden on in Bosnia, so he switched between the two, with occasional diversions to the loft space he was thinking about in Shoreditch. His clipped nasal voice barked out at several decibels above the necessary, and I could tell that it wasn't just me who was wondering hopefully if there were any landmines lying around the streets of East 1. I was reminded of something a journalist friend of Nicky's had once told me: foreign correspondents are usually the wankers the editor couldn't stand having around the office.

While I sat there failing to blank my heroic friend out, I had strange, odd thoughts, which I told myself were just stupidity, and paranoia. The product of several years without spending one single day in which at least one person wouldn't try to lie to me. I pushed the thought aside along with the last third of my steak sandwich, and at eleven I walked out to the car. I drove to Camley Street, halfway between Camden and King's Cross. I didn't know the exact address of the place I was going but I didn't bother looking it up. It wasn't the sort of place you could drive past and miss. In the car I pushed my Leonard Cohen tape into the machine but took it out again when I heard the song that was playing. It was the one about the storm of golden hair on the pillow, and eyes full of sorrow, and distance. I didn't really want to hear it right then.

* * *

It looked like a scene from the fall of Saigon. A huge crowd of people was queuing impatiently, six abreast, at a steel mesh security fence, many of them holding slips of paper like visa applications or letters of transit. Other people were arriving constantly, some pushing in with friends in the crowd, others joining on hopefully at the back. Behind the fence was a courtyard, policed by menacing dark shapes with headpieces, and behind them was an enormous old grain warehouse. Behind that I couldn't help imagining waves of helicopters taking off, crammed with desperate people, holding out their hands to those still left on the tarmac, screaming in pain and despair.

It was in fact one of the biggest clubs in Europe, and the people outside weren't trying to leave for America, although you could argue that most of them were there for some kind of escape. They looked eager enough as they shuffled forward slowly, eager but compliant.

I'd pulled the car onto a broad pavement across the street from the place. I killed the engine, and the uncertain groan of the Mazda was immediately replaced by a steady, upbeat hum. I got out and locked the door. Checking out the scene in front of me, I tied my fleece round my waist and slung my camera over my shoulder, before crossing the road towards the building where I expected to spend the next four hours or so. I looked at my watch; twenty minutes to midnight.

In contrast to the buzz in front of me, the night was still as a painting, a landscape of sombre, lumpen buildings drowned in shadow, topped by a sky that was the last gasp shade of a velvety, electric blue. The main horde of people was to the left. I walked right, straight to the front of what I assumed to be the guest list queue. I stopped for a second to take a laminated card out of my wallet, which Carl had run off for me a year or so ago. Then I stepped forward, maintaining a bored, slightly pissed-off expression.

'Hi,' I said, to a monosyllabic tower of junk food and steroids. 'William Rucker. I called earlier.'

The card was taken from me by a giant gnarled hand, one of the knuckles badly off-centre. It was inspected, then checked off against a long list held by a very stunning girl just inside the fence. As I waited I could feel the looks of the other people, standing hopefully in both of the queues behind me; respect, surprisingly, more than animosity. The card was given back to me with a nod that didn't meet my eye, a nod that showed me that I was who my card said I was; a staff photographer with a leading London fashion magazine. I was handed a small green ticket. The man grunted and pushed the gate, before pointing me past him.

Once in the courtyard I stood in a much smaller queue, waiting to be given the final clearance. I moved forward, listening to a group of four girls in front of me deciding where they'd meet if they got split up. Just then, a voice behind me took my attention, raised above the general hubbub. I looked round to see a balding, middle-aged man at the front of the original queue, arguing with the Man, who didn't say anything but just shook his head, and brushed the man aside. Under the glare of the security light it was easy to make out the man's features, and I recognized him. His name escaped me but I did know that he used to be a policeman, but was now working in the private sector; for Sirius Investigations. I just managed to restrain myself from giving the guy a wave. Then I lifted my hands in the air while my pockets were turned out and the insides of my shoes inspected. When the bouncer's finger slid round to my instep I squirmed a little because it tickled.

Wherever you went the music was loud, so loud it seemed like a physical thing, not emanating from the banks of speakers but coming from inside of you, trying to get out. The only times it seemed to ebb were in the narrow passageways between the pulsating rooms, like empty spaces on the radio dial, crossroads of sound. And then you would be in a different space, equally full of people, assaulted by the bass line like a straight right to the solar plexus. The sheer scale, the weight of the music, was like an immovable force, an insistent and powerful entity screaming for obeisance. And all around me it got it, from lean, sweat-shimmering teenagers, all having their own individual communion with the beast. I pushed my way through the noise, which made the air seem thick as syrup, and past a thousand baby-wide eyes dancing in their own space, as though everyone had plugged their own headphones into a giant super-Walkman. The whole place was like a huge, fleshy, madly pumping heart. I kept moving, because whenever I stood still for more than a minute someone came up and tried to buy drugs off me.

I thought I saw Lucy. Tight blonde plaits, teeth, a taut, slim arm. I tried to reach her through the swell but she vanished like a drowning girl, one minute there, one minute lost amongst the waves and breakers. I was kept from her by Donna, or Natalie, an ecstatic girl grabbing my arm, shouting at me that her breakfast had been lovely and why wasn't I dancing? I looked down and back and then there was no Lucy. I said wait there. Still no Lucy and then no Natalie either when I'd returned to where I was. Or had I returned, was this the place? It wasn't easy to tell, the space shifted and moved, there weren't any landmarks except at the edges. Just the roar, and elbows, and backs, shirts tied round waists, and armpits, hands, hairless chests, water bottles in back pockets, and armband tattoos, the backs of necks, of heads, eyes cast beyond me, upwards, at what? Donna had gone under too. I needed some air. I made my way to the exit. I saw a boy with a floppy bowl haircut dancing with some girls. His face was bruised and I was going to ask him how it happened

91

when I was twisted round again and then again and then he too disappeared.

I was outside, at the back of the building, in a well-lit cobbled area overlooking the canal. There was a canopy at the far end to my left, and a London bus halfway along, painted white. A couple of hundred people were milling around, or leaning against pillars, talking, taking a breather. No helicopters. I took a breath, suddenly disoriented by an emptiness, the lack of reverberations in my head. I put my fleece on but realized that the night was still warm. It was just the contrast with the heat from inside.

It felt good to be in the open air. I walked past the white bus and then stood leaning against a rail with my back to the inked-out water. I had my camera ready. The people coming in and out of the bus were better dressed than the majority, most with an air about them, so I figured it was a VIP thing. All around me, people were keeping tabs on the bus and pretending not to. I could see faces on the top deck, peering out. I saw two girls come out, arm in arm, obviously models. They turned to smile at someone going in, someone I thought I recognized. One of Luke's old friends? No. It was the guy from Take That, the one you don't hear from very much any more, the one who probably has daydreams about lynching Robbie Williams. I couldn't think of his name. I wondered how much longer he'd be getting into VIP lounges at clubs without having to tell people who he was.

A couple of people began to notice my camera, so I moved into the shadow of the canopy. I didn't want to be mistaken for paparazzi, and get beaten up by a pop star looking for a spread in the Sundays. From where I was standing I had a good view of each of the doors that led out from the three main rooms inside the club. Each time a door was pushed open I got a snatch of high velocity techno, or jungle, or drum and bass. When two doors were opened at once the sounds competed like angry witches screaming obscenities at each other.

As I waited, I couldn't help being impressed, by both the scale of the venue and the number of people willing to let themselves be herded and corralled, with only a fifty-fifty chance of getting in. I remembered what I used to do on a Friday night when I was seventeen, and the contrast made me laugh. I looked around at the people milling past me, some of them laughing, some talking, at least half of them happily whacked or on the way. The full-on bank lighting outside made everyone seem as separate and unreal as the memories of myself at that age were.

The courtyard got a lot busier, as the club inside filled up with people paying to get in round the other side of the building. I stayed where I was, figuring that everyone must want to come outside at some point. I was right. The boy came out. He walked past me, got a drink from the bar on my right and then stood by the stairs he'd walked down. I saw him chat to various people, mostly girls. Once or twice I thought I saw him passing over small packages but I never saw him take any money. I saw Donna-Natalie come out, walking carefully down the steps on her own, holding on to the rail. She was moving past the boy when, just as he had on the bridge, he held out his hand to stop her. They

93

started talking but I was much too far away to hear what they were saying. I suddenly felt worried for her, but I didn't know why. I looked away. My eyes flitted between the three doors, looking for Lucy, but I didn't see her come out of any of them.

It was only by chance that I did see her.

She walked straight out of the London bus.

I only saw her for a second, not long enough to get a shot of her. She was moving quickly. Almost immediately she was obscured by a group of gel-headed lads in Ben Shermans. She pushed through them and I got a shot of her back as she turned towards the stairs that I had walked down, where the boy was still standing. I still hadn't seen her properly but I was certain it was her. I didn't move. I was hoping she'd stop, to talk to the boy, giving me time to focus, but she didn't; the boy just turned when he saw her walk past him, and followed her. Donna followed too. I pushed myself off the railings. I walked towards the door, but not too quickly. I had to be a little careful; I had no reason to believe that Lucy knew who I was, but either Donna or the boy might remember me, and get suspicious. I got to the bottom step just as Lucy was at the top, pushing the door open with her arm and the side of her leg. I skipped up the stairs but had to step back when a big crowd of people gushed out through the door towards me.

When I got into the main room I couldn't see her. I made my way to the side, and perched on the stairs that led up to the DJ booth. A guy at the top of the stairs gave me a look but I ignored him. Above the heads of the clubbers I could see both doors. Lucy hadn't given me the impression that she had come there to dance. I saw a blonde girl and another girl forcing eddies into the crowd as they made their way towards the tunnel that led to the next room. I followed, eventually getting to the tunnel myself. The next room was the chill-out room, and it was small enough to see that she wasn't in there.

I went through the chill-out room, and down some steps. I was in the bar, a huge space like a students union. She wasn't in there either. I had a quick look in the long toilet queue and then walked up from the bar to the main entrance. I walked out into the courtyard, and looked towards the gate I'd come in.

There was no one in the courtyard now except for a couple of barmen smoking fags and a guy loading steel record cases into the back of a car. The queue had vanished as though I'd dreamt it, but the security still stood on the gate. I didn't know what to do, whether to go back in or take a look out on the street.

It was a risk because they weren't letting anyone back in now, but I strode over towards the three men on the door. I said a quick goodnight and the gate was held open for me. I didn't bother asking if a couple of girls had just walked out of there. It would have made them think I was Bill, and who knows when I'd have to go back there searching for someone else? Once in the road, I looked past the cab guy and the drivers hovering. I looked in both directions. Through the sparse crowd I saw two girls and the boy about fifty yards up on the right, crossing the road to the far side. I ignored the cab man's question, and walked the way the three were going.

The girls in front of me both wore minis, Lucy in elbow-length gloves. Reaching round behind me I made sure that my camera was wound on. I don't have an electric because they make too much noise and I don't like them anyway. I did want to be ready though, for when Lucy hit a patch of light. At the moment she was in shadow, and facing the wrong way. I thought about walking up ahead of her, and waiting, but decided to stay behind her for now.

Once the three had reached the other side of the road I crossed over too and kept pace with them. Three long shadows pointed back towards me on the broad pavement and then curved away, before shifting round again. I saw Lucy link arms with Donna-Natalie. Then, after no more than fifty yards, all three veered to the right of the pavement and stopped. I came to a halt too, moving towards the wall on my left, turning to the side, pretending to search my pockets for a cigarette.

Lucy stood fishing in her bag. Her two friends were a step back from her. Lucy was standing next to a car, but I couldn't see the make. She pulled out some keys. I pushed myself off the wall. As naturally as I could I turned round and headed back the way I'd come, back towards the club. I heard a car door being opened behind me, and then another, and then I heard them slam. I sped up a little, reaching into my pocket for my car keys.

When I got level with the Mazda I stopped and unlocked the passenger door. I took a look back up the street and the pavement was empty. I listened for a second and heard a motor starting up, nothing more than a 1.5, a small car, fairly new. I opened up the door of the Mazda and slid across the seat. Hurriedly I got the key in the ignition, and gave it a turn. Unfortunately, I didn't hear the sound of another engine kicking into life, another small engine. Very old. There was nothing. Only a click, not even a shudder, or that wheezing sound that says patience, we'll get there. I tried again. Nothing.

I gave a small sigh.

I didn't bother having another go. Instead I slid back across the seat and out onto the pavement. I locked the door quickly and crossed the road again, looking to my left. I saw a small car pull out from the row and head slowly up the street towards Camden. I couldn't believe it. No, please, not again. I looked back across to the entrance to the club, held open now to the first trickle of people starting to leave.

'You wanna cab?'

He'd stepped out into the road towards me, out from the throng of waiting drivers. He was a tall, loose-limbed Jamaican with shoulder-length dreads and a pale orange shirt with lots of growing room. His face was thin as a fox's and his smile was full of gold.

'You wanna taxi, my friend?'

I looked past him towards the cab man, holding a clipboard and ticking off cars as they left. Down the street, the only car on the road was stopped at a red light. If I was quick . . . just maybe. The cab man was pointing a young couple towards a Mondeo, and two groups of four were just coming out through the gate towards him. I wondered what to do. This guy would have been quicker, but I didn't want to get in a car with him only to be told to get out again because it was not the guy's turn. The cab man was in charge, and in a place like that a fly driver wouldn't stand a chance.

'It's OK, my friend, I'm up next. Where you wanna go?'

He stepped backwards against an old Renault 18. He opened the back door for me and waved at the man, who didn't even bother to acknowledge him. I walked towards him.

'Where to?'

'Clerkenwell.'

'Six pounds.'

'But I'll need to stop off first. Some friends of mine are having a party but I don't know the address. They're in that car.'

Up ahead the car was moving off through the lights. It was an Escort. I jumped in the back of the Renault, and the driver shut the door before getting in the front.

'If you show me where they stop first, then we can carry on,' I said.

'Sure thing, fella.'

He turned the key and got a lot more response than I had. He pulled out into the broad street, just in front of another cab moving out from the club.

I sat in the middle of the seat, looking forward through the windscreen. We just made it through the lights. The Escort was quite a way ahead, turning left with the road, round towards St Pancras Way, but I thought we wouldn't have much trouble catching it. We followed as it turned left onto Granary Street, up towards Camden. The Escort then took a right on Agar Grove and we stayed behind it, just catching sight of it as it hung a left, up into the grid of streets south of the Camden Road. I knew these streets were small, with a lot of turns the Escort could make, but my driver didn't seem too bothered about keeping up with it. I leant forward.

'Don't lose them,' I said, trying not to sound impatient.

'Don't worry, my friend, we'll get you to your party.'

We cruised into the quiet back streets, lined with dormant cars. The Escort was nowhere. I sat forward in the seat. We drove on. Then I saw it, down the bottom of a road to the right that we were driving straight past.

'Back up,' I said, 'we've missed it.'

'Alright, man,' the guy replied, with a quick smile behind him. 'Calm down. We'll duck down the next one.'

He cruised on. But the next street was one-way, and instead of taking the one after that the guy turned left, and put his foot down.

'Hey!'

He pulled another left quickly, and put his foot down again. There wasn't anything I could do. The car sped to the bottom of a dead end; a short street sided by five-storey council blocks with some sort of depot at the end. I thought we were going to crash straight through a red pull-down garage fronting, but instead the driver hit the break, yanking the wheel at the same time and we spun to the left. I flew forward and had to catch myself on the seat back in front of me. The car shuddered back on itself and as soon as it was stable the driver clicked his belt and reached for something on the passenger seat beside him. When he turned round to look at me he wasn't smiling any more.

'What the fuck are you doing?'

'Hush now,' he said. 'You've got to be cool.'

He shifted in his seat. Now the smile.

'I just want your camera is all, my friend.'

His face was in shadow but I could make out his gold-capped teeth, glowing in the light of a street lamp that just reached in this far. It wasn't the only thing that was shining. Before I could tell him where to get off he brought up a bowie knife with his right hand and rested it on the top of the passenger seat beside him. It was six inches long, and the hook on the end looked sharp enough. My eyes went straight to the point.

He held his knife tight and it twitched as he moved forward in his seat towards me.

'Hey!' I said. 'Jesus! OK, OK!'

I moved back from him, back from the knife.

'The camera.'

'Take it easy.'

I edged back further. I tried to put a blanket in my voice. Slowly: 'You can have it. All right? Just take it easy, OK? Please.'

Carefully, I slid back along the seat and leant backwards, as though that would make it easier for me to get the camera strap over my shoulder to hand it to him. My right hand went to the strap. The man didn't move. Good. I put a scared rabbit in my eyes. Without taking them off the driver I tried to get the strap over my head but I got nervous and the strap got tangled up. I moved back even more to compensate.

When I figured I was far enough back I yanked my leg up hard, and kicked it out even harder, straight at the thin gold face, pushing my shoulders back on the door arch with all I had. I saw the face change, and the flash of the knife as it found its light. I felt a connection, a good solid crunch with nice give, and I pushed through, letting my thigh extend to the knee. I felt his head go back against the windshield, and then a sharp burn on my shin bone. I pulled back my leg and scrambled for the door handle.

But the door was locked; it wasn't the side I'd got in. The driver was moving forward again, groggy with the blow to his head. I couldn't see the knife, he must have dropped it, so I lashed out at him again. I missed and he caught hold of my leg, but I still managed to yank up the tee on the door and pull the handle. The door swung open with my weight, but the driver still had hold of my leg. I kicked out, and again, madly, trying to get free before he could find the blade. I remember thinking what an amateur he was. I could feel him scrabbling for his weapon with his left hand. Another kick, then one more and I was clear, and I half scrambled, half fell out of the car, my camera still over my shoulder, landing heavily with my elbow on hard concrete. I tried to push myself to my feet and run at the same time, fell, and then righted myself.

Then I was up.

I was just about to break into a sprint when I saw the Sierra.

I was pretty sure it was the other cab, the one that had pulled out after us when we'd left the club. I'd been so busy watching for the car with Lucy I hadn't noticed it behind us. It had stopped halfway down the dead end, and the second of the two men inside it was just getting out. He joined the first one and they fanned across the road, walking slowly towards me. I turned round. I looked for a low fence, or a drainpipe to climb, but there was nothing. The depot had a chain fence topped with razor wire, and the two men had already blocked my path to the flats. I edged back towards the steel red pull-down door behind me. I could feel my leg, and looked down to see a rip in my jeans where the knife had gone through.

'The camera.'

He was West Indian too, but you couldn't have called him loose-limbed. Beside him the other guy was a similar size, but with the streetlight behind them I couldn't make either of them out. They just looked big. One was rubbing his hands together, the other had his behind his back.

'Give us that, we leave you alone.'

Slowly, they moved towards me.

'The camera,' he said again, snapping his fingers this time.

I didn't say anything. I took a few more steps back, keeping my eyes tight on the two men. I was thinking what to do when the door of the first car was pushed open, and my driver got out. He looked shaky. He pushed himself round the bonnet of the car and joined his friends, who had stopped about fifteen feet away from me.

'Just give us it and we'll leave you be, OK?'

There was something in the voice that sounded genuine, and I hesitated. But then I saw the driver. With one hand the driver was nursing his teeth, where my foot had caught him. The other hand held the bowie knife. He didn't look like there was anyone who could persuade him to leave me be, not after what I'd done to him. That was it. I made the decision.

The three men had stopped. I lifted the camera over my head by its strap. Without even pretending to hand it over to them, I swung it high over my head and brought it down hard against the concrete. The three guys looked stunned. I hadn't done too much damage to it, a fact that I knew would have made Carl very proud, so I did it again, and this time the lens flew off, the back opened, and various pieces of metal and plastic smashed out and skidded across the hard ground. On the third swing there was nothing much of any size left intact.

'You shit-stained motherfucker,' the third guy said. It was the first time he had spoken. When he let his hands drop from behind his back I could see he was carrying a short piece of metal tubing that was probably an exhaust pipe.

I let the strap drop to the ground and waited for them.

Chapter Nine

When I came to it was still quite dark. I was surprised;
I couldn't have been out for as long as it felt. Days. I
moved my eyes. Everything was very still. I was lying
on my front, pieces of loose stone biting into my
cheekbone. I didn't move for a second, mentally checking to see if there was anything seriously wrong with
me. The back of my neck was tight. I moved a leg. I
stretched an arm. I moved the other leg and felt a shout
of pain in my shin. Then, when I tried to push myself
up, my head expanded to the size of a nightclub before
returning to its usual size in the space of half a second.

What a rush. It took me right up to puking but not
quite there. When it was gone I stayed on my knees for
a second, feeling all around my head for cuts. There
was a soft patch at the back but I couldn't feel any
blood. I made it to my feet. I stood for a second, waiting
for aftershocks, but even though my head hurt and my
neck hurt and my right leg hurt, I felt stable. I took a
look around, to see if there was anything left of my
camera. I could make out various fragments and bits
and pieces but what little that could have been left of
the main body was gone.

It told me something.

Slowly, I straightened up, finding it easier than I

had any reason to expect. When I'd seen that pipe, and that bowie knife twitching, I'd expected a lot more than a quick and efficient dispatch to the canvas. I remembered the thin guy holding back while the other two moved in, and then I remembered landing a few shots before going over to a big right. Before I could get up the pipe had come down, and before I passed out I saw the thin guy walking forward. I remembered thinking, oh fuck. One of the other two must have stopped him, must have held him off. I felt grateful to him. The only thing I was really worried about was my shin. My jeans were ripped and there was a long cut where my calf muscle met the bone, probably made by the knife when I first lashed out in the car. It had stopped bleeding but when I rested some weight on the leg I felt it open up, a warm stream of blood heading down my ankle into my shoe.

I balanced on one leg and brushed myself down. Slowly, I centred myself, and thought back to the moment I'd got in the cab. I couldn't believe what had happened to me; this was just supposed to be a simple search and snap. I was angry. I wanted to work out what had happened but instead I tried to focus on the immediate problem of getting myself home. I looked up the road, the way the cab had taken me.

Hobbling, I made it out of the dead end, out of the shadow of the council blocks, and I saw that it was lighter than I'd thought, but it was still an hour or so from dawn. I needed to get back to the main road, or to a phone box. I checked my pocket for my wallet. It was gone, but I knew I hadn't been mugged. Not just that. Someone had wanted my camera or, rather, the film that was in it. I started to run a couple of scenarios through my head but I couldn't get them going. They could wait. My leg was throbbing and my head rang. I really could hear little birds singing.

I limped along, gingerly moving up the street, up towards the place where we'd lost the Escort.

I was through with this. I was going home. I was going home to bed and I was going to forget all about a certain Mrs Bradley and her two sexy flipside daughters. I thought back to the moment in my office when I'd had the impulse to tell Mrs Bradley where to get off. It felt like a golden chance I hadn't taken, the best tip on a nag I'd ever turned down. If only.

I stumbled up the slight incline towards Agar Grove, walking in the middle of the street to avoid the garbage. Even from there I could smell it, drifting up around me, staining the tense, pre-dawn air. I could feel the cut on my calf opening up more and more, and I started to worry about it. I moved over and leant back against the side of a house, ripping back the denim. It was worse than I'd thought. I managed to tear off a long strip of the fabric to make a tourniquet, thinking all the time that I had precisely no chance of persuading a cab driver to stop for me. My mind went back to my camera again. Lucy must have clocked me with it from the bus, or else the boy had told her. Actually, thinking about it, I didn't blame her that much. She didn't know who I was. I remembered my friend Olly, the paranoia he'd shown at the thought that his parents might find him. I even found myself being slightly impressed by the resources she must have had at her disposal.

I was in the process of winding the strip of denim round my leg when a loud crack echoed through the empty streets. It sounded like the hard smack of a door slamming without shutting, although I couldn't be sure. I didn't really care. I had more pressing concerns. I finished tying the strip in place. The sound wouldn't have bothered me at all but it was immediately followed by the insistent thwack of soft shoes on hard tarmac.

I didn't give a shit about the sound except that it was coming towards me, from round the corner. It sounded like a simple burglary gone wrong, but then I realized that the footsteps were coming from the street the Escort had driven down. Suddenly, I was interested. They were getting nearer. Without really knowing why, I pushed myself off the wall and went to look round into the street. I moved towards the corner, but before I could take more than three steps, a shape came steaming round it, smacking straight into me. It knocked me backwards and we both went over, the shape sprawling across me. I was winded, but I managed to get my hands in front to protect me. The shape wasn't in any mood for fisticuffs, however, it reacted instantly, trying to get up again as if I hadn't even been there, trying to make it up and keep going. I was all for that. I tried to get out of its way, to let it by, but suddenly our eyes met. It stopped. All of its forward momentum came to a halt as it stared at me.

As the boy stared at me.

His face went through shock to surprise and then to something else. For a split second he looked at me as though I was a ghost, as though I was the most terrifying thing he had ever, ever seen. His eyes widened and his still fat bottom lip began to tremble.

He scuttled backwards like a crab.

'You bastard,' he said. 'You fucking bastard.'

And then he was off and I made no better an

107

attempt at running after him than the fat man in the yellow shirt had done.

I sat there. I still wanted to go home, but there was something about his face. I looked after the kid but he was gone. I made it slowly to my feet for the second time that night, and leant back up against the wall. I peered round the corner, to make sure there weren't any more early morning Linford Christies in the area, my eyes fixing on a long street of drab, two-storey houses. Doors straight onto the street, bin bags, cars. I saw the Escort, and then my eyes went to a door halfway down on the right. It was open, still moving on its hinge, slowly coming back round to closed. I straightened myself up. With the cars on my left to support me I hop-walked down towards it.

I'd take a quick look. *You bastard.* What had I done? But only a quick look, I wasn't going to fuck around. I crossed the road and headed towards the house.

The door had stopped moving and was ajar. After listening to nothing for a full minute, I pushed it open slowly and found myself standing in a living room. There was no hallway. What there was instead was a mess. Foil food trays, pizza cartons and beer cans. One knackered old armchair and a mattress on the floor. I didn't look at it for long though because I could hear something. There was a door straight ahead of me, and the sound was coming through it. It was a low sound, a pressured hissing that wasn't very loud but seemed to be building. I stepped across the room, trying not to make any noise. It didn't sound human. I stopped halfway to listen. There were no voices of any kind that I could hear but it was late, there may have been people in the bedrooms. The noise in the room ahead took me again.

I told myself to be careful. Something had made that kid leg it. The noise intrigued me, it sounded like a snake, getting slowly madder. Is that what the boy was scared of, he'd found a boa constrictor going through his cornflakes? I made it to the door. I took a breath. Then I moved forward, my hand on the handle, turning and pushing at the same time. I made it through quickly, my left hand forward, my shoulders tense, ready to take on whatever it was that was making that increasingly sinister noise.

As I stepped through the door the red plastic button on the top of the kettle snapped neatly into place, leaving only the low rumble of boiling water, which was sending a plume of steam up to the ceiling of the squalid, sparsely furnished kitchen.

I let out a breath. My throat went through a dry swallow. Jesus. The great investigator, super-sensitive to active kitchen appliances but he couldn't see that a dodgy cab man was obviously trying to get him into his car, when there were hordes of other people he could easily have driven home. I walked over to the kettle, breathing in and out through my nose. There was a cup with a tea bag in it. The boy must have got spooked when he was waiting for the kettle to boil, while he was in the process of making his tea. The kettle was sitting on a set of units backed by a large, rectangular-shaped window. I walked over and looked out of it, into a small backyard with three-foot weeds forcing their way through badly laid concrete. Had the kid seen something out there? I couldn't. All I could see was a low wall leading onto waste ground, and beyond that the sunrise, a timid slice of red coming up behind Islington and Hackney like it really didn't want to. I had another listen for any voices. The house was dead.

The boy had legged it for a reason but I didn't know what it was. The reason could wait, and so could Lucy, who was probably sleeping whatever it was off upstairs. The tea bag looked inviting. I shrugged my shoulders, poured some water into the cup and then walked over to the fridge. But, like the front door, the fridge was ajar. There was a carton of milk on the floor, lying in a small white pool which was still seeping slowly through the dirty cracks in the lino. I stopped. Something was wrong. Very wrong. It was. I reached down to pick the carton up and my eyes went out through the glass of the back door, out to a huge mound of bin bags that were stacked up against the garden wall, a pile of bags four feet high, seven feet long at least. I dropped the carton. I guessed I wasn't the first to have dropped it.

I got the back door open using a key that was hanging from a hook on the wall. The bags smelled fetid and rank, and looked it too. I had no desire to touch them, no desire to see any more of what was beneath them. What I could see was a long, slim foot. An ankle. Part of a calf. The foot didn't have a shoe on it. It was getting lighter all the time and I could make it out easily. It was on its side. It didn't have a sock or any tights on it. It was quite long, and it had polished toe nails. A silver colour like the stuff I used to paint Airfix models with when I was a kid. It was a girl's foot, a young girl's foot, leading up to a girl's ankle and a girl's calf, and about six inches of instep.

I moved forward, slowly. I bent down but stopped. I

shouldn't touch this. I'd get into grief if I touched this. Did the house have a phone? I'd just wait for the law, I'd wait for Andy Gold and his team of toothbrush boys. I stood up again. I moved back towards the door. I had my hand on the handle when I heard the noise.

It was a rustling, a movement from underneath all that trash. Another. She was moving. That little cunt, that dirty little cunt, he hadn't even checked before he'd left her there.

I rushed forward and began pulling the bags aside, trying to get them off her. Another movement. I grabbed at the bags, yanking them back behind me, covering myself in shit. I put my foot through one, into a mess of old chicken bones, livid with maggots. I cut my hand on a can. But then I got to her, her body smeared with filth. There was blood, a lot of blood beneath her head. It wasn't sitting right. But she'd moved. I pushed more bags aside. When they were all gone I took her wrist, feeling for a pulse; nothing. I felt her neck. No. Her skin was pale. Too pale. I worked my finger into her mouth, clearing the mess out of it, and then I tried to breath life back into her, gagging on the taste, trying to block out the stink. Nothing. I tried again. Nothing. I started to press down on her chest. She'd moved, she had, she . . .

And then I saw the rat. It was sitting on top of one of the bags that I had thrown aside, less than three feet away from me. It was squinting at me curiously, with-out even the hint of any fear, looking slightly annoyed that I'd interrupted it. In its whiskers I saw flecks of its food, and I saw that some of them were held together by a thick, dark liquid. I held its gaze for a second and then I saw a movement to my right. It was another one, scurrying off along the side of the wall behind some boxes. Then the one in front of me broke its look and scrambled down into the pile of bags I'd created, making a loud, rustling sound as it went.

The sound I'd heard.

I turned away from it. Then, as the shy lidded eye of the sun took its first nervous look at a brand new day, I looked down at the naked, filthy body of Lucy Bradley.

Part Two

PART TWO

Chapter One

Over the last few days I hadn't given much thought to James Bradley. In fact, I'd never even known his name. I dare say that the overwhelming personality of his wife had somehow blanked him out, like a middle-aged father in one of those Jane Austen novels Sharon had lent me. So when he called me at my office one Wednesday morning ten days after his daughter Lucy had been found dead, and asked me to meet him in a café in Hampstead, I was a little surprised. I had imagined that it would have been his wife who would have contacted me, if anyone, or even his one remaining daughter. It was probably the fact that it was him, and not either of them, that had made me agree to go and meet the man.

As it was, meeting the Bradley family, or at least its female quotient, had not been a very positive experience for me. I had been bullied, followed, beaten up, knifed, and placed in the centre of a murder inquiry from which I had yet to satisfactorily extricate myself. All because of them. I wasn't too keen on continuing my association. Yes, I was sorry for them. No, I couldn't even begin to imagine what they were going through. But that didn't mean I had to have any more to do with them. Ever since the events of that Saturday night I'd been trying to shake off thoughts of them like a summer flu. It must have been the curiosity that had refused to let go of me, or else the bleak, flat tone of the man's voice, which finally persuaded me to go and talk to the only male member of the family.

Over the last week I had spent a lot of time in the company of men. A couple of men in particular. One of them was a sometime friend of mine and the other used to be my boss. Andy Gold and Chief Inspector Kenneth Clay had taken a great deal of interest in my involvement with the Bradley family, especially in my proximity to the corpse of their missing daughter. I hadn't known it at the time but Carr Street, where I'd finally found Lucy, is just within the borders of Islington Borough, which meant that it came under my former colleagues' jurisdiction.

'You topped her there on purpose, didn't you, Billy?' Ken Clay had announced, once he had got me safely ensconced in the station house on Calshot Street. 'Just so you'd have the pleasure of a little chat with me.'

That morning, ten days before meeting James Bradley, I hadn't stayed long kneeling by the side of his daughter. Just long enough to take in the artificial light of her silver-blonde hair, and too long not to be able to see what a beautiful girl she had been. I'd stood up and pulled my eyes away from her. I'd turned towards the door, but then turned back quickly when I'd heard the rats again. I'd kicked at the rubbish, trying to drive them away, and then I'd dragged myself back into the house where I did find a phone, sitting on the floor amongst the clothes and the cans and the fast food debris.

I'd called Andy Gold at home, wanting a familiar

face around when the cavalry came, and then I'd dialled three nines, just so that I would be registered as having done so. Andy was very pissed off that I'd called him, telling me angrily that he was pretty busy right then. I told him that I'd found Lucy Bradley. He wasn't interested. I told him how I'd found her. He was.

Andy arrived five minutes after the first patrol car, and by the time the last one came there were ten vehicles blocking the road outside, and more people in and around the premises than at a house-warming party. Andy led me straight outside, to show him what I'd found and tell him what I'd done. When I told him that I'd thought the owner of the ankle I'd seen was alive, and had shifted all the bin bags off to get to her, Andy looked at me as if I was either very stupid or lying. His manner changed to one of complete detachment from me. He spoke to me like he was the copper, and I was someone involved in something, which even if it wasn't murder, was something he wanted to know about. His voice had that you-must-think-I'm-very-stupid tinge. From that moment on I didn't have any illusions left about the gulf that separated him and me.

As the noise inside the house grew, the backyard began to look like a film set. The police activity had slowly begun to wake the neighbours and the first thing to happen was that a blue canopy was erected to shield Lucy's body, and the policemen acting on or about it, from the horrified eyes of the local residents. It was getting lighter all the time, but a trio of halogen lamps was set up to get the proceedings under way as quickly as possible. All the time I was allowed to remain on the spot, which didn't really surprise me. I guessed that Andy Gold wanted to monitor my reaction to having to look at Lucy, to see if I gave away signs of any sort of a connection to her.

The reaction of the other people present varied. A young policewoman who had helped erect the canopy maintained a professional look with a tinge of bitterness. Her eyes skirted round the prone, naked girl who was at the centre of her actions. She very deliberately did not look at me. A male constable in his late forties was similarly efficient in his duties but the look on his face was a mixture of sadness and fear, as he possibly connected the age of the victim with that of a daughter, or a niece. The rest of the uniformed officers were youngish men, and theirs was a confusion of revulsion and fascination. They all tried to look businesslike when they saw Lucy lying there but they couldn't help being affected by her, seeing her young body beneath the filth, beneath their job, beneath the fact of her death. Her breasts, her nipples, a deep armpit. Long elegant legs. I saw one, making an unnecessary journey from one end of the yard to the other, sneaking a hurried glance as he passed by her.

From my position next to the back door, I could hear officers knocking up those residents not aware of the drama unfolding in the neighbourhood, and beginning to ask questions. Beneath the canopy, a police photographer arrived, and took pictures of the entire scene before going over the same ground with a video camera. The duty pathologist arrived and had a quick chat with Andy before conducting a brief examination of the body. He bent over Lucy, checking her skin for cuts and bruises, and for lividity. He paid particular attention to the back of her head, and her neck. He took out a thermometer and went to take a vaginal reading, but stopped and bent to look closer. He reached in his case for a sample bottle and a spatula, and he took some swabs. When he'd secured the lid on the tiny bottle he turned to look up at me, his look one of blank but undisguised disgust. I could only guess what he'd found. Then he returned to his task, taking a temperature reading from the corpse, which he could use to ascertain the time of death.

A far more thorough examination would be conducted at the morgue, but the quicker the police can get information in cases like this the better. Even if the horse has bolted the door still needs shutting. Once the man had finished, and the position of Lucy's body was mapped onto a sketch of the scene, two officers lifted her onto a plastic sheet and carried her into the house. Then a set of plastic crates was brought out and, after they had been numbered and their position noted, all of the rubbish bags were loaded into them. I guessed it was the first rubbish removal to have occurred in that part of London for two weeks. The officers lifted up the bags gingerly, setting their faces against the stench, hardly talking. Andy Gold went as far as directing operations. Towards the end of the clean-up my friend the rat scurried out from his quickly vanishing habitat and ran straight between the legs of a young noddy carrying out a tray of tea. The boy stepped back quickly onto a broken bag and went arse over tit, something that would have been very funny at almost any other time. As it was nobody laughed, not even Andy Gold. He even helped the kid pick up the broken tea cups.

A tall, pinched-faced detective I recognized with much reluctance came out from the house and whispered to Andy. They both looked at me and then I was led round the side of the house, into the road, and sat in the back of a squad car where I was left in the company of the middle-aged constable. He didn't say anything. I watched the pinched-faced detective walk outside and hold the door of a large, shapeless Nissan open for an equally large, shapeless man. I watched the man being shown into the house, which was being guarded by two officers like the door of Number Ten.

The road was rammed now, milling with officers slowly walking up and down, looking at the floor as though the Queen had lost a contact lens. The street was sealed off, from the top to the bottom, and one angry householder was being told that he wouldn't be allowed to leave for his fishing trip just yet. Then, as I sat there, I suddenly remembered my leg or, rather, it remembered me. I could feel it, but when I bent down to check I was relieved to see that it wasn't bleeding. It was still quite open though, and looked a mess. I checked my hand too, clenched on a lump of toilet paper. Not deep, but it needed cleaning.

I was wondering whether I should ask my heavy-faced companion if he remembered his first aid training when the door of the house opened. Two officers were carrying Lucy, now in a body bag, swinging her a foot from the ground, one going backwards until he was out on the street. They carried her to a waiting ambulance where she was passed in by one of the medics, who had initially arrived on the scene. The doors of the wagon were closed, a couple of police cars moved, and the ambulance pulled away. I couldn't help but think of where Lucy was being taken, and what would be done to her, how she would be dissected and investigated, her organs removed and sewn back up, fluid taken from her eyes, her sexual organs probed into and examined. It made me almost as sick to think of as what had already happened to her. I followed the ambulance as it passed, and saw that the copper to my left was following it too. Then it was gone, into the brightening morning.

The door beside me opened. Ken Clay got in next to me, dumping his weight down on the springs, forcing me to move right up against the tired foot soldier on my left. He shrank back from me as though I had the plague. Another PC got in the front. Clay looked at me and sighed, letting me know that he hadn't bothered stopping to clean his teeth before leaving the house that morning.

'Home, James,' he said, rapping the back of the driver's seat twice. 'And don't spare the horses.'

The place we met was a fake French café on Hampstead High Street, a little piece of Disney Gaul to keep you going until your next trip over for the cheap vino. I had used the occasion as an excuse to wear a light, pale grey suit that had been conceived before I was born, and a sky-blue shirt without a tie. It was the first time I'd worn a suit in weeks and it had the odd effect of making me feel cooler than my usual shorts and trainers. The café was crowded when I got there but as James Bradley had arrived before me I didn't have to worry about finding a seat. I didn't know what he looked like, and we hadn't agreed on any carnations in buttonholes, but it didn't take me long to spot the man who had called me, sitting alone at a small round table in the corner. He was the only man there who looked like his daughter had recently been hit over the head with an as yet unidentified object and then strangled. To her death. I picked him out easily. There was just something about him.

When I had shaken James Bradley's hand and sat down opposite him, my first reaction was surprise. He wasn't what I had expected. In fact, I'd had no idea what to expect. No real image of the husband of the woman who had employed me had come to mind. I had vaguely pictured a tall, hearty man with the same self-confidence and direct manner as his wife, but the man I had met did not come across like that at all. Even before I'd spoken to him I was wondering how it was that he and his wife had come to be married.

James Bradley was a smallish man, possibly only about five seven. He was wearing an oldish grey suit cut a touch too small for him, the knot of his tie pulled fastidiously tight. He was thin, and he sat with his legs crossed and his arms folded in a way that made him seem timid, even slightly effeminate. The grey hair that I have already mentioned was still full and very soft, and the face it fell over had a withdrawn, awkward quality that I didn't think was due simply to the circumstances, although the pallid state of his complexion probably was. Irrespective of his current state, James Bradley seemed to me to be a shy, quiet man, totally unlike his wife. He made me think of a crumpled and sad version of Dirk Bogarde, or at least a character he might have played.

The table next to us was occupied by three well-dressed ladies approaching a certain age talking about the universities their children were applying to. A brisk but efficient waiter brought me an espresso and Mr

Bradley a fresh cup of filter coffee, to which he added a little milk before ignoring it completely. I asked him how his family was.

'Oh,' he said, in a thin voice, not that far back. He looked everywhere but at me. 'We're trying to cope. The police won't release the body yet though so it's all a bit of a strain. Maybe, after the funeral, you know . . .'

'Emma?' I asked.

Mr Bradley paused.

'She . . . I don't know.' He bit his lip. 'Mostly she just sits in her room and won't talk. My wife has spent a little more time with her than I have but she's very withdrawn. I hope she'll pick up when we go back to Sussex but it's difficult to know how she really is yet, what sort of effect this will have in the long run.'

'She's a strong girl,' I said, 'I'm sure she'll get through it eventually.'

Mr Bradley wanted to know how I knew that his daughter Emma was a strong person, and I told him about meeting her, and how she had tried to follow me. I was surprised that she hadn't told him herself. I'd told the police about it, just so they didn't think I was hiding anything from them, but they can't have informed Emma's parents. They can't have thought it very important which, to my mind, was the case. Nothing I had done was important, I had nothing to do with anything. I had, over the days following the incident, been at great pains to convince them of this.

Once my hand had been looked at, my leg bandaged, and samples of my blood taken, I was asked to remove my clothes and hand over my boxer shorts. I was then left to my thoughts in the same interview room I had occupied some months previously, in no less trying circumstances. The room was as grey and harsh-looking as I remembered it, designed to make those invited there want to leave as soon as possible; i.e. talk. Outside it could have been any time of the day, any season of the year. I was beginning to get tired now, and was grateful of the diarrhoea-thick tea I was presented with, though I only managed to get through half of it before the room's only door rattled. A uniformed officer came in and held the door open for Ken Clay, and his tall sidekick, who really did look like an angel had picked him up out of the mould by his face. The sidekick leant against the wall. Clay manoeuvred his bulk down at the table opposite, totally engulfing the flimsy wooden chair. Then he rested his two huge hands on the table in front of him and looked down at them, seeming to think of something.

I stared into Clay's raw, livid face, the colour of fresh liver, and thought how much more pleasant it would have been to look into a wound. His piggy little eyes flicked up and fixed on me. He started to speak but a thought changed his tack.

'You really are a queer one, Billy Rucker,' Clay said finally, his head shaking slightly. His voice, almost forgotten Glasgow menace, was loud and cheerful. 'I really, really don't understand you. I never have.'

'Tape recorder,' I said.

'You had a good job, good prospects.' He nodded to himself. 'People were saying nice things about you. Your name, as it were, was at the top of a lot of different lists. People liked the way you did things.'

'A tape recorder. On. Now.'

'But you had to chuck it all away, didn't you?' He waved a hand at me. 'Oh, I understand, I understand at the time what you were going through. We all did. A tough break, no doubt about it. But you couldn't get beyond it, could you?' His lumpen hands interlocked on the table top like octopuses mating. 'So what did you do? You bollocksed up, let it all go to shit. Handed in your book. The one way you could have dealt with it, maintain a structure, do something meaningful, you pissed away, you turned your back on it.'

He was waiting for me.

'I dealt with it. Playing your stupid games wouldn't have been dealing with it.'

He gave a shrug, just with his mouth. 'Your mate Gold got most of what you'd have got, you know. He'd have been polishing your magnifying glass now if you hadn't gone soft.' He smiled. 'And he knows it. Probably doesn't make him very happy, when he thinks about it. But what is the real shame, the *tragedy* here if you like, Billy, and what I'm trying to get at, is that if you'd stuck on this side of the table, you wouldn't be sitting on *that* side of it, would you?'

Clay reached over and took a swig of my abandoned tea, getting the skin stuck on his fleshy top lip. Then he smiled, wider this time, giving me a mouthful of livid pink gums scraped back too far over small, urine-coloured teeth.

'And that's what you call dealing with it, is it? Hey? Topping a pretty young girl you've been paid to find? Giving her one first. Or after? Is that what you call dealing with the fact that your brother's a cabbage? Golden Luke, the principal boy, getting his life out of a tube. And more to the point dealing with the fact that it was all, *all* because of you, because you wouldn't leave something alone? Fuck, Billy!' A shock of laughter burst up from somewhere within him. 'I'd hate to see what you'd have done if you *hadn't* been able to deal with it!'

Clay gave way to the laughter, and then to coughing, specks of phlegm falling on the table in front of me. I stared at him, containing a pale anger, the anger I knew he wanted to burst right out of me. Clay didn't think I'd done it. But that wasn't the point. He wanted to show me that he was perfectly willing to take me all the way for it, so that I'd give him everything I had. So that I'd go out there and solve the thing for him, scared that if I didn't I'd be back sitting there talking to him. There was something else too, something less tangible that I had never been able to pin down. I got the feeling that the control freak in Clay was afraid of me, afraid of the fact that I'd once been part of the team and was now out of there. Maybe he thought I knew something, something about the way he operated, that he didn't want me blabbing about. Sometimes I thought he was almost desperate to get me out of his hair. But whatever he was worried about he needn't have been. I didn't have a thing on him.

I waited until Clay had calmed down. I watched him sink the rest of my cold tea, nearly swallowing the mug. His throat shook as the liquid went down, and his body rippled with tremors as he shifted on his tiny chair. Clay looked soft. If you were a kid you'd want to bounce up and down on him. But he wasn't soft. He was the brick inside the snow football, the perfect plan to hurt you. His laughter focused me, set me hard.

'A tape recorder,' I said again.

I was kept at the station for twenty-four hours, during which time I told first Ken Clay, then Andy Gold, and then another two officers, almost exactly what I had been doing over the last four days. I told them everything, from originally seeing Lucy Bradley in Camden, to being run into by the boy just before finding Lucy's body. I did not, however, tell them what the boy had said to me, or anything about the look on his face. That look was surprise, and horror; I didn't think it was murder. I didn't tell them about the kettle or the tea bag either; facts that would maybe show he'd been just as surprised as I was. I was happy for the police to think that the boy had killed Lucy, at least for the moment. It might stop them wasting their time on me.

I told them about being followed by the murdered girl's sister, and seeing her outside the tube. I told them about seeing the boy at Camden Lock, and what happened at York's, and after with the cab driver and his friends. But one of the things I didn't give them was Donna-Natalie. At least not her name. As I'd moled down into those bin bags I'd actually thought it was her I was going to find down there, not Lucy. I didn't tell them about seeing her at York's because I wanted to have something of my own, a card to play if I needed it. Also, I couldn't believe she'd killed Lucy, and I knew that somehow her parents would find her if I gave her to the police. The police would want to know everything about her. Donna didn't need that. I could still see the look on her face when she'd told me about the life she'd led before she'd come to London.

As it was, I could tell that the two DCs who tried to pound me with logic were pretty certain I was the man they were after. Clay left them to it, probably telling them to take as long as was legal so he'd have something to tell the press. A man is helping the police with their inquiries. He could have just let me stew on my own, but probably just sicked the other two on me to give them a little practice. They certainly needed it.

As it stood, however, I could understand the officers' enthusiasm. Everything they came up with I had an explanation for, but the fact that my explanation was the truth did not alter the fact that their explanation, that I had killed the girl, also seemed to fit. I'd been seen following her for three days. I'd been seen following her on the night she died. Furthermore, my blood had been found, some of it on Lucy's body, some on three of the bags surrounding her. It was a can, I said, for the fifth time, check for a can with bloodstains on it. As for the state of my leg, the bruising on my head and neck, that could have been due to a struggle with the murdered girl, or with other parties involved. What witnesses did I have to the fight I'd had? None. What about getting in the cab? A guy with a clipboard. They'd most certainly check it out, they told me.

I didn't bother arguing with them or pointing out that they hadn't come up with any kind of motive for me to kill Lucy, or that I was hardly likely to report a murder I had myself committed. I knew it wouldn't make any difference to them. I just sat there trying to remain calm, to sit it out. I was now very tired, not having slept, mainly because I knew that if I did, Clay would have me woken after an hour or so to get at me while I was in REM haze. He didn't care what hour of the day or night he conducted his interviews. I spent the time tapping mental fingers, holding all the events in my head frozen still, waiting for the space in which to let them all move together. That space was not a police station.

At about ten a.m. the next morning Clay met me in the interview room, and didn't take long to get to the point.

'You've been placed at the scene,' he said. 'You sure you told me everything?'

I sighed. 'Placed at the scene by myself,' I replied. 'Remember? I called it in?'

'By a boy who saw you on the street outside. Says you were sniffing around after the Bradley girl for days.'

'You know that. I told you about him. Doesn't it mean anything to you that I also placed *him* there?'

'Maybe. But maybe you only mentioned him because you knew we'd find out anyway.'

'Whatever. What does it change? Where's the boy? Have you got him?'

'It was a phone call. But we'll find him. That might be enough on its own you know. How's your hand?'

'Fine,' I said. 'Find the can yet?'

'Maybe,' Clay admitted.

Clay looked thoughtful for a second, wistful even. He let his guard drop a fraction.

'You know what I hate?' he said after a second.

'As far as I can remember? Most things.'

'But particularly?'

I shook my head.

'It's these DNA fucking tests everyone's so frigging in love with. They really, really bug me sometimes.'

'Like when they make life difficult for you?'

'Exactly.' He leant forward on the table. I wasn't sure it could take it. 'When they cloud the picture so to speak, with information I could happily have done without.'

I left a second, watching while Clay tried to fold his arms over his chest. 'In this case referring to what?'

'Someone had tried to give her one,' Clay said flatly. 'Tried to but failed, so the report states. Ever had that problem?'

I shrugged. He looked like he had.

'Some laddie turned on the hose before he'd managed to get it into the garden so to speak. We thought it might have been you.'

'Not me,' I said.

'No. And thanks to DNA sodding testing I've got to believe you. Some other fucker. Or, rather, would-be fucker. Just like a mosque in Golder's Green apparently; no sign of entry. Just an offering outside. Sperm, Billy, in layman's terms. We've got a sample of his nasty nature and the boffins, bless 'em, tell me it didn't come from you.'

'I could have told you that.'

'Aye, but I wouldn't have *had* to believe you, would I? Even if I did.'

'What a shame. Things were much easier in the good old days, eh?'

'Too fucking right, mate,' Clay said. 'But as it is, Billy, sad as it makes me, for the second time recently, thanks to the damn scientists I'm going to have to let you go.'

Clay's hands spread wide like he wanted to hug me. Hearing him say what he had didn't make me consciously relax, but almost immediately a yawn fought its way from within me and I didn't bother stifling it. It seemed to annoy Clay. He was pretending to be very calm about the whole thing but I could tell that it irked him to see me walk away so easily, without giving him anything. Clay could tell that I knew stuff, I was closer to it than him. And he hated being in the dark, feeling excluded from the story. It was why he made such a good copper, because of his almost psychotic need: to know. He didn't want to bring people to justice, to put them away, he just needed to pry his way into things, to show them that he could get to the centre. I could almost picture him in the playground; the fat kid with a packed lunch on a bench, all the other kids with their backs to him without even realizing it.

I guessed that was why he was letting me go. He really didn't have to. Just because I hadn't tried to sleep with her didn't mean I hadn't killed the girl, and I wouldn't have been the first person to report a murder I'd committed myself. Clay had enough to keep me even if he knew I was clean. He just knew that I might be able to help him, something I wouldn't be able to do sitting there. And if I didn't, and if the whole thing stalled and he started getting flack about it, well he knew where I lived. He could easily give a little yank on the string.

Clay said, 'Keep me informed, Billy. Before I have to ask.'

And then he was gone.

James Bradley didn't think I'd killed his daughter. He knew that the main suspect for the killing was a young boy who had been seen with Lucy over the last couple of days and may even have been living with her. Bradley knew that I had seen him fleeing from the scene of the crime. So what he wanted from me was very simple. He wanted me to find the boy.

I shook my head and asked him why he wanted to waste money on me when my former colleagues were already onto it.

'You found Lucy,' he explained. 'You may have been too late but that wasn't your fault, you found her. Nobody else could, not the first people we'd tried, not the police.'

'They weren't looking,' I said.

'No, but even if they had been I'm not sure they would have found her any sooner. Tell me, how did you do it so quickly?'

I didn't think it ethical business practice to misrepresent my services so I told him the truth.

'It was a fluke,' I said. 'I saw her before I was looking for her, so I knew she hung around Camden. Then I went to the club she was fliering for.'

'But still, you found her. You specialize in young people?'

'I do.'

'And this boy is young. We'd like you to make some enquiries, see what you can find out. I know you've probably had enough of us, what with getting beaten up and everything, and I don't have much of a right, but I'm asking you, please, to help us again.'

I looked down at my coffee cup and thought about it. I touched my leg, which had just about healed. I'd gone along to meet Bradley with the intention of simply filling him in on Lucy's last hours, giving him information which, however meaningless, I would want to have known if my daughter had been killed. But I had to admit I was kidding myself. I needed to know myself, I needed to sort it out. I remembered the feeling I'd had about Lucy, how I'd thought of her as a selfish, spoilt little girl, when I hadn't known the first thing about her. It made me feel guilty, the way I'd dismissed her. I knew I couldn't dismiss her again.

I looked up and nodded. 'OK,' I said. 'But that's all I'll do.'

'Of course.'

'Anything I find out I'll take straight to the police. That's as far as I go.'

'Of course,' Mr Bradley said.

'And if I think things might get even the slightest bit hairy I'm going to back off immediately.'

'Of course,' Mr Bradley said, for the third time.

I took a sip of my espresso and Mr Bradley tentatively asked me how much I would charge him. I knew I could have taken him for a fortune but I didn't. Honest. After we had agreed a fee Mr Bradley wrote me a cheque, which I took without any fuss. This wasn't a usual case for me, and I wasn't going to feel pressured by this man the way I had been by his wife. I'd need to lay out some cash if I was going to get anywhere. I slid the cheque into the top pocket of my suit.

'Does your wife know you're hiring me?'

'Naturally.'

'Good. I'll probably need to speak to her. And to Emma. If that's OK.'

'I'll talk to her. I'm sure she'll agree. She's been very helpful to the police who've been round.'

'I'm sure she has.' I bit my lip. 'Have you spoken to her?'

'Yes, I mean as much as I can. It's her mother really who she's closer to. I know they've been speaking.'

'It's just that Emma told me she blamed herself for Lucy running away. An argument over exam results. I just thought I'd mention it because she probably feels it even more now.'

'Oh,' Mr Bradley said, very simply. 'Oh. I didn't know.' He was shocked, like I'd just woken him from a nap, and then he looked completely defeated. I couldn't tell whether it was at the thought of his daughter's feelings or at the fact that she had told them to me, a stranger, and not to him. He looked beyond me.

'Thank you . . .' he said. 'I'll speak to her. I didn't know she felt that way. No wonder she's withdrawn. It wasn't her fault, of course not, not hers at all. No. How could it be? It's just that Lucy . . . Lucy never . . .'

And then he sat back and his words dissolved into the smoke-filled air. I thought he'd finished but a look of horror came over his face. His mouth opened, as if searching on its own for the words it wanted to say.

'I haven't given Emma a thought,' he said finally. He shook his head in confused wonder, like he was watching a fireworks display. 'Not until you just asked me about her. Not really, not like I should have.' He paused again but I thought he had more to say so I waited. A bitter smile split his lips. 'Lucy . . . Lucy was my favourite, you see. It's a horrible thing to finally admit, even to a stranger, but she was. I've always known it really. Emma's always seemed to get everything she wants, she's never caused us any trouble, but there was just something about Lucy. Ever since she was a little girl. I always thought she needed more love somehow. And now I'm neglecting my other daughter, and do you know why? Because all I can think about is that boy. Just him and nothing else. I used to watch the news and wonder why parents of victims cared so much about bringing the killer to justice. It would never bring their children back, would it, no matter what happened? How could it? So why did they care?' He stopped again and then his eyes searched out mine for the first time, setting on me, fixed and hard. A bubble of outrage rose up through him, pushing its way into his voice. 'But now all I can think of, the *only thing*, is the bastard, the fucking, *fucking* bastard who killed my daughter.'

Mr Bradley had raised his voice, and just as he did so the conversation between the three women beside us suddenly died the way it sometimes can, and his words cut into the air between our table and theirs. The women all froze, the atmosphere between them turning to ice, but the man in front of me didn't notice. He sank back into his seat and his gaze transferred itself from me to the window, and through that into the street. The three women remained motionless for a second, and then they all turned back to their salads like a toy machine that's been wound up again.

Bradley was still staring out of the window. I watched his eyes narrow and left him there.

Chapter Two

Sleep. Beautiful, empty, drawn out sleep. It was all I'd wanted, but I didn't get it. I kept waking, seeing dark shapes coming towards me, a smile of gold. Seeing Lucy's body. I ripped myself out of one dream in which it wasn't bin bags I was pulling off her but the dark suited shapes of police officers, all slithering on top of her, all trying desperately to get to her. Try as I might I couldn't ever get them off her.

In the week or so prior to meeting James Bradley I'd tried to turn my mind away from it and take it easy. Once Clay had dismissed me, I'd gone straight home from the station and only made one call. I reached Sharon at work and apologized for not having returned her message about dinner. She was cancelling anyway so it wasn't a problem. She said I sounded tired.

'Just work,' I said. I hesitated. It didn't feel right to tell her about what had happened over the phone. I said I'd call her later.

I slept and woke and slept and woke. When I was fed up with the process I got up and made coffee, which made me feel hungry for the first time in days. I ate an English breakfast outside Fred's, eventually satisfying a sudden and violent need for fat and grease. The food made me feel slightly less stretched out and raw.

Alberto served me, and when he'd finished filling me in on his weekend he raised his eyebrows and asked me where my new friend was today. It took a second or so before I realized he meant Emma.

'At home I expect,' I told him. 'Very probably feeling more miserable than she's ever done before.'

'Oh, Billy,' he said. 'What a heartbreaker you are.'

I asked Alberto for some extra toast and some more coffee but he must have thought I'd eaten too much already and that my caffeine levels were advanced enough as it was because I never saw either.

Cats don't like water. For some reason they're suspicious of it, even though were you to chuck one in a lake it would swim OK. I had a similar irrational feeling, and that week I made a conscious, if largely unsuccessful effort not to think about the Bradleys. The newspapers didn't help, although they could have made a lot more of it if they'd chosen. I read them without wanting to and did my best to ignore my own curiosity. I'd decided not to act as Ken Clay's little helper if I could help it, let him do what he liked. As for what had happened to me, I wrote it off to experience, telling myself that what I would gain from looking into it would be, at the very best, precisely nothing. At worst, another load of trouble to add to my collection. I told myself this as sternly as I could and did my best to ignore the cold anger that gnawed my stomach when my mind went back to that wide, golden smile.

Instead of wondering about it I got my leg stitched and my hand looked at, receiving a tetanus shot that covered both wounds. I also went to pick up my car. It was still playing dead when I tried the ignition so I popped the bonnet and peered into the engine, just like I knew what the fuck I was doing. I didn't, but even someone as mechanically challenged as myself could see what the trouble was. A problem with my spark plugs. Actually, a rather obvious problem. There were no spark plugs.

Still, I wasn't going to go into it. It really wouldn't do me any good; I couldn't prove anything and I'd seen enough Shakespeare, a lot of it with my brother in, to know that revenge was a pretty pointless pursuit. That water feeling again; don't dive in. What I did do, however, was get the car fixed and drive it straight round to the photo lab, where I bought my old camera back off Carl. Luckily he hadn't sold it yet. I also put in an insurance claim for the Leica. On the form I stated that the camera had been irreparably damaged in the course of a mugging, and that I had reported the matter to the police. I didn't think it necessary to state that it had been irreparably damaged by myself.

Glad of something to occupy me, which had nothing whatever to do with the grim events of the last few days, I took my new old F1 down to Prior Street in Greenwich, and spent three pleasantly dull hours listening to Radio 4 on my car stereo. I sat in the quiet street until seven thirty p.m., when a Volvo pulled up outside the house I was watching and a man of about forty got out, carrying a briefcase. I got a shot of him as he closed his car door. He walked up to his front door and disappeared into his house but was outside again in less than thirty minutes, this time with his wife and two children. The way they were all dressed I reckoned he was taking them out for dinner. I got further shots of the man, and several of his children, some of which also included the wife. Once they'd disappeared round the corner onto Royal Hill I started the car and drove home.

I sent the shots to an old lady in Leicester, who hadn't seen her son for ten years. They showed a well-off Pakistani man, first on his own, and then holding hands with two very pretty little girls, both in loose, flowery summer dresses. The shots were very similar to the ones I'd taken of him before, except for the age of his children, and the fact that in the intervening two years he seemed to have filled out a little at the waist. He was now at that critical stage between the body he'd always had, and podginess. It could go either way. I sent the pictures with a short note saying that the man looked well and seemed happy as far as I could tell. I also included an invoice and, just like last time, I didn't include any pictures featuring the man's wife. They were not wanted. They showed a slim, attractive woman, a shade taller than her husband, wearing a simple black sleeveless dress that was designed to set off her long, very well-cut blonde hair. I threw those shots away.

No other work came up. I was pretty useless as far as the gym was concerned but I went down a couple of times anyway that week for the atmosphere. A young lad I knew was training a lot and it felt good to help him, give him what tips I could. I had a couple of drinks with Sal and some of the boys. I also hung out with Nicky for the first time in a while, telling him all about the Bradleys. Talking about it made me remember the pictures I'd taken of the boy in the alley, and I sent them off to Andy Gold, along with the shot of the man who had waylaid him. I also wrote a note saying when the shots had been taken. What with that, and the club, and knowing where he lived, I didn't think it would take the police too long to find him. As for finding the person who had killed Lucy, that was another matter. I still didn't believe it was him, although it was likely that he held the key to it all. But at that point I was happy to let Andy find him and start the chambers turning.

I'd had no contact with the police and I had done my best not to think about Lucy or her mother. For some reason, I half expected Emma to call me, but she didn't. I banked a few cheques, paid a few bills and tried to relax. I visited Luke. On the Wednesday night I eventually got to see Sharon. We went to a comedy show, catching Lenny Beige's act at the Talk of London. Sharon had got some free tickets through a friend of a friend, and even though I'd have much rather had a quieter time, with a chance to talk, I did enjoy the show. There was a party afterwards that Sharon wanted to go to, and so we went, and we ended up staying late, far later than Sharon normally wants to stay out on a week night. After that we went back to my place but we still didn't speak properly. Sharon was in a really good mood, she was vivacious and happy. She'd hardly let go of my hand all night. I found it hard to move the conversation to anything serious.

I'd already told Sharon about cutting my hand on a can, but when we got into bed she saw the scar on my leg and wanted to know the rest. The leg was healing fast, but when I told her about it, it still made her feel guilty.

'I knew you were being quiet,' she said.

'It wasn't because of that.'

'I knew there was something the other day on the phone. Why didn't you tell me?'

'I was going to, but . . .'

'God.' Sharon rested her head on my chest. 'That poor girl. And you for finding her. You've been going through all that and I've been . . . I've been so wrapped up in myself. It's been three days, you should have told me, you really should have.'

'Sharon . . .'

'Shush, Billy,' she said.

Sharon and I made love that night for the first time in weeks. To begin with I felt quite separate from her. Really, I wanted to talk, about Luke and his poems, but Sharon seemed focused on my body, she wouldn't be drawn away from it. Pretty soon, any worries I had were sandblasted away by her passion. I couldn't help but give way to the love I felt for this brilliant, beautiful girl, full of laughter and energy, who'd had coke-addled media types drooling over their William Hunt suits all night. God but she was incredible. If they only knew the half of it.

The second time Sharon and I made love that night I was totally there with her, and somehow, without realizing it, we seemed to go to a level that we had never visited before. I felt stripped and raw, my whole being gasping for her body like air. We both ended up in tears, gripping onto one another. Sharon wouldn't let go of me, and though I usually can't sleep unless I'm in my own world, I soon hit a place so sure and central that I didn't wake up until halfway through the next morning. I had absolutely no idea what time it was, whether I was at Sharon's place or mine, and for a second I thought that there would be a slow, heavy body lying beside me, a pool of warm skin to swim into. I stirred and reached out for her, but Sharon had gone to work long ago.

Chapter Three

Sitting in the traffic coming out of Hampstead, I couldn't help but think about the Bradleys and their daughters. It struck me that their relationship was almost exactly opposite to that of my own parents. Mrs Bradley was so strong, so direct, so different to my mother, whose spark and energy, if she ever had any, had been ground out of her like flour from a husk, leaving only a distant, wistful regret. My dad was the strong one. He had the Protestant Canadian drive, which was usually directed against my mother, but often enough against Luke and me. Mostly Luke. I wondered whom it was that Lucy had resented most, who had made her run away. It was probably the mother who never valued her like she did her twin, but it might not have been. When I was a kid I never blamed my father for what he did. I just wanted him to approve of me. Instead I blamed my mother. It was her fault, all of it. He didn't want to act like that, but there was something in her that brought it out, that awoke it in him like the bees round the lion on the syrup tin. When I grew up a bit I realized that this was crap, but it didn't change the fact that it was still all down to her. All of it. For the simple reason that she was still there. She didn't leave him. She stayed, and she took it, which meant we stayed too. She let him do what he did to her and, worse, she let him do it to us.

Andy Gold was already in Café Kick when I got there. He was nursing a bottle of French beer and watching two guys playing table football. I'd called him after leaving James Bradley, and asked him if he would meet me the next day at my office. He told me that Bradley had informed him of his intentions and he'd been waiting for my call, but as a meeting place he suggested Exmouth Market's temple to the beautiful game, miniature version, instead of my office. It was nothing to me, but he sounded oddly reluctant to come over to Highbury, even though he was always looking for an excuse to check up on me. I couldn't understand the man.

Andy downed his beer on seeing me and ordered two more, surprising me by also paying for them. After telling me that I looked like I worked in a frigging clothes shop he stood for a while, watching two guys playing, before turning to me.

'You come here a lot?' he asked.

'Sometimes.'

'Right,' he said. He moved over to the middle table, dropping a fifty-pence piece in the slot before I could stop him.

'I've got a rather nasty cut on my hand,' I told him.

'Bollocks. Put your beer down.'

'OK, but Andy?'

'Come on. Get on with it. What?'

'No spinning,' I said.

Andy did spin, and he also swore when I scored four goals in a row, before shouting very loudly when he managed to get one past me. The two guys on the other table looked sideways at him. I had the front view. There's a cliché that some coppers just look like coppers, and in Andy's case, in that hip bar, loosely populated with laid back out-of-work actor types and well-dressed city women on their lunch break, Andy's occupation didn't seem to me to be too hard to guess. All that I did wonder was if he did it on purpose, the way Ken Clay did, a sort of fuck-you bravado meant to make people feel uncomfortable about their secrets. Whatever, I was glad. As long as there were coppers out there who looked like coppers out there, there would always be room for me, someone to slide between their machinery unnoticed, their obvious assault on a world of people a lot more subtle than they are.

After realizing that Andy wasn't going to stand down from the table until his masculinity was no longer in doubt, I let him win the third game. After that we took one of the Formica tables by the bar, both ordering sandwiches and a couple more beers. When we'd finished eating Andy asked me how I'd been. I mumbled something, and then he thanked me for the photographs.

'And?' I said.

'And anything we learned from them is strictly police business. All announcements will be made through the press at the appropriate time.'

I sighed. 'Don't be any more of an arsehole than God made you, Andy,' I said. 'You know you'll get the usual.'

'Just want to make sure you're not taking me for granted, Billy love. Just making sure.'

We sat for a second. I knew what I wanted to ask

Andy but I couldn't quite get round to it. Instead, I asked him about the boy, and he said that in spite of the picture they still hadn't found him. They didn't even have a name.

'It shouldn't be long though, not with this new missing persons database. That's if he's on it. We've also got prints from the house, and the car.'

'I take it it wasn't registered?'

'You take it correctly.'

'What about the man?' I asked. 'In the alley.'

Andy reached in his pocket then flipped through his notebook.

'A Mr George Curtis,' he said, after finding the right page. 'Owner of the kebab place you saw him down the side of. He seemed very surprised when I showed him a picture of his very self getting rough with our mystery boy.'

'And?'

'And he didn't deny it. Said he remembered it very well. Claims he'd never seen the boy before and hasn't seen him since. Says he walked into the kitchen and found him in there trying to rob his freezers. Said he'd nearly called the police, but as the kid hadn't taken anything he let it go.'

'Believe him?'

'No way of knowing for sure till we find the boy, but it sounds plausible to me. The back door was open when we showed up and I can imagine it looking tempting to a fly young kid on the make. As far as it goes I'm sure he's on the level, but we'll probably visit him again to make sure. I made some noises about possible assault charges just to scare him, but he didn't seem fazed by it. He went on about his right to protect

his property etcetera etcetera. Can't say I disagreed
with him as a matter of fact.'

'He was doing a lot more than protecting his property when I saw him.'

'Whatever. You can understand, when you're trying
to run a business. There really isn't anything to do
about him until the boy shows up. I really wouldn't
worry about him if I were you.'

Andy ordered another beer but I wasn't finished
with my second. I asked him if he'd spoken to the
Bradley family himself and he said he had. He hadn't
got much out of them, other than the fact that Lucy had
always been the tearaway, had always been drawn to
low-lifes and scumbags. He said that Emma had given
him a list of names from Arundel where the family
came from, some guys Lucy had been seeing over the
last few years. He'd sent some men down there to talk
to them but none of them were in London when Lucy
was killed. So that, in Andy's opinion, just left them
with the boy. Andy was sure that the semen sample
would turn out to have come from him.

'Now that we know it didn't come from you,' he
smiled.

I didn't respond to that, and a silence settled
between us for a second as our minds both moved on
to the next obvious subject. Andy looked serious all of
a sudden as though, actually, he might be a human
being after all. He had a briefcase with him, which he'd
left on a chair near the football tables, and without my
having to say anything he went and fetched it before
setting it down on the table. He produced a folder.
Making sure that no one was paying any attention to us
he laid the contents of the folder out on the table. I

picked them up and went through them quickly, setting them down where they had been, making sure that none of the photographs I had been looking at were face up. As it was, in that part of town, we could have been an art director and a photographer going through prints. You wouldn't, however, see pictures like that in *Arena*.

It had been over a week since I'd found Lucy Bradley's body, and looking at the pictures in front of me didn't make me feel sick, not the way I'd felt when I finally realized she wasn't moving, or even when I'd seen the ambulance taking her away. They just spread a wave of pure greyness through me.

'So,' I said, resting my hand on top of the prints. 'What actually killed her?'

'Difficult. She received at least one blow to the back of the head. It could have been that, or that could have just knocked her out. It was a severe blow though and it might have done it. Time of death three to six hours before discovery. Difficult to tell with this heat apparently.'

'Where?'

'In the bedroom, top of the stairs. We think she was sitting down, by the angle of the wound. Her skull was fractured, probably by a hammer, definitely coming down. We found blood on the back of a chair and more on the carpet.'

'Right,' I said, jotting notes down in my book. 'Then what?'

'She was suffocated. Burg thinks a bag, after she was unconscious. Burg also found bruising on the neck, so some kind of ligature was used, probably a belt. We didn't find one, or a bag with any blood inside, but that doesn't mean anything. Neither would be difficult to remove. The boy, was he carrying anything?'

'I don't know,' I said. 'Maybe. He could easily enough have had the belt round his waist and the bag in his pocket, though.'

'He could,' Andy said.

'So, she was hit over the head and then suffocated?'

'Suffocated or strangled. Difficult to know which or whether she was dead anyway from the hammer. We don't think it matters that much as long as we have the sequence of events.'

I could see his point. 'No.'

'The doctors care though. Anyway, we're pretty sure that whatever the actual cause, she died upstairs. Then she was dragged down and dumped under the garbage, and then the belt was untied and the bag removed from her face.'

'How do you know it was removed then, not in the bedroom?'

'There was no blood on the stairs,' Andy said. 'Or anywhere else, which meant that the bag was still on. It must have been.'

'Right,' I said. 'And then she was dragged outside, and left, not quite completely covered by bin bags.'

'That's right.'

I thought for a second. I wondered if leaving her foot exposed was intentional or a mistake. I figured a mistake.

'She could have been there for days,' I said. 'She could have lain there for days before—'

'Weeks,' Andy said. 'The boy wouldn't have reported her missing, not if he killed her. And there was no sign of anyone else living there. As for the smell, she

149

wouldn't have made a lot of difference, I don't think. It was pretty rank out there anyway.'

I thought about the newspaper reports, the scant space they'd given Lucy. Her murder didn't make a lot of difference there either. It was on the same page as a story about a minor soap star cheating on her husband. I had another thought.

'Why would she have been sitting on a chair naked?'

'Why not?'

'I don't know,' I admitted. 'It's just not what you do really. She was definitely naked when she was killed?'

'Yes.'

'How can you be sure?'

'There weren't any bloodstained clothes, simple. So she must have been. Unless he took those too. But why should he?'

'No reason', I said, 'that I can think of.' I tried to see the bedroom, to see Lucy there. If she was naked with her back to someone then surely she must have known them. It very probably was the man whose semen was on her, but was it the boy I'd seen?

'So, run me through it.'

'Through what?'

'Through what you think happened. With the boy.'

Andy laughed. 'Isn't it obvious?'

'Patronize me,' I said.

Andy opened his hands and spoke slowly. 'OK,' he said. 'They're in the club. She wants to leave. He agrees and goes with her.' I saw Donna. I didn't say anything. 'Then they come home with you following but, unfortunately for Lucy, you get mugged.'

'Then what?'

'They arrive home, oblivious to your interest in them. After a while they go upstairs. They start getting it on.'

'Was she consenting?'

'Nothing to suggest she wasn't, no bruising or anything. Anyway, they get down to it but he shoots his bolt too soon and feels like an idiot. Probably his first time or he's really stuck on the girl. Anyway, Lucy gets out of bed.'

'Why?'

'To take a piss, how the hell do I know? Wash the come off her. Doesn't want to be in bed with someone who can't control himself . . .'

'OK. And she sits on a chair?'

'Yes.'

'A mirror?' I asked. 'Was there a mirror?'

'No, not there. There was one but it was over the other side of the room. I see what you're getting at but it wouldn't have made any difference. It doesn't change anything.'

'Probably not. So, she's sitting there. Why does he kill her?'

'Come on!' Andy leant back in his chair. 'She starts laughing at him, taking the piss, making him feel bad. Maybe they've tried it before and he was useless that time too. We're pretty sure they were both living there, although there was nothing to ID the boy. Anyway, her laughter is getting to him so he tells her to shut up. She won't. He shouts at her. She just laughs. Maybe it's happened to him before, with other girls. Maybe the kids at school used to laugh at him for having a little todger, how the hell do I know? But he just cracks and then our Maxwell picks up his hammer.'

151

'A hammer. In the bedroom?'

'We're not sure it was a hammer. But even if it was, why not? People keep things in the strangest places.'

'So then he hits her, with whatever, and after that he sticks a bag over her head. Why?'

'He's scared. He knows he has to make sure. Or else he's suddenly enjoying himself, he hasn't got his humiliation out of his system yet.'

'And . . .'

'And then he thinks, oh shit, and he drags her downstairs and sticks her under the garbage. Finish.'

'And I see him running down the street.'

'Bingo,' Andy said. 'And he makes a call about seeing you there to dump you in the shit. Which you were in anyway, at least until the DNA test. After that he disappears. That's it.'

I sat back in my chair and I nodded reluctantly. It wasn't bad. I'd have probably been satisfied with it myself if I hadn't seen the kid's face. I leant forward.

'The neighbours,' I said. 'Did they see anyone else? Going into the house that day? Another guy perhaps, someone else.'

'No, they didn't. The neighbours didn't see her with another bloke. No.' Andy stopped and looked at me. 'One of them thinks she *may* have seen her earlier in the day, but not with a bloke, with a girl. It's only a maybe, but there were other recent prints in the car. It might not mean anything and it's not something we want to rely on. No, the thing to do is collar the boy, and that, believe me, is not going to take too much longer. Especially as we've now got the added help of your very talented self, William.'

Andy went off to use the toilet, and I had another

look at the pictures, for no reason that I could think of.
I then put the pictures back into the folder but somehow the rest of the file, about fifteen pages of photo-
copied typewritten notes, ended up propped against the
wall behind the cigarette machine. Odd that. I thought
about what Andy had said about another girl, and I
figured that if she was with another girl that day it was
probably Donna. From the way they'd linked arms
they'd obviously known each other. I was beginning to
have doubts about keeping Donna out of it. I'd go back
to the office and give it some thought. I didn't want to
give her up to her family, and I knew from experience
that having something Ken Clay didn't was a good way
to play him, but I was beginning to think that she might
be involved in something that could turn out to be
worse than the thing she'd run away from. Maybe, if it
was the same thing as Lucy had been into, it could turn
out to be much, much worse.

When Andy came back he told me what else he'd
been doing. He'd been to the club, of course, and
spoken to a lot of people who worked there, but no one
remembered much. A barmaid remembered Lucy, and
so did one of the promotions assistants who'd given her
a load of fliers to hand out. She only met her a couple
of times. Neither of them could say whom she'd been
with that night. The promotions assistant also claimed
never to have seen the boy, and had definitely not
employed him in any way. Lucy must have shared her
fliers with him, she said.

None of the guys on the door remembered either
the boy or Lucy, citing the weight of people coming in
and out, and though the incident room was still getting
calls from some of the clubbers themselves, they were

still sifting through these, seeing which sightings or possible sightings turned out to have any value. Andy also said that none of the cab drivers could recall her walking past them on her way out. Neither did the club have CCTV.

'And what about me?' I asked.

'You?'

'Did anyone remember me leaving?'

'No one.'

'What about the cab man, the controller on the gate?'

'Nope.'

'And no one remembers a tall Rasta with gold teeth in an old Renault 18? Another car following?'

''Fraid not. Not that they'd tell us. You think they've got some kind of mugging racket going on, organized through the cab drivers?'

'Maybe,' I said, although I knew that whoever set me up did so for more personal reasons. 'Had any other complaints?'

'I'll check it out,' Andy said.

We chatted a little more. Andy didn't seem especially psyched to the case; there was no sense of urgency about him. It was maybe the weather, or else he thought it was a simple matter of finding the kid and locking him up. I asked him what sort of state the family had been in.

'The usual,' he said. 'Sister sitting on the sofa with her shoulders hunched over, lip going, one-word answers. Father aged about ten years. That woman though, Jesus.'

I thought for a second.

'Don't worry,' Andy said. 'She's accounted for. The

whole family were in before eleven and didn't leave. We told them it was just routine, but I was interested in her for a while. She didn't seem so much upset by the whole thing as furious.'

'But she was in?'

'It's a controlled building,' Andy said. 'The security on the desk would have clocked her if she'd left.'

'Right,' I said.

And that was about it. Andy asked me if I wanted another game of table football but I told him no. He opened his case and I dropped his file into it for him, before he could pick it up and notice how light it was. We both stood up and walked to the door together, emerging into eye-watering sunlight. Andy's car was parked, very illegally, right outside. He strolled towards it but stopped and turned back.

'Oh,' he said, 'congratulations by the way.'

'Sorry?'

'On your new job.'

'What?'

'With *Esquire* magazine.' Andy held a finger up. 'Or was it *GQ*? That's a very nice gig you've got there, taking pictures. I didn't know you were so talented. Get you into many clubs does it?'

'A few,' I admitted.

'Not York's any more though, I'm afraid.' Andy shook his head. '*Unfortunately*, one of our boys blew your cover.'

'Never mind,' I said, 'not my kind of place anyway. The music's too loud and it's not music. Tell him not to lose any sleep over it.'

'I won't,' Andy said, giving me a big smile.

Andy pulled the parking ticket he'd acquired from

behind his windscreen wiper and tossed it onto a pile of rubbish. He got in his Cavalier and wound the window down.

'One more thing, Billy.'

'Yes?'

'Ken Clay asked me to remind you that impersonating a police officer, even over the telephone, is a very serious criminal offence, and one he doesn't take particularly kindly to. Especially when the officer impersonated is himself.'

'I don't know what he means,' I said, folding my arms and leaning against a lamp-post. 'But why don't you tell him to mention that to those two clowns who interviewed me last week. They weren't impersonating police officers over the phone, they were doing it in a bloody cop shop.'

Andy laughed and drove off, his left front tyre popping open a bin bag that had rolled down from the pile. I walked back into the bar and retrieved the photocopies from behind the back of the fag machine. Impersonating a police officer, what about simple theft of classified documents? I sat back down and read through them quickly and made more notes in my book. When I'd finished I turned a new page and wrote several names down, names of people I wanted to talk to. I put Donna-Natalie's name down of course, and the word 'boy', and then I had an odd, nebulous sensation, the cross between a concrete thought and a vague feeling. I wrote another two words, in capitals, underlined them, and followed them with a question mark.

GEORGE CURTIS?

I slid the photocopies into my jacket and walked outside.

Chapter Four

Back at my office I thought about changing into my shorts but decided against; I was hoping to talk to Mrs Bradley later and a suit might make her take me more seriously. I called the number she'd given me and arranged to go round later that afternoon.

I took Kojak through to the café where Ally filled him up. Mike was there too this time and seemed to be in a good mood. Chelsea and Forest were once again in the same league, and even though any game between them was months away, Mike started baiting me about the likely result. It wasn't like I was exactly passionate about it but I mixed it up with him anyway. Mike put an arm round Ally's shoulder and said, 'Being at The Bridge, it's just like watching Inter, isn't it, darling?' Ally, a Milanese, forced a weak smile and turned to froth some milk. She still seemed a little distant.

'The only difference at Stamford Bridge is you've got more Italians,' I said.

I walked back to my office. I had to decide about Natalie. I didn't have a clue why Lucy had been killed but if it wasn't a *crime passionel*, if it was something Lucy had got herself into, then it didn't matter if I betrayed Natalie's confidence. All that mattered was she didn't get involved. I called Andy Gold. After he told me what a bloody liberty I had just taken I told him I might have something.

'Listen,' I said. 'I've been thinking. I'm pretty sure I saw someone at York's who might have known Lucy.'

'Who? Who did you see?'

'A girl. Donna Appleby's her name, though she's now calling herself Natalie. A young kid I was looking for. I saw her there, and I saw her talking to Lucy in the street, a few days earlier. In Camden. Then, when I was at York's, I'm pretty sure I saw her talking to the boy we're after too.'

'What? Why the bloody hell didn't you—?'

'I only just clicked it,' I lied. 'I've been trying to ignore the whole thing, at least until today. Anyway, I've got a couple of shots of her and I'll drop them round.'

'You do that, Billy, and don't take too long about it. She was in Camden you say?'

'That's right. And Andy?'

'What?'

'If you could keep her parents from knowing where she is I'd be grateful.'

He thought for a second.

'Dodgy Daddy?' he asked.

'Something like that. And she's a really sweet kid. Well?'

'They won't find her through me,' he said.

I'd left the Mazda in the shade of a huge truck belonging to a ballet company so it was only like stepping into a Belling on gas mark 3, not as bad as it had been recently. It took me half an hour to drive up to Chalk

Farm, during which time I was tuned into long wave, listening to English wickets falling faster than Italian governments. I decided to hell with it, I was half Canadian anyway if I cared to think about it, though unfortunately it wasn't quite the weather for ice hockey. By the time the last man had gone the score was only just higher than the temperature.

Mrs Bradley had informed the management of the building the family's pied-à-terre was in that I was arriving, so I was allowed into the private car park and told that I could leave my car in any of the unnumbered spaces. I did this, and was very proud of the fact that my car was the elder statesman of the lot, a veritable antique compared to the soft-shouldered saloons and sporty little numbers all around it. I straightened the tie I'd put on and walked through the car park to the back door of the building, but found it locked, with no entry bell. I strolled round to the front where I was buzzed in by Mrs Bradley.

Although the outside of the building was Victorian, the foyer of the complex was more like the lobby of a modern, five-star hotel. A marble floor led past a small fountain to a desk, behind which sat a well-dressed young woman and a security guard. I wasn't sure if I was supposed to register with the desk but I couldn't be bothered and ambled past nonchalantly, heading for a row of four lifts to the right-hand side. No one said anything to me. It was only then that I realized I had no idea where the apartment belonging to the Bradleys was located. I retraced my steps and approached the desk.

The girl was talking on the telephone and didn't notice me. The security guard was gone. Eventually I was told that the Bradleys lived on the fifth floor of the south side of the building, flat 516. Left out of the lift. I took the lift, which spoke to me quite sternly, and did what the girl told me, getting out on five. I was in a sombrely lit corridor also reminiscent of a hotel, with a thick brown carpet and apartment doors on the wall in front of me. I padded my way along until I reached 516 and then pressed the door bell. I could feel a presence at the door and a movement behind the peephole. The door opened.

'Please,' Mrs Bradley said, 'this way.'

I followed Mrs Bradley into a very spacious living room with a homely feel. It had block wooden flooring mostly covered by an old Persian, two black leather sofas and a smoked glass coffee table cluttered with copies of *National Geographic* and *The Economist*. A breakfast bar acted as a partition to a small, brown tiled kitchen. The whole place looked like it had been decorated in one go, very fashionably, but that this had occurred quite a few years ago. The human-shaped indentations in both of the sofas increased the effect. The only recent additions seemed to be an office table in one corner, replete with the usual fax machines and VDU.

The room led out through large French windows to a veranda-cum-roof garden made up of pale stone slabs, on which sat a profusion of tubs and plant pots overflowing with brightly coloured flowers, the only ones of which I could identify with any certainty being geraniums. A wooden rose trellis bordered two sides. Mrs Bradley turned in the frame of the window and folded her arms over her breasts. She was wearing burgundy trousers and a blue sweater with a gold chain over the top. Her hair was tied back in a ponytail. She seemed nervous, chewing her full bottom lip, trying to be brusque and natural but looking everywhere except at me. In contrast to her husband, she didn't seem to have aged any since we met, and the slight vulnerability that I thought I detected even made her seem younger. She gave a short cough before asking me if I would like any tea or coffee. I told her that a glass of something cold would be welcome, and watched as she walked into the kitchen and opened the fridge. She had a strong, deliberate walk, moving her arms though she only took a couple of steps.

'Grapefruit juice OK?' she asked.

'That'll be fine,' I assured her.

I took the glass of juice and sat on one of the sofas, looking at Mrs Bradley across the coffee table. She sat with her hands in her lap, very still. She wasn't drinking anything, which made me feel a little like I was a kid again, visiting my best friend's house. I put the glass down on a coaster. A welcome breeze meandered in from the roof garden, casting a light pall of scent across the room. I pursed my lips and said how sorry I was about Lucy. Mrs Bradley nodded at the token, taking it for what it was. A ritual. Some words to exchange, nothing more, but words that must be given and must be taken.

'You look a lot different,' she said eventually, studying me like she had done in her office.

I smiled. 'I can make an effort,' I told her, 'if I know I've got an appointment. You have to admit you caught me on the hop last time.'

Mrs Bradley smiled to herself and lit a cigarette, instantly snuffing out the aroma of the flowers. I watched her, slightly puzzled. She still made my back straighten, but this was not the difficult, impatient woman I'd met in my office. The lack of impatience I could understand – there was no hurry any more – but not the uncertainty. It made her more attractive, and I almost wondered if she had a twin, like her daughters had. I would have put it down to what had happened to Lucy, but Andy Gold had said she'd been very tough with him. Now she seemed, not timid exactly, but ever so slightly unsure of herself, like a boxer with a secret injury who's trying to pretend to be the fighter he used to be naturally. Suddenly I had an idea as to why, something I'd not thought of before but seemed quite obvious as soon as I had. I folded my arms and looked her in the eye.

'Did you get anything off the film?'

Mrs Bradley let out a breath and looked down, the shame on her face mixed with a little relief. She reddened, setting her lipstick-smudged cigarette down in an ashtray.

'No,' she said. 'There was nothing on it. You must have broken the casing.'

'That was my intention,' I said, quietly. I looked at her for a second, holding her gaze. 'As I told you when we met, I don't tell people where their children are, and I do my best to ensure that they don't find out where they are either. And if you knew what reasons some of the children I look for have for leaving home, you would understand why I do this.'

'I'm *sorry*, Mr Rucker, I really am.' Her sorry was explanatory rather than apologetic. I'd put her down but she was on her feet again. 'It was unforgivable to have had you waylaid like that. But you must understand that when you've lost a child, then you'll do anything, *anything*, to get her back. I really didn't know you'd get hurt.'

'But you didn't know I wouldn't either, did you?'

'No,' she admitted. 'I can't say that I knew that but—'

'Tell me,' I said, 'did Sirius suggest it or was it your idea?'

'It was them,' she said quickly. 'Though I did agree. I got a call from the man they were using, telling me where you were, and that Lucy might be in the club. For an additional fee I could probably have your camera stolen. I'm afraid I didn't stop to think how it would be done.'

'No,' I said. 'And if you had?'

'I would have told him no,' she insisted. 'I promise you.'

Her cold slate eyes and pursed lips told me she had no doubts about her own justification. I took another sip of juice and sighed. It was too late to care about the morality of what she'd done but I was annoyed that it was Mrs Bradley who'd had me followed. If it had been Lucy I could have found the guys; there would have been a connection to her. Maybe they would have known something. Instead, all it was, was some useless bastard at Sirius trying to cut corners when all he'd had to do was stay there himself until the girls had come out of the club. He couldn't be bothered to stay up all night, or else the bouncers had told him to get lost, so he paid the three guys to get my camera. They'd given me a beating because, by exposing the film, I'd probably lost them a bonus. They hadn't, however, had to get my camera at all – he should have just told them to follow me. Sirius. Ha. No one could claim that their man was the brightest star in the universe.

I told Mrs Bradley that I didn't hold any grudges against her. I may have received a kicking but she had lost a daughter after all. I took out my notebook and looked down a list of questions I'd written out. The first was whether Lucy had ever spoken of anyone in London whom she'd had any contact with here.

'No. Lucy didn't meet anyone when we were here, outside of the family. Or not that I know of. She may have known people in London of course, people she'd met elsewhere. Lucy was always going to music festivals, things like that. We used to get a lot of people staying. I wouldn't have them in the house but James used to let them camp in the back field . . .'

'I see,' I said. 'So she may have known the boy who I saw, before she came to London?'

'Possibly. We wouldn't have known about him though. Lucy wasn't exactly communicative.'

'So I understand. But would you happen to know if she kept a diary at all?'

'The police asked me that. I don't know. Emma had a look for one but she said she couldn't find anything.'

'Emma?'

'Yes, she's been at home, although she's back now. I wanted her to stay down there but she wouldn't. She wants to be here. I'm sure it's not doing her any good. This whole thing has been awful for her. I only hope she gets over it.'

'I'm sure she will in time,' I said, taking out a pen. 'I'll need to have the number in Sussex if you don't mind? Are you planning on going down there at all?'

'No,' Mrs Bradley said. 'At least not yet, although

I'm going to have to at some point. I've got a ton of things to do, I really have. A business can't run itself, and no matter how good your staff are, they're either just not committed enough, or else—'

Mrs Bradley stopped suddenly and looked at me. My face must have given away what I was thinking because her mouth set firmly and she sat up in her chair.

'You think I'm very callous I expect.'

'Not at all,' I said quickly. 'Life goes on, there's nothing you can do here really, just so long as you can be reached. And work is probably the best thing to do to deal with a thing—'

'You think I'm very callous.' She nodded to herself and then lowered her head slightly. 'And no doubt I am, concerning myself with work at a time like this. But it's all I can do, you see? I don't know how to be otherwise.' Her eyes flickered. 'Not like James. Or Emma. He's just gone to pieces and she's disappeared inside her own head, hardly letting anyone within ten feet of her. I'm not saying it's easier for them, but at least they both seem to know. To know what to feel. I . . . I'm like an actor without a part. I haven't got a clue how to be.'

'Losing someone is hard. I don't think there are any rules, any fixed answers on what to feel afterwards.'

'Don't you?' Mrs Bradley's eyes flashed and she suddenly raised her voice. 'For a *mother* who's lost a *child*? I would have thought there were, wouldn't you?! A long list of answers. Grief perhaps? Or sorrow? Anger at the killer? Loss? Emptiness? Misery? Hopelessness? And what about despair? Shock? Or guilt? They're all fixed ways of being, wouldn't you say? They're what most mothers would feel I should imagine. And any of them would do,' she added.

I waited for Mrs Bradley to go on, but even though I could tell she hadn't finished thinking about it she didn't add anything. She just stared at the coffee table, at a huge lump of jet that was acting as a paperweight. I took the chance to study her, and thought once again about the contrast between this haughty, attractive woman and her husband. They both seemed over-whelmed by what had happened but he had somehow seemed to accept it, he had let it enter and become him, so that his whole essence seemed to be grief at the loss of his daughter. But his wife was resisting, holding herself up against it and refusing to let it appear in her behaviour. She squeezed herself tight, only letting out hints. She was like an empty house with many rooms and I was following the footsteps. As soon as I pushed open one of the doors, only her perfume remained.

Mrs Bradley sat in silence for a while, her look far heavier than the lump of jet it fell upon. I stared at her and wondered how she really felt about the loss of her daughter, the tearaway disappointment who would never cause her trouble ever, ever again.

The breeze had given up, and my host's cigarette smoke clung to itself in the air, twisted rings and knots that stubbornly refused to disperse. I looked at my list again. I asked for any other pictures of Lucy that I could use, and my host fetched me some from a drawer in the kitchen. I told her that I'd take care of them but she didn't seem too bothered. Then I told Mrs Bradley that the main reason for my visit was that I wanted to ask her if it was all right if I visited her home.

'I want to look through Lucy's things,' I explained.

'If she did keep a diary she may have hidden it. Teen-agers do that. I want to see if there's anything that might give me a clue to people Lucy might have known. You told me that Lucy went to festivals. She may have met the boy there, the one we're after. He might be in a photograph somewhere. The police have probably gone through them all but I've actually seen the boy, I'd be more likely to pick him out.'

Mrs Bradley was instantly defensive but when I told her why I wanted to go she agreed. Reacting against things in the first instance was evidently just her way. She told me that the woman who ran the post office was holding a spare key at the moment, and that she would phone ahead and tell her it was all right to give it to me.

I finished up my juice but declined another glass. I asked about Emma, and Mrs Bradley told me that she thought she was in shock. She'd barely said ten words since her sister had been killed. I could picture her, running the events over in her mind, blaming herself. I asked Mrs Bradley where she was.

'I sent her out to get some sun,' she replied, her voice softening. 'There's a small park we go to some-times. I sent her out there with a book.'

'I'll pop over and see her if you think it'll be OK?'

'Yes, yes I'm sure that will be all right. Just so long as you don't make her talk about anything that she doesn't want to.'

I stood up and put my notes away. A bee flew in through the open window but quickly decided that the atmosphere didn't suit him.

'That's a lovely roof garden you have,' I said, my eyes following the bee back to the flowers.

'Oh, that's all James's work,' Mrs Bradley replied, sounding glad to be talking about something mundane, but at the same time slightly irritated. She stepped round the sofa and walked out of the French windows. I followed her into the heat and the aroma. 'He's the one with the green fingers. I don't have the time, or the inclination really. I've never seen the point of gardening. It's the sort of thing if you have enough money you get someone else to do. I work hard enough as it is.'

Mrs Bradley stood in the centre of the patio and turned round, suddenly seeming to wonder why she'd led me out there. She picked up a plant sprayer and awkwardly started sending plumes of water out. I was pretty sure that it was the wrong time of day, that she was liable to burn the leaves, but I didn't say anything. She had her back to me, and she'd only got to half of the plants when she stopped, as if she'd thought of something. She stood quite still, for a little too long. I was about to ask her what she was thinking, when the hand holding the sprayer dropped to her side. Then, very deliberately, Mrs Bradley sat down on a flat wooden bench, built into the side wall. Having moved her position I could see a patch of cement in front of her that had been left deliberately bare. Three words had been etched into it before the cement had dried. They were 'Lucy, Emma, James' followed by the date: 2/6/1991.

Mrs Bradley was looking at the names. The truth of the situation she was in suddenly seemed to find her. I thought she was going to say something, about the names she was looking at, but she didn't. But neither did she look away. Instead she squinted, her eyes seeming to hurt her, like someone deliberately staring into a fire. Her grey eyes clouded and I thought that she might give way to tears, but instead she gave a short, harsh laugh. An ugly smile took possession of her mouth but she didn't move. I didn't know whether to say something or just to leave her there with her thoughts. I was stepping back into the flat when she stopped me.

'She nearly killed me.'

It was the softest I'd ever heard her speak, barely more than a whisper. It didn't sound like her voice, it didn't seem to come from her.

'I . . .?'

'She nearly killed me.'

Mrs Bradley looked straight ahead, her motionless head framed by rose petals shifting almost impercept- ibly in the light air. She wasn't looking at me but she must have sensed my reaction. She gave another, sour laugh.

'Lucy?' I asked.

'Don't worry,' she said, 'Mr Detective. It was before she was born. They didn't have scans in those days, not in Saudi at any rate. Somehow the doctor missed her. He didn't even know she was there, the useless, patron- izing old fool. And I didn't have a clue, I mean, why should I have? What did I know? Emma came out fine and I thought that was it, but then . . . there was this pain.' She stopped for a second and shook her head in wonder. Her face paled at the thought of it. 'Another child. The nurse said it like it was the most amazing thing in the world, but all I knew was *agony*. I've heard women say that they forget the pain of childbirth, but I'll never forget *that*. And it wasn't like it was before, it was pain that felt . . . wrong. Then she started to come.

I was so relieved, and for a second I thought everything would be all right. But she stopped. She just, stopped. And then she was in the wrong place for a Caesarean. She was all twisted up. They had to hurt me to get to her. Cut at me. And the pain then . . . They had to do it quickly because the cord was strangling her. All they cared about was her, it was as if I wasn't even there. I was nothing. They used things . . . you wouldn't believe what I watched them use to get her out of me, before they put me under.'

Mrs Bradley stopped, and I could tell that she was back there, giving birth to her dead daughter.

'I used to think of the pain later,' she went on. 'When I was looking after her. What I went through so she would be there. Even as a baby she was impossible. Never being able to sleep, crying, screaming all day and all night, until I just wanted to *scream* back at her. I put Emma in a separate room, because Lucy was always waking her, but it didn't make any difference, Lucy somehow managed to make herself heard wherever she was. I used to think I'd given birth to a devil. As a man you'll never be able to understand what feelings a mother can have towards a baby like that. The dark feelings, the feelings that make you cringe with guilt, when you leave her crying in her room because you're afraid to go in to her. You're afraid that her yelling will send you mad, you're afraid that you'll do anything, *anything* to make her quiet.'

Mrs Bradley's eyes were wide open, her breath short and shallow. I left a second, then spoke quietly. 'And is that why you didn't have any more children?'

The eyes I was looking at turned heavy as cobblestones. 'No. That wasn't the reason.' Again, that ugly smile. 'It wasn't a choice. After Lucy was born I nearly died. And I couldn't have any more after that. I wanted to, it was what I'd always wanted. It was what women did, I wanted to be a wife and a mother. I wanted lots of them, lots of lovely, pink babies. But my insides were torn. Torn up. I still get problems. I went to some different doctors, some proper English ones when we came back, but they all agreed it was useless. They all said the same thing. When Lucy came, all sorts of things got ripped, ripped and broken.'

Her face was blank now, pale as mildew. She looked down from the patch of cement she was staring at to her hands, folded on her lap, and I had the curious impulse to take one of them, just as I had with her daughter Emma. But then she raised her head and once again she was the woman who had come to my office. Her back straightened and her jaw trembled, quenching the sheen that had found its way into her stone grey eyes. She looked at me almost as if she was challenging me to something.

'And now she's done it again,' she said.

Chapter Five

I got the *A to Z* out of my glove compartment and looked
for the nearest park. It was a couple of minutes walk
away. Not a park really, more like a green or a garden. I
tossed the book onto the seat and locked the car.

I hadn't asked Mrs Bradley where the park was. I'd
thanked her for her time and then asked if I could use
her toilet. I didn't really want to but I did want to see
more of the flat. There were two bedrooms that I could
see. The door to one was open and through it I could
see two single beds, one of them strewn with the
clothes of a teenage girl. The other bed was turned
back. The room was dark but I could make out a
hairbrush lying on the floor. There were some posters
on the wall and a stack of CDs piled on top of a mid-
range hi-fi, a lot of them out of their cases. The second
door was closed but I pretended to have got Mrs Bradley's directions wrong and I pushed it open. The room
was bigger than the first and contained a double bed
and two wardrobes, as well as a built-in sink unit. I
closed the door as quickly and nonchalantly as I could
before turning to the door that Mrs Bradley had told me
was the bathroom. She was standing at the top of the
narrow corridor with her arms folded. I don't think I
fooled her.

I found the small park and I found Emma. The park was littered with bodies, buzzing with toddlers and the odd frisbee. Emma was wearing cut-off jeans and a pale green vest top. She was lying on her side on a rug, a fat Dostoevsky novel unopened beside her. I sat on the nearest bench, next to an old drunk the colour of ketchup, watching her. Emma was asleep. Her face was resting on her left arm, her mouth slightly open, a line of saliva making its way down her cheek towards the rough tartan cloth she was lying on. Her face was all squashed up and this made her look even younger than she was. I sat there for ten minutes and she didn't move once. Emma was so completely asleep that she looked shocked, almost like she'd been frozen in suspended animation. It was the kind of sleep you wake from not knowing where you are, the kind of sleep that the body occasionally demands, which it will not be denied no matter what. Emma looked about as far away from her conscious life as she could possibly be.

And so I left her there. Her body and her mind both obviously needed to go to another place, somewhere far away from the events of the last few weeks. I wasn't going to wake her up, jolt her back to reality, and I wasn't going to wait for her either. For one thing she wouldn't be in any sort of state to talk to me properly, and I didn't think it fair that as soon as she came round by herself she would instantly be reminded of what she had been so thankfully removed from. I was a little concerned for her legs though, but when I looked closer I noticed a bottle of Ambre Solaire lying next to the paperback. I glanced at the drunk and stood up. He was staring at the girl too, and I could tell that he had his own thoughts about Emma's legs. I hesitated for a second, but reasoned that there were plenty of people around. Also, I wasn't absolutely sure the old man could stand. I walked out of the gardens and back to my car.

Sitting in the Mazda I almost enjoyed the weight of traffic I had to negotiate. I didn't bother lane-hopping or diving through amber lights. I sat listening to miserable old Mr Cohen whose dolorous tunes perfectly underlined the sombre mood, which was not so much my mood but which seemed to hang in the car nonetheless. I thought about my employers, and wondered whether it would have made any difference if I had found Lucy, and passed on her sister's message to her. Would she have gone home? I didn't know. Such a fuck up, such a glorious fuck up, the seeds of which were planted so long ago. And how arbitrary it seemed, how terrible, that instead of the simple estrangement and resentment that may very well have followed the feelings I had heard about from all the members of the Bradley family bar one, there was this death, this death so awful it seemed almost surreal. This death that came out of nowhere and broke open a family like a spade rammed straight into a wasps' nest.

I was heading for the other side of Camden, and though I didn't have to I drove straight through the middle, past the place where I'd first seen Lucy. As I stopped at the lights I saw her again, and remembered the feeling I'd had as she bent over to Donna. How, in an instant, I'd seen myself screwing her. And how stupid I'd felt when the car behind had sounded its horn. Caught out and foolish. Maybe that's why I'd taken against Lucy initially, because she'd made me feel stupid and I'd never even met her. Maybe I liked her sister more because she was just a girl, she had confided in me, made me feel wise and solid, someone in control of himself, someone with the answers, someone to lean on. Not a guy in his thirties getting the horn for young girls. The reasons why we like people or we don't are so bound up with the way they make us feel about ourselves.

My reveries were broken by the sight of the top of the street I was headed for. I looked at the corner where the boy had slammed into me. It seemed strange to be back there. I turned into the sun-baked road and drove along slowly, passing the house in which I had found Lucy. There were plenty of spaces but I parked right at the bottom and walked back up. I stopped outside the door. The door was bolted tight with industrial padlocks, and there was also a cross of fluorescent tape announcing the fact that the police would be very grateful if persons did not try to enter the premises or touch the locks in any way. I heeded the request, going only so far as to lean against the wall of the house while I took some sheets of paper out of my jacket pocket, the ones I had removed from Andy Gold's file. The sheets were stapled in the top left-hand corner and I flipped them over until I'd got to the page I needed.

The house I was standing outside of was registered in the name of a Mrs J. Anthony, a woman who had died five years earlier. At the time of her death Mrs Anthony was not officially divorced and the house had reverted to her estranged husband, a Mr Henry Anthony who, if he was still alive, was now resident in Auckland, New Zealand. Mr Anthony had apparently been informed of his good fortune at the time of his wife's death but had made no effort to claim the house, and it had remained empty for a year or so before, as

a couple of residents who had been there a while
reported to the police, some young people moved in.
They were soon replaced by other young people, leading to a succession of different 'tenants' during the
intervening period, all of them young.

The curtains in the front window were open a touch
and I peered through the gap into the living room. It
was dark, so I couldn't see very much, not that there
was very much to see. I thought about what the report
said; a succession of young people. I was surprised. A
good squat like this was a gold mine, I couldn't imagine
why people would leave it. Also, it had a phone, as well
as gas, water and electricity, so someone had been
together enough to pay the bills on time. This didn't
seem too plausible if the kids living there only stayed
for short periods.

I walked back down the street to number fourteen,
and knocked on the door. No one answered. I looked
down the list again. There were five other houses in
which residents had lived for more than five years and
I crossed the road to number twenty-three. My hand
went up to the brass knocker but the door was opened
before I could reach it.

'You from the *Sun* then?'

I stopped and shook my head.

'Saw you looking through the window over there.
We've had a few like that. Must say you're the most
normal looking, which is why I knew you were one of
them paparazzi. We've had all sorts of fucking weirdos.
Right morbid if you ask me.'

'I'm not from a newspaper,' I said. 'I'm investigating
the murder that took place over there.'

'Blimey,' the woman said, closing the door a fraction. 'Haven't your lot asked enough questions round here?'

'You can never ask too many questions,' I said, as seriously as I could.

The woman standing in front of me was in her mid to late thirties. She was small, barely over five feet, and quite chubby. She used one hand to shield her eyes and the other to hold a cigarette. She wore large, gold earrings and was dressed in a loose white tee shirt with thin red stripes, which she evidently felt was long enough to simultaneously perform as a dress. She wasn't wearing any shoes. I took out the sheets of paper, letting the woman see the Met's logo on the top, and then asked her if she was Mrs Iris Chortney.

'Juliet Chortney,' she said. 'Iris is my mother-in-law, for my sins.'

'Right,' I nodded. 'Can I ask you whether you knew the woman who used to own the house where the murder took place? A Mrs Anthony.'

'Who?' Juliet squinted, and looked past me into the street. 'I didn't think anyone did own that place, I always thought it was a squat. I know one thing, it was full of little druggies . . .'

At that moment there was a movement behind the woman, and I looked over her head into the dim hallway. An old lady was struggling into the passage from a doorway on the left-hand side, manoeuvring a Zimmer frame in front of her with head-down determination. Juliet followed my eyes round towards her.

'Mum!' she exclaimed. 'What are you doing?'

The old lady didn't look up. 'I'm not your mother. I heard my name.'

Juliet moved down towards her but the old lady was

ADAM BARON

head on to me now and moving with the steady determination of a glacier. She didn't slacken her pace. Juliet
hovered in front of her.

'Go and sit down, Mum, or this nice policeman'll
think that we don't need our care allowance.'

'There's no such thing, not any more. And what do
I care what he thinks?'

'Mum—'

'Get out of my way,' the old lady said. 'And put
something on before you open the door to strangers.'

The younger woman made a strangling gesture with
her hands that she didn't bother hiding from the old
lady, but she gave up the fight. I put my notebook away
and waited for the old lady to make it down towards
me. Once she'd established herself at the door she
stopped and leant against her frame, getting her breath
back. I looked down at her. Mrs Iris Chortney was
almost bald, wisps of white hair like wool caught on
barbed wire providing scant cover for the liver spots
that gave her head the look of an old football. She had
once been taller than her daughter-in-law but was now
about the same height. When she finally looked up at
me, raising her head with apparent effort, I could see
through her glasses that there was a brightness in her
milky-blue eyes, which managed to fight its way
through two heavy, crusted lids. The old lady's hands
gripped the frame like an old vine clinging on to
wrought iron.

'What do you want now?' she snapped. Juliet,
behind her, stood leaning against the wall, shaking her
head, pulling on her fag. I hesitated.

'Before I ask you anything, Mrs Chortney,' I said,
'I'd like to say that I'm not a police officer.'

178

Her eyes narrowed until there was almost nothing there. 'What are you?'

'I'm a private detective. I'm working for the family of the girl who was killed. Lucy Bradley. Across the street. They're very keen to know what happened to her.'

Behind her, Juliet raised her head.

'It's all right for them after, isn't it?' she said. 'Feeling guilty. What about before? It's the families I blame for not looking after 'em. Well-off too, weren't they? I read it in the paper.'

The old lady grimaced as though she had a bad taste in her mouth.

'They already asked me lots of things,' she said, shaking her head. Her voice was a good ten years younger than she was. 'But I was asleep, of course I was. I don't go to bed till late most nights, but not that late. All I knew was when the lights were all flashing and they started knocking on the doors. I'd like to help you but how am I to know what happened . . .?'

'Yes, Mrs Chortney,' I said. 'I understand. I'm not interested in that. How could you know anything?'

'Exactly.'

I smiled and nodded. 'But what I'd like to know is whether you knew the woman who *used* to live in the house. Before.'

'Kids,' she said. 'All kids. Nice enough, most of them.'

'A Mrs Anthony,' I said, 'who died some time ago? She lived here before the last five years, before the kids moved in. She lived here all her life as far as I know. Do you recognize the name? Mrs J. Anthony?'

The old lady seemed surprised. 'June? June Anthony?'

'Yes,' I said. 'Did you know her?'

Mrs Chortney looked at me as if I was stupid. 'Yes,' she said, 'yes I did. Of course. In those days you did know people. June, you want to talk about?'

'If I can.'

'Well then you'd better come in,' she said. 'No use standing out here, is there?'

Juliet shook her head and drew a sharp intake of breath. She muttered to herself as she and I processed behind her mother-in-law as the old lady made her way back down the hall and into the front room, where she eventually backed herself up into her chair like a fork-lift. In a voice laced with sugared irritation Juliet asked the old lady why she hadn't just stayed there all the time and let me come through to her.

'You'll wear yourself out, Mum,' she said.

'I'll wear you out, you mean. Care allowance! Sitting on your fat backside all day or else gadding about all night. How do you care for me? If I hadn't come out you'd have stood there all day trying to chat this man up and he would never have found out what he wanted.'

The younger woman looked at me as if to apologize for her mother-in-law and smiled. I just nodded. She came and sat a little too next to me on the springy sofa, but was soon informed that the best thing she could do was get out of our hair and make some tea. She gritted her teeth but did what she was told. When she came back into the small, neat room, with its flower pattern brown wallpaper and photos on the mantel, and I took a sip of the tea she handed me, I wondered if she had a part-time job in catering at the police station on Calshot Street.

Mrs Chortney and I spoke for an hour. She was an entertaining old lady with a sharp sense of humour. She told me a lot of stories about people who lived on the street, sometimes remembering that it was Mrs Anthony I was interested in, sometimes not. Though most if not all of what she told me was just by-the-by, I did enjoy listening to her. I think she enjoyed the chance to remember.

I put together a picture. Mrs June Anthony was the only daughter of a tailor and had lived in the house opposite ever since both she and Mrs Chortney were little girls. Though they went to different schools, the girls were friendly. June, who had changed her name with each of her marriages, was, apparently, a rather large lady, and had had three husbands, the first of whom Iris could only describe as a spiv. He had tried to avoid serving his country, she told me, but had eventually ended up in Burma in 1945. He didn't come back.

'At least not to her,' Iris said, leaning forward in her chair. 'Though my late husband Frank swore on his very life that he saw him one day on Oxford Street, right as rain, live as you are, in a nice new whistle and a shiny pair of shoes. Frank reckoned he just got one of his mates to write the letter so he could hop it. He never told June though, Frank didn't. He said she was better off out of it.'

Mrs Anthony was left with a son, but married again soon, this time to a man who didn't leave her until fifteen years later, when he definitely *was* dead.

'I helped lay him out,' Iris said. 'Frank told me to offer. He said he would never be able to be sure if I didn't, the silly old fool.'

Iris began to laugh at the memory, and then became a little subdued at the thought of her husband. She got herself together though and then told me that June had married again, but had been left by her final husband who had gone to live in Australia, she thought. That was ten years before she died.

'She was very sad after that, June was,' Iris said. 'And her son didn't help, only coming round when he wanted money off her, the mean sod. Right piece of work he was, though Juliet was friendly enough with him if I can remember right, weren't you, dear?' The look she gave her daughter-in-law left no doubt as to what she meant. Juliet didn't say anything. 'She saw to him though, June did. Never even left a will as far as I'm aware. He certainly didn't get the house. It's something which I'm considering myself if the truth be told.' Mrs Chortney's face looked deadly serious as she turned once again to her daughter-in-law.

'Seriously considering.'

I ignored the tea as politely as I could and if Juliet was offended in any way she chose not to show it. When I stood up to go Mrs Chortney insisted on showing me out, telling Juliet to stay where she was.

'Your Australians are on soon, aren't they?' she said. 'Wouldn't want to miss them, would you, dear?'

Mrs Chortney told me that her son would be home soon, if I needed to speak to him, but I told her I probably wouldn't. When we finally got to the door I thanked her for her time and said that I hoped very much to see her again some day. She gave me that look old people sometimes give you when you say that, accompanied by a nod and a distant smile. She stayed standing in the doorway while I walked back down to the Mazda, and then held up a hand as I drove past. I waved back to her. In the window I could see Juliet using the telephone. I slowed a little. Then I hit Leonard Cohen again and drove up towards Agar Grove.

Chapter Six

When I got home I unlaced my shoes rather than my trainers, eased my tie loose, and returned my suit to the hanger instead of pulling a tee shirt over my head. It made me feel like someone who had a real job. I poured myself a vodka and tonic and thought how much I'd actually got done in one day. And there was more to come. It reminded me of being on the Force and I remembered those intense periods, trying to break a case, working all hours God or the devil sent. For a second or two I even missed it and Ken Clay's words came to mind about why I left. Was he right? Was I just running away? Would it have been better after all to have stayed and got on with it? No. I only had to look at him to know that in many senses I'd been lucky. I'd have become just like him. A slicker version maybe but no different; using the most sensitive parts of people to get to them, making people hate me on purpose just so they would tell me things. I might even have become like Andy Gold, hustling the odd fifty quid out of his contacts, making dodgy plays for every woman he went anywhere near. It must just be the heat, I decided. I got under the shower and let an almost painful torrent of water pound the thoughts out of me.

Drying myself off I took a look at my leg and at my hand and saw that they were both a lot better. I cut up a banana on a bowl of cereal and ate it quickly before pulling on some sweatpants and a tee shirt. I packed a bag, locked up my flat, decided against the bike and walked downstairs to the car.

It felt good to put in a workout and then get in the ring. I was tentative at first, feeling my way into my body like it was a new pair of shoes. But I soon got into it. Being able to move freely felt like repossessing myself, getting control of my limbs again. It gave me a real sense of freedom to be able to work out, or stand up opposite another person, to push my body to do things it naturally resisted but naturally responded to at the same time. I was pretty fucked after a couple of hours but I felt invigorated, and I told myself to make sure that I reinserted my training into my schedule. It's as easy to get out of good habits as it is to get into bad ones. Sal said it was nice to have me back off my holidays.

Before taking a shower I stood in front of the mirror. I don't cultivate an overly bulky physique but I do like to be trim, and I saw a slight decline from the previous month, caused no doubt by my lay-off. It was something that was probably only noticeable to myself, but it was there. Something else was noticeable too, a faint though still visible area of purply-green bruising just below the hip bone on the top of my left leg. I touched it with my hand and it was a little tender. I wondered for a second where I'd got it. It hadn't come from the ring and nor was it a remnant from the fight I'd had. Odd. Then I did remember where it came from and the memory made me smile. Bad lass. I could even remember the sharp, sweet pain. The memory was then followed by another response, an immediate one that made me glad that I'd ducked out of training a little earlier than usual and that none of the boys were about to see it. It might have given them the wrong idea.

* * *

I sat in the car outside the place for a while, watching people coming in and out, waiting to see if George Curtis did either. I thought about the kid, sneaking in the back to rob his freezers. Maybe he did, and maybe Curtis caught him as he said. Right now, nothing seemed amiss. There were the usual sort of customers, lads going to or from the pub, and also four or five men dressed in suits or else still quite smartly, who didn't look like they were used to frequenting scuzzy little fast food joints. They probably knew the boss, I reasoned, and this impression was enhanced by the fact that only one of them actually bought anything, and this just a can of Coke. None of them stayed long so I figured Curtis was out, though I sat in the car for an hour to make sure. Then I moved the car to a side street and walked back down the High Street, tucking three photographs into the back pocket of my Levi's.

I stood in front of the counter behind a couple of lads wearing Jamaica football shirts. When they'd been served I stepped up and the man who was serving asked me what I wanted. He was a small, thin man with lank greasy hair tied up in a sad attempt at a ponytail. A Shetland ponytail. I told him I wanted a chicken kebab with salad and chillies in pitta, no mayonnaise. He nodded his head but didn't say anything.

He picked up a long knife and started slicing top to bottom down the cone of processed meat, sending long strips of greasy white chicken curling and then falling into a catch-tray at the bottom. I took the opportunity to glance beyond him into a kitchen area, but I couldn't see anyone. The man picked a pitta up off the grill and split it, before using his fingers to add salad from a row of plastic tubs between us. I leant against the counter.

'George in tonight?' I asked, with a yawn.

The man behind the counter rested his eyes on me as he stopped what he was doing. He left a second.

'No, he's out.'

'Never mind.'

'Who shall I say's calling?' the man asked.

'Sorry?'

'Who's calling?'

I looked at him. 'What does it matter? You said he was out.'

'Never mind,' the man said. He got the meat from the tray, assembled the kebab, laid three pickled chillies on top and then asked me for as many pounds. I handed the coins to him, took the food and left.

Camden was beginning to really smell now. The trash was piled up like trenches so that in some places you could hardly see over it onto the street. They were really going to have to do something about this soon. The sticky odour that hung in the breathless night air all around me even made the thing in my hand smell tempting. Almost.

I was about to dump the greasy crap I'd just bought on top of the nearest pile but I caught myself in time. I saw my mother's face, over a plate full of cauliflower. Some things never leave you. I looked round for a worthy recipient for my largess and then thought of Olly. I walked along amongst the late-night revellers, crossed at the lights and saw that Olly was at his pitch, trying without any success to get rid of his last copy of the *Issue*.

I said hi and went to hand him the package but I stopped. An old man ambled past and I handed it to him instead. He took it in amazement, telling me that I was high up in the hierarchy of the Catholic Church. Olly was of a different opinion.

'What? Hey? That was for me that was. You can't offer something to someone and then—'

'Follow me,' I said.

I gave Olly a ten-pound note and told him to go to the kebab shop on the High Street. He knew which one I meant. I said he was to sit at the small ledge by the window, and eat whatever he liked. I didn't expect any change. I asked him to stay there as long as he could and listen out for anything unusual. I said that if a very fat man came in he should come and tell me at once. I didn't want to do it myself because I'd already been in, and I didn't want to get my face known. Olly couldn't see anything wrong with the deal.

'Where will you be?' he asked.

I thought about it. 'Outside Café Delancey,' I said.

I left Olly, walking with him as far as the lights to make sure that he didn't head for Thresher instead, and then strolled round the corner to Delancey Street. I stood at the bar of Café Delancey for ten minutes until a smart young couple left a small table outside. I beat a couple of suits to it, sat down and ordered a chicken salad, immediately changing my mind to fresh tuna. I was off chicken. I drank a glass of red and some water and thought about my brother. I recognized a waitress who was still working there after all those years. She either didn't notice me or else didn't know who I was. I thought about visiting Luke in his time there, and about one night in particular, not long after he'd left, when we'd both gone there and got hammered after hours and not had to pay anything for the privilege. I'd gone home with one of the chefs, as far as I could remember. He, of course, had gone home with Sharon.

I try to avoid thoughts like this, getting drawn into the past like a wasp into syrup, getting its legs caught more and more as it tries to drag itself out. But this time something was different. The memories came but not the deep, pulling regret that normally came with them. They were just pictures, they didn't have any hold over me. It felt very curious, like looking at photographs in a second-hand shop of someone else's family. I felt a pang of guilt for a second, but then I began to feel light inside. Sharon's clear green eyes stood up in front of me. I felt that somehow I was very much part of the present, the here and now, and the things that were part of my life there. Not a product of the past, not a flipped-out ex-copper who couldn't take it any more. I remembered reading somewhere that the cells in your body change completely every seven years and that, therefore, every seven years you are a completely different person than you were. It wasn't seven years but it was approaching it. I felt like I had earlier at the gym, that somehow I was retaking possession of myself. I couldn't change the past, and though the present was full of trauma and pain for a lot of people, just then it wasn't for me and I couldn't pretend it was. Unlike the Bradleys, my past was gone. I finished my glass of wine and ordered another one. The tuna came and it tasted as fresh and clean as I felt.

Olly came by after about an hour. I'd sat outside so that he could come and meet me; there was no way they'd have let him through the door. There'd been no fat guy, he told me, and nothing unusual that he could see. I had a thought. Remembering the people I'd seen from my car, I asked him if anyone had come in to the place, but not ordered anything.

'I wish I had of, the kebabs are shite. Burgers didn't look bad though—'

'Did anyone?'

Olly looked at me. 'If I happen to think of it, yes. A couple of blokes actually. Not together, one after the other like.'

'What did they want?'

'They wanted a bloke called George I think it was.'

'Right.'

'But he weren't in. So they both left.'

'Right. You didn't recognize either of them, did you, by any chance?'

'No, sorry.' Olly shook his head but then looked pleased with himself. 'Got their names though for ya.'

'Nice one, Olly.' I took out my book and flipped over a couple of pages. 'Well?'

'Vincent,' Olly said, decisively. I wrote it down.

'And?'

'Vincent,' he said again. I looked at him.

'Thanks, Olly. What was the other guy's name?'

'Vincent, I told you. Both of them.'

'Really? Are you sure?'

''Course I am! What are the chances of that, eh?'

I shrugged my shoulders and put my book back in my pocket.

I paid my bill and ignored the waiter's discomfort at seeing the state of the man who was now sharing my table. His obvious disdain made me almost decide not to tip the guy, but as he hadn't actually been serving me I let it go. The girl had been nice enough and the guy didn't actually say anything. And Olly, Lord love him to bits, *is* one hell of a scruffy bastard.

Looking at my friend made me imagine Sharon sitting there instead and I resolved to give her a call. Olly and I handed the table over to an American couple in their fifties, who both looked uncertainly at the chair Olly had been using. We walked back down to the High Street where we stood leaning against the railings. Olly pulled a couple of cans from his coat, which were still cold. We stood drinking for a while, watching the people, and then I showed Olly the pictures I had with me.

Lucy, of course, was dead, but Olly squinted at her face and bit his lip. I understood his confusion and helped him out of it.

'You may have seen her sister in the last week or so,' I told him. 'Her twin. She was hanging around the tube looking for her.'

Olly nodded. 'Different though? Different kind of person. Not identical.'

I thought about it. 'No,' I said, 'identical, but you're right. Very different indeed.'

I showed Olly the other two pictures and though he obviously recognized Donna, and had seen the boy around a lot, he hadn't seen either of them recently.

'If you do, Olly . . .'

'Yeah, yeah, yeah,' he said. 'I'm more than happy to do your job for you, Billy, you know that. Though I do expect you to do the same for me sometime.'

'Fine,' I said, nodding, and I slid my hand in his jacket pocket before he could stop me. I took out his last remaining copy of the *Issue* and then walked up to a very, very beautiful Chinese girl, waiting for her friends to finish using the cash machine.

'Excuse me,' I said. She turned round. 'Would you like to buy my very last copy of the *Big Issue*, and make me the second happiest man on this entire street?'

'The second?'

'Behind your boyfriend, that is.'

I held up the copy and smiled. The girl hesitated for a second before handing me a pound coin, taking the magazine with a deep smile. I thanked her.

'Charm, Oliver,' I said, spinning the coin in the air. He held a hand out but I frowned at him and slid it into my back pocket, before turning to go. 'C-H-A-R-M.'

'Badged vendors only, mate,' Olly said. 'Badged vendors only.'

I flipped Olly the coin and left him there.

I walked twenty yards to the nearest phone box, a sex Tardis, catering for an unbelievably huge spectrum of tastes and desires. I was in a good mood. I held the phone and was about to dial Sharon's number when something started to nag at me, an impression that it was far too early to be calling it a day. But no. I'd been at it since eight that morning and I didn't have a very clear idea as to what to do next anyway. The kid could be anywhere, and I didn't want to start slogging around until I was sure that George Curtis didn't have anything to do with him. The image of Emma Bradley came to mind and I felt slightly guilty at putting the hunt for her sister's killer on hold, but the image I had of Sharon was too much and so I shrugged the feeling off. I could still see her, the other night. I tapped in Sharon's number, enjoying the familiarity of its pattern on the keypad, and she picked up after a couple of rings. I could hear people in the background, and I even recognized one of the voices; a brassy Geordie girl from Sharon's office whom I remembered meeting in some pub or other, and liking a lot. I asked Sharon if she was having a party and had forgotten to invite me.

'As if,' she said, taking me a little too seriously. 'Just people from the office. We were going to do some work on this pamphlet thing but, well, we got distracted.' She was talking about a report on racial inequality in asylum procedure that she and a group of other lawyers had got together to commission.

'Well, is it an all-legal affair or would a lovesick private investigator fit in to the evening?'

At that point a male voice asked Sharon where the loo was and she broke off for a second to tell him. She came back and told me that people had already said they were going soon.

'Even better,' I said. 'No, that sounded wrong.' I laughed. 'But I can come over anyway, if you want that is.'

Sharon didn't speak for a second. I had the feeling that she was going to say maybe tomorrow but then, very decisively, she said, 'Yes. Yes I want you to come over, Billy. I really need to see you.'

'Great,' I said. 'I'll be half an hour—'

'Oh,' Sharon said. 'That policeman phoned.'

'What?'

'The one I could never stand. You know.'

'He phoned you?'

'Uh huh. He said that if I spoke to you I should get you to call him. He wasn't too polite either. I don't know why I can't think of his name. I wrote it down, just a . . .'

'Andy. Andy Gold.'

'That's right. He left his number. He said he'd tried you at home and at your office. Here it is, 0973 534 826.'

'It's OK,' I said, 'I've got it.'

'Right,' Sharon said. 'You know, Billy, I think I'd better come over to yours . . .'

'Don't be silly,' I said, 'I don't mind at all. Really. I'll see you later.'

'OK then,' she said.

I put the phone down. Andy wouldn't have called Sharon unless something was going on. He would have had to get hold of the number somehow. I ran into the nearest newsagent and asked the man for some change. Even as the words left my mouth I could see him forming his response.

'Sorry, my friend . . .'

I picked up a handful of chocolate bars and slapped them down on the counter before thrusting a fiver at him. His till rattled open and I took the coins he offered me.

'Wait a minute, you forgot . . .'

The phone box was occupied. I pulled open the one next to it and found that it only took cards. I went outside again and waited, but when I peered in over the shoulder of the woman who was using it I saw that she still had ninety pence left. I ran off up the High Street towards Café Delancey again, trying not to make the very disappointing decision that it really was about time that I bit the bullet, gave in to the modern world and got a mobile. I ignored the maître d', pushed through the crowd and eventually got to the little plastic call box that was sitting on the end of the polished wood bar. I pumped two pound coins into the slot.

'DS Gold.'

I pressed the heel of my hand into my right ear.

'DS Gold.'

'Andy,' I said. 'It's Billy.'

'Billy. You have to meet me. Where the hell are you?'

'In a bar. What is it?'

I moved aside to give some room to a waitress carrying a tray of drinks. It was the same one I'd seen before and after doing a double take and spinning her mind back six years she did recognize me. I saw all sorts of cogs turning, which were replaced by a look of concern. I held a just-a-minute finger up to her and let her go past.

'Did you find the boy?' I bellowed.

Andy left a second. I could hear a siren in his background and then a door slam.

'No,' he said.

'Then what the hell—?'

'The girl,' he said. 'We found the girl.'

'The girl?'

'The girl you told me about, from York's. For God's sake keep up, will you? Donna Appleby. Natalie, as you said she calls herself.'

'And you want me to ID her?'

The waitress had come back. She was waiting, wanting to say hello to me. Her nervous look told me she wanted to ask about my brother.

'No, not really, Billy,' Andy's voice was a distant crackle. 'She had a rail-pass on her. We know who she is. But I think you should come over anyway.'

I held another finger up to the waitress and then covered my ear again. 'Where is she?' I shouted. 'Calshot Street?' My heart sunk at the prospect of spending any more time in that building.

'No,' Andy said. 'No, she's not there.' I was relieved. But then Andy's voice died for a second and I thought that my cash had run out or else the signal had gone. I was about to hang up and redial when he came back on the line.

'She's not at the station,' he said.

'Then where the fuck is she?'

'She's at the Whittington, Billy.'

Chapter Seven

It was the second time I'd been to the Whittington Hospital on Highgate Hill and I tried not to think of the first time. Instead I thought of what Andy had said over the phone about not needing me to come and identify Donna-Natalie. At the time I'd been confused – even if she did have ID on her, I'd still have to say that it was her I saw leaving York's that night with the murder victim. But now I knew what he was getting at. Looking at Natalie through the seeming confusion of tubes and wires connecting her to the insulin, and oxygen, and heart monitors, which were all there to try to keep her alive, I didn't think that her own mother would have been able to tell who she was. Her face was covered in so many bandages, and what was visible was so swollen and misshapen that she could have been just about anybody.

Andy Gold and I sat on canvas chairs by the side of the curtained-off bed and looked down at the girl who was occupying it. A nurse walked by, who obviously knew who Andy was, and she gave us both a look that had a warning in it. Donna-Natalie had had brief moments of lucidity apparently, and the staff didn't want anyone badgering her with questions if she came round again. Andy was staring at Natalie so hard he didn't seem to notice the nurse but I gave her a slight nod of acknowledgement and a serious smile that was supposed to say, don't worry we won't bother her. The nurse allowed herself to be fractionally reassured before bustling off down the ward to see to another patient.

I looked down at Donna-Natalie and tried to fix in my head the odd thought that the messed up inert body in front of me was the same sunny girl with the clear face and the quick smile I'd seen that morning in Camden. I let out a breath and Andy put a hand on my shoulder.

'I'm sorry,' he said.

I was surprised. 'I didn't know her. I just took her picture.'

Andy smiled, and let the sounds of the ward float over us for a second. Steel sounds, electronic sounds, so different from the smell, the all-too-human smell that hid just behind the disinfectant but was always there. I looked at Andy and was puzzled, as I often am by him, to see that he seemed genuinely affected by the sight of Natalie lying there.

'You liked her though.'

'She was a nice girl,' I said, somehow feeling that I had to justify myself. 'She was a nice, bright, fucked around girl, who should never have come to London. She should have been riding her pony around the field near her house, or else if she did come it should have been to wander round Madame Tussaud's holding hands with her mum and dad. Not lying here or sitting on the street or doing whatever else she was doing.'

'Which is why I'm sorry,' Andy said. He pushed

himself up on my shoulder and walked out of the ward to get some coffee.

Donna-Natalie had been in hospital for twenty-four hours, ever since being brought there by the ambulance that had rushed down to King's Cross to pick her up. She was admitted suffering from major concussion as well as excessive cranial fluid caused by severe trauma, and by the time I'd got there she had already had two emergency operations to remove shards of her skull, which had splintered and become embedded in the soft tissue of her brain. Her nose and both of her cheek-bones were shattered, as was her jaw, which had almost disintegrated into miniature rubble under the impact it had suffered. As I sat there trying to focus on the fragile, almost imperceptible sound of her breathing, Andy came back and told me what the doctor had told him. It was close to a miracle, he'd said, that Andy had been called to see Donna lying in an intensive care unit on the ground floor of the Whittington, rather than on a cold piece of clean steel downstairs.

At approximately nine o'clock that morning Donna-Natalie had caused what London Underground refer to as a passenger incident, when they are trying to explain to irate customers why a particular line is being subject to delays at a given time. At nine o'clock she had jumped in front of a tube train, a Victoria Line service coming into the platform at King's Cross. She had been at the near end of the platform and had, according to the very distressed German tourist who had been standing only feet away from her at the time, been acting very strangely. For at least ten minutes she had been wandering aimlessly about the platform in a daze but had then started screaming, very suddenly, and very loudly, for no apparent reason, as if she had suddenly seen something terrible. The tourist had then watched in horror as Donna held her hands up in front of her face and sprinted towards the steadily increasing sound of the incoming train as fast as she could. The tourist managed to make it to her feet but there was no way she could have caught up with the girl to stop her.

Donna did not, however, go in front of the train. Instead, in what was a bizarre fluke that may well have saved her life, she had left her run too late, and had been struck by the corner of the driver's carriage instead of the front of it. Any sooner and she would have been killed almost immediately, and then dragged underneath the train until it could have stopped towards the end of the platform. Any later and she may well have fallen down into the gap and been ripped to pieces by the onrushing wheels. As it was she hit the corner of the train and was hammered backwards onto the platform. Like a man punched in a comedy western she was thrown back thirty feet before sliding along the floor another twenty and hitting the wall. Andy said it was lucky it was so early on a weekend and the station was quiet, or else she may well have caused serious injury to anyone else waiting for a train that morning.

The tourist who had seen Natalie had tried to phone for assistance, but on picking up the emergency phone had found herself unable to speak. She had forgotten all of the English she'd learned, even though she was almost fluent in it. It was only four hours later that she was able to say what had happened, by which time the police had viewed the CCTV cameras anyway. It was the driver who had notified the control room and asked for an ambulance. When it came he got in the back of it too.

I asked Andy how come it had taken so long for him to get over here.

'They didn't know who she was,' he told me. 'They had no idea we were interested in her and a couple of the locals caught it. They simply established that she hadn't been pushed or anything and then left it to the medics. It was only a couple of hours ago that some nurse found her rail pass, and called the station, who ran it over the computer. It was in her sock, for some reason, as well as fifty quid or so. I don't know why she kept it there.'

'It's about as safe a place as you can get when you're on the street,' I told him. 'I've watched homeless kids putting paper money in their shoes before now. They change it up whenever they get enough, it saves carting coins around.' I thought about the guy in the newsagent an hour before. 'If you ever need change for a fiver', I said, 'go to the nearest doorway.'

We sat for a while, and then Andy's face took on a frown. He looked up towards the ceiling and then at me.

'It was here, wasn't it?' he asked me. 'I mean this ward? Further up the other end. Christ, I can remember it as if it were last week. You and that girl. Sharon, one I called earlier. You were both here. Fuck, it must be hard for you to come back and look at—'

'Have you seen the tape?' I said, cutting Andy off. My eyes found his.

'Not yet,' he said, quickly. He turned his head back to Natalie. 'Spoke to the locals though, they say it's

201

pretty clear cut, no one else anywhere near, hardly anyone on the platform . . .'

Right then there was a slight commotion at the far end of the ward. We both stood up and looked round the curtain. I could see a nurse and a doctor arguing with a couple of men, one of whom was holding a camera. They were trying to get onto the ward.

'Officer!'

The doctor called back over his shoulder. Andy walked towards him and the nurse, who was practically being pushed backwards by the man trying to get past her. I took a step forward but thought I'd better let Andy deal with it. Andy quickened his pace and I watched as he pulled out his badge and stuck it in the faces of the two guys before asking them to wait out- side. They didn't do it and so I heard Andy telling them. They weren't too happy but most policemen soon learn ways of telling people to do things so that they do them, and the two men reluctantly backed out through the thick plastic doors. The nurse, who was the ward sister, stood with her hands on her hips.

'Like I don't have enough to do,' she said. 'Arse- holes.' She let out a breath before following the men out of the ward.

The doctor stuck his hands deep in his pockets. I could see him thanking Andy, and then Andy followed him back down towards where I was standing. As he walked along Andy reached into his jacket, and while I was shaking the doctor's hand and telling him who I was Andy punched some numbers into his mobile. The doctor was about to tell him not to use it but it was already too late.

'At least a couple,' I heard him say. 'Four if you can

spare them. We've just got the first wave now and there are bound to be more.' He waited a second. 'Yeah,' he said, 'drugs. The first whiff of kids and drugs and these bastards start circling like buzzards. And I bet if I searched these two now I'd find enough coke to make a paperweight.' I saw the doctor smile. 'OK,' Andy nodded into his phone. 'Will do.' He snapped it shut and slid the phone back into his jacket before turning his attention to the doctor.

'So, you confirmed it then?'

'I'm afraid so,' the man said.

The doctor, who was one of those very affable, posh Englishmen with fluffy blond hair who it is impossible to dislike no matter what class you are, took Natalie's chart off the end of the bed and tucked it under his arm.

'We do that,' he explained, 'when the media are around.'

The doctor explained that tests had shown a high concentration of Ecstasy in Natalie's blood, a sample of which had been taken earlier. The doctor would have been within his rights not to tell Andy this, but I imagine that Andy impressed on him the need to get on and find out what had happened to Donna as soon as possible. The fact itself didn't surprise or shock me. It was true of 90 per cent of London's teenagers at some point in their lives, if not quite in that amount. Natalie had probably had four tablets, the doctor said, although it was impossible to tell given the range of concentrations available. I heard what he was telling me but couldn't peg it to the presence of the two bloodhounds Andy had just ejected. It was so commonplace. I'd done it, Andy had done it, the two guys who were now waiting outside had done it and so, probably, had the doctor at some stage. I asked him why he thought they were so interested in Donna particularly.

'A new angle,' he explained. He dug his hands so far into his pockets that his arms were almost straight down by his sides. 'A new way to package it. Some bad Ecstasy kills you, or you dehydrate, or you drink too much water and your brain swells. All been done. But now it makes you suicidal. Can't you see it? "Ecstasy Girl In Suicide Lunge".'

I could see it.

'But it's supposed to make you happy!' Andy said. 'Christ, it made me feel like a fucking prince.'

'It all depends', the doctor said, 'on your state of mind. But I have to say, it's the first time I've heard of it, which was why we took so long with the tests, expecting to find something else. But we didn't. Just Ecstasy, and a small amount of alcohol. Which is why those boys will have a field day.'

'If she dies,' Andy said.

'Either way,' the doctor said. 'But you're probably right. They'll have more to say if she doesn't make it.'

The doctor took us aside and explained that Natalie was very seriously injured and that there was a chance she would never regain consciousness. Andy asked that they should call him immediately as soon as she did wake up, assuming she did. The doctor left, but Andy and I stayed with Natalie until the uniforms Andy had ordered showed up. We sat by the bed just looking at her. Andy shook his head and wanted to know what sort of person tries to break into hospital wards to take pictures of sick children. I couldn't tell him. I wondered who it was in the hospital who had let these people know about her. A porter? A nurse? An intern?

'A nice little earner that from time to time', I said, 'for someone.'

'Some cunt.'

As we waited, Andy asked me if I had any ideas about Natalie, and why she'd done what she had. I told him what she had told me in the café that time, when I'd bought her breakfast, and he nodded like it was all the explanation he needed. But I said that I found it hard to believe it *was* just because of that. She'd been strong enough to run away from it, she'd seemed able to cope with it when she'd told me about it.

'But maybe the drugs did make it bigger,' I shrugged, 'who knows?'

'Not me,' Andy said. 'At least not until I've seen the video. Probably not even then by the sound of it. You want a look?'

'Thanks,' I said, again a little surprised. 'Thanks, Andy.'

When the two noddies came Andy filled them in. He put one of them by the bed and the other on the door. We walked out into the waiting area and there were now four other people there, all press, all being spoken to severely by the ward sister, who was looking at them as though they were all contagious with something very nasty indeed. Andy and I tried to slip past but they spotted us and ran over. Most of London's crime press know most of London's police, at least by sight. I pushed my way through them to the corridor that led to the exit while they besieged Andy with questions, which he did his best to ignore. One of them, however, had a long memory. He darted over to me.

'You back on the beat then . . .?' He was searching for my name. I wasn't going to give it to him. He was a small man in his mid-forties, whom I vaguely recognized, largely due to a huge epiglottis that swayed below his chin like a plum in a plastic bag. His voice whined like a kettle boiling on a deaf man's stove.

'No,' I said.

'No? What you doing here then?'

'Ingrowing toenail.'

'Bollocks.' He stepped closer to me and lowered his voice to a simple hiss. 'Come on, give us a hint. She full of smack or what? Horse? E? It's E, isn't it?'

'Big toe, left foot. Very painful.'

'Oh, fuck you then.' He waved a hand at me and turned to go. '*Rucker*, that's it.' He turned back with a grin. '*Rucker*. Shouldn't give you a hard time really, should I? Nah. Got a lot of good copy out of you at one time if I remember. Very good copy. Dramatic. Five years ago? At this hospital, wasn't it? In fact, wasn't it in this very . . .?'

I watched, almost as amazed as he was, as my right hand reached out and took a handful of the man's collar, catching hold of a fair chunk of loose skin too, cutting off air to his windpipe. I watched as my hand twisted him against the wall. I saw my hand squeeze tighter and my arm push him backwards, hard, and his eyes widen with surprise as he fought for breath. My hand gripped tighter and we were both very still for a second. Then, as I saw his tongue reaching forward and the panic beginning to well behind in his eyes, my arm became mine again and I pulled my fingers apart and let him go, setting him gently on his feet like a toy boat on a glassy pond. We looked at each other and then I drew my hand back slowly before walking towards the exit. The guy didn't follow me, simply choking out

'Twat!' before turning back to Andy, who was reluctantly giving up a very bland statement.

I unclenched the left hand, which I hadn't realized was clenched, and walked along the flatly lit corridor until I reached the main foyer. I stood with my back against the reception desk, pinching the bridge of my nose against the first jarring vibrations of what I prayed would not be a migraine. I winced, rubbed my temples with my thumbs, and shook my head at how stupid I'd nearly been. The desire to hurt the guy had been huge, I didn't know where it had come from. I let out a long breath and looked back down the corridor.

I thought about just leaving but I decided to wait for Andy, to fix up a time to see the videotape. There was no point wasting this amenable mood of his. There's no A and E unit at the Whittington now and so the foyer was empty but for a couple of black guys in overalls, stood by a coffee machine, sharing a quiet joke. There was something comforting about their soft laughter. I took another look back towards the ward and then glanced at my watch. I was amazed to see that it was after two. I wondered how the hell it got that late. And then my arms dropped to my sides, my eyes closed, and I let out a long breath.

I hadn't phoned Sharon.

'Fuck.'

I hadn't meant to say it out loud, let alone quite as loud as I had, and the nurse behind the desk raised an eyebrow at me. I was embarrassed, and was about to apologize, and ask her where I might find a phone, when her eyes moved from me to the entrance. Two people were hurrying through the door, moving straight towards her. They were middle aged, a middle-aged couple and they both looked exhausted, but manic at the same time. Especially the woman. She held one hand out in front of her, holding the other to her chest. She beat her husband to the desk. I looked away, not interested, and willed Andy to get a move on. But then I turned back to them.

'Our daughter. Our daughter. She's here.'

The nurse spread her hands. 'Just a moment, madam, if you could—'

'Donna,' the woman said. She was a slightly tubby fifty-year-old, and her face was a white Chinese mask, painted with worry. 'Donna. Donna Appleby. The police, they phoned us. We've driven for hours. Where is she? Please take me to her, I'm her mother.'

The man had caught up with his wife by now but he didn't say anything. He stood beside her, resting one hand on the counter, the other on his wife's shoulder. He was a tall, military-looking man, with very full grey hair and thick eyebrows the colour of barbed wire.

'If you could wait a second, madam, I'll find out where she is. Please, take a seat, I won't be long.'

'Donna, Donna Appleby, I have to . . .'

I saw the husband's hand grip his wife's shoulder and she was silent, though her whole body seemed to be urging the nurse to hurry up. They stayed where they were while the nurse picked up her desk phone and spoke into it quietly, her back to them. They hadn't noticed me. I pushed myself off the desk and took a step towards them. The nurse put the phone down and turned back to the couple.

'Now, if you'll please just take—'

'Nurse,' I said. I spoke loudly, looking straight at her. She was confused but turned to me. The couple

turned too. 'Nurse,' I said again. 'I need you to page Dr
Fursten for me. It's very important. I need to speak
with him. Urgently. Please could you do it now.'

The woman hesitated. But I knew she'd seen me
with Andy Gold and she wavered. She broke my look.

'If you'll just take a seat,' she said, to the couple by
my side, neither of whom had ever seen me before or
had any idea who I was. 'A nurse will be through in a
second. And I'm sure that she'll take you to Donna.
Please.'

The nurse put a little firmness in her look. Reluctantly, the two people stepped away from the desk and
shuffled backwards to the empty lines of blue plastic
seating, where they sat, the wife perched on the edge
of her seat, her husband sitting with his elbows on his
knees, staring straight in front of him. Beside me, the
nurse picked up the phone again.

In a nearby side room I told Fursten why I had
called him. I told him why the girl in his care had run
away to London and changed her name to Natalie. I
told him that her parents had now arrived to see her,
which he already knew. He looked at me steadily and
nodded gravely, biting his bottom lip when the impli-
cations of what I was telling him were absolutely clear.
It didn't take very long, he was an intelligent man.

'If she comes to,' I said, 'and she looks up, and sees
the people who—'

'Yes. Yes.' The doctor nodded quickly. He didn't
look too thrilled at the prospect of some of the decisions
he was going to have to make in the next minutes and
hours. Days even. 'Thank you. I'd . . . They *are* still her
parents though. Maybe she'll still want to speak to
them, even in spite of . . . you know?'

I shrugged, which told him I couldn't help. He nodded, knowing it was down to him.

'I'll go and speak to them now,' he said.

I yawned, and followed Dr Fursten out of the room. I let him get ahead of me, and watched as he introduced himself to the couple waiting for him in the foyer. I hung back further and then stopped, looking at the entrance to the unit. I saw a trolley crash through it, fast, people holding bottles connected to tubes, others pushing, some shouting out instructions, some simply trying to keep up, trying not to get in the way. One of them was me. I heard a voice.

'Sir?' It was the nurse. It sounded like the third time she'd spoken.

'Sir? The policeman. The one you were with? He asked me to tell you that he's gone home.'

'Oh,' I said. 'Thanks.'

'He said to say you should call him.'

'Right.' I stayed staring at the empty doorway. 'Thank you.'

'He said . . . Sir? Are you all right?'

'Yes,' I said. 'I'm sorry.' I shook my head and turned to her and did my best to smile. 'I was somewhere else.'

She smiled back. 'Lucky you.'

'Or, rather, I was here.'

'I'm sorry?'

'I was here, six years ago. Right here, right here where I am now.'

The nurse laughed nervously. I wished her goodnight and walked towards the entrance. The doctor was sitting with his back to me, talking to Mr and Mrs Appleby. I walked right past but I didn't look at them.

Chapter Eight

In the hospital car park I stood for a minute, trying to breathe the thick, warm air through the resonating pain behind my eyes. I breathed into my ribs, the way Luke had once shown me, and tried to imagine the air leaving through the top of my head and taking the pain with it. It didn't work. I couldn't focus on it. I kept getting distracted by the crowd of people running through my brain.

After Luke's accident on the Westway they brought him here, to the Whittington, which in those days had an Accident and Emergency Unit. Sharon had gone in the ambulance with him but there wasn't room for me, and so I'd gone with Andy in the unmarked car we used. We had weaved and pushed through the dregs of the rush-hour traffic, the sirens of three police cars and an ambulance screaming the way I wanted to scream.

From the time we arrived at the hospital it was all a bit of a blur. The confusion, which wasn't really confusion but actually professionalism on the part of the hospital staff, made me feel helpless, as I followed the trolley with Luke on, saying his name, wanting to do something for him but knowing that I could do nothing, that once again I was the wrong person. The feeling of isolation and helplessness I felt that night sustained itself for so long over the next few weeks and months that gradually it began to define me. It was only thanks to one person that this ever ceased to be the case.

I don't remember how long we stayed there, Sharon and I, in that miserable foyer, waiting for news. All I could see was a car crushed like a toy, a body, far too still, calm drops of blood dripping off the inside of a shattered windscreen. All around me in the hospital I saw other distressed people, accident victims, victims of stabbings, of bar brawls, of domestic incidents. It was like standing in a whirlwind and it was so completely awful it seemed surreal. I remembered looking at all the employees of the hospital, unable to imagine why anyone would go there every day, voluntarily, to fill their daily lives with so many images of pain. I remembered the nurses, and the doctors, and the cleaners, and the porters, how comforting they all were, how they actually did seem to help with their words, and their advice, the simple tone of their voices or their smiles as they cleared some plastic cups away or mopped the floor around us at four a.m. And then another feeling; when Sharon turned to me for support. How inadequate I felt when faced with this girl whose whole life had just been screwed up into a ball and tossed into the waste-paper basket because, as Ken Clay said, I wouldn't leave something alone.

I let the images pass through my head and when they were gone I felt leaden and hard, pissed off that I had been pulled back into the place I seemed to have finally started distancing myself from. I tried to shake the feeling off, telling myself to think about the present but that didn't help because, when I thought about it, nothing in the present seemed to make any sense to me. Not this case, not my job, anything. I never seemed to make decisions, I just seemed to be constantly trying to catch up. And what was worse, it seemed to be affecting the one thing in my life that did make sense. Sorting out other people's problems meant that I was always calling Sharon to break dates, always having to work at night when I should have been with her. And now I hadn't called her because once again things had overtaken me. She would be fucked off. She would have waited up. And if I called her now she would probably have gone to bed and that would only make it worse. Added to this was the fact that I just really, *really* wanted to see her, and I couldn't.

It was a bad end to a long, long day, which had begun with a father in turmoil and finished with a young girl fighting for her life. I had a headache and I was frustrated and all that I could think of now was to get home, soak in the bath, then fall into bed. I opened up the Mazda and pulled out onto Highgate Hill, before driving down to Archway. There was no one about. I drove home quickly, with the feeling that somehow I was never going to get there. But I did. There was no space outside my flat, however, and the delivery bay I sometimes park in was full too. I cruised around but I couldn't find anything, my headache slowly building like the accelerator was stuck. Eventually, I'd had enough, and I abandoned the thing in the car park of the GP surgery around the corner from my flat, which meant that I would have to get up before eight and move it if I didn't want to get clamped. Less than six hours' time. But I didn't care. I locked up and walked back up the street to Exmouth Market and then down the side street to my flat. I unlocked the outside door. I closed it behind me and headed up the stairs. But when I turned the bend in the stairwell I stopped.

There was a light beneath my door.

I was halfway up the stairs. I held on to the handrail and didn't move. I listened, but I couldn't hear anything. I couldn't see much light but there was definitely some, just one lamp perhaps, or the light from the kitchen. I hadn't left any on. No way. I'd left the house when it was still light outside. Why would I have had a light on? I took a step backwards, then a few more. I put my hand on the street door and pulled it open as slowly as I could. Carefully, I twisted round and peered outside, left then right. There was no one around. No one I could see. I stepped into the street and pulled the door to without making any noise, leaving it slightly ajar.

This had happened to me before. Someone had broken into my flat and the subsequent events had been as unpleasant as any I could have imagined. No, more so. As quietly as I could, I stepped over to the other side of the street, which is a one-way passage with just room for a single car at the most to squeeze past those that are parked there. I crouched behind the bonnet of a black cab and looked up the multi-tagged brickwork, to the window on the third floor. Yes, there was a light on, behind the curtains that I had definitely not left closed. I moved further behind the cab, knowing that if anyone had been watching for me they would probably have seen me by now.

I felt a tightness in my chest. Was I just going to walk into something? I thought about it. Maybe I should call my own number, see if anyone picks up the phone. I didn't know. What about calling the police? What about just going to my office for the night? I really didn't need to deal with anything right then. My head hurt. But then again, what if I *had* somehow left a light on, what if . . .?

And then I had another thought. No longer bothering to hide myself I walked up alongside the row of cars to Exmouth Market, checking the models. Then I walked back down again. Right at the far end of the street I found it. I let out a sigh of relief that seemed to take everything with it. Suddenly, I was absolutely fucked. Sharon's Fiat Uno was squeezed in between an Audi and an old Jag. I leant against the bonnet. Sharon, thank God. And not because it wasn't some hoods out to break my legs or worse, no. Thank God because it was her. Up there, waiting for me. I looked up at the window and smiled to myself, wondering if I'd make it up the stairs. It seemed like a long way, but then I felt the last vestiges of energy within me come to life and move me up the street.

I made it to my door and I pushed it open and then hopped up the stairs. I felt like a man running through the desert into the Red Sea. Sharon, she was the one I told about days like this one, she's the one who took some of it off me. I felt so grateful to her for coming over. Once I'd got my hall door open I called out hi, up the stairs inside my flat. Then I pushed open the inside door at the top. Sharon was sitting cross-legged on my bed, with only the light of my desk lamp for company, leaving half of her face in shadow. She was fully clothed and she wasn't watching the TV, or reading a book, or doing anything. She seemed very still and her stillness stopped me, though all I wanted to do was collapse on the bed beside her. I took her stillness for annoyance.

215

'I'm sorry,' I said. 'I am.'

'What for?' Her voice was too quiet for anger. I took a step forward.

'Not coming over. Not phoning . . .'

'I don't blame you. I understand.'

'Do you? How? Did Andy tell you about the girl?'

I felt relieved that I didn't have to explain, but Sharon hadn't seemed to hear me. A bitter, wistful smile broke the half of her face that was visible.

'I could tell that you knew,' she said, slowly. Her voice was so distant it sounded as though she had left it for me and gone. I didn't know what she meant. 'I mean, how could you not? I've been a bitch to you recently.'

I still didn't understand. 'No you haven't,' I said, squinting into her. 'It's just been tough. Your work, the course—'

'Not wanting to see you. Making excuses. Christ. I knew you knew, you're a detective for God's sake, but I just couldn't . . . That stuff about my dad's boat. Christ, I'm not surprised you didn't come over tonight. And I'm glad. You shouldn't have had to go all the way over there. Which is why I came over here when I knew you weren't coming . . .'

I still hadn't closed the door. Sharon's voice stopped and I turned and pushed it shut. When I turned around again she was looking at the floor. I knelt and put my hand on her shoulder but very firmly she took it and put it down on the bed.

'I should look at you I know, but I can't,' she said. 'And though I know you must already know by now I owe it to you to just say it, so I will. I've been seeing someone else, Billy.'

Part Three

Part Three

Chapter One

I feel comfortable in the part of London I live in.
Exmouth Market. It has an urban, international quality
I like. It isn't so very English, I don't think, and if you
were suddenly planted inside it, and asked where you
were, it might take you a moment or two to say Britain,
let alone London. It reminds me of places on the
outskirts of Paris. Of Madrid, or Milan perhaps. Even a
couple of areas of New York I've visited. I liked it when
I moved in and, surprisingly enough, I still like it. Even
though it has changed.

When I moved into the area the bar on the near
corner, Fred's, was a Wimpy. The pubs on the street
catered mostly for postal workers from the Mount Pleasant depot, and though a couple of them still do, postal
workers are no longer the target clientele for the
majority of outlets now found in the vicinity. The area
used to be a complete backwater in the minds of
fashionable people, simply a place you passed in a cab
on your way up to Islington from the West End. But
there are now three trendy bars here. There are four
minimalist coffee shops. There is a fashionable jewel-
lery store that is always empty, a hip tailor and a store
selling magazine fashion for men. There is also a shop
purveying brightly coloured ornamental items, which

ADAM BARON

you hope you don't get for Christmas, a chain Japanese noodle bar, which is like eating in a goldfish bowl, and one truly excellent restaurant.

It has been interesting living where I live during all this. While Camden, say, gives the impression of being finished, complete in and of itself for good or bad, Exmouth Market has seemed like frontier territory; the front line in the battle for the city. The battle is still going on; the old wine shop is still not an Oddbins, there is still an Afghan grocer, and the pie and mash shop still does good trade. But most of the old places are gone and those that remain are really just pockets of resistance. Anyone can see that the war is over.

As a resident of the market I don't know how I feel about this. I like having nice bars to sit in. I like being able to buy sandwiches with roast peppers in. If you've ever been inside Moro you'll appreciate that I like sitting at the bar and eating the tapas there. I even like the odd game of table football with Nicky. But at the same time I'm afraid that I'll wake up one morning and they'll have glassed the street over and I'll realize I'm living in a shopping mall. It hasn't happened yet, most of the big boys have been kept out, but it's probably only a matter of time before I'll be able to have coffee in an Aroma, buy milk from a Tesco Metro, get a plastic tasting lunch in a Dôme, a drink in an All Bar One (me) and dinner in a Pizza Express. When all the people who saw potential in the street won't be able to afford to do business there any more. I hope it never gets to that, but if you take most other 'rejuvenated' areas as a guide I'm afraid it probably will, eventually.

Still, while I don't exactly own my flat, I don't pay

anything to live where I do and I could rent the place out for a small fortune if I got fed up. I could go and live in a different part of London, or a different city altogether. I could live anywhere I wanted to. I could even leave the country and never, *ever* come back, never have to look at or deal with the things that depress me here. But if I did that I would be leaving my brother. And he would be even more alone than he is now if that is possible, and there would be absolutely no one to go and visit him, or to talk to him, or to shave his face, or tell him how his poems had been received.

No one, no one at all.

They started loading the rubbish at eight. I saw them when I went out to move my car. There must have been emergency talks or something because it wasn't soldiers who were doing it, or the long-term unemployed, but real bona fide bin men. I stood watching them move the two trucks slowly up the market, throwing the bags that hadn't split into the back, sweeping the rest into piles. I don't know why but what they were doing was strangely mesmerizing and I stayed watching until they'd finished. They did a good job. After half an hour or so it was as though none of the shit that had stunk the place up so much over the last two weeks had ever been there. Just a clean, empty space. When the trucks pulled off onto Rosebery Avenue I stuck my hands in my pockets and wandered round the corner to Zack's for a cup of tea. I stayed there twenty minutes before walking back up to my flat again. I thought about driving up to my office, or calling Emma Bradley, but I couldn't find the energy. I spent the rest of the morning looking out of the window, down across the rooftops to the dome of St Paul's, the only curve on a horizon of hard grey lines.

* * *

'Yes,' the doctor said, 'I'm positive. The tests are quite clear. Just Ecstasy and alcohol. A lot of the former, not much of the latter.'

'It just seems odd,' I told him. 'Have you seen the tape? From the tube station?'

'No.'

'I think you should look at it,' I said. I held the cassette up. 'Or at least someone should, a specialist in drugs maybe.'

'I'd be glad to', he said, 'if you think it would help me care for Donna.' He shrugged, his hands deep in his pockets again. 'But didn't she just run off the platform? I mean, what good would it do to see it? I know what's wrong with her, she got hit by a train. Hard.'

'I know,' I said, 'but she didn't just jump. It was more than that . . .'

At that moment we had to step back from the desk, out of the way of a delivery trolley. It was mid-afternoon and the hospital was hot and heaving. We had to move again to let a man on crutches struggle through the mêlée, and then one of the doctor's colleagues tapped him on the shoulder and tried to set up a squash game with him on Sunday. When the man had gone I took hold of the doctor's elbow.

'Listen,' I said, 'is there somewhere we could go and watch this?'

He looked at his watch.

'Yes,' he said. 'I think so. I'll have to ask . . . Oh no, sod it. Follow me,' he said.

Just after two that afternoon, the phone had rung. I stared at it for a while but let the machine get it. After my message I heard Andy Gold announce that he was leaving the tape he'd promised me at the station, and that I could collect it any time I wanted, if I wanted. I nearly picked the phone up to thank him but didn't bother. I didn't trust my voice to sound normal with anyone I knew.

Andy rang off. I sat for a while longer and Lucy Bradley came into my mind. I remembered how one minute she'd been a sassy young girl in control, walking along the street with a kick in her step, and the next it was all over for her. I almost knew how she felt. But I hadn't been left for dead, it only felt that way. Glad of something to do I stood under the shower for a while and then stepped into some jeans. I cycled down to Calshot Street and picked the tape up before peddling straight back home again. I watched the tape three times and then got on the phone to David Fursten, the doctor from the Whittington, and he agreed to give me twenty minutes or so before his shift started.

Fursten led me through the shifting tide of walking wounded to a personnel lift where we rode up to seven. Upstairs, the hospital didn't look much like a hospital. The carpeting was thick and new and the furniture was a lot more expensive than that which members of the public were given to sit on. I followed Dr Fursten through an encoded security door into a warmly lit corridor that we padded along quickly. There was taste-ful art on the walls and we passed a couple of stands for fresh flowers, today's selection of which was made up mainly of lilies whose sweet scent spread like tentacles before and behind us, strong enough to resist the suction of an air conditioning unit humming quietly overhead. We turned a corner and then stopped. Dr Fursten seemed a little on edge and he looked both ways as he tapped quickly on the dark wood of an anonymous-looking door to our right. When he got no response he turned the handle. The door opened inward and he ushered me past him.

'They don't like us up here,' he told me, shutting the door and locking it behind him. 'It reminds them that there are sick people around – somewhere in the building.'

I laughed.

'Something that they try to forget,' he added.

We were in a large room with a long, modern conference table running down the middle, which looked to me like three thousand pounds worth of teak. The table was flanked by high-backed chairs and at the end was a wide-screen monitor with a video recorder underneath. Fursten walked down the far side of the table, flicked a few buttons and slid the cassette I'd handed him into the machine.

'They bring us up here occasionally to show us how to do our job,' he explained. 'Which is saving money.'

Fursten hit play and we both sat back on either side of the table, in the chairs closest to the screen. After a second or two of black space we were presented with a view of a station platform taken from a camera high up, at the near end. It was, of course, a single, locked off shot, and it showed several people, some sitting on benches, the rest either milling, leaning against the

long wall or else just standing. There was no sound.
Amongst the people it was possible to see Donna,
wandering around, about halfway up the shot, and I
used my finger to point her out to the doctor.

'Right,' he said.

Donna was moving in a seemingly aimless fashion,
first one way then the next. When a train pulled into
the platform the passengers moved towards and then
boarded it and when the train pulled out again there
was only one person left on the screen. Donna. She
hadn't seemed to register the train's arrival. She obviously wasn't going anywhere in a hurry. The doctor
and I both watched as she walked up to the far end of
the platform and sat down on the floor. She held her
head in her hands, and she looked like she was crying,
but it was difficult to see whether this was in fact the
case.

Nothing happened for a minute or so. Donna just
sat there, hardly moving. Then a few more people
walked onto the platform. When a woman walked into
the shot and sat on the nearest bench to the camera I
put my finger back on the screen.

'The tourist,' I said. 'The German lady.'

The next train didn't come for another six or seven
minutes, during which time Donna walked right down
the platform and into much clearer view. She was
wearing baggy, burgundy coloured trousers of a thin
material and a green top with a cross-laced front, the
laces untied. She had on a pair of black Converse boots
and her hair was tousled. Whereas before she had
seemed simply lost, now she was clearly distressed. Her
mouth kept opening and closing and she looked all
around her, as if afraid that someone was trying to

harm her. Then she stopped, and seemed to just think, before looking round again. Most obviously she seemed confused, as if she had mislaid something, something very important. When she got as close to the camera as I knew she ever did, I hit pause.

'Look,' I said.

I pointed to Donna's face and though the picture was less than clear I thought I saw bruising. I hit the button again and watched as Donna wandered round a bit more, before sitting next to the woman on the bench. The woman looked at Donna and gathered her bag to her. In her statement she said that Donna had been talking to herself, odd random words that didn't seem to make any sense. She couldn't remember any of them. On screen the woman continued to glance nervously at Donna and twice looked at her watch.

I gave a look to Fursten that was supposed to warn him but he was staring hard at the screen. After two or three minutes of sitting on the bench Donna simply took hold of her hair in both hands and started scream-ing for no apparent reason. The woman beside her looked shocked and uncertain. Donna stood up quickly and just as quickly my hand reached out to hit the button again.

'You don't have to watch the rest. What I wanted you to see was that reaction. Why would . . .?'

Fursten's lips were pursed and his eyes were focused in front of him. He still didn't look at me. Instead he reached for the recorder and touched the pause button, sending the figure of Donna into motion again. She ran straight forward with her hands in front of her face, into the path of the incoming train, which sent her flying backwards up the platform. Because there was no sound, the impact looked unreal, as if Donna were just a puppet, jerked backwards by an invisible wire. She flew backwards and then landed on the floor. Then she slid along the wall until she was rammed into the iron legs of a low bench and jolted suddenly to a halt. After that she was completely still. It was all over in less than a second.

The train slowed quickly but carried on along most of the rest of the platform. The lady on the bench had stood up. The doctor and I watched as she began to move, slowly at first, before running the rest of the way towards Donna. I reached forward and turned the video off.

I hit eject on the machine and sat back in my chair with the cassette. I turned to the doctor. He let a breath out of his nose.

'It's very strange', he said, shaking his head, 'to watch that. We normally only ever see the aftermath.'

I nodded, and slid the cassette back into its case. 'But you can see why I think it's odd?'

He thought about it. 'Yes, I can.'

'I mean, if she'd been on acid, or mushrooms even. To just suddenly scream like that. And then run.'

'I know what you mean.'

'It just looks so sudden. She's distressed, sure, but then she just flips, like she's seen, I don't know ... giant green ants or killer spiders. If she'd been on acid, I could understand it.'

Fursten nodded and folded his arms. 'I was chased by ten-foot razor blades,' he said. '1977. I locked myself in my room but they tried to slice their way through the door. It was my friends, actually, but I didn't know that. I nearly jumped out of the window and I still don't know what stopped me. Terrifying. My first and only experience of LSD.'

'But Ecstasy?'

The doctor hesitated. 'I know what you're getting at. Between you and me, I have used it a few times and no, it never made me act that way. Or anyone else I know about for that matter. But we don't know what was going through Donna's mind. She's a very messed around girl, as you know. You told *me*, remember?'

'But to act so *suddenly* . . .' I said again. 'I don't know. It just doesn't seem right . . .' Fursten gave me another big shrug.

'What can I tell you?' he said. 'I agree it looks off, and it's not what I would have guessed if I had just seen this, but the tests are very clear. A limited amount of alcohol, a lot of E. Nothing else. I wish I could help you but faced with that, there really isn't anything else I can say. Except that it is, of course, very, very sad indeed.'

I knew that Fursten was right but nevertheless there was a story there, a series of events that produced Donna's behaviour, something we didn't know. I was sure it was something other than the obvious but Fursten couldn't tell me what it was. There wasn't anything else to ask him so I thanked him for his time, and he apologized for not being of any more help to me. A cleaner knocked on the door and looked at us strangely when we opened up, but she didn't say anything. We then snuck out of the office wing as furtively as we had entered, and waited for the lift. Fursten told me he would get in touch with Andy if there was any news about Donna.

I parted with the doctor on the fourth floor, where

he got out. Once downstairs again I spoke to the ward sister and she said it was OK to sit with the girl for a while. She told me that there was no change in Donna's condition: stable but critical. I sat in the same seat I had before, and the constable, who recognized me from before, took the opportunity to wander off up the ward to chat to his colleague minding the door. When he was gone I looked at the flowers by the side of the head that was still swathed in bandages. There was a name tag by the bed, placed there I imagined, so that any nurse with a free second could come and chat with the girl. The name tag said Donna. But she called herself Natalie. I'd come to think of her as either, or both, and I wondered which name referred to her most, which person she really was; the girl she had run away from being or the body lying still in front of me? I decided she was Natalie, not Donna, and I admired her for trying to reinvent herself, for not accepting the hand she had been dealt by life. I thought of the girl in the photograph, with the pony, and then of Natalie's dyed hair and eyebrow ring and the contrast they made with the person she was before. It moved me to think of the fragile, ephemeral foundations we use to build our personalities upon.

I smiled down at the girl and even spoke to her, telling her simple, inconsequential things, nothing that would have been at all important to her. I chatted for twenty minutes or so before the constable came back. It wasn't difficult. I'm an old hand. I left her at about five and walked back out into the corridor.

Chapter Two

I was back in the hospital foyer but this time I didn't see any ghosts. I found a phone next to a vending machine and took a sip of coffee as I dialled Andy's number. He was back at the station and I thanked him for the tape. He didn't tell me that my voice was any different. Andy said he'd been through the tape himself and I asked him what he made of it. I told him what I thought. He'd noticed the possible bruising on Natalie's face himself, but wouldn't say it was there for certain.

'The doctors?' I asked him, suddenly thinking of it. 'Could they tell how fresh it was?'

As soon as Andy laughed I realized it wasn't very likely. 'If she hadn't nutted a tube train, maybe,' he said. 'As it is, forget it.'

Even if there had been bruising on Natalie's face prior to the train hitting her, Andy couldn't see that it changed anything. She wasn't exactly leading a risk-free life. He pointed to the fact that we were looking at clear and unambiguous proof of an attempted suicide, in which no one else was directly involved.

'It's just one of those things,' he said.

Andy wasn't too interested, either, in my qualms about Natalie's behaviour.

'Its not a controlled drug,' he said, 'Ecstasy. Who

knows what it'll make you do? When I took it I ended up tonguing one of the most hideous, disgusting bints you have ever seen in your entire life, and thinking she was Denise van fucking Outen.'

I could hear him wincing at the memory.

'And she ended up tonguing you,' I told him.

I hung up and walked outside to my car. Huge, dense clouds squatted over the city, still and heavy. My shoulders felt heavy too and my stomach cramped at the coffee. I pulled out into the traffic. I'd intended going home to catch up on some of the sleep that I'd done without the night before but after a minute or two I thought better of it. I knew it wouldn't work. I'd tried earlier without any success. I'd laid down and shut my eyes but my mind had kept looking for answers, some sort of way round what I'd been told. And it kept showing me pictures I didn't want to see. Eventually I'd given up and returned to the window, as if something out there would suddenly let me know what was going on. St Paul's didn't tell me anything.

At Archway I took a right, and drove towards Camden. The video was niggling the hell out of me but I put it to the back of my mind with all the other crap I couldn't work out. I focused on the boy; I still had to find him, and as yet I hadn't really started looking. I knew I'd probably end up walking the streets or sitting in cafés until he either turned up or I gave up, but while there was something more positive to do first I'd do it. I had one possible link to the kid. I parked the car right outside George Curtis's kebab shop and killed the engine, knowing that I could keep an eye on it and move it later if I needed to.

I clicked my belt loose and went to open my car

door, but as my hand reached for the handle I stopped. I suddenly wondered if actually it might not be such a good idea to let Mr Curtis see the car I drove. In fact, I couldn't see any point either in simply asking the man the same questions Andy had. He'd be sure to tell me what he'd told him, if he even agreed to speak to me at all. I took my hand off the door handle and turned the key again. I pulled out, back into the traffic. I cruised round the one-way system and pulled into the car park thoughtfully provided by the Sainsbury's people.

I sat in my car for a couple of minutes, tapping my thumbs on the steering wheel. Then I got out, opened the boot, and from amongst the pile of stuff I keep in there I pulled out a leather bag. Inside it was a non-iron blue shirt, which I buttoned up over my tee shirt. I dug out a nondescript tie and put that on too, before untying my shoelaces. I ignored a middle-aged woman loading groceries into the back of a Volvo and pulled down my jeans, before stepping into a pair of dark trousers and some old black loafers with a nice polish. A jacket finished the effect. I picked up a briefcase that was also in the boot, took out half of what was in it while making sure that what I needed was in there, and walked back up the High Street.

'Mr Curtis?'

I'd waited until the shop was almost empty, pretending to look at the illuminated menu on the side wall. Then I laid my briefcase flat on the counter. I opened it up, took out a blue plastic clipboard and turned over a few pages. The man behind the counter stared at me.

'Could I speak to . . . Mr George M. Curtis please?'

'He's out,' the man said. It wasn't the same guy as

232

the time before, though there was something very familiar about him. He was a balding, pit bull of a man wearing an Arsenal tee shirt, and if I'd still been on the Force I'd have arrested him just for that. 'Who are you?'

'I'm a health and safety officer, sir,' I announced, with a brisk, professional smile.

I reached into my briefcase again and handed the man another set of credentials that Carl had whipped up for me on his Mac about a year ago; another laminated photocard, but also this time a much folded piece of yellow A4 detailing my rights of entry as a health and safety officer of the Crown. And had I been such an officer I would indeed have had such rights. They explained that I was allowed to inspect all areas of the premises without warning, at any hour of the day or night that I saw fit. That hour, I explained, was now.

'If you'd like to show me through,' I said.

The man shuffled. The one remaining customer had obviously overheard our conversation and thought better of it – the door clanged shut behind him. I was about to ask the man again if he would please show me into the kitchen when the doorway behind him was filled by a large figure in a plain yellow button-down, which gave ample space to the little polo player galloping above the breast pocket on the left-hand side.

'George,' the man said. 'You are in.'

George Curtis didn't look quite so big as I'd remembered him, but then he was no longer doing battle with a very thin kid a good foot shorter than he was. He was still pretty large though; a good six two with round shoulders that didn't look to have gone all the way to fat yet. He had glasses on, which was a slight surprise, as was his manner. He didn't seem fazed to see me, or if he was he didn't show it. He must have been highly confident of his hygiene standards.

'Can I help you?'

His voice was a bigger surprise, perhaps the deepest bass I ever heard. It was pure, cartoon bulldog.

'John Hammond,' I said, feeling like Aled Jones, dueting with Tom Waites. 'Health and Safety.' The other guy handed Curtis my documentation, which he glanced at before giving me a shrug.

'Follow me,' he rumbled.

Carl had created this new ID for me some years ago, when I'd been looking for a thirteen-year-old Turkish boy whom I suspected of working in a restaurant kitchen in Ladbroke Grove. I'd taken his picture in the course of photographing the entire place. But this time I didn't need the camera. I followed George Curtis into a small, clean-looking kitchen space with a chip fryer, a grill, a hotplate and four gas rings. Trying to look as official as possible I set my briefcase down on a steel work surface and took out a thermometer. I opened up the fridge that was nearest to me, slid the thermometer onto the top shelf and closed the door again.

Curtis stood watching me, with his arms folded and a bored though patient expression on his face. He had a broad, flat face with cheeks that did all they could to push themselves forward, his nose small, his forehead slightly scorched from the sun, and a dirty three-day beard. He stood watching me, breathing through his mouth. Remembering the man outside I asked him if the staff wore hats at all times while preparing food.

'Of course,' he said.

I asked him to please show me the hats, which he

did, opening a drawer to reveal a pile of white paper berets.

'In that case can you tell me why the man on the counter isn't wearing one?'

Curtis looked to his right and barked over my left shoulder. He'd hardly left a beat. 'Steve! Put a fucking hat on! How many times do I have to tell you? Huh?'

The other man scurried through and put a hat on before disappearing again. Curtis's mouth opened again and he took a few breaths. I opened the fridge and retrieved my thermometer. I nodded and wrote the reading down, having no idea whether it was cold enough or not.

After that I poked around, looking in cupboards, pulling open drawers and nodding to myself now and then. Curtis didn't seem to mind. I did the job systematically, with occasional glances to see if he looked any more relaxed at all. If he did it would mean I'd missed something, but he just looked bored and stoical; a small businessman having to endure more ridiculous bureaucracy. When I'd finished taking temperature readings and making sure the fire exits were clear I asked Curtis if he could show me the back of the building. He shrugged again and walked past the work surfaces to the rear of the kitchen.

The back door was ajar. Curtis held it open for me and I stepped into a small yard with a mini-skip at one end and a rubbish bin on the left-hand side. There was a small, circular drain in the middle. The yard was enclosed by a seven-foot wall with pieces of loose glass on the top. There was a wooden door in the centre of it, presumably leading out into the alleyway, and after a cursory look around I put my hand on the handle. I pulled, but the door didn't give, and I tried again with the same result. I made a tick on my pad and then held it with both hands down in front of me.

'I take it you keep this door shut,' I said, turning round.

'Of course.' Curtis stuck his hands on his hips.

'At all times?'

'All times.'

'Are you sure, Mr Curtis?'

'Yes I'm sure.'

I left a second and looked the man in the eye.

'I'm afraid that is not what we have been led to believe,' I said. 'We received a report from the police that you had a break-in here.'

'What?'

'A break-in. The police report all such matters to us, when they involve places where food is prepared.'

'They do?'

How the hell did I know? It sounded plausible.

'In case the security of a building threatens public health,' I explained. 'This door, for instance. If it were left open, anyone could have access to your kitchens. People could tamper with the food. And, with the recent problem concerning rubbish removal, there have been a lot of cases of rat infestation reported to us. If this door were left open, rats could easily gain access to your kitchens.'

'It's closed, always.'

I glanced down at my file. 'The police report says that a boy stole in here and that you ejected him. Is that right?' He nodded. 'I find it hard to believe he could have done so if the door was locked,' I said. I looked upwards. 'That's a pretty high wall you've got there.'

George Curtis didn't bother looking upwards but instead he looked at me, very deliberately. He took three slow breaths before a look of sarcastic tolerance settled on his features.

'Watch this.'

Curtis walked over to the dustbin and tied a knot in the bag. He then lifted the bag out of the bin and walked towards the door. Holding the bag in one hand he opened the door and walked out into the alleyway, and I followed him as far as the door. He disappeared into the street and it was a minute or so before he came back, during which time the door was left open.

'See what I mean?' he said.

'I do,' I nodded, 'I do.'

'Normally it's locked. The kid who broke in must have been watching for an opportunity. The door has to be left open sometimes, but it's not for long. What do you want me to do, take the bleeding bags out through the frigging shop?'

I told Curtis that in future it might be an idea to shut the back door on such occasions and come back in the front, or else take a key with him. He shook his head but he didn't argue. He showed me back into the kitchen where I lay my pad and my thermometer in my suitcase. I clicked the clasps and Curtis made as if to show me out.

'Now if you could just show me the staff toilets,' I said.

Curtis definitely hesitated.

'They're upstairs,' he replied. 'I'll just—'

'Up these stairs?'

I pulled open a door before Curtis could get ahead of me and turned right up a narrow stairway. He was right behind me.

'It's the door on the right,' I heard him say. 'Hang on, I'll show you.'

I got to the top quickly and stopped opposite the door. As Curtis lumbered up the stairs I glanced to my left into a large, open-plan apartment with a smooth wooden floor and a huge TV. It was all I could take in before Curtis reached the summit and ushered me into the toilet. I checked it out diligently but I could find no fault with it. When I stepped back out Curtis was standing with his back to the rest of the flat, blocking any view I might have had of his living quarters.

Ten minutes later I was wandering round Sainsbury's, absent-mindedly loading my basket. I don't normally use supermarkets but it was either that or pay a fiver for the car park so I thought, what the hell. I picked up some flat green chillies and some turkey to make a stew later, and bought a couple of bottles of wine. This last activity normally takes me some time but I didn't really concentrate; I was thinking about Curtis. And his flat. His flat was a whole lot nicer than I'd expected and he'd certainly been a tad edgy about me going up there. But what did it show? Not much. He could have simply been fixing his taxes for years to pay for it and that's what he was nervous about. What did interest me though was his explanation about the door. I didn't go for it. I hadn't seen him out there with any rubbish before he threw the boy into the alley. I was sure I would have noticed him, I was watching the street after all, if not for him. It meant that he had either left the door open, and therefore lied to me, a health and safety officer, or else he hadn't and he had lied to Andy. He hadn't simply found the boy in his kitchen after all.

He knew him.

And if he was so keen to hide the fact, he probably knew a lot more besides.

I loaded up the car and pulled out of the car park. I didn't know what to do, but I knew it had to be something, and I didn't want it to be at home. Beachy Head? Instead I drove to my office and opened the mail. I'd hoped that there would be a lot; people to reply to, bills to pay, anything to keep me occupied. But there were only three letters and dealing with them used up as much time as it took my hand to reach over to the waste-paper basket. I stood up and walked down to the café, where Mike poured me a coffee and let me have a couple of rolls that he'd only have binned anyway, seeing as it was the end of the day. Mike didn't say too much. I chewed off half of one of the rolls, and as I was leaning over to drop the remnants on top of the circulars the phone rang. Again I didn't answer, but the call was from Emma Bradley so I picked up before she'd got to the end of her message.

Emma's mother had told her that I wanted to speak to her and that was why she was calling. I arranged to meet her the next day. After putting the phone down I stepped over to my filing cabinet and took out a file containing the self-assessment tax form I'd got from the post office. I took a calculator from my desk drawer and started on my accounts. It seemed as good a time as any to do them. I was making steady progress when Nicky called.

'Hey,' he said, 'Mr Elusive. Where've you been?'

'Hospital mostly,' I said.

'Nothing serious?'

'Very. But not for me. I'm fine. How about your good self?'

'Never better,' Nicky said. He was in a cheerful mood and it was good to hear his voice. 'Thanks for the card by the way.'

'What?'

'My birthday card. Twenty-one today.'

'Your birthday? How the *fuck* was I supposed to know that?'

'You weren't, unless of course you really cared, in which case you would have used your incisive powers of investigation to find out.'

'I'm afraid I don't know which powers you're talking about.'

'Anyway. You know, at least, that my sister is living in London now?'

'I do.'

'Well,' Nicky sounded resigned and I could see his eyebrows raising. 'She's insisting I have some sort of party. It's an excuse for her to meet people more than anything I think, but I can't talk her out of it.'

He seemed as enthusiastic about the idea as I was at the thought of going.

'Tonight?'

'Tuesday. She wanted to hire a place but I managed to talk her into doing it at the bar. So I don't have to move.'

'Right.'

'Which will probably end up costing me a fortune

but also means that I can chuck everyone out whenever I feel like it.'

'Clever.'

'Aren't I? Anyway, I won't be mortally offended if you can't make it, you know that. But you'd better fucking be there anyway.'

'Nicky—'

'And, the lovely Sharon of course. In fact, if you can't make it just send her.'

'Nicky—'

'Just kidding, but it really is about time my sister was in the same room with a woman who's better-looking than her. She comes in the bar all the time and acts like it's hers, like she's some sort of society hostess holding court. I've never seen her even attempt to pay for a drink. And the amount of dickheads I've been introduced to over this last month, Jesus.'

'Nicky—'

'I don't want to hear it. You've got excuses lined up, I can feel them. Come on! Shulpa's invited all the people from her new law firm. Solicitors. They special-ize in corporate mergers. Can you imagine? If I slash my wrists it'll be on your conscience.'

I sighed.

'Billy, come on—'

'I'll do my best to make it,' I said.

'Good man, thanks, and, Billy?'

'What?'

'You don't have to spend *too* long looking for my present.'

I put the phone down and tried to get back to my accounts. But I couldn't concentrate. Her presence was too strong. Instead I went over and over what she'd said to me, refining it, paring it down to the major details. I kept seeing her face, hearing the tone of her voice, as she used all her strength to summon it up from inside her, to tell me what she had to tell me. I felt the same hollowness that I had felt, in my arms and in my chest, and the same dead stillness in my stomach.

Sharon loved me, she hated to hurt me. She told me that the guy, Ronan, had come to work in her office before she and I had ever even got it together, and that she'd started to see him, her first since Luke. She explained to me how liberated she had felt being with him, how she had begun to feel like herself again, for the first time in two years. How she could talk about Luke and what had happened in her own way, how it was just a shit thing that had happened, it wasn't everything, it wasn't her whole life.

Sharon told me that she had been seeing this Ronan for a month. But then she had decided it was me she wanted, and that she was seeing this Ronan because she couldn't really face up to the fact that she was in love with her fiancé's brother. She'd ended it with him, and she and I had been together for more than a year, and everything was fine. Until six months ago. Then it had all started to get too much for her; this living in a cloud, the past in her face all the time, feeling like she could hardly see two feet in front of her. Reading his poems over and over, seeing herself as the tragic lover, holding on to the past through her lover's brother. And then her thing with this Ronan had started up again and she realized that it was him she wanted, not me. Not the memory of my brother, and that night, casting a shadow on even the lightest of things. How we laughed the same, walked the same, and cooked the same food. How we even made love the same. That's what she told me. And how guilty she felt wanting to be free of what had happened, but how she had decided that it just wasn't her fault, that she didn't have to keep paying for it all of her life.

'And neither do you,' she'd said, standing in the doorway, about to leave. 'Neither do you.'

I let the images run through my head until they played themselves out, leaving just a pall of lethargy behind them. I sat back in my chair for ten minutes staring at nothing, until my eyes found the photograph in the frame in front of me. Then I dumped the paperwork I'd been looking at in a file and walked downstairs.

Chapter Three

I got to the gym at seven that night, which was earlier than usual, and I did some work on the machines and the treadmill before the circuit training and the bag. I tried to focus completely, pushing and pulling myself through the strung out tiredness I felt to the borders of a sustained, satisfying pain, squeezing the sweat through my pores in an effort to feel purified, concentrated to a simple, physical experience of the equipment I was using. I felt the initial objections of my body and then the slow change as it took up the challenge I was putting to it. After an hour and a half I felt tight and self-contained, centred on the breath I was moving in and out of my chest.

Sal was working with some young kids in the ring, and watching them made me think of the boy, fighting Curtis in the doorway. He hadn't looked bad. Sal could have done something with that kid. When she'd finished she called me over, and put me in with Des Formay. He had a fight coming up and needed some sparring time. I put thoughts of the kid aside and nodded hi to Des. We touched gloves and waltzed round each other for a few seconds. I tried a few jabs and he responded in kind. In the first I managed to keep him out of the centre of the ring, my reach being an inch or so longer than his, and he had to use up his energy moving round me, trying to get me to chase out after him. But I didn't take the bait and after the bell I felt good. When Des stepped into his corner I saw Sylvester, a wiry old pro who liked to help Sal out, waving his finger, giving him a hard time.

Des got out quicker than I did for the next round and he upped his punch rate. He was working harder now. Des is small for a light heavyweight but he's quick and he's fit, doesn't mind getting hit when he has to and generally gets in more punches than the average. He unsettled me. I began to lose my rhythm. Des wasn't exactly hurting me but he was making it hard for me to put together combinations, constantly making me cover up. It was annoying. I could see Des's eyes beneath his helmet; fixed and hard. He started punching my arms, hitting them as I was forming my punches. It was what Marciano, another undersized fighter, used to do, trying to wear his man down. He went for my arms and my body, putting in more and more effort to close me up. His shots were jarring but they left me irritated rather than in pain. I remembered that Des could be an arrogant fucker sometimes, and that really, I didn't actually like him that much. When we broke for the second I saw Sal, standing with her arms crossed, watching me from behind the ropes. With a confused look on her face she said, '*Concentrate*, will you?'

I took some water from my friend Pete.

In the third, Des carried on with the same tack, but I'd anticipated that. I decided that he could have his flurries; they looked good but they weren't doing that much to me. Des was all show; it was why he'd never made it. I had a bigger punch than him and if I could just rock him with a couple he wouldn't feel so confident in coming forward any more. Then I could use my reach to pick at him. I looked into Des's eyes. I began to have this real desire to beat him, which I hadn't had when I'd been in with him before. But I just couldn't land. His dark eyes were there in front of me and then they were gone. He peppered me with more flack in the ribs and I could feel myself getting more and more angry; he was trying to make me look stupid, relying on his speed. He thought he was Hamed, he wanted to win without respect. I looked into his eyes again; was he laughing at me? I could almost swear he was. I bit down on my shield. I could feel my jaw set, tight.

I let Des do the punching. But then he came too close and I caught him with a left worth about five times what he was throwing. It slid off the top of his helmet but it got him. It felt good. I found myself in the middle of the ring again. He danced to my right. I cut him off. He ducked the other way and I launched another left, harder this time, almost straight through his guard. It was a brave punch, I just stepped in and hit him. His eyes flickered. Yes. I had him, I knew I did. He wasn't laughing now. He started on my arms again but again I stepped in with another big left. He didn't have an answer. It straightened him up. It knocked aside his concentration, for the split second, which was all I needed. His hands were no longer his, they just hung there in the air. He was wide open.

I bit down harder into the shield. I dropped my right shoulder and let it go, my right, all it could be, balance perfect, straight through the centre of his guard, right dead centre between his small, nervous-looking eyes.

Except that it didn't hit him between the eyes. It didn't hit him at all. There was a gap of about two feet between my glove and the top of his head, and the next thing I knew was my back making contact with the canvas. It was followed by my head, bouncing a little with the protector, until I saw light in my eyes. The light was white and uniform and very quiet.

I lay there for a second or two, until the light had stopped being uniform and had become two long strips, two feet apart. I blinked my eyes and focused on them, and a breath let itself out of my body. I closed my eyes. I said fuck, very quietly, and then I pushed myself up onto my elbow.

Sylvester was already unstrapping Des's helmet. When it was off he walked over, and knelt down to me.

'You OK?' he said.

I nodded, and spat out my shield. 'Yes. Fine. Great shot.'

'You're sure you're OK?'

'Absolutely. Really.'

'Good. Well, thanks, Bill, see you later.'

Des went back to have his gloves untied and I got to my knees. I expected Sal to come over but she didn't. She walked round to the other side of the ring and spoke to Des. She didn't even look at me until I'd got myself to my feet. Pete came in and helped me with my helmet and my gloves. When they were off Sal looked at me again.

'Get changed,' she said.

Ten minutes later I was standing with my eyes closed, letting a torrent of steaming hot water gun into the top of my head.

'What the fuck did you think you were doing?'

I opened my eyes. There was nowhere to go. Sal was standing six feet away.

'Christ,' I said. 'Sal, for Chrissake.'

'Makes you feel vulnerable, does it?'

'Sal . . .'

She had her arms folded and she was staring straight at me.

'Much like sparring with a fucking lunatic I should think,' she said. 'Makes you feel real vulnerable. What the hell did you think you were doing?!'

I started to speak but I couldn't find an answer. I looked away from her.

'It's not a real fight, Billy. We have rules, you know. If you wanted a real go at Des you should have told me. More to the point, you should have told him. Think you could beat him, do you?'

'No,' I said. 'No—'

'If that bloody idiot haymaker you tried had connected, Des wouldn't have been back in the ring for months. You were *sparring*. It's a good job he's quick. You could really hurt someone, you know?'

'Sal,' I said. 'I'm sorry. I . . .'

I let the words trail away and shook my head. I put my hands on my hips. I could feel the water running down the small of my back and Sal's eyes on my body. But it wasn't them that made my face burn. Sal's voice softened.

'All right, Billy,' she said. 'All right. I didn't mean to yell.' She left a second and all I could hear was the sound of the water running down into the shower stall. Sal let her left hand fall down to her side. Her face relaxed.

'I'll be upstairs if you want to talk about it,' she said.

I didn't say anything. 'OK?' Her eyes widened and found mine. Then she gave me a tight smile, turned and left me there.

I flipped the shower to 'Off' and stepped out. I dried myself slowly, embarrassed at what a jerk I'd been. Then I caught my reflection in the mirror and my eyes went immediately to my hip bone; but there was nothing there. I dressed quickly and packed up my bag.

Chapter Four

Back in the gym I found Des to apologize to him and he was as gracious as a real prince, saying it was nothing. Sal had got changed herself, and now looked more like an attractive forty-something PR lady than a woman who came from the school of hard knocks, and now ran one. She asked me if I wanted to go for a drink but I shook my head.

'Any time though, Billy, you know that.' She did that John Powers smile and I nodded into it.

'Thanks, Sal,' I said.

It was just about dark now. I walked up the stairs to my flat. There was no flashing light on my machine but I checked it anyway. I thought that maybe one of the Bradleys might have called. But there were no messages. From anyone. I sat on my bed, looking around me at the things I owned: the table, the lamp, the Salgado print on the wall. Everything in the flat looked odd, alien to me. I thought, is this it? Is this what I amount to? This space I live in, the few things in it? There didn't seem to be anything else. I didn't feel like a person, just an amalgamation, a collection of the things on the outside of myself. I shut my eyes, and sat listening to the faint murmur of traffic heading down the Farringdon Road. Then I picked up my copy of the

Tao, but put it back on the bedside table without opening it. I took three cocodamil and got under the covers.

* * *

I was waiting for Emma Bradley in the happily air-
conditioned foyer of the family's apartment complex in
Chalk Farm at nine thirty. Personally, I could easily
have slept much longer, about three days, but Emma
had suggested the time; she always got up early, she
said. I'd buzzed up and been told to wait at the desk,
which I did, watching all the people coming to and fro,
mainly fro. I was reminded of a very orderly, laid-back
hotel, especially seeing as a lot of the residents had
foreign, predominantly American, accents. I guessed
that a lot of the apartments were owned by international companies, who put their overseas staff up
there. I was shaken out of my hypothesis when Emma
stepped out of the lift. I held a hand up to her and she
walked towards me, her hair still wet from the shower.

I followed Emma through to a covered atrium past
the lifts, with comfortable sofas and pot plants surrounding a small pool overfilled with indolent, fantail
goldfish. We sat, and Emma handed me the coffee she'd
brought down for me, asking me if milk no sugar was
OK. I said it was, and took a much needed hit.

Emma wasn't drinking anything. She sat very still,
with her hands folded in the lap of the same cut-off
shorts I'd watched her sleeping in. She wore a simple,
baggy blue tee shirt, a pair of clean white trainers and,
most noticeably of all, a look of real exhaustion. There
were no lines or wrinkles on her clear skin, but nevertheless her young face looked old, as if the ghost of an

ancient woman were living inside her skin, looking out through her heavy brown eyes.

Before I'd managed to say anything to her, Emma asked me if I was making any progress tracking down her sister's murderer. I smiled at the girl and put my coffee cup on a side table.

'I've only just started,' I said. 'And as I told your father, it'll probably be the police who do that. What I can do probably won't mount up to much, and it might not even mount up to anything at all.'

Emma nodded, seeming to accept what I'd said. She tucked her legs underneath her on the sofa. 'But, you're still looking for that boy?'

'I am,' I said. 'That's all I can do really. I might find him before the police do, but either way he'll turn up.'

'And he did it, didn't he? It was him?' She sounded desperate to be told that it was.

'I don't know, but it does seem most likely. He was there at the time and we do know he was living with your sister. The fact that he ran away does seem to indicate that he had some sort of involvement in some-thing that wasn't legal.' Emma nodded again. 'But we have to find him first,' I said.

'Right. But you'll tell me, won't you? The police won't tell us anything.'

'I will,' I said.

I'd put a suit on that morning in an effort to feel more together. I took a notebook out of my jacket pocket and asked Emma to run off the names of all Lucy's friends that she could think of. I'd check these against the names Andy had collected, to see if there were any extra. I also got Emma to tell me the names of all the festivals Lucy had gone to, and all of the gigs she could remember. I asked her if she knew of any places in London Lucy had ever spoken of, clubs, bars and the like. Emma just remembered that Lucy really liked Camden, that they had both gone there a couple of times with their father. Then I asked her a question that had suddenly occurred to me.

'You were looking for her, weren't you?' I said. 'At Camden tube.' She nodded, warily. 'You told me that you wanted to speak to her, to tell her how sorry you were, how much you loved her.' Her eyes flicked down. 'You didn't see her, did you, Emma?'

Emma's eyes flashed up to mine and her mouth opened. She looked horrified at what I'd said. Then she shook her head and pulled her knees up in front of her chest.

I didn't have anything else relevant left to ask. Instead I asked her how she was.

'I'm OK.'

I smiled. 'You don't have to tell me that,' I said. 'It can't be true. It's a horrible thing that has happened and you can't deny that.'

'I know, I know.' Emma pushed out a long breath. 'But you can't be upset *all the time*. You have to pretend, don't you?'

'If it gets you through the day.'

'Not the day,' she said. 'That's easy. It's the rest that I need to get through.'

It felt good to focus on someone else's problems. I asked Emma how her parents were and she had a lot more to say about them. I think that parents often forget that their children worry about them as well.

Emma said that her father had gone very quiet and distant, and that her mother was trying to be the strong one.

'But I know it's all rubbish. She doesn't sleep either, and unlike me she works all the time. She's like a car that's run out of petrol but just doesn't stop. And you can't tell her, you can't say a word. She doesn't listen. I can't get anywhere near her.'

'I'm sure your concern is a great help to her,' I said. 'I'm sure she can feel that.'

Emma stood up and made to show me out, but I asked her if her mother was home. Emma said she was. We rode the lift together and I let Emma get ahead of me to announce my arrival. When she told me to come in, I followed her into the apartment, where her mother was sitting at her desk in the corner working on the computer that I'd noticed idle before. Mrs Bradley swivelled in her chair but didn't get up. She did say hello, and she held her hand out, which I moved forward to shake.

At that moment I saw Mr Bradley through the French window, sitting on the slab bench with his back resting between a gap in the profusion of roses. He was reading a newspaper. When he saw me he folded his paper hurriedly and got up.

'I'm sorry to interrupt,' I said, trying to sound matter-of-fact. 'Please don't get up. I'm afraid it isn't anything much.'

Mr Bradley was up now though and he came inside. His shoulders and arms still had a heavy cast to them and the hope that had rushed into his eyes on seeing me reverted to the look of resignation that was planted deep in his face. He asked me if he could get me anything.

'No, no. I just wanted to ask Mrs Bradley if she had had time to mention to the woman in the post office that I'd be coming down? To Ravensey, to look through Lucy's room?'

I turned to the computer table, where Emma was standing by her mother, her mother's hand in hers.

'Yes,' Mrs Bradley said. 'Mrs Dearing. She wanted me to ask you when you'd be going.'

'I'd planned on Thursday,' I told her.

'What time?'

'Early afternoon, I think. If that's OK?'

'Of course. I might even be around to let you in myself. I can do a lot from here but there are some documents I need.'

'Right,' I said. 'Well, I'll see you there then.'

I thanked Mrs Bradley and said goodbye to her husband, who immediately turned back to the roof garden with his paper. I walked to the door and Emma followed me. I said there was no need, but she insisted on accompanying me as far as the lift and pressing the button for me.

'Thanks for coming round,' she said, as we waited.

'It's nothing, I did need to speak to you.'

'I know. But it was good. I mean, it's good to have someone to talk to. I can't talk to them.' She looked back towards the flat. 'And there's no one else in London. And at home, they're just so full of sympathy. I feel like a leper. Everyone *knows*. So, thank you for listening.'

'It really is nothing,' I said. 'Any time you want.'

The lift came and the door opened and I stepped in. Emma held her hand out, probably having seen her parents do the same and I leant forward to take it. We shook hands awkwardly and then I took my hand away, pushed the ground floor button. I smiled at Emma as the door closed.

Downstairs I stood by the atrium and let out a yawn, which had been waiting inside my body like a racehorse that can see the paddock. I rubbed my eyes with the heels of my hands and thought for a second. I walked behind the reception desk towards the back door that leads out of the building to the car park. I got to the door and looked at the lock. It needed a key from the outside but not the inside. There was a latch right inside the mechanism, just by the bolt, and I clicked it down. Then I walked back into the foyer. I walked past the reception desk towards the front entrance but stopped when I heard a voice I recognized.

'Mrs Bradley, please,' the voice said. 'Apartment 516.'

'Are you expected?' the receptionist asked.

'I will be, when you tell her I'm here.'

'And your name, *sir*.'

'Clay.'

'Right. And you have a first name I presume, or is it just Mr?'

'It's Chief Inspector, laddie. That'll do.'

I stood by the door and watched Clay lumber slowly towards the lifts, swaying gently from side to side like an ocean liner in a light swell. It seemed that he was beginning to have the same idea I was.

Chapter Five

I spent the rest of the day showing the boy's picture round Camden, wearing a baseball hat in case George Curtis came by, but more to keep off the sun; it was hotter than ever, and muggy too, a smudge of haze putting the air out of focus. Camden looked strange without the bags of rubbish, which had all finally been removed from the kerbs and pavements. The place was emptier but it still had that tatty, tired feel to it. Even though the bins were now empty, Coke cans and polystyrene chip cartons still found their way onto the tarmac.

None of the people I showed the photograph to had seen the boy. I left copies with several of the people I spoke to, which all had my number on the back, and told them that it would be worth calling me if they saw the boy. I dished out change to most of the people, figuring that it wouldn't hurt to spread a little goodwill. I ate dinner in a Mexican place with a view of the street and spent the rest of the night standing outside various pubs with a pint in my hand, keeping my eyes open.

And that's basically what I did for the next three days. I got good at pinball in video arcades round Leicester Square, and drank a gallon of espresso outside cafés in Soho. I drove to Finsbury Park to see my friend

Joe Nineteen, a former bus conductor who gets his mates on the network to keep their eyes open for me sometimes. He dished out some of his famous goat curry to me and we chatted for a while. I read the *Evening Standard* at bus stops in Hoxton, and Kilburn, and Brixton, and down by the Embankment, and handed out a lot of pictures at Liverpool Street, Waterloo, on the Strand and outside theatres, anywhere the homeless hang out in any numbers. I went to the squats that I knew of, the basements of tower blocks waiting to be pulled down, and I kicked aside used needles and used condoms and got told to get fucked by gangs of kids giving off as much suspicion and hostility as I'd felt at their age. I smelled a lot of stale piss and read a lot of graffiti, though nowhere did I see the words 'Missing murder suspect woz ere'. I got up early in the mornings and went to bed late at night, spending the entire day wandering around, glad of the dull, routine nature of what I was doing, glad of the simple, effortless concentration it required.

I didn't speak to Sharon. I picked the phone up a few times but never managed to dial all of the number. It seemed that I had a lot of things to say to her, but that they were all of them too late. They'd only sound like I was making them up. I thought perhaps that she might phone, and I really didn't know what I'd say if she did, but as she didn't I was saved having to confront that particular dilemma.

So, work. While I searched for the boy I tried to run various scenarios through my mind, of the different people I thought might have been involved in Lucy's death. It was more to cut the boredom than anything else. The boy was involved, but how? Her family were

involved, insomuch as the seeds of Lucy's disappearance from home seemed to have been sowed amongst
them, by a tough mother, an indulgent father and a
brainy sister. But did it go any further? And Curtis, did
he know the boy after all? Was it him who had killed
Lucy, and set the lad up? And if so, how could I prove
it? The answer was that I couldn't, not while the boy
was out there. So I just kept looking, with something at
the back of my mind, which nagged at me, which
mocked me for not noticing it. It was something off to
the side like a member of the chorus who's actually the
biggest talent in the show, something I'd looked at,
stared at even, but I hadn't seen.

Whatever it was, and however hard I scoured my
mind it didn't come to me. I couldn't find the boy either
and the time I spent looking for him was pretty dull.
Only two things stood out. On the third morning Andy
Gold caught me at home. He had some news.

'Lee,' he said, shouting above the usual incident
room mayhem. 'He's sixteen and his name's Lee Finch.'

I jotted the name down. 'How'd you find out?'

'We got a call from a care home. Don't you love it
that they're called that? They used to look after him, on
the infrequent occasions that he hadn't legged it from
the place. Anyway, some of the beat boys have been
doing the rounds and one of the staff pegged him from
the photo you took. They sent one from their files, it's
the same kid.'

'Where's the home?'

'Lambeth,' he said. 'Nicholas Court's the name.
They sent us a biog too.'

'And?'

'The usual stuff. Taken from his mother, fostered,

too unruly, five different homes. No real form though. The good thing is he's never been outside London, so he probably won't know of anywhere else to go. Other than that it doesn't help much. He's an elusive little bugger.'

'You're telling me. I haven't come up with shit.'

I drove down to Nicholas Court, which looked like a former workhouse, and was situated in the streets behind the Stockwell Road, in what is primarily a Portuguese area. I'd been to one of the restaurants there a few times for the bacalau. The home itself was sterile and basic, very much an institution with its wire mesh windows and hard fibre carpets. But the staff were friendly enough, and they told me what they could about Lee. He hadn't been there for that long, and quite a few of the staff themselves were new, but Janet, the head of the place, remembered him well. She was a kind-looking woman in her fifties with very short, grey hair.

'He was a cocky young boy,' Janet told me, with a smile. 'Very sure of himself. Not like most of the ones in here, who just pretend that they are. You got the impression that one day he might do very well, he might even be one of the ones you see being interviewed on TV in ten years' time – if he stayed out of trouble. Something which, it seems, he hasn't managed to do.'

The home catered for twelve- to sixteen-year-olds, and Janet let me speak to some of the kids. They had more to say. I wrote down a list of the places they told me Lee hung out, and some names of people he hung out with. I got the impression that Lee was a popular kid, especially with the girls. They all teased each other about fancying him and one girl, who hadn't said anything, was accused by the rest of sleeping with him.

'I never,' the girl said. 'I never. You're just jealous.'

I asked the girl if she'd heard from Lee since he'd left, six months ago, but she said she hadn't. She had no idea where he was.

'And I don't care neither,' she said. 'Anyway, what's he done? You and the filth, what you want him for?'

'Maybe nothing,' I said. 'We just need to speak to him.'

'Yeah, right,' the girl said. 'You just need to speak to him.'

I handed out my card, and the staff and kids all told me they'd give me a call if they either saw Lee, or thought of anything else I might want to know. I didn't really hold out much hope.

The other thing that stood out was the conversation I had later that same day, with one of the girls at King's Cross, a tall girl who'd told me she was Italian but was probably one of the growing number of Albanians now working the street in London. She hadn't seen the boy I was looking for, she said, but she'd definitely seen Natalie. She'd watched her walking around in front of the station, only minutes before she'd gone down to the underground, minutes before she'd jumped in front of a train. The girl had even spoken to her, asking if Natalie was OK. Natalie had been wandering around aimlessly, crying and talking to herself.

'I read what happened to her,' the hooker said to me. 'Those drugs, it's terrible.'

I asked her to tell me what she remembered and the girl said that Natalie had been dropped off at King's Cross, by a woman who gave her some money. The hooker thought the woman was her mother, but she didn't fit the description of the woman I'd seen at the Whittington; she'd been small, the girl said, only in her late thirties, and it wasn't a very expensive car that Natalie had got out of, though she couldn't tell me what make it was, or the colour. Neither could she tell me what the woman looked like beyond her size.

'I just know this girl was not happy. Her face, not happy. It make me feel bad. Maybe I should have talked to her more, help her, I don't know . . .'

'You didn't know what she was going to do,' I said. 'How could you have?'

The girl nodded and I gave her the rest of the pack of cigarettes that I'd bought to hand out. She lit one and I took the chance to see what an attractive girl she was, far too good-looking for the area, really. At that point the girl's pimp came up. He'd obviously been watching us talking and he wanted to know whether I wanted to stop messing around, and fuck the girl, or not.

'She good,' the man said. 'Believe me. She fuck you good.'

The girl looked a little embarrassed but smiled at me. I thanked her for her time and left her there, walking up to a café on Judd Street.

*　*　*

I saw him later that night. I was standing outside Centrepoint, having just walked along Oxford Street and through Soho handing out photographs. He simply walked past me and down the steps into the tube station. I was shocked. I stood there for a second or two. I didn't have any kind of reaction at first but then it started to come. The fucker. The little fucker. Without having any sort of a plan I followed him into the station and just caught sight of him through the rush-hour crowd, walking onto the Northern Line escalator. The feeling in me grew. It had lain dormant ever since that night when I'd found Lucy. I'd tried to ignore it. But I couldn't ignore it any more.

I bought a ticket and passed through the gate, walking quickly down the escalator. I still didn't know what I intended doing and I didn't take any measures to stop him seeing me. I didn't care if he did. He was out of sight, having turned towards one of the platforms, the northbound or the south, and I hurried up, not wanting him to get on a train before I could catch up with him.

I checked the northbound platform first and he wasn't there. Knowing he must be on the other one made me slow down and be a little circumspect. I still didn't know what I was going to do but I couldn't see the point of letting him notice me. The feeling in me was now a coldness, and my arms felt unnaturally light. I remembered the feeling I'd had that night; not the pain, more the outraged helplessness, the sense of being used, so casually set upon. I went down to the furthest platform entrance and carefully moved back up. He was there, standing close to the edge, his nose in an *Evening Standard*. When the train came I let him step aboard and then hurried to get on the carriage next to his.

I stood by the door in the crush, looking at him through the window. He'd managed to grab a seat and was still immersed in the back pages. I stared at him, not able to stop my nose setting into a frown of pleasure at seeing him. He got off at Kennington and I merged into the crowd behind him in the lift and then out through the gates onto the street. He turned left out of the tube, and even though quite a few other people did the same thing I began to worry that he'd be bound to notice me as the crowd thinned out, he'd be sure to feel me behind him. I was beginning to have a plan now, not one of my own but something that was just coming to me as I trailed after him. Not something rational but which I knew I was going to follow nevertheless. Sometimes life just blows you along like a dandelion seed in the breeze. There's nothing you can do.

I didn't need to worry about being spotted because he only lived a minute from the tube, in a small yellow-brick property that looked like a council house. He opened a small iron gate and then turned a couple of locks on a dark brown wooden door. Then he was gone. He hadn't even looked round. I walked past the house, turned a corner, and then crossed to the other side of the junction. I stood for a minute or two, wishing I had my car, and then turned towards the fleapit of a pub I was standing outside. I went in the place, empty except for me, and sat next to the window with a pint.

Sitting there I realized exactly where I knew him from. When I'd seen him outside York's, arguing with the man, I couldn't place him. But now I saw him clearly. He was at Hendon, the police training college, barking out orders to us new recruits, pulling that cliché got-to-be-tough-you-bunch-of-pussies line. I was OK, he had nothing on me, no way in, but I remembered the grief he gave a young Asian woman there, the snide viciousness that stopped about a centimetre from sexist and racist abuse, but never quite got there. How he

loved making her look stupid. I remembered resenting
the power he had, which was especially galling knowing
as we all did that he must have been a pretty fuck
useless copper to have ended up doing his time teaching us.

I waited an hour or so, until the street was much
emptier. I was worried that he might not be alone in
his house, but I'd seen him use two keys to unlock, and
no one else had shown up. That was clear enough. I
left the pub and stepped into a utility store next door,
where I bought various items including a selection of
magazines and a pack of gum. I crossed over, opened
up the small gate the man had gone through, and
walked up to the door. I took the gum from my mouth,
stuck it over the eyehole and rang the bell.

The door had a wooden hood over it, a kind of mini
porch. I put my shopping bag down. When I heard
footsteps from inside I took hold of both sides of it and
lifted myself up, so that my feet were suspended in
front of the door about two thirds of the way to the top.
I figured that even if the door had a chain on, it
wouldn't hold if I caught it right. I heard the guy stop,
probably to take a look at who was there, but then
decide to open up anyway when he couldn't see anything. As soon the latch gave I kicked out with all I had
and the door smacked hard into the man on the other
side of it, jolting him fast back into his house. There
was no chain. I dropped down from the porch and got
inside quickly where I saw him, on the floor of a short,
narrow hall, dazed, on his back. I pushed the door to,
gently, and took the couple of steps towards him. I
kicked him in the balls about as hard as I could.

He was in too much pain to see me. Not that I cared

if he did. I really didn't think he'd call the police. Not after what he'd paid three guys to do. In the living room I found a large cushion and took the cover off it, before placing it over the man's head. Before the cover went over I remember thinking that he looked like Van Morrison, and hoping that I didn't see this little prick's face every time I fancied listening to *Astral Weeks*. I saw that there was no blood on his head but he was going to have a bump that would have scared Tiger Woods. When the cover was on him I went out and brought in the shopping, before shutting the door behind me. And there was a chain. I shook my head and tutted. Some people can be *so* careless.

I didn't hit him very much more. Just enough to calm him down, and to persuade him it would be best if he did what I told him. I got his shirt off OK and his slippers weren't a problem, but he began to squirm when I dug my fingers into the doughy flab of his white belly for the button to his trousers. I don't know what he thought I had in mind. I got the trousers off though, in spite of his resistance, and when I saw the state of his pants I figured he must just have been a little embarrassed at his level of personal hygiene. They weren't nice. They came down easily enough though and pretty soon he was lying there clad only in a pillowcase for a hat, and his birthday suit. Neither of them suited him.

Through the cushion cover he demanded to know what the hell I wanted, but I told him to hush up. I'd bought some washing line from the store but I had an inspiration. He was a former policeman who was now a private dick with the renowned Sirius Investigations. He was bound to have some handcuffs lying around somewhere. I found them, and used them, and then dragged him into the living room where I had a quick look around. Then I fetched the bag from the hall. I took out the washing line and the gaffa tape and the golf ball that I had, bizarrely, been able to purchase in the store opposite. I didn't have a clue where the nearest golf course was.

My mind saw exactly how it should be, and though it was a bit of a struggle, eventually I managed it. First, I got him standing up, and I used the belt from his trousers as a ligature for his neck. Then I attached the belt to some clothes line, which I then wound round a built-in cupboard door a foot or so above his head. I wound another section of line round his balls, tight, and tied that to the handcuffs, which I had transferred to the front of his body. Following which, standing behind him, I pulled the pillowcase from over his head.

'You have a cleaner,' I said. I'd seen a note he'd left her on the kitchen table. 'When's she coming again?'

He shook his head, trying to get free. There was no way he'd manage it. 'Not till the morning. Please, if you want money . . .'

I pulled a stretch of gaffa out and wound it round his eyes, and then stood in front of him again. I dropped the key to the cuffs on the carpet beneath him, so that it may have looked like he'd dropped it by mistake, and got stuck. Then I opened his mouth like a horse's, and managed to stuff the golf ball in there without getting bitten, before securing it in place with more gaffa. I made sure he could breathe through his nose. Before I left I took a couple of pictures of him with his own camera, removing the film. I made a mental note to explain it to Carl at the repro shop, before getting it developed. I didn't want Carl thinking they were my holiday snaps. I put the film in my pocket, wondering how long I should leave it before sending copies in to his colleagues at Sirius, and I took the gay porn mags I'd bought and spread them liberally around the room. Finally, I went in the kitchen, where I found a banana, which I left on the floor just behind him.

The little fat man standing trussed and naked in front of me looked absolutely terrified, even though I couldn't see his eyes. I slapped him lightly on the cheek, in kind of an affectionate way.

'Try not to struggle,' I said, in as soothing a voice as I could find. 'It'll just tighten things up. Your cleaner will come eventually. You're just going to have a very, *very* long night. Oh, and in the morning you're going to have quite a lot of explaining to do.'

He started to protest at that, but of course I couldn't make out what he was saying. I walked out into the hall but turned and popped my head back into the living room.

'I hope you've learned a lesson,' I said. 'Always, *always*, put the chain on.'

Chapter Six

The light on my machine was blinking at me. I'd got back from Kennington at around seven.

'Billy.' It was a female voice, followed by a long gap. 'This is Emma Bradley. I was just calling to, well just to chat really. I hope you don't mind me calling, you did say I could. I'll try you again.'

'Billy, Nicky, just reminding you about tonight. Come any time. The earlier the better, but Shulpa's in a feisty mood so we'll probably be up late. See you later.'

There was no message from Sharon. I hadn't spoken to her and I had begun to wonder if I would ever do so again. I sat back on my futon as the machine rewound itself, and looked round my flat. It seemed like the first time that I had been there in ages, just hanging out. The idea of Nicky's party almost made my skin crawl; noise, people, idiots asking me the same stupid questions about my job. And the questions Nicky would ask. There was also the fact that I was in the middle of something, and I never feel right about going out with a big case on the go. The thought of it gnawed away at the almost decent mood that I was in; I could feel myself sinking down into a dark, dank lake, right in the very centre of myself.

But I knew I had to go, at least for a while. I let

myself imagine a really strained and miserable evening but then I thought no, fuck it. I sat and thought how I could handle it. Drugs sprang to mind, but though Nicky was bound to be able to put his hands on some decent stuff, their outcome was unpredictable. Alcohol, the same. Then I had an idea that struck me as both odd and perfect at the same time and I reached for the phone.

'Hello.' Her voice was deep and relaxed.

'It's Billy.'

'Oh, hi. How are you?'

'I'm fine,' I said. 'I'm just calling to apologize for the other day.'

'Don't worry,' Sal laughed, 'really. Actually, I think I should apologize too, running in on you like that.'

'That's OK, you were concerned for Des. Anyway, I just wondered what you were doing, how late you were staying tonight.'

'Not much later than now, as it happens. It's pretty quiet and Sylvester said he doesn't mind closing up. Why, do you fancy a pint?'

'Well,' I said, 'it's a friend of mine's birthday and he's having a party in the bar he owns. The Old Ludensian, on St John Street?'

'I know it! Pete goes there. You both helped your friend out, is that right?'

She was talking about the time that my pal Pete from the gym and myself had 'talked' a cuckolded and very angry minor crim into letting Nicky keep his kneecaps.

'That's right. Anyway, do you fancy it?'

'Sure.'

'And how about supper first?'

'At your place? Great. I've always wondered where tough Mr Rucker goes home to when he hangs up his gloves.'

I was going to settle for reheated chilli that night but I thought it was a bit of an insult so I nipped out onto the market, filling a couple of bags with chicken, sweet potatoes, polenta, plantains and coriander amongst the usual. I enjoyed the shopping, talking with the shy Afghan lady, and when I got back I cranked the Red Pony Suite and rolled my sleeves up. I put the chicken in to roast, on top of the sweet potatoes, lemons and some lime leaves, and I mashed the plantains with some polenta, mixing in some chopped fresh chillies, a little beer, the coriander leaves and an egg. I left that to settle and jumped in the shower and this time Sal waited until I was out of it before arriving. The buzzer went just as I was pulling on a tee shirt.

When Sal reached the top of the stairs I told her it was good to see her and we kissed hello. It felt a little awkward; I'd never kissed my boxing coach before. Sal followed me into the flat and stood, taking a look around.

'Nice place. Very minimal.'

'Yes,' I said. 'Some people go on about Feng Shui but I've got another method. Laziness.'

'Whatever works. Great smell too, by the way.'

'Thanks,' I said.

Sal handed me a bottle of wine, which I was almost astonished to see was a Montus '85. She saw my face and smiled.

'It was my husband,' she told me, following me into the kitchen. 'He was into wine in a big way. He invested in the stuff but he couldn't half drink it. I've heard you banging on too so I thought I'd dig out something decent. This all right?'

'It's more than more than all right.'

'Well, good,' Sal said.

I asked Sal to choose some music and she put on Oscar Peterson's versions of Bach, a CD that had been Luke's, while I fried up the sticky mixture I'd made. The Madiran deserved decanting, which I did, and it was unbelievable. The plantain fritters weren't bad either, going well with the chicken. We had a green salad and I dug out some goat's cheese that I'd picked up at the Neal's Yard store near Borough Market, when I'd been on my travels over the last few days. I put some coffee on the stove and Sal and I both munched away at cantucinni biscuits. Sal told me that my cooking was just as good as my boxing, but I didn't know whether this was a compliment.

'I don't often find myself flat on my arse in the kitchen,' I said.

The conversation was easy and interesting and the evening turned out exactly as I'd hoped. I tried to keep my mind off Lee Finch and Lucy Bradley but every once in a while I could feel them hovering at the edge of my consciousness. They would have come a lot closer if I was with someone I didn't care for, but Sal had an ironic sense of humour and a rich laugh that sat close to the surface, and even though we'd never been alone like this before the time went by and I never felt even slightly uneasy. We joked about some of the people at the gym and then spoke about fighters, the ones who inspired us. After kicking round various names we had to agree that in the end it all came back to Ali.

'People forget,' Sal said, 'when they talk about all the important stuff he did, the race stuff and throwing his medal in the river. They forget just what a simply amazing fighter the man could be.'

Sal talked about the fighters she'd seen when her husband was alive, the people she'd met. They included a very old and frail Billy Wells, whom her father had actually seen box as a boy. She told me about being ringside at the Nigel Benn–Gerald McLellan fight, what an amazing night it had been, until it all went wrong and McLellan ended up fighting a second battle, this time for his life.

'You could tell as soon as he took the count,' she told me. 'Just sitting on his heels. You could tell what was wrong. One man shouldn't have that much courage. It took him way past what his body could stand, it made him deaf to what his body was telling him. If there's one thing I'd tell any boxer, it's try your best but know when you're beat. Anything more, it just can't be worth it.'

She told me that the look on Benn's face, after what was in reality an amazing victory, was one of the most terrible things she had ever seen.

At ten thirty I excused myself, telling Sal I was just going to have a quick shave.

'Don't bother,' she said, 'it suits you.'

I took her advice but did decide to put a shirt on and change out of my Levi's. I also used the phone to call the police, telling them I was a neighbour who'd seen something strange through the window of the house next door in Kennington. I didn't want the little shit strangling himself to death trying to get out of the position I'd left him in. When I came back into the kitchen Sal was halfway through the washing up. After dragging her forcefully from the sink we caught a cab on Rosebery Ave and rode down to Nicky's, making the journey in less than five minutes. She insisted on paying for it. The door was open and we pushed our way through the mêlée to the area at the back that Nicky reserves for parties. Once we'd made it along the length of the bar on the left-hand side we were met by a very tall, Asian beauty with luxuriant, jet-black hair, in a red sheath dress, which looked like Mr Valentino had spray-painted it on her himself. I told her who I was and she broke into a wide smile, holding out five long red talons for me to negotiate. I found her hand, shook it, and introduced her to Sally.

Shulpa told me that Nicky often mentioned me, and that she was very intrigued, never having met a private detective before. She began to ask me exactly what I did, not taking a whole lot of notice of my friend, when Nicky appeared at her elbow.

'Leave him alone,' he said. 'He's taken.'

Shulpa screwed her nose up at Nicky, smiled, and said she'd see us later, before disappearing into the crowd, which was largely made up of middle-aged men still in their work suits, their ties pulled open like loosened nooses. I handed Nicky the two bottles of Ridge I'd brought along and asked him how he was.

'Terrible,' he said. 'Terrible. Everyone keeps telling me how great my bar is. If this lot start coming in regular I'm going to have to sell the place. It looks like something out of Ally Mac fucking Beal. They'll start dancing in a minute.'

I laughed, and introduced Nicky to Sal. Nicky is a tall, long-boned guy around my age, with thick, shiny crow-black hair and light dark skin given by his Indian mother and English father. Nicky is very rarely found without a smile on his face, be it felt or worn, and he is *always* found in a very well-cut suit. Probably even in the shower. As well as maintaining his own style, the word handsome, an old-fashioned word, could have been invented for him. Sharon used to assure me that he was, in fact, too good-looking, but I think she was just being kind. Added to this is the fact that he is witty, intelligent, and has a quality so seldom found in London that it really stands out in my friend. He is genuinely interested in people. When I first met him this was what struck me most of all. How many people in the city ever even bother to ask you what you do, let alone what you think about things?

Nicky smiled broadly at Sal, making a big fuss of her, and called over to Carla behind the bar for a bottle of champagne. I noticed that it wasn't the house brand. He asked Carla to put the Ridge somewhere safe. When the fizz came he poured three glasses and led us to a table littered with cards and wrapping paper. All the time he was his professionally charming self but I could tell that he was puzzled, even though I knew he wouldn't say anything until we were alone. He knew that I would have offered apologies, if there were any to offer, without him having to ask.

We sat at the table for the half an hour it took for Sal and Nicky to finish the champagne. I didn't feel that much like drinking. They made impressive inroads into a second one too. Nicky joked with Sal about the gym, asking her if it was OK for him to come down sometime; not to train, but to watch me getting hit, preferably by someone very big. Sal said sure, and asked Nicky about the time when Pete and myself had had to help him out. He shivered, and said he still got nightmares; but not about the villain. About the guy's wife.

'Now she *was* terrifying,' Nicky said.

Shulpa came over and dragged Nicky off. He excused himself, and when he was gone Sal's laughter relaxed into a look of gentle concern, and she rested her arms on the table.

'So?' she said. I didn't need to ask what she meant. I shrugged.

'The obvious, I suppose.'

'Bugger.'

'Bugger indeed.'

Sal smiled. 'Didn't need me yelling at you then?'

'Shouldn't have been there in the first place,' I said.

'No. But we don't always do what we should when that happens. It's not just some girl either, is it?'

'No. No it isn't.'

'I didn't think so,' Sal said.

Sal let out a breath and smiled at me. I smiled back, and lifted my glass. I was glad Sal realized that there was some sort of excuse for the way I'd acted in the gym, and I was glad too that she could tell there wasn't a lot more I wanted to say on the subject. She didn't press me. Instead, she told me what it had been like when her husband had been killed. Her simple frank manner surprised me, making me feel very quiet inside. She told me that it had happened as a result of a long-running feud between the people he worked with and another local gang. She'd heard the car bomb from her flat, she said, and thought it was the IRA. She told me that she always knew it was possible Mike would get hit, but that nothing could have prepared her for the way she felt when he did.

'I know it's a cliché,' she said, 'but something in me died too, as soon as I found out. A whole part of me went dead, just as dead as Mike was, and it never came back to life.'

Sal's dark amber eyes took on a look of real frailty, as memories of her husband came to her. She poured out the last of the champagne and it struck me as odd, given what we were talking about. She told me about how she had met Mike Dawes, how her lower middle-class family had hated the handsome East End tearaway their daughter fell for.

'I still don't talk to my mum that often,' she said, with a deep frown. 'She never said as much, but at the funeral I could tell she was thinking, "I knew this would happen" rather than "my poor daughter". I could see the shame on her face at having to stand in the same church as some of the people who were there. I think she might even have been glad it happened, hoping I might be able to start again. I was still only thirty-one. But there was no way. Mike was a hard act to follow.'

'There's been no one else?'

'No one serious,' she said. She laughed at some flash then shook her head. 'I've tried pretending once or twice but it's no use. I've accepted it now. I'm happy the way I am.'

Sal sat back and thanked me again for dinner and we chinked glasses. Our eyes met and we both smiled at each other. Sal pushed some hair behind an ear, but kept smiling at me. For some reason I thought of her standing there in the shower and I suddenly felt very embarrassed and very young. I broke the look and there was silence for a second, until Sal remembered a joke she'd been told. It was something about a man who had an orange for a head, and though it was pure nonsense it struck me as the funniest thing I had ever heard. We both ended up screaming with laughter, which resulted in Sal going off to use the toilet. I sat back, and Nicky took the opportunity to come over. He looked concerned and it annoyed me at how perceptive my friend could be. I was actually having a really good time, enjoying listening to Sal talk, finding her strong forty-something candlelit features very easy on my eyes. I knew it would help to have a long chat with Nicky sometime soon, but right then, as they say, I just didn't want to go there.

I could tell he was going to ask me but I was saved by Shulpa, who joined us at the table and took control of the conversation. She chatted away about all the things she'd been doing in London, while Nicky sat back in his chair with his arms folded, looking bored as a Brazilian at a test match heading for a draw. I gave him a secret wink and he moved his head from side to side. He made me laugh. He tried to look pissed off, but I could tell how much he loved his sister, how happy he really was to have her around. I'd noticed earlier, how he kept his eyes on her, from wherever he was in the room.

Sal came back from the toilet and the four of us chatted for a while. I say the four of us, Sal didn't say that much. I could see her looking at Shulpa without a lot of fondness. When Nicky asked if she wanted anything else to drink she thanked him, but said it was time she made tracks. I stood up too, and said I'd call her a cab.

'You'll be lucky,' Shulpa said. 'We've just ordered five, and they told us they'd be thirty minutes, minimum. Why don't you stay?'

Sal said that she was happy to wait, but I said I'd drive her home; it was only a fifteen-minute walk to my flat where we could pick up my car. Nicky reached in his pocket and came out with a set of car keys.

'Take mine,' he said, 'it's right outside. And more to the point, it works.'

'Ho ho ho,' I said. 'There's no need.'

'Go on, I'll probably kip here tonight anyway.'

'Well, if you're sure. Cheers. I'll drop it straight back.'

'Whenever,' Nicky said. 'And thanks for coming. And the Ridge.'

'Just make sure you don't drink it unless I'm here,' I told him.

'Oh, I get it. Don't worry. But let's make it sooner rather than later, OK?' Nicky stood up and came round to us. I kissed Shulpa goodbye and she told me that it was up to Nicky's friends to show her round London. Nicky told her that she wouldn't want to go to the places I'd take her. He shook my hand and kissed my friend.

'Sally, it was lovely to meet you.'

'You too,' Sal said. 'Thanks a lot. And come down any time.'

'I might just do that,' Nicky said.

Sal and I didn't say a lot as we drove to Crouch End in Nicky's four-year-old Audi. The atmosphere was as

279

quiet and comfortable as the car. As we were pulling into her street, she said, 'That was a real treat, Billy. I want to thank you.'

'For me too. I was dreading it, if the truth be told.'

'Yes,' she said. 'I know that one.'

I slowed down and looked for a space.

'Nicky's a very nice guy.'

'He is,' I agreed. 'One of the best.'

'And his sister. Stunning.'

'If you like that kind of thing,' I said. Sal told me which of the houses was hers, and I pulled into the kerb and killed the engine.

'She liked you,' Sal said. 'I could tell.'

'Oh, really.'

'Really. Women can always spot it. She was flirting with you like crazy. You should go back, you really should. I think you're in there.' Sal laughed, nervously.

'With my best friend's sister? Right.'

'You think he'd mind? Don't be silly. I'm sure Shulpa's old enough to decide for herself who she gets it together with.'

'And so am I,' I said. 'So am I.'

Sal and I sat kissing for twenty minutes, Sal's fingers curling round the back of my neck, her mouth finding mine, and then leaving it for my cheekbones, my chin, my eyelashes. It felt like I was swimming through warm amber. After a while she pulled away. I thought she'd had second thoughts but it was only to ask me if I drank grappa, which I said I did, and then we were inside, on the sofa, not drinking grappa. After ten minutes she led me through her big, stripped-pine Georgian house to her bedroom, and her bed, where her hands found my chest, and my neck, and mine found her long, lean back, and my mouth found her breasts and her legs and her belly, her pale skin almost luminous from the light of the moon, and the streetlights coming in through the big bay window.

'Wait here.'

Sal got out of bed, walking out towards the bathroom. She was gone for a minute or two and the room was very quiet. I sat back on the bed, resting on one elbow. When Sal came back she was naked. Very slowly she undressed me too, and she lifted the sheet and invited me beneath it, and we slipped under and into each other's arms. Our mouths locked again, and Sal pressed her body against me. But I was gradually feeling myself becoming separate, as if I were drifting away from what was happening, as though I were gradually breaking up, into pieces that were slowly beginning to move apart. It was odd. In the car I'd really needed to kiss Sal, to feel her body, her passion locking slowly into me. But I was losing it, the spell was breaking. I tried to focus, to bring myself back on line to her, but when Sal reached for the condom she'd brought through, I knew it wasn't going to happen. I kissed her again and went down on her, trying to find the desire that had scurried out of me, but I felt dead and empty, as if the flower that had begun to grow in me had turned out to be a puffball, cold and white. Suddenly, touching Sal became unbearable, I didn't want to do it, and when she moved out from under me, and went to slip the condom out of its foil she could see that I didn't want her. She put her hand on my stomach and then her head moved down my chest, but it was like I was watching it on TV, I was so far away from it.

Sal stopped what she was doing and I lay back. She

didn't look at me. I didn't know what to say. We lay there for a long minute until I felt her turning to me.

'Too old for you, Billy?' Her voice was a soft soup of bitterness and understanding.

'Sal,' I said. My throat was as dry as my chest. 'Come on. It's not that. Come on.'

She left a second, and then pulled the duvet up over her breasts. She said, 'It's OK. I understand.'

We lay there side by side. A group of lads passed beneath her window, Arsenal fans proclaiming their loyalty to the world. It seemed like ages until their voices had trailed away. More time seemed to pass until, gradually, I could feel Sal move closer to me. I responded and her hand found mine.

'It's so hard to pretend,' she said eventually, her quiet voice filling the room. 'Why is it so hard to pretend?'

Sal moved right next to me and I held on to her, only vaguely realizing how hard her teeth were biting into the side of my chest. I couldn't feel them. I couldn't feel anything.

Outside there was no one, the street was empty and city-quiet, the leaves on the plane trees almost unnaturally still. It was just gone two and I was wide awake. I took three measured breaths, knowing that sleep would be impossible, and wondered if Nicky was still up. That talk, maybe. Then the Bradleys came to me. My mind seemed clear, sharp as crystal. I sat on a low wall and ran the events through my head, clicking from person to person like a slide show. I wanted to do something, to act. But I had no point of focus, nothing to get to grips with, only a number of places I could hang around on the off chance of seeing the kid. Maybe I should go and see Nicky after all. I couldn't decide.

Then I realized that I had Nicky's Audi, and that therefore no one would recognize me if I was in it, no one who knew my car. I had a thought. Why not make use of it? I stood up, and walked the twenty yards towards it, disabled the alarm and got in. I drove quickly, but not too fast, getting to the place in about twenty minutes. I was lucky. I found a space right opposite and parked. I suddenly worried that I was in fact too close, that I'd be seen, but I told myself not to be stupid. You wouldn't notice someone in a car at night, especially if it was just another car you didn't recognize. All the same, I pulled it a yard or so backward to get it out from beneath a streetlight.

I waited. I didn't have my camera but it didn't matter. I didn't really expect anyone to be around. Not really. It was just something to do, something to do instead of lying in bed staring at the ceiling. I sat, with the radio on low, telling myself I was being stupid, eventually hoping that nothing would happen. After twenty minutes I was convinced that nothing would happen and my hand reached forward for the ignition key.

But then, before I could turn my wrist, two figures appeared at the end of the road. They were obviously on their way home from somewhere, and they walked towards me. I stayed still, knowing that if I did, then they wouldn't be able to see me through the dark windscreen. Not that they'd be looking – it was just an anonymous Audi. Then the two people walked closer and I could tell that yes, it was them. Definitely.

The two figures stepped up to the doorway. I thought for a second that Sharon was wearing a top that I'd bought her, but it was a different one. She disengaged her arm from that of her friend and as she fished in her bag for her keys the man she was with turned round to the square. He looked as though he could tell I was watching him. He looked around. He was a very tall, very thin man, with the beginnings of a slight paunch, and a chin that was beginning to give a bit. He had a suit on that hung off him rather, and I could see a tie poking out one of the side pockets. He wore round glasses, a little too big to be fashionable, and he had a studious expression on a long, tight-lipped face. I looked at his face hard, drilling my eyes into it, and a quizzical look narrowed his features. Then he turned round into the doorway. Sharon held the door for him and I got to see her face too for an instant, before the door swung shut.

A few moments later a light snapped on, in a window on the fourth floor. Nothing happened for a while until, just for a second, I caught a glimpse of a naked girl, walking into the frame to pull the curtains closed. Then she was gone. For the next ten minutes I stared at the curtains, still able to make out two thin strips of light at the edges. Then the house was dark.

Back at the bar, Shulpa was sat talking to three friends whose cab was taking ages. Nicky had already gone upstairs to bed, she told me. When her friends left Shulpa asked me if I wanted a drink, and I told her whisky, please. She walked behind the bar and fetched the bottle, setting it down on a small table. I drank a lot of it. Shulpa had a fair go too. When it was finished she asked me if I wanted any more but I said no. Then she asked me if I was OK to drive her home, which I said I was. She lived in Bayswater, she told me, in an apartment block right next to the park. It would have been about a half-hour drive at that time of night I expect but I didn't find out. We didn't go there. We went to Exmouth Market instead.

Chapter Seven

Andy woke me up. His voice on the answerphone telling me I should call him. How come I never, ever got round to turning the damn sound down? I let the message end and reached for my alarm clock, which was facing the wrong way. It told me the time was 10.16. I rolled over onto my side.

Shulpa was lying on her front, still very much asleep, her head buried in the pillow, her arms either side of it. I let my eyes trace the outline of her light dark skin, from her elbow down along her breast, to her hip bone, where the rest of her body disappeared into the sheet. I pushed myself up from the futon as quietly as I could and made it into the bathroom.

In the mirror was a creased and unshaven face, which looked about as good as it had only a few weeks ago after my encounter with a cab driver and his friends. I took a razor to it, making a conscious effort to keep my hand steady, and then ran the shower. I then knelt in front of the toilet bowl, and tried to make myself vomit, hoping that the noise of the shower would mask the sound of retching if Shulpa happened to be awake. But there was no noise, because all I could manage was a few dry heaves. I gave up, showered, and raided the medicine cabinet.

Three ibuprofen went down with a glass of water, and I squirted some stuff into my eyes to clear away the red. I power-scrubbed my teeth and used some after-shave balm that was supposed to make people think that I was not an ineffective private detective/dumped boy-friend who'd just screwed his best friend's sister as if she was a twenty-quid tart, and still too pissed to have a hangover, but a forest glade instead. I put a towel round my waist and headed back into the living area, where I noted that there was no change in the condition of my guest. The room smelled of whisky, smoke and sex. I picked up the phone and pulled the wire as far as I could towards the kitchen, letting the receiver cord fill the rest of the gap. The kitchen smelled of chicken bones about to go, and old garlic. I pushed the door to quietly and dialled the number for the station.

Andy wasn't there so I dialled his mobile and left a message on his voice mail. I put the kettle on, and made myself eat a few spoonfuls of bio-yoghurt with wholegrains. My, I was a healthy fella. After only a couple of minutes the phone rang again and I managed to get to it after only one ring.

'Billy Rucker.'

'Billy,' he said. 'It's Andy.' He was using a payphone and my mind automatically tried to make out where he was calling from. 'I'm at the hospital.'

My breath stopped still and my stomach tensed. I waited for him to say it.

'It's the girl.'

I knew that. Who else could it be? 'Yes?'

'She woke up,' Andy said.

'What?' I let the breath out and sat back against the sink unit.

'She woke up,' he said again. 'Very briefly, this morning. Only for a minute or so. They called me and I came right over.'

'How is she?'

'The same,' he said. 'She's the same as she was, except her vital signs have improved. Not much, but a little.'

'I'll come over.'

'There's no need, but you can if you want. They won't let us in anyway. They've put a nurse with her full time for us though, in case she says anything else.'

'Anything else?'

'Yes. But don't get too excited. She mumbled something, nothing much apparently. I'll get the noddy to tell you if you're coming.'

'Give me half an hour,' I said.

I stepped back out of the kitchen to put the phone back down and saw Shulpa, sitting up in bed, the duvet beneath her arms like a lady in a Cary Grant film. She must have heard the phone ringing. She was looking slightly nervous.

'Good morning.'

'Hello,' she said. She bit her lip. 'Was that . . .?'

'What?'

'Was that my brother?'

'Your brother? No.'

'No? I thought you might be . . . I don't know. Thank God.'

'Thank God indeed.'

Shulpa smiled, and relaxed. I walked across the room to my wardrobe and pulled out a shirt.

'What's that for?' she said. It was a childish, mock petulant sound.

'The usual.'

'Oh! Not yet. Come here.' Shulpa stretched out her shoulders and stifled a delicate yawn. She was one of those women who can drink like a Russian sailor and wake up looking like a Polish nun.

'Listen,' I said. 'That call. I really have to go.'

'I wasn't asking,' Shulpa said. She laughed and her eyes narrowed. 'Just for a minute.'

'A minute.' I tossed the shirt on a chair.

'Oh,' she said. 'You shaved. Let me feel.'

I walked over and sat on the bed. Shulpa sat up, but kept herself covered. She ran a lazy hand over my face.

'I was very drunk last night,' she said, in a teasing voice.

'You were,' I agreed. 'Very. Me too.'

'Everything seems . . . a bit hazy.'

'Yes.'

'Yes. What a waste. It's a shame.' She took my hand and pulled me towards her.

'Listen, Shulpa. I've just arranged—'

'Shh,' she said. 'I want something I can remember, something I can really see later. Don't you?' Her hand went for my towel. 'Something like this,' she said.

* * *

'Half an hour, you said.'

'I'm sorry, Andy. The traffic. How is she?'

'The same,' he said. 'Like I told you. I don't think there's any point hanging around. They won't let us in, they think we're as bad as that lot.'

We were in the ante-room outside the ward. Andy nodded to the corner where a group of bored men sat twitching beneath a No Smoking sign. Natalie's mother and father occupied the seats opposite them.

Andy introduced me to the PC who had been sitting with Natalie and he told me what the girl had said when she'd woken. It was simply the words 'I can see things', repeated over, until she'd faded back out. Andy told the PC that he'd done good work.

'Be nice to the nurses,' Andy said to him, quietly. 'Flirt with them. Tell them you want to sit with her. That you were talking to her and that's what made her come round. Anything. Yes?'

'Yes, sir.'

'Make them trust you, show them that you really care for the girl. OK?'

The guy seemed a bit shocked at what he was being told; he looked as if he did care about Natalie, but he nodded anyway. I thanked him again and followed Andy outside. I was pretty tired but I didn't feel as bad as I deserved. I was going to go straight back home to a hopefully by now empty bed, but Andy thought it might help to go over the scene again, and he asked me if I wanted to come.

'Without young Mr Finch there's fuck all else left to do,' he said.

I had already made a note to ask Andy if I could have another look at the house where Lucy Bradley died, and even though I would have rather done it on my own I took him up on his offer. I followed his Astra in my Mazda, parked on the quiet, drab street, and met him outside the door. Andy used a set of keys to open the police locks, before breaking open the tape seals. I followed him into the living room, taking in the stained chairs and the ripped sofa and the rest of the skip-salvaged furniture. I told him about my meeting with the old lady opposite, and about the history of the house. Andy nodded. I stood in the centre of the room as he poked around, opening some drawers, looking behind a built-in bookcase. I checked to see if any of the skirting was loose, and got a chair to look inside the lampshade, but neither of us found anything more than a spider, a take-out pizza menu and an old copy of *The Face*.

It seemed odd to be there in the daylight. I wandered into the kitchen, and then Andy found the key to the back door, and we both dutifully stared at the spot Lucy had lain in, before going back inside the house, and upstairs. We looked in the two sparse bedrooms, one with a single mattress, the other with a double bed that had probably stood in the same spot for forty years. Maybe it was even the same one in which Mrs Chortney from opposite had laid out June Anthony's second husband. We looked under the bed and flipped over the mattress but of course we didn't find anything. Andy even took his Swiss Army knife and cut both mattresses down the middle, but there was nothing inside except stuffing.

There wasn't much else to see. The clothes had all been removed for forensic analysis that hadn't yielded anything, and all that was left was a tube of toothpaste in the bathroom, some empty hair-dye bottles and an aerosol spray on what must have been Lucy's dressing table. There were also traces of fingerprint powder, which had shown up prints matching those taken from the dead girl, plus mine from the kitchen, the back door and the phone, and those assumed to belong to the kid we were looking for. Lee Finch.

'They're being checked against the prints in his file,' Andy told me. 'They'll match.'

No other prints were found in the house.

Andy went through his version of the sequence of events again and I followed him as we walked it through. Something didn't seem right to me, but it wasn't necessarily what I was hearing, which sounded perfectly plausible. After Andy had finished we walked back into the living room and Andy started to reseal the house, before adding his signature to the list of officers who had been on the scene in the last week. Ken Clay's name was one above Andy's. Andy held the door open for me and I was just about to duck under the tape when I stood up again.

'It's very clean,' I said.

'What?'

'The house. The whole house. It's not tidy but it's clean.'

It was something I hadn't noticed the time I'd been there before. It had been too late, too dark. There'd been too much else going on.

'So?'

'Young people aren't known to be house proud', I said, 'at the best of times. But squatters?'

Andy shrugged. 'So they got fed up, and had a spring clean. What are you getting at?'

I thought hard for a second but then shrugged back. 'Fucked if I know,' I said.

Once we were outside, standing in the sticky heat, I asked Andy if any of the team showing Lee Finch's picture around had had any bites. When he told me they hadn't, I suggested using a different one, a different shot from the ones I'd taken.

'It can sometimes help,' I said. 'Sometimes a photograph just doesn't look like the person, you know? The angle or the lighting or something. The expression on his face might not be the way he usually looks.'

Andy said it couldn't hurt to post an alternative image, if I had one, and I said I did. I asked him if he wanted to come over to my office and pick one up, telling him I'd buy him lunch for helping me out. Andy looked uncomfortable. He said he'd prefer it if I sent it, or else dropped it off at the station.

'You see, Bill,' he said, 'and this is between you and me. I'd just as soon steer clear of your place.'

'Why?'

'Well.' Andy folded his arms and sucked some air in through his teeth. 'It's just that I've been screwing that little piece from your café.'

'What?'

'The girl, the Italian bird. I know, I know. You'd have thought she'd have better taste, go on, say it. But I dropped by one day and you weren't there so I asked her out. Bingo.'

'You and Ally.'

'Yeah. She's a fiery little thing, believe me, didn't take much persuading. But the thing is, she's been getting a bit keen.'

'She has?'

'Talking about ditching her boyfriend, that kind of thing. And don't get me wrong, I'm up for giving her the benefit now and then, who wouldn't be? But hold on. Anyway, I'd be grateful if you could pop the picture round. For one, her old man might be there, which I can do without, and I really don't want to give her the wrong idea.'

'No,' I said.

'Cheers then.'

Andy walked off down the street to his car. After a few steps he turned but kept walking.

'I still think you got to her first,' he laughed.

Chapter Eight

I drove back and ate lunch in the relative cool of the Sand Bar. Upstairs in my flat I discovered that Shulpa had left me a note, to the effect that Nicky had been wrong about my not taking her anywhere she'd want to go. I dropped the note in the waste-paper bin and spent the rest of the afternoon asleep on my futon, lulled by the remnants of an unfamiliar scent.

Sal called at about four, after I'd already woken up and made myself a cup of tea. She thanked me for the night before and then said it was her turn to apologize.

'I'm sorry,' she said, 'I really am. You were vulnerable and I was pissed. I hope we can still be friends.'

'Sal, of course. And there's no need—'

'There is, Billy. There is. There's no excuse for emotionally blackmailing you.'

'What?'

'Talking about my husband, acting the sad lonely widow. It was pathetic really, and I knew what I was doing as well, I'm ashamed to say. I was just having such a good time with you I didn't want it to end. It's been a long time since I was so easy with a man – when he's not wearing gloves that is.'

'I understand. And I wanted to be with you too,' I said. 'So don't worry.'

'OK,' Sal said. 'But I wanted you to know that I am sorry about Sharon, I really am. I could tell you were hurt. The last thing you needed was to get it together with someone else last night.'

'Yes,' I said, 'yes. You're probably right about that.'

I told Sal I'd try to make it down to the gym that night, if nothing else came up. But as it happened I didn't really feel like it much, and I drove down to see Luke instead, at about seven. Faber had sent through the finished copy of his book, which I set by the side of his bed. I even read from it to him, a long poem about a childhood friend of his whose father had died suddenly, how the boy's mother had brought him round for Luke to play with that afternoon. I noticed one of the nurses stop what she was doing to listen, and though I don't claim to read well she did say she enjoyed it. I told her she was welcome to have a look at the rest of the book if she wanted. When I told her it was by Luke she said, 'Oh,' quietly, and when I left she was leafing through the pages.

At eight I met Nicky for dinner, at Randall and Aubin on Brewer Street. Once we'd sat ourselves down on a couple of long stools and had a quick look at the menu, Nicky turned to me.

'So,' he said. He didn't look that friendly. 'What happened last night?'

'I . . .'

'With that woman? Sally. And don't give me any bollocks.'

'Nothing happened. Not a lot anyway.'

'Billy,' Nicky said. 'I'm your friend, you know that, and I liked Sally, I really did. But are you being fucking stupid or what? You are going out with one of the most

beautiful, brilliant women I've ever met, and she certainly doesn't need treating like—'

'Nicky,' I said. 'There's a lot that I have to tell you.'

I filled Nicky in and he said he couldn't believe it,
and then said that he didn't believe it. I assured him it
was true, but what he meant was he didn't believe what
Sharon had told me.

'I've seen the way you are,' he said. 'It's right. I
don't care about this other guy. She's kidding herself.'

'I don't think so,' I said. 'I saw them together. The
way she clung on his arm. She looked . . . she looked
happy. What can I do?'

'Nothing,' Nicky said. 'Nothing. Don't do anything.
She'll realize, she will. I know it.'

Nicky continued to express his shock at what I'd
said but it was still too early for me to talk about it. I
just didn't have a clue what I felt, I still couldn't look at
it, the bare fact that she was with someone else. That
another man had been making love to her at the same
time I had, that she hadn't really been there, not like
I'd been there. It seemed ludicrous; the whole idea of it
was as ridiculous to me as it was to Nicky, but it did
nothing to change the fact. She was with this guy,
Ronan. A tall, slightly seedy-looking man in a suit that
didn't fit him. I would have trusted them alone on a
desert island where the only food was oysters.

I changed the subject, asking Nicky how he liked
his new friends, and he pulled a face. Then, after we'd
had a couple of glasses of Rueda he insisted on getting
in a bottle of Langi Ghiran at thirty-five quid, and
paying for it. When I told him he didn't have to do that,
just because I'd been dumped, he said that wasn't the
reason.

'It's to make up for the Ridge,' he said.

'What?'

'The Ridge. Carla put it with some spare bottles of house red that wouldn't normally have been touched. But, well, we got busy.'

I put my hands in front of my face.

'One of the waiters, and they're all denying it, gave it to a couple of city boys. Both bottles. I saw them finishing it off. I didn't even get a sip.'

'Oh, Jesus.'

'And when their bill came they complained.'

'Huh?!'

'The menu said the 'ouse wine was French, mate.'

After dinner Nicky suggested one of the clubs he's a member of but I told him I wasn't up for a big night. We caught a cab back to Clerkenwell and he persuaded me to stop into Fred's for one, the bar at the near end of Exmouth Market. The place was fairly busy and we had to stand at the bar. I bought him a pint of Guinness and he asked me how I liked his sister.

'She was lovely,' I said.

'A pain in the arse. And you'd better watch out, she liked you. Whatever you do, don't tell her you're single.'

Nicky moved to let a couple of girls into the bar and I took a deep breath, thinking that I'd better just get it over with and tell him, but I was saved by Alberto. He just tapped me on the arm and nodded over my shoulder. I turned to see Emma Bradley, standing nervously at the far end of the bar, with a small bag over her shoulder. I sighed to myself and walked over to her.

'Emma,' I said. 'What is it?'

'It's nothing. I'm sorry. I was just sat at home . . . I

just needed someone to talk to, and you did say anytime. I didn't know you were with your friends, I'll
go—'

'Don't be silly,' I said. 'Stay. Really.'

'OK,' she said. 'Thanks. But can we not . . .? I mean,
it's hard to talk here.'

'Right,' I said. 'Right. Just give me a second.'

I said goodnight to Nicky and Alberto and took
Emma upstairs to my flat. She spoke for about twenty
minutes, telling what she was feeling, expanding on the
kinds of things she'd already said to me. I nodded now
and then but I couldn't really concentrate on what she
was telling me. The light on my machine was flashing,
and when she went out to use the toilet I hit 'Play' and
there was a message from Sharon on it. She was asking
me how I was. Her voice sounded nervous, and I was
glad she hadn't tried to mask that and put on a fake
kind of bonhomie. I almost felt that she was in the
room with me, and I couldn't help but wonder why she
was calling. Was Nicky right? Had she realized she'd
made a mistake? As soon as I had the thought I told
myself not to be stupid, but I couldn't dismiss the hope,
it had found its way into me before I could stop it.

When Emma came back from the toilet she asked
me again what I'd found out. I had to tell her not a lot,
but I did mention going to the care home the boy had
been at. Emma nodded, and then asked me if she could
have a drink. I thought it couldn't hurt and poured
some wine.

Emma drank a lot of it, quickly, and it wasn't long
before it got to her. She started to sob. I held her until
she'd finished crying and then made to move away, but

she held on to me. I waited, then tried again with a little more force, but she held on to my hand and pressed it to her face.

'Emma,' I said. I held her wrist and pulled my hand from her as gently as I could. She smiled, grimly.

'I get it.'

'You're upset,' I said.

'Thanks, Mr Patronizing. I'm not a child.'

'I know that . . .'

Emma moved nearer to me and took my hand again.

'I'm not a virgin, you know,' she said.

I pulled my hand away and told her that I'd better drive her home. When she started to pull off her top I stopped her, and told her that there was no way this was going to happen. She stayed still for a moment and then turned and ran out, slamming the door on the way down. I took a few deep breaths and walked down after her and was just in time to see her mother's Peugeot pulling away from the kerb, towards Rosebery Avenue. Well, if she got there, she could get back home. I walked upstairs.

I replayed the message from Sharon. It sounded different the second time over. She'd probably phoned at a time when she'd hoped I was out. She didn't say she needed to speak to me or anything like that. I couldn't decide what to do about it and instead of thinking about it I picked up the *Tao*.

'Learn the value of non-action.'

I didn't call her back.

Chapter Nine

'Beautiful roses.'

The man with his back to me looked up and turned. He was a good-looking guy in his early to mid-twenties, dressed in old jeans and a long-sleeved plaid shirt, even though the heat was already getting up. I figured it was to stop his arms getting scratched.

'I thought Mr Bradley did the gardening,' I said, with a smile.

'He does,' the man replied, leaning on his edge trimmer. 'Usually won't let anyone near his roses, though he can't do everything himself. But just at the minute he hasn't been able to do much at all, what with . . .' He tailed off and looked at me. 'Who are you?'

'I'm working for the Bradleys,' I said. 'Trying to find out what happened to their daughter. Are you going to be around long?'

The man looked ever so slightly flustered. 'Until about three,' he said.

'I'll talk to you later then.'

On arriving by train at the small village of Ravensey, Sussex, that morning I'd gone immediately to the post office, a small general store facing a well-kept green on which some kids were playing football and using a set of swings. The postmistress, Mrs Dearing, had told me that yes, I was expected, but she didn't need to give me the key to the Bradleys' house because Mrs Bradley had phoned to tell her that she'd be there to let me in herself. Mrs Dearing obviously knew who I was, because she went into a five-minute speech about how shocked she had been to hear about what had happened to Lucy, and what a lovely girl she had been, during which I nodded my head when appropriate.

'She used to come round you know, just to talk. I think she liked someone to listen to her. Anyway . . .'

Eventually I had to interrupt Mrs Dearing, and she told me where the house was. I took the short walk over there, feeling the space, breathing the air, thanking God I was out of the city if only for a day.

I left the gardener and walked on up the curved drive, breathing in a mélange of scents that I'd forgotten existed, listening to the crunch of my feet on the gravel biting into the insistent backdrop of birdsong. When I got to the end I found a house that was slightly smaller than the drive had led me to expect, with a yellow alarm box above the door. There was a black BMW estate parked outside and a sit-on lawnmower, the kind I always wanted as a kid when my dad made me cut the grass to within an inch of its life. Or mine. I was wondering if Mrs Bradley would let me have a go, when the woman herself walked out of the front door and greeted me with a look that gave away neither pleasure nor annoyance. We shook hands and I followed her into a wide hallway that turned into a reception area for her husband's dental practice. James Bradley had obviously cancelled all appointments for the foreseeable future, however, rather than get a locum; there were no patients waiting and no receptionist in attendance.

The inside of the house was pretty much as I expected; it was light and airy, done out in a modern, though still *Country Life* style, which I could never have lived in but was a lot more tasteful than most. Mrs Bradley led me into a modern kitchen with a huge old Aga shining on one side, which I told her I admired. She curled up her nose.

'You're welcome to it,' she said. 'Stupid bloody thing. I'd cart it off tomorrow and get a real cooker, but James won't let me.'

I tried not to show my surprise at the fact that Mr Bradley had his way about anything, and let Mrs Bradley pour me some coffee. I took a sip and then asked her if she could show me into Lucy's room. I really did want to get on. She showed me upstairs and opened the door, but didn't enter herself. I wondered if she had gone in there at all in the last week. I tried to smile at her sympathetically and she turned back to the stairwell heading down to her office, where she'd be if I needed anything. I'd half expected her to stand over my shoulder while I searched Lucy's room and I was thankful that she wasn't going to.

I shut the door behind me and let out a breath. Then I began looking for anything that might give me a clue about Lucy. The room was medium-sized, the walls covered in an eclectic mix of rap star posters, modern art, postcards and gig tickets. On her bedside table was a purse, which the police had returned, and I went through that. In her wardrobe I was surprised to find a shoebox full of photographs that I thought the police would have taken, and I went through them, primarily looking for anyone I recognized – Lee Finch in particular. I didn't see him in any. Nor did I see Lucy's mother or her father, or even any of her sister. I put the pictures back in the box, intending to take them with me so that I could go through them later with Emma. Then I went through all of Lucy's drawers, rummaging through the clothes that were there and checking her cupboards for a hidden diary or address book, anything she hadn't wanted her parents to find. I looked at the labels inside some of the clothes, and wrote down the names of any shops that I didn't recognize and which came up more than once. I looked in her pillowcases, and underneath her mattress, in each of her CD cases, of which there were a vast number, and inside every book on her bookshelf, of which there were considerably fewer. I read her old schoolbooks, and checked inside a Bart Simpson water-bottle cover, and I took every poster off the wall to see if there were any notes tucked away behind them. I removed each and every postcard and put them in the box with the photographs.

I was in there for three hours, during which time Mrs Bradley made an appearance with another coffee and told me that she had left some sandwiches out for me downstairs in case I was hungry. When I was done in the room I found that I was, but before going downstairs I used the bathroom and then checked the other doors on the landing. I found Emma's room, which was a much more ordered affair, with Mr Darcy taking the place of Tupac Shakir. I also found the spare room, a walk-in linen closet, and a boxroom filled with old computer equipment and piles of software magazines. The last door that I came to was locked, which didn't really surprise me. I was about to do something about that when I heard Mrs Bradley walking around in the kitchen. I thought better of it, knowing it wasn't really necessary, and I wandered downstairs to meet her.

Mrs Bradley was putting the kettle on for more coffee. She told me to help myself to the sandwiches, which I did, and she asked me if I'd managed to find anything. She didn't sound exactly interested, almost as if she knew I was wasting my time, and she was right. Apart from getting the impression that Lucy was a girl very much out of synch with those living around her, which was not a very unusual thing to surmise after looking in a teenager's bedroom, I hadn't come up with anything, and I told Mrs Bradley so.

After finishing up I asked Mrs Bradley if there were any other places in the house that Lucy was particularly fond of, where she tended to hang out. She told me no, not that she could think of, in the house, at least. When I asked her what she meant she told me that Lucy used to spend a lot of time in the tree house in the wood at the bottom of the garden, that her dad had built for her one birthday.

'It was just for her,' Mrs Bradley said. 'Not for Emma, just for her. The twins always complained when we gave them things to share, so James said that was just for Lucy. When they were eleven, I think. He spent hours on it, when the girls were on a French exchange, it wasn't your average tree house, and it was the only time I've ever seen Emma jealous of her sister. Oh, we got Emma something of course, a bike I think, and she was pleased, but it didn't match the look on Lucy's face. To think her dad had done that just for her.' Mrs Bradley stopped. 'She wouldn't let Emma anywhere near it. She used to sit in it all the time and if Emma did try and get in she'd run and tell James and he'd tell her to get out, that it was Lucy's to do with as she liked. Even when James asked Lucy to let Emma in, she wouldn't.'

I asked Mrs Bradley if the police had looked in the tree house but she said she hadn't thought to mention it. I asked if I could check it out and she shrugged, before opening the back door for me and leaving me to stroll down a long, smooth lawn. Once I'd worked out how to get the rope ladder down, by using a bamboo cane hidden in a conifer, I climbed into the house, which was built around the bottom two branches of a horse chestnut. It was ten feet by twelve, with a branch running through the far corner, and looked stable enough to live in. The inside had been painted orange a few years back and was perfectly dry, with two small stools and an old table.

There was nothing to see, but I sat in the house for five minutes looking at the walls, which were all covered with one word carved into the wood. Lucy. I got down and found the gardener, spoke with him for five minutes and then went back indoors.

Back in the kitchen, I apologized for disturbing Mrs Bradley, but told her that I had needed to come down there.

'You never know if something's necessary until you do it,' I said.

Mrs Bradley nodded and then we chatted for a while, until she asked me how I'd travelled down. I told her by train, and asked her if she knew when the next one left. She had a timetable pinned to a board in the kitchen, which she looked at, and then she insisted on driving me to catch the 4.10 to Arundel, which I would just about make if we hurried. Otherwise I'd have had to wait another hour. I don't think either of us relished the thought of that much small talk so I thanked her for her offer and we got to the station in time to see the two-carriage hopper pulling onto the platform. I got out of the car, told Mrs Bradley that I'd call her, and jogged through the tiny station entrance where I was just in time to step aboard. The train pulled out and I watched Mrs Bradley's BMW pulling up the quiet lane, back towards Ravensey.

I let out a breath and relaxed my shoulders, which I always seemed to do after meeting Mrs Bradley. I looked around the empty carriage and perched on the nearest seat. I had the box of photographs with me, and I could have gone through them again for something to do, but I didn't. I didn't even get comfortable. The next stop was only ten minutes away. When the train pulled into Dalcombe Heath I stepped off and walked out of the station into the small car park where I found my Mazda. I put the box on the back seat, got in, and had a look at an ordnance survey map that was in my glove compartment. After that I went and found the local pub, where I sat over a ploughman's and a couple of pints until about seven thirty. Then I made a phone call, and when I got an answerphone I put the receiver down without speaking, set my pint glass on the bar, and left.

I glanced at the map again and drove for ten minutes. I parked the Mazda at a crossroads and set off across a field full of sheep. I came to a very dense wood after five minutes, and had to use my Maglite to pick a way through the brambles and pines, and over a dried up stream. I climbed over a barbed wire fence dissecting

ADAM BARON

the wood, and found that on the other side the trees
thinned out and were better cared for, and bigger. I put
the light away. Very soon I was standing underneath
Lucy's tree house. I walked up to the back of the house
and skirted round to the front. Taking a quick look
round the corner of the house onto the drive I saw that
the BMW was gone.

Mrs Bradley hadn't come down to work all day. She
just wanted to be there when I was, which was perfectly
natural given that it was her house, or else very suspicious. Either way, I wasn't having it. I retraced my
steps to the back door, which was built into an old glass
porch. I moved to the left of the door and pushed at the
bottom of a window, which was the type that swings
upwards. It hadn't looked open, but I was pretty confident that it would be, as I'd fixed it that way earlier,
tossing an old coat over the latch so Mrs Bradley
wouldn't notice it when she locked up. The window
moved beneath my fingers and I reached in underneath
it to keep the latch from falling back into place. Then I
made sure that neither of the Bradleys' neighbours was
being overzealous about their civic duties and I stepped
through the window into the porch.

The tone was continuous and loud, and it began as
soon as I pushed open the door into the kitchen. I didn't
know how long I had, but I tried not to hurry as I made
my way through to the front door, where I'd already
noticed the alarm disabling box fixed to a wall in the
hallway. I got the cupboard open, while simultaneously
pulling a crumpled post-it note out of my back pocket,
which I'd found in Lucy's purse only a few hours ago.
On the note was the number C237Y, which was too
long for a bike lock and couldn't have been a PIN

308

number. I punched it into the keypad, said a small prayer, and the alarm stopped as suddenly as it had begun. It was replaced by a ringing silence. I said another prayer and stood in the fading light for a second. Then I closed the door of the alarm box and headed up the stairs.

An hour later, in the local pub, I stood waiting for the young gardener, who had reluctantly agreed to meet me. I hadn't really left him any choice. When I'd gone to find him earlier I'd told him straight out that I knew he'd been having an affair with Lucy Bradley. It was something that I'd only guessed at, from what Emma had said about her sister, plus the look on the gardener's face when I'd first mentioned Lucy's name to him. I'd obviously struck lucky though because as soon as I said it he went as white as the lilies he was tending, and began to protest his total innocence in regard to Lucy's murder. I didn't really doubt that but played it a bit heavy with him anyway, and he said he'd see me in the pub at nine. When he came in he led me through to the very back of the place, and into a step-down snug with a flagstone floor, which we had to ourselves.

Ian Williams was saving up to go travelling by working for his father, who owned a couple of garden centres and a contracting company. He'd known Lucy for years, he told me, ever since he'd been at school. He had an alibi for the night Lucy was killed but I told him I wasn't really interested in that. I got him to tell me how he knew her. Ian said he'd been sleeping with Lucy on and off for a couple of years, mainly when he was home from college. He was not under any illusions that he was the only one, but I got the impression he had been more than slightly fixed on her. Williams told me that he'd been really shaken by what had happened to Lucy, and that he hadn't come forward because he knew he had nothing to tell, and couldn't see the point of getting himself into trouble. I nodded, and asked him what kind of girl Lucy was.

'Fucked up,' he answered.

'How so?'

'About her family. Her mother particularly.'

'Go on.'

'Her mother was a bitch to her. I heard her yelling at her a few times. It drove Lucy mad. It was like a constant preoccupation with her. And she couldn't do anything. Emma, that's the other one, she's a bit of a stuck-up cow, but her mother was really into her. She got the grades and stuff but Lucy couldn't compete. I think that's why she went a bit wild. It got her mother's attention at least.'

Ian shook his head at some memory or other, something Lucy must have done.

'You know', he said, after a second, 'if I'd have been told that there was a murder in that family, and had to guess who, I'd never have said it would have happened to Lucy. I'd have said it would have been the mother they'd found. And Lucy's fingerprints on the murder weapon.'

I walked back to my car through the quiet, darkening lanes, listening to the distant, rasping call of a corncrake somewhere in the fields surrounding me. I opened the door and sat for a while, enjoying the quiet, running a few thoughts through my head, trying them out like film scenarios to see if they'd work. Then I drove back to London, with the radio off, thinking all the way. I felt focused and clear, like I hadn't for ages. Somehow, I managed to keep everything else out. It felt good; just me, a car, and a series of problems. When I thought about them, the last few weeks felt surreal, as if someone else had been living them for me, someone who kept turning the wrong way, saying the wrong thing, leaving things too late. Someone else had been living my life and it wasn't someone I liked very much.

When I got back home at about eleven there was a message from Andy, to the effect that Natalie's condition was the same and the boy was still nowhere. I set the box I'd taken from Lucy's room on the kitchen table and made a note to go through the photographs and the postcards with Emma. Not that I thought it would help. I was 80 per cent sure I had it now. Not everything, but the main deal. The rest would either fall into place or else fall out of the picture. I just wanted to be certain, and I wanted to know that I had something for Andy Gold, so he'd be certain too. I pushed the box to one side. Then I slid out another photograph, not from the box, this one out of my jacket pocket. It was a ten by eight, folded in two, which I'd found in a file in Mrs Bradley's bedroom, and taken with me. I laid it out on the table.

I studied it carefully, using a plastic eyeglass Carl had given me. And then I was certain. I reached for the phone.

Chapter Ten

I reached for the phone but it rang. It always throws you when that happens but this time I was even more confused. The person who was calling me said her name was Dana, and said it like I'd know who she was. It was a foreign accent.

'At King's Cross,' she said. 'You give me your card. That girl who jumped in front of the train. I saw her with woman, I told you.'

'Of course,' I said.

'Well, she is here. Now.'

'What?'

'The woman. I am using public phone and I see her.'

'Where are you?'

'Right outside station.'

'Wait there, please.'

'I will if I can. My man, he doesn't like me not to work—'

'Please,' I said. 'Tell him I'll pay you. I'll be fifteen minutes. Please.'

'I'll do what I can,' she said. 'Any man who approaches me, I'll tell them I'll bite his fucking cock off.'

I put the phone down and grabbed my camera. In

ten minutes I had cycled down there and found the girl where she said she'd be. When I jogged up to her she shrugged.

'Too late.'

'Fuck,' I said. 'Fuck. Why is this always happening to me?'

The girl's pimp hovered fifteen feet away, checking us out. The girl glanced at him and pushed a breath through her teeth.

'Can we go somewhere?'

'Yes,' I said.

'You have money?'

'Yes.'

'For him. For Bela Lugosi. I have to give him something.'

'I understand, it's fine.'

'Follow me then,' the girl said.

I trailed after Dana as she led me towards the lights at the bottom of the Pancras Road where we stopped. I figured she was taking me to the underground car park across the street where I knew that a lot of business went on. I hoped she'd be able to give me a much better description of the woman she'd seen. But just as we were about to step through the light traffic she stopped.

'There!'

She was pointing at a yellow Ford Fiesta. I looked at the car and stepped back onto the pavement.

'There!' Dana said again. 'It's her!'

The car slid past us, before coming to a halt, and then moving on again. I got a good view through the windscreen. A young girl I had never seen before was sitting in the passenger seat. She looked about as old as

Natalie was. Then I saw the face of the woman driving the car. She was in her late thirties, quite short, with a round face. I stared at her, only just managing to pull my eyes away before she noticed me. Then I turned my back on her, pretending to sneeze, not wanting her to see me. I did it because I didn't want her to recognize me, the way I'd just recognized her.

The Fiesta pulled off up the Pancras Road and I stood, watching it go. Dana had seen my reaction and was saying something to me but I couldn't hear her. Once again my head was full of people, all demanding my attention. I made them quieten down, stop running around, and line up. One by one. Then they had lined up. I thanked Dana quickly, thrust some notes in her hand and ran off to my bike.

Forty minutes later I was standing in the living room of the Chortney house, talking to Iris, who had once again backed into her chair and was curled up on herself like an old toenail. Her daughter-in-law was not home, she said, which I already knew; there was no yellow Ford Fiesta parked on any of the streets nearby. It was her who'd been driving it. Once again I apologized for my late appearance, but added that I knew she wouldn't have gone to bed yet. Mrs Chortney assured me that she didn't mind in the least. Then I asked her the question that I'd come to ask her.

'The woman who owned the house opposite,' I said, 'where the young girl died?'

'Yes.' Mrs Chortney nodded her head.

'She didn't make a will, and her house went to her third husband, who moved to New Zealand.'

'Yes.'

'But what I want to know is the name of her son.

You said that you didn't like him. The son from her first marriage?'

Mrs Chortney frowned. 'He'd be fifty now.'

'Yes,' I said. 'But do you remember his name?'

'Of course, it was George. I never—'

'George what, Mrs Chortney?'

'George Curtis,' the old lady said. 'His name was George Curtis.'

'And your daughter-in-law, she knew him?'

'Yes. And my son. They helped him out at his shop. Kebabs, he sold, don't know what he does now. I could never stand them.'

'No,' I said, and glanced up at the mantelpiece where there was a picture of her son, sitting on a palm-fringed beach, the man who had served me the last time I'd been in Curtis's shop.

'Nasty piece of work that George, ever since he was a nipper. I haven't seen him for years but I don't suppose he's changed much.'

'No,' I said, 'you're almost definitely right.'

Olly was at his usual place. He followed me to the cash machine where I gave him a twenty. I'd parked on a side street, but while Olly walked off to the kebab shop I pulled out onto the High Street and sat in the Mazda, keeping my eye on the place. After thirty-five minutes Olly came out and sauntered across the road towards me, and I leant over to unlock the passenger door. He got in.

'Well?' I said.

'Not bad. The hamburger that is. Better than the kebabs.'

'I think you know what I mean.'

'Oh, sorry. Yeah. Only one geezer came in and asked for George.'

'Right,' I said. 'I think I saw him. Guy in his thirties, looked like a third-division footballer. He was in and out fast, didn't buy anything.'

'That's him.'

'So what happened?'

'He asked if George were about and the bloke behind the counter said no, then asked his name. It sounded a bit weird, that way round.'

I nodded. 'Then what?'

'He said his name was Jeffrey. Not Jeff, Jeffrey. Then he shook the man's hand. I reckon he palmed him something. You reckon they're pushing from there?'

'And the rest. I don't know.'

'You want me to go back in?'

'It's OK. I think I know what to do. Thanks though.' I pulled out another twenty for Olly, which he hadn't expected to get, and which I hadn't actually expected to give him. He took it with a smile, punched me on the arm and disappeared.

I sat for a while wondering what to do. It was about one a.m., the streets packed with revellers, and I suddenly had a flash of my night in York's; all those people churning around together in the semi-dark. I found that I couldn't get anywhere near to understanding it, and the realization made me feel old. I looked at the people walking by, the girls mostly laughing together but most of the men depressed-looking and defeated, in their weekend duds, as if they'd tried to find something and failed. As if there was some sort of secret out there in the pubs and bars that they hadn't been let in on.

I wanted to go into the kebab shop and tell the guy my name was Jeffrey, and see what he'd hand me, but I knew he'd be bound to recognize me. Instead, I waited until two men pulled up in an Audi and one of them got out. He was only a couple of minutes in the shop and when he emerged he got back into the driver's seat and handed his friend what looked to me like a small piece of paper. Then, through the window I saw the passenger hand the driver a book. When he turned immediately to the back I knew it was an *A to Z*.

The Audi pulled out and I followed. In less than ten minutes we'd driven down past King's Cross and up the Pentonville Road towards the Angel. The car took a right at the lights onto Amwell Street, and cruised along until it took another right onto Margery Street, the one-way cut-through used mainly by cab drivers. The car slowed, prowling for a place to park. When it had found one I cruised past, turning my head away. I continued down towards the lights at the bottom of the street, keeping an eye on the two guys in my mirror. They were getting out of their car. I'd hoped the lights would be red so I could see where the men went, but they were green, and I couldn't risk being spotted. I turned right, almost straight back on myself onto Lloyd Baker street, and did a circuit back up and round onto Margery Street again, where I parked.

I looked around, but the men were nowhere. I got out of the car and walked up the street, but couldn't see any sign of them. Their car was parked at the top end of Margery Street, near the old Merlin's Cave pub, which was now derelict. I walked past it, and up onto Amwell Street, and then back down, wondering what had happened to them.

They could have gone into any of the nearby buildings, and I was trying to work out a way of finding out which one it was when I realized that once again I didn't need to worry. I stepped into a doorway across the street from the Audi and waited. I figured there were bound to be more people coming this way and I didn't have to wait long before finding I was right. This time it was a black Jeep Renegade, which pulled onto the street and slowed. It parked close to the Audi and three men got out, all in their forties, all looking like they had a few quid. Without looking around or checking any instructions they walked back up the street towards the Merlin's Cave. They walked down the side of the building, past the boarded up windows, until they were out of sight.

I waited five minutes. The street stayed quiet. I stepped down from the doorway and crossed the road towards the derelict pub. I walked to the right of it, where I'd seen the three men turn. I was faced with a wooden door, leading towards what I assumed must have been the backyard of the pub, or the beer garden if it had had one. There was no latch so I pushed the door open, walked through it, and found myself in a narrow passageway lit only by some security lights from the builder's yard next door. I walked to the end. The passageway had been blocked off by some pretty shoddy but effective brickwork and I turned round. There was nothing on my left. All that I could see on my right was a steel security door, the type they put on empty council houses to stop squatters moving in. I stood in front of it listening, but I couldn't hear anything. The door had no handle, and there was nothing to show that it had been opened in years.

But it must have been. The door itself was largely in shadow, but when I looked closely I saw that someone had cut a tiny peephole into it, at eye level. I looked round, then knocked, lightly. Then I knocked again. After a few seconds a section in the top of the door, that I hadn't even noticed, opened a touch.

'Who sent you?'

'George,' I said. 'Big George.'

'What's your name?'

'Jeffrey,' I said, hoping that Olly had heard right.

'Wait.'

The shutter closed. I waited for a minute, and heard some shuffling behind the door. Then it opened again.

'Quickly.'

The door opened a foot and I slid through it.

I was at the top of a flight of stairs, at the bottom of which I could hear a faint hubbub, which I could tell was quite a loud noise reaching me through at least one other door. To my left was a heavyset black man, wearing a tee shirt three sizes too small. His face was calm and assured – he didn't need to assume a menacing expression. In a ring next to Lennox Lewis he may have looked a touch slender, and not in such brilliant shape. Nowhere else. He was standing in front of another doorway, this one covered by a curtain, his legs spread, his hands folded across his chest.

'Fifty.'

I reached for my wallet and handed him three notes, all twenties, which he passed back through the curtain without looking round. A hand must have taken them because when he pulled his back out it was empty.

'Sorry, no change.'

I shrugged my shoulders and smiled. A tap came on the steel door. The man ignored it, and then nodded me down the unlit stairs, towards the sound, which was increasingly of whooping, and cheering. Hey, maybe I was in for a good night. All on expenses. I turned away from the guy and took a step forward.

I walked down the stairs carefully, noting that if I were a health and safety officer I would have demanded a handrail, or at least more adequate lighting. I turned a corner and came to the bottom, where I was faced with another door, guarded by another guy of similar proportions to the first. He didn't look at me or ask me any questions. Instead, he reached out to the handle of the door, pulled it open for me, and the hubbub I'd heard before turned into real noise. I made to step forward. I was going to walk through the door but there was a man blocking my path.

'Hello,' he said. 'Come for another inspection?'

What light there was inside the door had leaked into the stairwell. I saw the shadow of the arm, going up behind me, and I just managed to move to the left before it came down. Whatever the guy was using still made contact with the side of my head though, raking down onto the back of my neck, making me lurch forward into Chortney, who had to take a step backwards. I caught a glimpse, beyond him, and beyond a crowd of people to a stage, lit by a spotlight, a foot off the ground. It can't have been her, but in that second I could have sworn it was Natalie who was standing on it, her naked arms high above her head. Then the girl on the stage was swamped by people and I couldn't see her. I made to push myself backwards, into the guy who had clubbed me, but I stopped. My eyes found the gun in Chortney's hand.

'This way please,' he said, tucking the gun into his jacket pocket. 'There's someone who's dying to meet you.'

Part Four

Chapter One

They sat me in a booth at the back, Juliet Chortney next to me, her husband opposite, with his back to the empty stage and his hand underneath a jacket on the table, holding the gun. He told me he wouldn't hesitate to use it, and I had no reason to disbelieve him. The gun had a silencer on it, and getting a body out of there would be easy. They'd just say I was drunk, and no one there would argue even if I was a drunk who was bleeding. Chortney told me to sit back, with my hands on the table, as we waited for George.

'Why not enjoy the show?' his wife said.

A tape played an old Dean Martin album and the place, which was already very busy, filled up. If everyone had paid fifty quid, someone was making a lot of money, and I didn't imagine the bar would be cheap. I looked round for any faces I might know, but apart from the stage the place was very dark, and dense with smoke. I thought I maybe saw a couple of people, but certainly no one who would be likely to help me out. I turned my attention to the stage, which was now empty, except for a trapeze-like structure hanging from the ceiling.

So. Curtis had keys to the house Lucy had died in, and when his mother died he used the place, knowing that it would be a long time or never before his mother's last husband came back from Oz to claim it. He put Lee Finch in there, and Lucy too, for whatever purpose. I wondered how many other girls had stayed there, and what had happened to them. I didn't really want to know the answer to that, but I had the feeling that pretty soon I would do. I kept my eyes on the stage, and it stayed empty for another twenty minutes, during which the bar grew busier and all of the seats were taken.

But then there was a movement to stage left, as Luke had taught me to call it, and the crowd settled down. After a second or two the music went dead.

I sat with my hands in front of me, keeping my eye on Chortney and the coat in front of him. Over his shoulder, two men dragged a girl into the centre of the stage and began tying her wrists to the trapeze, about three feet above her head. I say dragged, she was very slight and they didn't have to put much effort into it. One was the man from the lower door, and the other was smaller, wearing a Kangol fisherman's hat, with his back to me. The girl looked startled rather than afraid, her eyes wide as new coins, shining in the spot. I was pretty sure she was the girl I'd seen earlier, in the car with Juliet Chortney. She looked out of it, hardly even noticing what was happening to her, but still making a feeble effort to fight the men off at the same time. It almost looked as if she was badly pretending to resist, but there was something about her that told me she wasn't.

Right in front of me Chortney smiled, but didn't look round. On the stage the two men had finished and the girl was secured to the trapeze, her thin arms high in the air. She stood, panting slightly, as the man in the fisherman's hat turned and moved towards the front of the stage. Not a man really, just a lad. As he stepped down into the crowd at the apron I saw it was the boy. Lee Finch. He disappeared into the crowd, and I gave myself a gold star for finding him.

Throughout the auction that was held for her, the girl on the stage remained quiet, finding her position uncomfortable, shifting from one leg to another. She was in her underwear. She didn't seem to be listening to what was going on. Then, when the auction was over, two masks were thrown into the crowd and when they had found their targets, two men got up on stage wearing them. One of them, a youngish-looking guy in a grey suit, held his arms aloft and the crowd cheered. The other seemed more eager to get on with it. He strode over to the girl and yanked her bra down. That got a cheer too. The guy from the door, who had remained on stage, warned him to be careful, and then stepped back. It wasn't until the second guy had turned his back on the audience and approached the girl, that she started screaming.

'What have we here then?'

It would have had to be a loud voice to cut through the noise, and it certainly was. It was pure, cartoon bulldog. George Curtis sat down opposite me, next to Chortney.

'If it's not Mr Rucker. The private eye stroke health and safety man.' Curtis laughed, and raised a glass at me. 'I take it our sanitary conditions meet with your approval this time. Or are you going to report us?'

I looked at Curtis but didn't say anything. Curtis put his glass down, leant across the table and hit me, a hard punch full in the face. Juliet Chortney immediately shuffled herself up against me.

'Stop it,' she said, in a syrupy voice. 'Leave his nice face alone. At least let him enjoy the show. You *are* enjoying it?'

I ignored her, and looked back towards the light. On the stage the girl had had her underwear torn off her and she was naked. She was a skinny girl, thirteen or fourteen, with small white breasts and pubic hair so light it was almost invisible in the white glare that was making her squint. She was limply struggling to free her hands, as the two men began to paw at her, pulling her legs and elbows apart as she tried to close in on herself. Once again the auctioneer stepped forward and told them to be careful. One of the men got down on his knees, and forced his head between the girl's legs.

I looked at Chortney and saw his hand tense beneath the coat.

'Go on,' he said, though I could hardly hear him. 'Try it.'

I told myself not to be stupid, but my body was tense, ready to go for him. Then I felt Juliet Chortney's hand on my thigh. I felt the tug of her fingers as she pulled at my jean buttons. She kissed the side of my neck and my hands clenched on the table, but her husband was still looking me in the eye.

'Go on,' he said. 'Please. Just move your hands.'

I kept my hands still. Getting shot wouldn't change anything. My eyes went to those of the girl on the stage, trying to send some sort of compassion to her. I wondered what was going on in the minds of the people, the men watching this, and decided that they thought it was a show, that the girl was acting. But I knew she wasn't. Natalie had been up on that stage. I kept my eyes on the girl's eyes, but when one of the men stood up in front of her, forcing her legs apart, and the other moved behind her, I pulled them out of focus. It made me feel guilty to do this, as if I were abandoning her, but I wasn't able to watch what was happening. They were both standing now, both pressed against her. All I saw was a haze of lights and a mass of dark shapes, but I couldn't shut the sound out, which was so loud it cut through the yelling of the crowd like a siren through traffic. The girl managed to keep it up for probably no more than five minutes, but to me it sounded like it would never stop. Then it was just noise, and shouting, and I don't know how long that went on for. After a while all I became aware of was a feeling in my stomach, which was one of sickness and disgust, laced with the thought that if I'd been allowed to see this, I was in deep, deep shit.

Eventually the noise died, the focus began to break up, and there was a movement to the small bar just behind us. I came back into the room, sat up a little and looked at the stage. For a second I thought that the girl had gone but she was still there, lying on the front of the stage. Now there were three men, different men from the ones who had started. I hadn't noticed the change. As the noise evened out, Juliet Chortney stopped what she was doing and sat up.

'He must be a poof,' she said to her husband.

'That true, mate? We don't cater for your sort here, sorry about that.'

I ignored them and looked back at the girl, who was conscious but still out of it. The men moved away from her and the doorman came forward and picked her up. He carried her off, through a door at the back. She wasn't moving much. As soon as the stage was empty, Juliet Chortney disappeared from the booth, and headed through the crowd. I saw her step onto the stage before going through the same door the girl had been carried through, and then I turned to Curtis.

'What do you feed them?'

'Huh?' He'd been turned to the stage but now he looked at me.

'What do you give them, dose them with?'

'Oh,' he said, as though I'd just asked him what sort of oil he put in his car. 'Rohypnol. Benzodiazepine. You heard of it?' I shook my head slowly. 'You probably have. Roofies. The date-rape drug, they call it. Causes almost complete memory loss. Sometimes flashbacks, but not always, and never very clear. Sure you don't know it?'

'I've heard of it.'

'It's very popular Stateside, which is where I get it. Made in Mexico. It's effective and almost untraceable, unless you're looking for it of course, which isn't likely, at least not over here.'

Curtis stood up and I nodded to myself. I thought about Natalie. She had said she could see things. Now I knew what they were. Now I knew why jumping in front of a tube train had made sense to her. While I was thinking, Curtis had stepped behind the bar. He came back with a bottle of Canadian Club and a glass.

'And Juliet Chortney finds the girls?'

'Very good,' he said. He bowed his head in apparent appreciation of my logic. 'Yes. But the boy too, don't forget the boy.' Curtis picked up his drink and downed it, before pouring himself some more from the Club, and half-filling the empty glass.

'The boy? He's been hiding here?'

'Here and there. A right babe magnet he is. Or used to be, when we let him out. Can't any more of course, too dangerous, but he'll soon be back in action. He can sometimes get three or four girls at a time if he's at the right club. You know, you've seen him. Give 'em some pills, tell them it's a party. It was even better when young Lucy helped him, it made them feel more secure to have another girl along.'

'Lucy,' I said. 'Oh yes. Now why don't you tell me about her?'

Curtis stopped, and I waited for him. He looked almost wistful. '*You* know what happened to Lucy. The poor kid was in love with her, you know? Wouldn't let me so much as touch her – though she would have made me a small fortune. We had a few arguments about it, believe me, to begin with, until she began to prove useful. After a week or so she was even good at getting girls back here on her own. Young girls, they just want to be told what to do, they want to be told that they're where it's *at*.'

I nodded to myself again and thought of the girls at Nicholas Court. Had Finch got them along here? Was he planning to? 'And so when you get them back here you just dose them up, that it? Before . . . this?'

Curtis looked reflective. 'The trick is to get them to swallow the stuff *before* we get 'em back here, or any of the other venues we use. We use the house for that usually, if we can't get it down them before. Stick it in some vodka. After that, only *after*, the mind's a complete blank until it wears off. It really is amazing.'

'And afterwards you just dump the girls?'

'We drop them off in the morning with a few quid in their pocket. They're none the wiser and no harm done. Usually,' he added.

Curtis sat back in his chair and stretched. 'Still early for me,' he said. Then he made me drink the measure of Canadian Club sitting in front of me, and when I'd done it he made me drink another, and another after that.

I drank what I was told to drink, pretending I was gagging on it, finding it hard to swallow. But Canadian Club was a good choice, it went down easily. I was wondering just what Curtis planned to do with me once I'd drunk enough of it not to be a problem, when my eyes were drawn to something in the crush. It was a fisherman's hat, moving my way. I saw the boy pushing through the crowd to our table, where he immediately started to say something to Curtis. But whatever it was he never finished it. The words disappeared and he turned to me.

Finch hadn't expected to see me sitting there. It jolted him like a cattle prod. It was a second or two before he was able to take in my presence. I looked up at him, and his jaw began to tremble. I could see his mind going back to that night, when he'd seen me on the street at four a.m., and the look on his face was the same. Horror, and shock. But this time he didn't run away.

'You bastard,' he managed to say. It was almost a whimper. 'You fucking, fucking bastard.'

He still thought it was me, that I'd killed the girl he'd been in love with. I was there that night, and he'd seen me in Camden and at York's. He couldn't think who else it could have been. I thought he was going to break down, to collapse on the floor, but instead he launched himself across the table at me, sending the drinks flying, managing to get his nails into my neck before I could stop him. It hurt, but that was OK. He was lying across the table, trying to throttle me, but he didn't have the strength. I got my hands under his armpits. I pushed back in my seat and twisted him round towards Chortney, slamming Finch's thin body against him and Curtis.

The two men both put up their arms to protect themselves. As Finch slid back across the table his hands were wrenched off my neck and he tried to get hold of my arms. I shifted to the right, trying to slide out of the booth. I didn't know what sort of a chance I'd have of getting out of there, but it was better than no chance at all. There was only one thing Curtis would do with me if I didn't get out. I hadn't had any Roofies, there was only one way of making me forget what I'd seen.

The upholstery on my left ripped open as the gun in Chortney's hand went off from underneath Finch, who was twisting round to try to get to me again. I made a move along the bench but Curtis shoved the table forward, sending it hard into my guts. Again the bench-back to the left of me jolted as another bullet went into it, closer this time. I got my hands on the table and forced it forward, against Curtis, as far as I could, and just managed to get my shoulder beneath it. As I did so I was vaguely aware that the music had gone off, that there was more light than before. I didn't stop to think about it. I planted my feet and launched myself up and forward, upending the table, sending the kid to the floor, ramming it straight into Chortney and Curtis as hard as I could. I saw the gun in Chortney's raised hand, above the table top. I grabbed for it, but only succeeded in knocking it down onto the floor where the kid was lying. While Curtis reached for it I lunged to the right, towards the crowd, which was splitting open now, scattering this way and that. I could hear shouting and screaming, my eyes were full of people rushing, chairs going down, tables being knocked over and drinks flying everywhere.

As I staggered up from the mess of Curtis, Chortney, Finch and the table, my left foot caught a broken glass, which sent me lurching towards the ground, up against two legs that had been running towards me. I sent a fist out wildly, trying to find my feet before Curtis's hand found the gun. I caught the guy in front of me in the groin, doubling him up, but then there was another guy, in the same dark trousers. I swung for him too, still trying to get up from my knees, but then there was yet another guy. I managed to make it to my feet, and sent out a right that only found air. But I wasn't going to let them just take me, I was dead anyway whatever happened. I was about to launch another swing, aiming at the nearest face, when I noticed that all of the three men standing in front of me were police officers.

I stood, surrounded by the three men. The lights were full on. I looked through them. There were about twelve uniformed officers in the room, all in flack vests, four of them armed as far as I could see. Ken Clay stood in the middle of the room, shouting, telling people what to do. Behind him, two were blocking the exit I'd come through while several more were streaming across the stage to the back door, where the girl had been carried.

Those still in the room were shouting at the crowd of people to lie on the floor and not move. Most had already done it, their hands behind their backs, some of them already cuffed. I stopped trying to lay hell into anyone and turned round.

Chortney was still on the bench, his hands on his head, covered by an officer holding a pistol. Curtis was slumped on the floor beneath me, his back against the upturned table, blood streaming down his face where the table had broken his nose. I hadn't even noticed that. Next to him was the boy. He was also leaning back against the table, his shirt and the top of his trousers soaked with blood where Chortney's bullets must have gone through his stomach. He had the gun in his hand and he was pointing it at me.

'Give it up!'

It was the nearest armed officer. He was pointing his sub-machine gun at Lee Finch, from no more than fifteen feet. Lee didn't move.

'Put-it-down-slowly.'

The kid still didn't move, even though I could tell that holding the gun upright was costing him a lot of effort. I spread my hands out and took a step back, looking into his already pale face. The room went silent.

Finch's gun was pointed at my chest. His finger was tight on the trigger. I tried to find his eyes.

'I didn't do it, Lee.'

I heard the rattle of metal as the guy beside me tensed. I held a hand out to him. I shook my head.

'I didn't do it. It wasn't me.'

'You must have. I saw you there, you were following her, taking pictures . . .'

The gun in Finch's hand twitched. There were tears beginning to run down his cheeks, almost colourless now. His jeans were soaked from sitting in a puddle of blood.

'I didn't do it. And I know that it wasn't you either.'

He looked surprised, but still wary. Beside him, Curtis didn't move. 'Then who was it?' He was almost breathless. 'Who did it to her? Who then? Who was it, who . . .?'

I was about to tell him when the gun he was holding wobbled. The officer beside me took this as a sign that the boy was about to shoot. Once again I could feel him tense and once again I managed to stop him opening up by holding my hand out to him. But it didn't make any difference. The hand holding the gun moved down slowly towards the floor, as if the boy were a toy whose spring was winding down. His head rolled gently to the side. His eyes stayed open but after a few seconds I could tell he wasn't seeing anything. The man beside him still didn't move. The boy had let the gun fall only a few inches from Curtis's hand.

I looked down at Curtis and found his eyes. They were small and empty. Then I looked across at the gun and his eyes flickered down to it too.

'Go on,' I said. 'Please. Go on, George. You can make it. Please.'

But the only movement he made was to shift his leg out of the way of the thick, dark pool spreading slowly towards him.

Chapter Two

When the lift got to the fifth floor it told me where I was, the doors opened and I got out, before padding along the carpet to flat 516. I knocked. After a few seconds Mr Bradley opened the door for me, and we shook hands. I followed him into the apartment where he told me he had just put a jug of coffee on, and he asked me if I wanted one. I thanked him and he walked into the small kitchen area.

It was about noon. At nine that morning the Bradley family had been informed by telephone of the events of the previous night, and told that a police officer would call on them later that afternoon, or the next day; when certain tests had been carried out on the dead boy, specifically to see if his semen matched that found on their daughter. The police were confident that it would, but needed, of course, to check. At five minutes past nine I called the family myself and told them that I was more than happy to come round in person, and give them an account of what had transpired the night before. I took the coffee Mr Bradley handed me and perched on one of the chrome stools at the breakfast bar, setting the cup down next to the cardboard file I'd brought along.

I'd come straight from Camden, where I'd met up

with Olly. I bought Olly breakfast, which really was the least I could do. It was Olly I had to thank for getting me out last night. He'd called the police. He'd gone back to the kebab shop with the money I'd given him, hoping to score with his unexpected bonus. He'd used the password, Jeffrey, and been handed what he thought was a wrap, but was simply an address. The Merlin's Cave, it said, Margery Street. Olly was about to shrug his shoulders, bin the address and find something on the street, when George Curtis had rushed into the shop from the back.

'I heard him say to the geezer on the counter that they'd caught that snoopy twat,' Olly told me. 'So I knew he meant you. I heard him say he was going to deal with you, and by the look on his face I could tell how. So I thought I'd better come to your rescue, like.'

Olly had thought about coming to the place on the piece of paper himself, but instead he did something as natural to him as synchronized swimming for cats. He called the police.

'I've been after Curtis for years,' Ken Clay told me, half an hour later. We were sitting in the light, airy foyer of the Bradleys' building, with only the gurgling fishpond to keep us company. 'He's been in the background of a few drug busts. We've known about his illegal drinking holes for a while but we've never been able to pin him down to one long enough to get anyone in undercover, see what he was really doing. I always had the idea he was probably paying one of our lot for tip-offs, but I could never find out who.' I had my own ideas about that but I let them ride. 'When your mate Olly told me what he'd heard, and that you'd gone off like you had, I knew it was our chance. We got a man in, Myers, using the password Olly gave us, and we were waiting outside. He saw that you were in *difficult-ies*, shall we say, and he also caught the last dregs of what had been going on in there. He called us and we called in the cavalry, and Myers got the door open from the inside. The rest, you know. We found a shitload of that drug they were using. Curtis was pushing it, and that's one of the ways he got people along to his club – he'd only sell it from there. God only knows what he's been responsible for. We found that, as well as Ecstasy and the usual porn shots he was selling. A good night for us.' Clay sat back and gave a good scratch to about half of his chins. 'For once, Billy my boy, you've actu-ally done me a favour. I'm sorry for the way we went for you over this, but you know the drill. I couldn't give you an easy time just because we were *friends*, could I?'

Clay turned his attention to some holiday brochures in front of him, which he'd picked up on the way. He'd already told me that he was surprising his wife with a trip to the Caribbean for their twenty-fifth wedding anniversary.

'Friends! Jesus!'

I shook my head and laughed all the way to the lift. When I got there I turned. 'You sure this is a good idea?'

'The only way, Billy. The only way.'

Mrs Bradley was resting on one of the two sofas, and she gave me a quiet smile as she said hello. She was sitting with her daughter's head in her lap, casually stroking the girl's hair, pushing it behind her ear. Emma was very still, her brown eyes looking at me nervously, a little embarrassed. It looked to me that she'd been crying; probably with relief. Mr Bradley looked relieved too. There was something lighter about the way he moved, as he eased himself back into an armchair. Behind them, the door to the roof garden was open, and I cast a glance towards the soft array of flowers out there. The roses were the same shade of crimson as those in the Bradleys' garden in Ravensey.

When I had set myself, I told the family what had happened the night before, once I'd got back into London. What I had to recount was pretty gruesome, especially concerning the stage show, and I could see Mrs Bradley worrying that Emma should be hearing it all. I didn't have any qualms about it, so I pretended not to notice Mrs Bradley's concern. When I began to describe what had happened to the young girl at the Merlin's Cave, Mr Bradley went grey.

'And that,' he said, 'that happened to Lucy? They drugged her,'and then—'

'No,' I answered. 'No they didn't.' I paused and let out a breath. 'I'm afraid that Lucy was a part of it, but not as a victim.'

'I don't understand.'

'When your daughter came to London', I said, 'she had very few contacts. But she was resourceful. She knew she was attractive, and she had money from her account. She probably found a cheap B&B, and then hit the club scene. She knew she could make men pay for her drinks, give her somewhere to sleep, do anything she wanted them to really. And then she met the boy, the one we were looking for, Finch. He was getting girls for Curtis's club, and he probably tried to get Lucy, but she was too clever for him. Rather than get drugged up and raped she joined him. She helped him find the girls, and then get them whacked on drugs, Roofies, they're called, the date-rape—'

'No!' Mr Bradley made to stand up.

'Yes, I'm afraid. Yes. There's no doubt about it. Curtis has made a confession, and so have two of the people he worked with. They all said Lucy helped them. She showed them she was just as good at luring girls to Curtis's clubs as Finch was, and they started to pay her good money, and gave her a place to live. And in the meantime the boy was falling in love with her.'

'I can't believe Lucy would—'

'Your daughter was no angel, Mr Bradley. She did a lot of things you didn't know about, like most teenage girls I suppose. But Lucy went a lot further. Your wife knows what I mean.'

I turned to Mrs Bradley and reached for the folder beside me. I passed the folder to her and Emma sat up. I sat back as Mrs Bradley opened the folder, but as soon as she saw what it contained she closed it up.

'Where did you get this?'

'From your office,' I said. 'I came back to your house after you left, and broke in.'

'How dare you?!'

Her husband held his hand out, and then stood up out of his chair.

'You don't want to see this, James.'

'Your wife's right,' I said, but it didn't stop the man grabbing the folder from his wife's hand. I wanted to warn him. 'It's a porn shot,' I said. 'It's about five or six months old, semi-professional quality, taken just before Lucy sat her A levels, from the date on the bottom. At a little studio in Arundel. It's quite hardcore I'm afraid.'

James Bradley had opened the folder and was now looking at the photograph, going through something I had often imagined and hoped to hell I never had to experience. Looking at your little girl with her legs in the air. I didn't envy him.

'She was part of it,' I said.

Bradley let the photograph fall onto the low table. He looked at me, hard.

'OK. OK. But she was tricked, tricked into it. She didn't know what was going on there, not really. And then that little bastard killed her, left her in the garbage. Was it because she wouldn't let him have her? Or she finished with him? Maybe she even threatened to go to the police. To be honest I don't care. When the detective called this morning I almost laughed. Is that bad, to be glad that little shit's dead? Is that—?'

I interrupted him. 'No, Mr Bradley,' I said. 'You shouldn't be glad. But not out of any moral sense. It's just that Lee Finch didn't kill your daughter. It wasn't him. He did a lot of things to a lot of girls but none of them to Lucy.'

Bradley stopped. He looked at me as though I were mad, then shook his head. The photograph of Lucy was lying face up on the table. Mrs Bradley picked it up and folded it in two. I turned to her.

'I wondered for a long time yesterday why you didn't just burn that, Mrs Bradley,' I said. 'But then I realized there'd be no point. Lucy had plenty more spare if you had. Did she threaten to show them to your husband?'

Mrs Bradley paused, then crossed her legs. 'Yes.'

'And you knew how much it would hurt him. Lucy probably said she was going to get them published, didn't she, or at least show the neighbours?'

'Yes.' Mrs Bradley's mouth hardly moved. 'It was in

342

June. I yelled at her for not studying one day, and she told me she didn't need A levels for what she wanted to do. That's when she went upstairs and came down with that. She gave that to me, I didn't find it. Can you believe it, showing your mother something . . . like that? She laughed when I looked at it. She'd had some boyfriend take it, she said. I'd threatened to stop her allowance if she didn't start behaving differently, but she said that if I did she'd have to earn money that way, and what would Daddy think?'

'And what did you say to her?'

'I told her she was a slut.'

'Victoria!'

James Bradley had stood up again. I realized that it was the first time I'd ever heard his wife's name. He moved towards her but she didn't look at him.

'I thought she was a slut. And she was.'

'Stop it. Lucy's dead—'

'No, you stop it.' Now she did turn. 'Look what she's done. Oh, so she's dead, what does that change? She was a horrible child. She always was. What sort of person bribes her mother like that? What sort of person lures young girls to be raped? Your lovely little angel, all alone in her tree house for a cloud? Well?! Well?! What sort of person does that, James?! Tell me!'

Bradley turned his head away.

'And how did it make you feel, Mrs Bradley?' Her eyes levelled on mine. 'Do you want me to guess? Shall I?' I took a sip of coffee. 'You probably wished she was dead,' I said. 'Didn't you?'

Both Victoria and James Bradley were looking at me. There was silence in the room. Bradley stepped

ADAM BARON

back from his wife, his mouth opening. He was about to protest when I saw him deciding not to. He was waiting.

'Both Inspector Clay and I wondered about you, Mrs Bradley,' I said. 'From the off.' I stepped back and leant on the stool again. 'The problem was that the doorman had sworn that you hadn't left the building that night, so the police crossed you out. But I did a little experiment. The last time I was here I put the door on the latch. The back door. Later, that night, I waited until someone used the car park and I strolled into the compound. Then I sat, for an hour or so, outside. At about two a.m. I came in through the back door, which no one had fixed. I walked behind the security booth, got in the lift and rode all the way up here. Nobody saw me. When I went out I walked up to the desk and the guy hardly noticed me, he was ploughing through a John Grisham. I asked him if he had seen anyone come in in the last ten minutes and he said no. There was no one. So you could have snuck out. You could have done it and not been spotted coming back in, either.'

'How would I have known how to find her?'

'You could have found her ages ago.' I shrugged. 'A resourceful woman like you. Employing me would have been a good way of pretending you had no idea where she was. You could have guessed that she would hang out in Camden. You could have found her, and you certainly had a motive to kill her. Get her out of your hair once and for all. Young Ian Williams, your gardener, heard you two fighting all the time, he wasn't fazed in the least when I suggested to him that you had done it. I don't say you necessarily planned it, though you could have, but there's one thing I do know. I know

344

what she made you feel like and you do too, don't you? You know how you felt.'

'Yes,' she said.

'And how *was* that, Mrs Bradley? How did she make you feel?'

'I hated her,' the woman said, slowly and deliberately. 'I used to think sometimes of the other children she stopped me from having, and then I'd look at her. At who she was. And I *hated* her.'

Mrs Bradley was poised and still. When she'd finished speaking the room was almost completely quiet. The only noise was that of weeping, coming from the French window. The Bradleys' daughter had moved over there, and was standing in the doorway with her back to us.

'You hated her. And how does that make *you* feel?' I asked. The girl made no response.

'Lucy,' I said.

No one said anything.

'Lucy,' I said again. And then again. Bradley looked at me.

'Why do you keep saying that?' He took a step forward but I didn't take my eyes off the girl.

'Why shouldn't I say it?' I asked her. 'Lucy. That's your name, isn't it?'

What took place after that seemed to do so in slow motion, an unreal haze.

'Don't be ridiculous. Emma, say something.' Mrs Bradley stood up off the sofa and turned to her daughter. The girl didn't move.

'You met Emma at the tube. Didn't you? Didn't you,

345

Lucy?' Still the girl was motionless. 'You phoned Emma and told her to meet you. She was so glad to hear from you and she went. You took her back to the house you were staying at, and you told her that she had no idea what it was like being you. Being the second best, having a mother who hated you. You said the two of you should swap, for a week maybe, see what it was like. That's what happened, isn't it? She loved you, Emma did, she wanted to be your friend. So she agreed. You cut her hair, and bleached it. You told her you'd both go home, and then she'd know what a bitch her mother really was, by the way she treated her, thinking she was you. Tell me if I've got anything wrong.'

No one said anything. The girl in the window was still turned away from me.

'You did a spot of cleaning that night, dusting the surfaces so that only one set of girl's prints would be found in the house. Didn't you? It was why the house looked so clean. You told Emma that you had to go out, and you left her at the house, telling her to wait for you. Then you went to York's and later you got Finch to drop you off at home. But before Finch left you went down on him, didn't you? In the car, probably, with Natalie watching. Then you ran inside and you killed her. You hit your sister on the back of the head with a hammer, and then suffocated her, while Finch was taking Natalie to Curtis's club. You put his sperm on her, knowing that he'd go away for it—'

'Get out. Now. This is the most—'

Bradley was shouting but his wife cut him dead. 'Shut up, James. Shut up. Go on. Go *on*.'

The girl still hadn't flinched. I took a breath. 'Finch didn't come back for an hour at the very least, so you had plenty of time. You killed her. Then you stripped her – you had to get her out of her own clothes. Then you dragged her downstairs. You weren't able to look at her face though, were you, which is why you covered it up. Then you dumped her out the back. You had gloves on by this point, long elegant satin ones, which I thought looked naff earlier on, but which meant that you didn't leave prints in the house or on the car or anywhere. Emma's prints were already on the car from earlier.' I didn't take a sip of coffee for dramatic effect. My mouth was dry. I set the cup back down on the counter.

'When you were finished, you came back here. It's not that long a walk. You may even have had your mother's car. You snuck in past the guard, which you must have done any number of times before, after a night out. Then you had to deal with your hair. When I first saw you, in Camden the time I wasn't even look-ing, I thought your hair was shorter than Emma's. It was how I could tell you apart. But it wasn't – it only seemed like that, because of the bunches you had it in. It was clever of you. When you'd crept back in here you spent the next hour dyeing your hair black, and then you were Emma. It still hasn't been that long, I bet if we tested your hair, Lucy, it would have black dye on it. You killed your sister, didn't you? You killed her because you wanted her life. Her grades, her university place. Everything.'

Nothing happened for a second. Nobody moved.

'That wasn't what I wanted.' Lucy's voice was ten years old. She turned round to her mother, staring at her, her eyes open, her hands in front of her.

'*I wanted you to love me. I wanted you to love me like you loved her.* I love you. I wanted you to love me. These

347

last few days, you've loved me, you have. You've held me. And touched me. And kissed me. You never did. It's been . . . the best time in my life. You came in my room and slept with me. I . . . You *never ever* loved me.'

Mr Bradley couldn't move. His face was a maze of confusion as he realized that Lucy was still alive. His favourite daughter. The scream that came out of his wife's mouth sounded like everything she had ever felt. Nothing could have stopped her rushing towards Lucy. She ran over the sofa as if it weren't there. She reached her daughter and forced her backwards. Lucy didn't resist, she tried to hold onto her mother, to bury her head into her chest. But Mrs Bradley pried her arms free and lashed at her, trying to get at her eyes, forcing her backwards towards the bank of roses. James Bradley was closer than I was. He was through the windows after them, trying to pull his wife and daughter apart. But he was a small man, totally blown away by what was happening. Lucy was being forced back towards the balcony, into the wooden trellis. Her mother was trying to throttle her, her nails deep into her daughter's throat. Lucy was choking, she was kicking at her, trying to get free.

I made it out onto the patio but I was too late. In his efforts to prise the two women apart James Bradley got caught between them and was thrust back against the flimsy trellis of roses, which gave way beneath his weight. He went over the balcony backwards, landing on the concrete five storeys below. When I got through the French windows, and looked over the edge, a thousand red rose petals like weightless drops of blood were rocking on the breathless air, floating down towards him.

Chapter Three

There were a few things that had made me think of it. The first inkling I had was when her mother had said she'd gone down to Sussex. It didn't seem like something Emma would have done, leaving her father and mother. Then, when she was asleep, sunbathing. I'd noticed something; a faint mark that I only realized later was the place where Lucy's belly had been pierced. I was pretty sure that Emma wouldn't have had that, though Lucy could have got one later to cover the mark. It was lucky that I'd found her asleep. Following that, at my flat, I'd mentioned seeing Emma at Camden, looking for her sister. Lucy hadn't acted surprised, having assumed that I'd spoken to Emma, but Emma would have been surprised, and maybe asked why I hadn't stopped my bike to speak to her. It was then that I first had the thought, a real suspicion.

After that, in the dental surgery that I broke into at the Bradleys' home, I was unable to find dental records for either of the girls. Lucy must have trashed them, knowing that they could be checked. That made me almost sure, but when I'd looked over the porn shot with Carl's eyeglass, and saw that yes, Lucy had definitely had a belly ring, I knew what had happened.

And really, it wasn't such a bad plan. The two girls

were exactly alike. At various times all throughout her life Lucy had pretended to be Emma, so she wouldn't get into trouble for things. Lucy knew her sister, she knew how to act like her, and any inconsistencies could be put down to having had a sister murdered. She would have been given a lot of latitude, would perhaps have been able to behave in all sorts of ways that would have been put down to bereavement. Later, when she'd taken up her college place she could have relaxed, loosened up a little, met new friends. She was a clever girl and probably would have got by at Oxford. She may well have stayed being Emma for ever, coming home at weekends to be spoiled by her mother. As long as she never let her father look inside her mouth ever again, she was safe. I was convinced that if she was careful her mother would never have guessed, she would never have let the thought anywhere near her. When I think of how Lucy had looked, her head in her mother's lap, I almost wish I hadn't upset the apple cart.

When I think of James Bradley I do wish it. But as Clay said, surprising Lucy with it was the only way. There was no proof, and no way of proving it. She had to confess. DNA tests wouldn't have worked, because there were no definite samples to cross-reference. The same with fingerprints; Lucy had wiped the bedrooms in Ravensey as well as those in Camden. In Camden this was assumed to have been done by the killer, after the murder. In Ravensey no one bothered to check until afterwards – why should they? – and even afterwards it wouldn't have been seen as strange not to find any prints because the Bradleys' had a daily. Even the tree house was clean, except for my prints. Any other prints that wouldn't be too old were in areas both of the girls had used.

If Lucy had denied the accusation then that would have been the end of it, in terms of the law if not Emma's friends, who probably could have caught her out if they'd known to try. I wanted to take her into Calshot Street, and try to force it out of her, but Clay was right; in a police station she would have been on her guard. But not there, not in the family apartment, not after I'd practically accused her mother of killing her daughter, and her mother had effectively told Lucy that she hated her. She had always suspected it, but hearing her mother actually say it was too much for Lucy to bear. Lucy had come out with it and Clay was right. What happened to Bradley couldn't have been foreseen by anyone.

When Lucy was taken into the station she was in shock and had to be removed to hospital. She kept screaming, and scratching at her eyes, as if, like Natalie, she was seeing something, an image she wanted to erase. I thought it might be the body of her sister, left in the garbage, which I can't help seeing myself from time to time. But I decided it wasn't. It was her father, the only person who had truly loved her. Knowing that it was all because of her that he was dead.

The police are still waiting for Lucy to be released, so they can charge her with her sister's murder, and also with being a party to abduction and rape. But I think they'll have a long wait. Lucy was strung out on so much resentment and self-disgust that when she broke, I think she broke for good. As the psychiatrist told me when I went to visit her, when a rubber band snaps, there's really not a lot you can do to make it whole again. If her mother ever visited her, he told me, then maybe she'd have a chance. In that case, I said, she didn't have any chance at all.

I actually went down to Ravensey to see her. In the chaos that followed her husband's fall I wasn't able to talk to her, to apologize for the things I'd had to say, and to commiserate with her for the loss of her daughter, Emma. I really did take the train this time, all the way, and once again I walked through the quiet village. I passed the woman from the post office, who lowered her eyes and nodded at me. When I got down to the house I found some workmen just packing up their van, parked on the gravel drive. They told me that Mrs Bradley was round the back. I walked round and found her, at the bottom of the lawn, wearing gardening gloves, tending a big fire that was cracking and spitting viciously. I told her how sorry I was. I said a few words about Emma, and about her husband, but Mrs Bradley neither heard me, nor saw me, nor gave any sort of recognition of the fact that I was standing there, speaking to her. She just went on tending her fire. Nevertheless, I said what I had to say. Then, just before leaving her, I looked up at the horse chestnut behind her, where I'd sat a few days earlier, thinking about Lucy, wondering if a girl really could do such a thing to her sister. Mrs Bradley saw my glance and turned to face me with a look I'll never forget.

The branches above her head were empty.

I didn't have a lot to do in the days that followed. I hung out with Nicky quite a bit, staying up late a few nights talking. I told him about Shulpa and he didn't mind. He said that he looked forward to my finding out what a pain she was, so that there would be two people in the world who didn't think the sun shone out of her admittedly shapely arse. I also spent a lot of time in the gym, and went with Sal to watch Des's fight at a hall in Lewisham. He was put in with a guy from Deptford, and even though the guy had a lot of local support, he only lasted four rounds. Barely more than I had. Des was made up, and there was a good party afterwards, following which I drove Sal home. I felt slightly awkward as we pulled up outside her house, and stopped my car, but when I turned to look at her we both burst out laughing. Sal kissed me on the cheek and ran upstairs.

'You don't get that lucky twice in a lifetime, Billy Rucker,' she said.

I spent some time in the office, doing chores. I spent some time chatting to Ally, about this and that, and managed to get past the reserve she was showing towards me. Thinking of Andy Gold made me just shake my head. I saw him too. I had to go into the station a couple of times to give statements, and then add to them. Curtis was charged, and was looking at fifteen years, minimum. Juliet Chortney and her husband the same. Iris Chortney didn't know anything, of course, and I asked Andy if I could break the news to her. The poor woman was so horrified when I explained everything that she couldn't speak. She started to tremble and eventually to cry, but she got it together to tell me that it wasn't for them, not for her daughter-in-law, not even for her son.

'For those girls,' she managed to say. 'For those girls.'

* * *

When I got to the gallery on Regent's Park Road, where Faber were hosting the party, the place was already quite busy. People were chatting, saying hello, and generally being gregarious in a muted way suitable for such an event. I was on my own, having told Shulpa that I didn't really want her to come. Our first fight. The gallery was a roomy, bright space, with polished beech flooring and soft music in the background. I drifted around, with the obligatory glass of cheap white in my hand, looking at the posters Faber had put up; huge shots of each of the poets, accompanied by a short poem, or an extract, printed in large type. I had to admit that while it all seemed a bit glitzy to me, the concept did seem to work. There was definitely a buzz about the event, with several people taking pictures and someone from Radio 4 making a feature.

I strolled around, picking up the odd book, flicking through the pages. I may have been biased, but nothing I read seemed to have the immediacy of my brother's work. I chatted away to the editor for a while, a woman I'd met before, but I didn't talk to any of the poets. They were surrounded by their friends, some of them laughing, some of them having serious discussions. They didn't know me. Eventually I found myself gravitating back towards Luke's stand, where I stood to the side by myself, feeling slightly foolish at being there on my own, almost wishing Shulpa had come after all. At least I'd have someone to go to dinner with after. It all

seemed, well, something of a disappointment after all
the expectations I'd had, and I found myself feeling
slightly let down. I was looking at my watch, wondering
how much longer to give it, when a middle-aged lady in
an expensive suit took hold of my wrist.

'Congratulations,' the lady said. 'Your work is lovely.
I bought your wonderful book, and I was wondering if
you would do me the honour of signing it.'

I thanked the lady, and smiled. I was halfway
through explaining when something else caught my
attention. It was two eyes, green like river moss in the
sun. Sharon walked up slowly, and waited quietly until
I'd finished. The lady, almost tearful, took her leave
after five minutes, clutching the book to her chest as if
it were the Bible.

'Hi.'

She had a copy of Luke's book too, folded between
her hands. A smile appeared on her face, like a candle
flame blown out before it could take. I couldn't look at
her.

'Hi,' I said. 'Thanks for coming. It's good of you to
come.'

Sharon nodded. She took a look round the room. 'I
can't believe I said I wasn't going to come here,' she
said. 'I was always going to come. Always.'

I took a sip of wine. 'Whatever. Anyway. I'm glad
you did.' I glanced at my watch. 'I'm going to head off
soon though, I think.'

'I know I'm late,' Sharon said, stopping me with a
hand on my sleeve. 'But I was with Luke. I've just come
from there.'

'Oh,' I said. I put the empty glass on a table and
stuck my hands in my pockets. 'It's OK, the ward, don't

you think? Not as nice as Lewis House but it won't be long before they move him back. I think they told me the 27th—'

'I've been telling him what a fuck up I've been making of my life recently.'

I met Sharon's eyes but she looked down at her feet. I sighed. 'Listen, you don't have to say that, Sharon—'

'Oh but I do, Billy. I really do.' Sharon let out a harsh laugh. She went a long way inside of herself and then looked at me. 'You haven't asked me how I am,' she said.

It was because I didn't want to hear it. 'I'm sorry,' I said, with a little sarcasm. 'How are you? How's . . . Ronan?'

'Fucked if I know.' She left a slight pause, possibly for me to ask. I didn't. That laugh again. 'We split up,' she said.

I didn't mean to react but I couldn't help it. I hoped Sharon didn't see my reaction. Once again I thought about what Nicky had said. I wondered if he could have been right? Had she realized? If so, was I going to blame her? Could I just forget it? I looked at my fingernails.

'What happened? I mean—?'

'He dumped me.'

'Oh,' I said.

Again, I hoped she didn't see what my reaction was. Sharon's eyes narrowed. She seemed to be waiting for me to ask why, but once again I didn't say anything. What did it matter? Again I made to go.

'He said he didn't believe it,' she said.

'Believe what?'

'What I felt for him. He said I'd never really loved him. He said it wasn't him I wanted.' Sharon was trying to look at me. 'He said he thought I was using him as an excuse. A get-out clause.'

I did look at her. 'From what?'

'You,' she said. She turned her head towards the huge blow up of Luke, sitting on an upturned fishing boat. 'From you, and from him.'

'Oh,' I said. 'Oh. Look, I'm sorry. I mean . . .' Something rose in my chest. 'What, what do you think? About . . . what he said. Is he right? I mean, how do you feel . . .?'

At that moment a young woman wearing large round glasses walked up to us and introduced herself as Lisa March. She was from the *Express*, she said, and had been trying to get in touch with me. I nodded. She said she wanted to do a profile of Luke, which would really help his book sales, and then began to ask both myself and Sharon the questions I had anticipated when I first knew about Luke's book. I answered her questions but I knew what she wanted. Eventually she got to the point.

'And, it must have helped you get over what happened to . . . well to have each other. I understand that you, you are friends.'

'Yes.'

'And, is there any more to it than that? I mean, I think our readers would find it very heart-warming to know that you have, have found—'

'Why did you think to ask us this?' I said. The woman ran a hand back through her hair.

'Well, I don't know really, I think someone at Faber may have mentioned something. I mean it's nothing to be ashamed of, is it? What with your brother in a . . . I think it would make a lovely story. I . . .'

My eyes had found Sharon's, and she was staring straight back at me. Her mouth opened slightly. I couldn't hear the girl talking any more. Then, suddenly, I saw Sharon. I saw her with Ronan, walking towards her flat, holding onto him, her head against his arm.

'Well, is it true? The publicist at Faber *did* seem pretty sure . . .'

I saw her, holding onto him, fishing for her keys, and then the door close behind them. I saw the light go on and the figure in the window. I saw the light go off.

'She's wrong,' I said, turning back to the journalist. 'Sharon and I are friends. I'm afraid that there's nothing more to it than that.'

'I see,' Lisa March said. 'I see.'

Ten minutes later I was sitting in the front seat of my car. I'd intended driving down to see my brother, to tell him how the whole thing had gone. But I changed my mind. I didn't feel like it. I sat for a while. Then I took the irises that I'd bought him from the back seat, and I walked up through the Lock, where the last of the Sunday stalls were being taken down by council workers. No one else was about. I walked through and up to the bridge. When I got to the High Street I turned right, towards the tube, and when I got there I waited for the lights to change. When the signal came, I crossed, and then I was standing outside a greasy spoon café, opposite the Marks and Spencer store, with its give-away green store fronting and its deep porch, refuge for many a homeless or tired person, resting in their weariness from the heat of the day. I stopped for a second, and looked at the small pile of flowers that had been placed there. There were several bunches of roses, and some lilies, and two bunches of cheap, yellow daisies, all neatly laid out in the doorway. I guess there must have been seven or eight bunches in all.

She was a pretty girl, with an open, sunny expression and bright green eyes, smiling up at passers-by when they gave her money. She had a lovely face, a lovely, lovely face, and I decided that the absence of freckles actually suited her. Not everyone needed freckles. I waited for some cars to go by and then I stepped out into the road.

I left the flowers in the doorway at the foot of the pile, and was about to cross back over when a ticket on one of the others, a bundle of roses, caught my eye. It said, 'To our darling Donna. You are always with us. Mum and Dad.' I picked the roses up and crossed the road again. I stood outside the café, just looking over at the empty doorway, listening to the tired sounds of the evening, finding it hard to leave. After a minute or so an old bag lady shuffled up. Carefully, she moved some of the flowers aside, and sat, setting her weight down on the pavement like a mother hen. Then she was comfortable. I watched as she gathered her belongings around her, huddling herself beneath an old duvet with a flower pattern just visible beneath the grime. I stayed for another minute, as she pulled out a penny whistle and began to blow. I don't know why she was bothering, there was no one about. I stood there until a slight breeze moved past me and I shivered, wishing I had a coat. I rubbed my arms. Then I dumped the bouquet of flowers I was holding in the nearest bin and walked back to my car, with the thin sound of the music fading away behind me.